ERLE STANLEY GARDNER

The Case of The
TERRIFIED TYPIST

The Case of The
GRINNING GORILLA

WALTER J. BLACK, INC., ROSLYN, N.Y.

THE CASE OF THE TERRIFIED TYPIST

Copyright © 1956

BY ERLE STANLEY GARDNER

THE CASE OF THE GRINNING GORILLA

Copyright 1952

BY ERLE STANLEY GARDNER

Published by special arrangement with
William Morrow and Company, Inc.

The Case of The Terrified Typist

CHAPTER 1

PERRY MASON EYED THE BRIEF WHICH JACKSON, HIS LAW clerk, had submitted for his approval.

Della Street, sitting across the desk from the lawyer, correctly interpreted the expression on Mason's face.

"What was wrong with it?" she asked.

"Quite a few things," Mason said. "In the first place, I've had to shorten it from ninety-six pages to thirty-two."

"Good heavens," Della said. "Jackson told me he had already shortened it twice and he couldn't take out another word."

Mason grinned. "How are we fixed for typists, Della?"

"Stella is down with the flu and Annie is simply snowed under an avalanche of work."

"Then we'll have to get an outside typist," Mason told her. "This brief has to be ready for the printer tomorrow."

"All right. I'll call the agency and have a typist sent up right away," Della Street promised.

"In the meantime," Mason told her, "I'm going over this thing once again and see if I can't take out another four or five pages. Briefs shouldn't be written to impress the client. They should be concise, and above all, the writer should see that the Court has a clear grasp of the *facts* in the case before there is any argument about the *law*. The judges know the law. If they don't, they have clerks who can look it up."

Mason picked up a thick blue pencil, held it poised in his hand, and once more started reading through the sheaf of pages, which already showed signs of heavy editing. Della Street went to the outer office to telephone for a typist.

When she returned Mason looked up. "Get one?"

"The agency doesn't have one at the moment. That is, those they have are rather mediocre. I told them you wanted one who is fast, accurate and willing; that you didn't want to have to read this thing through again and find a lot of typographical errors."

Mason nodded, went on with his editing. "When can we expect one, Della?"

"They promised to have someone who would finish it by two-thirty tomorrow afternoon. But they said it might be a while before they could locate just the girl they wanted. I told them there were thirty-two pages."

"Twenty-nine and a half," Mason corrected, smilingly. "I've just cut out another two and a half pages."

Mason was just finishing his final editing half an hour later when Gertie, the office receptionist, opened the door and said, "The typist is here, Mr. Mason."

Mason nodded and stretched back in his chair. Della started to pick up the brief, but hesitated as Gertie came in and carefully closed the door behind her.

"What's the trouble, Gertie?"

"What did you say to frighten her, Mr. Mason?"

Mason glanced at Della Street.

"Heavens," Della said, "I didn't talk with *her* at all. We just rang up Miss Mosher at the agency."

"Well," Gertie said, lowering her voice, "this girl's scared to death."

Mason flashed a quick smile at Della Street. Gertie's tendency to romanticize and dramatize every situation was so well known that it was something of an office joke.

"What did *you* do to frighten her, Gertie?"

"*Me!* What did *I* do? Nothing! I was answering a call at the switchboard. When I turned around, this girl was standing there by the reception desk. I hadn't heard her come in. She tried to say something, but she could hardly talk. She just stood there. I didn't think so much of it at the time, but afterward, when I got to thinking it over, I realized that she was sort of holding on to the desk. I'll bet her knees were weak and she—"

"Never mind what you thought," Mason interrupted, puzzled. "Let's find out what happened, Gertie. What did you tell her?"

"I just said, 'I guess you're the new typist,' and she nodded. I said, 'Well, you sit over at that desk and I'll get the work for you.'"

"And what did she do?"

"She went over to the chair and sat down at the desk."

Mason said, "All right, Gertie. Thanks for telling us."

"She's absolutely terrified," Gertie insisted.

"Well, that's fine," Mason said. "Some girls are that way when they're starting on a new job. As I remember, Gertie, *you* had *your* troubles when you first came here, didn't you?"

"Troubles!" Gertie exclaimed. "Mr. Mason, after I got in the office and realized I'd forgotten to take the gum out of my mouth, I was just absolutely gone. I turned to jelly. I didn't know what to do. I—"

"Well, get back to the board," Mason told her. "I think I can hear it buzzing from here."

"Oh Lord, yes," Gertie said. "I can hear it now myself."

She jerked open the door and made a dash for the switchboard in the outer office.

Mason handed Della Street the brief and said, "Go out and get her started, Della."

When Della Street came back at the end of ten minutes Mason asked, "How's our terrified typist, Della?"

Della Street said, "If that's a terrified typist, let's call Miss Mosher and tell her to frighten all of them before sending them out."

"Good?" Mason asked.

"Listen," Della Street said.

She eased open the door to the outer office. The sound of clattering typewriter keys came through in a steady staccato.

"Sounds like hail on a tin roof," Mason said.

Della Street closed the door. "I've never seen anything like it. That girl pulled the typewriter over to her, ratcheted in the paper, looked at the copy, put her hands over the keyboard and that typewriter literally exploded into action. And yet, somehow, Chief, I think Gertie *was* right. I think she became frightened at the idea of coming up here. It may be that she knows something about you, or your fame has caused her to become self-conscious. After all," Della Street added dryly, "you're not entirely unknown, you know."

"Well," Mason said, "let's get at that pile of mail and skim off a few of the important letters. At that rate the brief will be done in plenty of time."

Della Street nodded.

"You have her at the desk by the door to the law library?"

"That seemed to be the only place to put her, Chief. I fixed up the desk there when I knew we were going to need an extra typist.

You know how Stella is about anyone using *her* typewriter. She thinks a strange typist throws it all out of kilter."

Mason nodded, said, "If this girl is good, Della, you might arrange to keep her on for a week or two. We can keep her busy, can't we?"

"I'll say."

"Better ring up Miss Mosher and tell her."

Della Street hesitated. "Would it be all right if we waited until we've had a chance to study her work? She's fast, all right, but we'd better be sure she's accurate."

Mason nodded, said, "Good idea, Della. Let's wait and see."

CHAPTER 2

DELLA STREET PLACED A SHEAF OF PAGES ON MASON'S DESK. "Those are the first ten pages of the brief, Chief."

Mason looked at the typewritten sheets, gave a low whistle and said, "Now *that's* what I call typing!"

Della Street picked up one of the pages, tilted it so that the light reflected from the smooth surface. "I've tried this with two or three sheets," she said, "and I can't see where there's been a single erasure. She has a wonderful touch and she certainly is hammering it out."

Mason said, "Ring up Miss Mosher. Find out something about this girl. What's her name, Della?"

"Mae Wallis."

"Get Miss Mosher on the line."

Della Street picked up the telephone, said to Gertie at the switchboard, "Mr. Mason wants Miss Mosher at the secretarial agency, Gertie. . . . Never mind, I'll hold the line."

A moment later Della Street said, "Hello, Miss Mosher? . . . Oh, she is? . . . Well, I'm calling about the typist she sent up to Mr. Mason's office. This is Della Street, Mr. Mason's secretary. . . . Are you sure? . . . Well, she must have left a note somewhere. . . . Yes, yes . . . well, I'm sorry. . . . No, we don't want *two* girls.

. . . No, no. Miss Mosher sent one up—a Mae Wallis. I'm trying to find out whether she'll be available for steady work during the next week. . . . Please ask Miss Mosher to call when she comes in."

Della Street hung up the phone, turned to Perry Mason. "Miss Mosher is out. The girl she left in charge doesn't know about anyone having been sent up. She found a note on the desk to get us a typist. It was a memo Miss Mosher had left before she went out. The names of three girls were on it, and this assistant has been trying to locate the girls. One of them was laid up with flu, another one was on a job, and she was trying to locate the third when I called in."

"That's not like Miss Mosher," Mason said. "She's usually very efficient. When she sent this girl up, she should have destroyed the memo. Oh, well, it doesn't make any difference."

"Miss Mosher's due back in about an hour," Della Street said. "I left word for her to call when she comes in."

Again Mason tackled the work on his desk, stopping to see a client who had a three-thirty appointment, then returning to dictation.

At four-thirty Della Street went out to the outer office, came back and said, "She's still going like a house afire, Chief. She's really pounding them out."

Mason said, "That copy had been pretty badly hashed up and blue-penciled with strike-outs and interlineations."

"It doesn't seem to bother her a bit," Della Street said. "There's lightning in that girl's finger tips. She "

The telephone on Della Street's desk shrilled insistently. Della Street, with her hand on the receiver, finished the sentence, ". . . certainly knows how to play a tune on a keyboard."

She picked up the receiver, said, "Hello. . . . Oh, yes, Miss Mosher. We were calling about the typist you sent up. . . . What? . . . You didn't? . . . Mae Wallis? . . . She *said* she came from your agency. She said you sent her. . . . Why, yes, that's what I understood she said. . . . Well, I'm sorry, Miss Mosher. There's been some mistake—but this girl's certainly competent. . . . Why, yes, she's got the work almost finished. I'm terribly sorry. I'll speak with her and—Are you going to be there for a while? . . . Well, I'll speak with her and call you back. But that's what she said . . . yes, from your agency. . . . All right, let me call you back."

Della Street dropped the phone into its cradle.

"Mystery?" Mason asked.

"I'll say. Miss Mosher says *she* hasn't sent anyone up. She's had a hard time getting girls lined up, particularly ones with qualifications to suit you."

"Well, she got one this time," Mason said, fingering through the brief. "Or at least *someone* got her."

"So what do we do?" Della Street asked.

"By all means, find out where she came from. Are you sure she said Miss Mosher sent her?"

"That's what Gertie said."

"Are you," Mason asked, "going *entirely* on what Gertie said?"

Della Street nodded.

"You didn't talk it over with Miss Wallis?"

"No. She was out there waiting to go to work. While I was talking with you, she found where the paper and carbons were kept in the desk. She'd ratcheted them into the machine, and just held out her hand for the copy. She asked if I wanted an original and three carbons. I said that we only used an original and two for stuff that was going to the printer. She said she had one extra carbon in the machine, but that she wouldn't bother to take it out. She said that she'd only make an original and two on the next. Then she put the papers down on the desk, held her fingers poised over the keyboard for a second, then started banging out copy."

"Permit me," Mason said, "to call your attention to something which clearly demonstrates the fallacy of human testimony. You were doubtless sincere in telling Miss Mosher that Mae Wallis said she had been sent up from her agency, but if you will recall Gertie's exact words, you will remember that she said the girl seemed frightened and self-conscious, so Gertie asked her if she was the new typist. The girl nodded, and Gertie showed her to the desk. At no time did Gertie say to us that she asked her if Miss Mosher had sent her."

"Well," Della Street said, "I had the distinct impression—"

"Certainly you did," Mason said. "So did I. Only long years of cross-examining witnesses have trained me to listen carefully to what a person actually says. I am quite certain that Gertie never told us she had specifically asked this girl if she came from Miss Mosher's agency."

"Well, where *could* she have come from?"

"Let's get her in and ask her," Mason said. "And let's not let her get away, Della. I'd like to catch up on some of this back work tomorrow, and this girl is really a wonder."

Della Street nodded, left her desk, went to the outer office, returned in a moment and made motions of powdering her nose.

"Did you leave word?" Mason asked.

"Yes, I told Gertie to send her in as soon as she came back."

"How's the brief coming?"

Della Street said, "She's well along with it. The work's on her desk. It hasn't been separated yet. The originals and carbons are together. She certainly does neat work, doesn't she?"

Mason nodded, tilted back in his swivel chair, lit a cigarette and said, "Well, we'll wait until she shows up and see what she has to say for herself, Della. When you stop to think about this, it presents an intriguing problem."

After Mason had smoked a leisurely cigarette Della Street once more went to the outer office and again returned.

Mason frowned, said, "She's probably one of those high-strung girls who use up a lot of nervous energy banging away at the typewriter and then go for a complete rest, smoking a cigarette or . . ."

"Or?" Della Street asked, as Mason paused.

". . . or taking a drink. Now, wait a minute, Della. Although there's nothing particularly confidential about that brief, if we keep her on here for four or five days, she's going to be doing some stuff that *is* confidential. Suppose you slip down to the powder room, Della, and see if perhaps our demon typist has a little flask in her purse and is now engaged in chewing on a clove."

"Also," Della Street said, "I'll take a whiff to see if I smell any marijuana smoke."

"Know it when you smell it?" Mason asked, smiling.

"Of course," she retorted. "I wouldn't be working for one of the greatest trial attorneys in the country without having learned at least to recognize some of the more common forms of law violation."

"All right," Mason said. "Go on down and tell her that we want to see her, Della. Try and chat with her informally for a minute and size her up a bit. You didn't talk with her very much, did you?"

"Just got her name, and that's about all. I remember asking her how she spelled her first name, and she told me M-A-E."

Mason nodded. Della Street left the room and was back within a couple of minutes.

"She isn't there, Chief."

"Well, where the devil *is* she?" Mason asked.

Della Street shrugged her shoulders. "She just got up and went out."

"Say anything to Gertie about where she was going?"

"Not a word. She just got up and walked out, and Gertie assumed she was going to the washroom."

"Now that's strange," Mason said. "Isn't that room kept locked?" Della Street nodded.

"She should have asked for a key," Mason said. "Even if she didn't know it was locked, she'd have asked Gertie how to find it. How about her hat and coat?"

"Apparently she wasn't wearing any. She has her purse with her."

"Run out and pick up the last of the work she was doing, will you, Della? Let's take a look at it."

Della Street went out and returned with the typed pages. Mason looked them over.

"She has a few pages to go," Della Street said.

Mason pursed his lips, said, "It shouldn't take her long, Della, I certainly cut the insides out of those last few pages. That's where Jackson was waxing eloquent and bombarding the Court with a peroration on liberties, constitutional rights and due process of law."

"He was so proud of that," Della Street said. "You didn't take it *all* out, did you?"

"I took out most of it," Mason said. "An appellate court isn't interested in eloquence. It's interested in the law and the facts to which it is going to apply the law.

"Good Lord, Della, do you realize that if the appellate judges tried to read every line of all of the briefs that are submitted to them, they could work for twelve hours each day without doing one other thing, and still couldn't read the briefs?"

"Good heavens, no! Aren't they supposed to read them?"

"Theoretically, yes," Mason said. "But actually, it's a practical impossibility."

"So what do they do?"

"Most of them look through the briefs, get the law points, skip the impassioned pleas, then turn the briefs over to their law clerks.

"It's my experience that a man does a lot better when he sets forth an absolutely impartial, thoroughly honest statement of facts, including those that are unfavorable to his side as well as those that are favorable, thus giving the appellate court the courtesy of assuming the judge knows the law.

"The attorney can be of help in letting the judge know the case to which the law is to be applied and the facts in the case. But if the judge didn't know what the law was, he wouldn't have been placed on the appellate bench in the first place. Della, what the devil *do* you suppose happened to that girl?"

"She must be in the building somewhere."

"What makes you think so?"

"Well, there again—well, it's just one of those presumptions. She certainly is coming back for her money. She put in a whale of an afternoon's work."

"She should have stayed to finish the brief," Mason said. "It wouldn't have taken her over another forty or fifty minutes, at the rate she was working."

"Chief," Della Street said, "you seem to be acting on the assumption that she's walked out and left us."

"It's a feeling I have."

Della Street said, "She probably went down to the cigar counter to buy some cigarettes."

"In which event, she'd have been back long before this."

"Yes, I suppose so. But . . . but, Chief, she's bound to collect the money for the work she's done."

Mason carefully arranged the pages of the brief. "Well, she's helped us out of quite a hole." He broke off as a series of peculiarly spaced knocks sounded on the corridor door of his private office.

"That will be Paul Drake," Mason said. "I wonder what brings *him* around. Let him in, Della."

Della Street opened the door. Paul Drake, head of the Drake Detective Agency, with offices down the corridor by the elevator, grinned at them and said, "What were *you* people doing during all of the excitement?"

"Excitement?" Mason asked.

"Cops crawling all over the building," Drake said. "And you

two sitting here engaged in the prosaic activities of running a hum-drum law office."

"Darned if we weren't," Mason said. "Sit down, Paul. Have a cigarette. Tell us what it's all about. We've been putting in our time writing briefs."

"You would," Drake told him, sliding down into the big over-stuffed chair reserved for clients, and lighting a cigarette.

"What's the trouble?" Mason asked.

"Police chasing some dame up here on this floor," Drake said. "Didn't they search your office?"

Mason flashed a swift, warning glance at Della Street.

"Not that I know of."

"They must have."

Mason said to Della Street, "See if Gertie's gone home, Della."

Della Street opened the door to the outer office, said, "She's just going home, Chief."

"Can you catch her?"

"Sure. She's just at the door." Della Street raised her voice, "Oh, Gertie! Can you look in here for a minute?"

Gertie, ready to leave for the evening, came to stand in the door-way of the office. "What is it, Mr. Mason?"

"Any officers in here this afternoon?" Mason asked.

"Oh yes," Gertie said. "There was some sort of a burglary down the corridor."

Again Mason caught Della's eye.

"What did they want?" Mason asked.

"Wanted to know if everyone in the office was accounted for, whether you had anyone in with you, and whether we had seen any-thing of a girl burglar."

"And what did you tell them?" Mason asked, keeping his voice entirely without expression.

"I told them you were alone, except for Miss Street, your confi-dential secretary. That we only had the regular employees here in the office and a relief typist from our regular agency who was work-ing on a brief."

"And then what?"

"Then they left. Why?"

"Oh, nothing," Mason said. "I was just wondering, that's all."

"Should I have notified you? I know you don't like to be disturbed when you're working on correspondence."

"No, it's all right," Mason said. "I just wanted to get it straight, Gertie. That's all. Good night, and have a good time."

"How did you know I have a date?" Gertie asked.

"I saw it in your eyes," Mason said, grinning. "Good night, Gertie."

"Good night," she said.

"Well," Drake said, "there you are. If you'd happened to have had some woman client in your private office, the police would have insisted on talking to you and on getting a look at the client."

"You mean they searched the floor?" Mason asked.

"They really went through the joint," Drake told him. "You see, the office where the trouble occurred is right across from the women's restroom. One of the stenographers, opening the restroom door, saw this young woman whose back was toward her fumbling with the lock on the office door, trying first one key then another.

"The stenographer became suspicious. She stood there watching. About the fourth or fifth key, the girl managed to get into the office."

"What office was it?" Mason asked.

"The South African Gem Importing and Exploration Company."

"Go on, Paul."

"Well, this stenographer was a pretty smart babe. She telephoned the manager of the building and then she went out to stand by the elevators to see if this girl would come out and take an elevator. If she did that, the stenographer had made up her mind she'd try to follow."

"That could have been dangerous," Mason said.

"I know, but this is one very spunky gal."

"She could have recognized the woman?"

"Not the woman. But she knew the way the woman was dressed. You know the way women are, Perry. She hadn't seen the woman's face, but she knew the exact color and cut of her skirt and jacket, the shade of her stockings and shoes; the way she had her hair done, the color of her hair, and all that."

"I see," Mason said, glancing surreptitiously at Della Street. "That description was, of course, given to the police?"

"Oh, yes."

"And they didn't find her?"

"No, they didn't find a thing. But the manager of the building gave them a passkey to get into the office of the gem importing company. The place looked as if a cyclone had struck it. Evidently, this girl had made a very hurried search. Drawers had been pulled out, papers dumped out on the floor, a chair had been overturned, a typewriter stand upset, with the typewriter lying on its side on the floor."

"No sign of the girl?"

"No sign of anyone. The two partners who own the business, chaps named Jefferson and Irving, came in right on the heels of the police. They had been out to lunch, and they were amazed to find how much destruction had taken place during their brief absence."

Mason said, "The girl probably ran down the stairs to another floor and took the elevator from there."

Drake shook his head. "The building manager got this stenographer who had given the description, and they went down to stand at the elevators. They watched everyone who went out. When the police showed up—and believe me, that was only a matter of a minute or two; these radio cars are right on the job—well, when the police showed up, the manager of the building briefed them on what had happened. So the police went up and the girl and the manager continued to stand at the elevators. The police weren't conspicuous about it, but they dropped in at every office on the floor, just checking up."

"And I suppose the restrooms," Mason said.

"Oh, sure. They sent a couple of girls into the restrooms right away. That was the first place they looked."

"Well," Mason said, "we seem to be doing all right, Paul. If I don't go out and get tangled up in crime, crime comes to me—at least indirectly. So Jefferson and Irving came in right after the police arrived, is that right?"

"That's right."

"And the manager of the building was down there at the elevators, waiting for this girl to come out?"

"That's right."

Mason said, "He knew, of course, the office that the girl was burglarizing?"

"Of course. He told the police what office it was and all about it. He even gave them a passkey so they could get in."

"And then he waited down there at the elevators with the stenographer who had seen this woman burglarizing the office?"

"That's right."

"A lot of elaborate precautions to catch a sneak thief."

"Well, I'm not supposed to talk about clients, Perry, and I wouldn't to anyone else, but as you know, I represent the owners of the building. It seems this gem importing company is expecting half a million dollars' worth of diamonds before long."

"The deuce!"

"That's right. You know the way they do things these days—insure 'em and ship 'em by mail."

"The strange thing," Mason said thoughtfully, "is that if Irving and Jefferson came in right on the heels of the police, with the manager of the building standing down there at the elevators, he didn't stop them and tell them that they'd find police in their office and—

"What's the matter?" Mason asked, as Drake suddenly sat bolt upright.

Drake made the motion of hitting himself on the head.

"What are you trying to do?" Mason asked.

"Knock some brains into my thick skull," Drake said. "Good Lord, Perry! The manager of the building was telling me all about this, and that point never occurred to me. Let me use the phone."

Drake moved over to the phone, called the office of the manager and said, "Paul Drake talking. I was thinking about this trouble down at the gem importing company. According to police, Irving and Jefferson, the two partners who run the place, came in while they were searching."

The receiver made squawking noises.

"Well," Drake said, "*you* were standing down at the foot of the elevators with this stenographer. Why didn't you tell them that police were in their office—" Drake was interrupted by another series of squawking noises from the receiver. After a moment the detective said, "Want me to look into it, or do you want to? . . . Okay. Call me back, will you? I'm up here in Perry Mason's office at the moment. . . . Well, wait a minute. The switchboard is disconnected for the night, I guess. I'll catch the call at my—"

"Hold it, Paul," Della Street interrupted. "I'll connect this line with the switchboard, so you can get a call back on this number."

"Okay," Drake said into the telephone. "Mason's secretary will fix the line, so this telephone will be connected on the main trunk line. Just give me a buzz when you find out about it, will you?"

Drake hung up the telephone, went back to the client's chair, grinned at Mason and said, "You'll pardon me for taking all the credit for your idea, Perry, but this is my bread and butter. I couldn't tell him the idea never occurred to me until I got to talking with you."

"No credit," Mason said. "The thing is obvious."

"Of course it's obvious," Drake said. "That's why I'm kicking myself for not thinking of it right at the start. The trouble was, we were so interested in finding out how this girl vanished into thin air that I for one completely overlooked wondering how it happened that the manager didn't stop Jefferson and his partner and tell them what was happening."

"The manager was probably excited," Mason said.

"I'll tell the world he was excited. Do you know him?"

"Not the new one. I've talked with him on the phone, and Della Street's talked with him. I haven't met him."

"He's an excitable chap. One of those hair-triggered guys who does everything right now. At that, he did a pretty good job of sewing up the building."

Mason nodded. "They certainly went to a lot of trouble trying to catch one lone female prowler."

The telephone rang.

"That's probably for you," Della Street said, nodding to Paul Drake.

Drake picked up the telephone, said, "Hello. . . . Yes, this is Paul Drake. . . . Oh, I see. Well, of course, that could have happened, all right. Funny you didn't see them. . . . I see. Well, thanks a lot. I just thought we ought to check on that angle. . . . Oh, that's all right. There's no reason why that *should* have occurred to you. . . . Not at all. I'd been intending to ask you about it, but it slipped my mind. I thought I'd better check up on it before knocking off for the night. . . . Okay. Thanks. We'll see what we can find out."

Drake hung up, grinned at Mason and said, "Now the guy thinks I was working overtime, cudgeling my brain on his problem."

"What about the two partners?" Mason asked. "What's the answer?"

"Why, they evidently walked right by him and got in the elevator. Of course, the manager and the stenographer were watching the people who were getting *out* of the elevators. At that time, right after lunch, there's quite a bit of traffic in the elevators.

"The manager just finished talking with Jefferson on the phone. Jefferson said *he* saw the manager and this girl standing there and started to ask him a question about something pertaining to the building. Then he saw from the way the man was standing that he was evidently waiting for someone, so the two partners just went on past and got in the elevator just as it was starting up."

Mason said, "That sounds plausible, all right. What do you know about Jefferson and Irving? Anything?"

"Not too much. The South African Gem Importing and Exploration Company decided to open an office here. Their business is mostly wholesale diamonds. They have their main office in Johannesburg, but there's a branch office in Paris.

"This deal was made through the Paris office. They wrote the manager of the building, received a floor plan and rental schedules, signed a lease and paid six months' rent in advance.

"They sent Duane Jefferson out from South Africa. He's to be in charge. Walter Irving came from the Paris office. He's the assistant."

"Are they doing business?"

"Not yet. They're just getting started. I understand they're waiting for a high-class burglarproof safe to be installed. They've advertised for office help and have purchased some office furniture."

"Did those two chaps bring any stock of diamonds with them?" Mason asked.

"Nope. Unfortunately, things aren't done that way any more, which has cost us private detectives a lot of business. Gems are sent by insured mail now. A half a million dollars' worth of stones are sent just as you'd send a package of soiled clothes. The shipper pays a fee for adequate insurance and deducts it as a business cost. If the gems are lost, the insurance company writes out its check. It's an infallible, foolproof system."

"I see," Mason said thoughtfully. "In that case, what the devil was this girl after?"

"That's the sixty-four thousand dollar question."

"It was an empty office—as far as gems go?"

"That's right. Later on, when the first shipment of gems arrives, they'll have burglar alarms all over the place, an impregnable safe and all the trimmings. Right now it's an empty shell.

"Gosh, Perry, it used to be that a messenger would carry a shipment of jewels, and private detective agencies would be given jobs as bodyguards, special watchmen and all of that. Now, some postal employee who doesn't even carry a gun comes down the corridor with a package worth half a million, says, 'Sign here,' and the birds sign their name, toss the package in the safe and that's all there is to it.

"It's all done on a basis of percentages. The insurance business is tough competition. How'd you like it if an insurance company would insure your clients against any loss from any type of litigation? Then your clients would pay premiums, deduct them as a business cost, and—"

"The trouble with that, Paul," Mason said, "is that when they come to lock a guy in the gas chamber it would take an awful big insurance check to make him feel indifferent."

Drake grinned. "Damned if it wouldn't," he agreed.

CHAPTER 3

WHEN PAUL DRAKE HAD LEFT THE OFFICE MASON TURNED TO Della Street.

"Well, what do *you* think, Della?"

Della Street said, "I'm afraid it could be—it was about the same time and . . . well. sometimes I think we don't pay enough attention to Gertie because she *does* exaggerate. Perhaps this girl really was frightened, just as Gertie said, and . . . well, it could have been."

"Then she must have come in here," Mason said, "because she

knew her escape was cut off. There was no other place for her to go. She had to enter some office. So she came in here blind and was trying to think of some problem that would enable her to ask for a consultation with me, when Gertie let the cat out of the bag that we were expecting a typist."

Della Street nodded.

"Go out and look around," Mason said. "I'm going out and do a little scouting myself."

"What do you want me to do?" Della Street asked.

"Look over the typewriter she was using. Look over the typewriter desk. Then go down to the restroom and look around. See if you can find anything."

"Heavens, the police have been all through the restroom."

"Look around, anyhow, Della. See if she hid anything. There's always the chance she might have had something in her possession that was pretty hot and she decided to cache it someplace and come back for it later. I'll go down and get some cigarettes."

Mason walked down the corridor and rang for an elevator, went down to the foyer and over to the cigar stand. The girl behind the counter, a tall blonde with frosty blue eyes, smiled impersonally.

"Hello," Mason said.

At the personal approach the eyes became even more coldly cautious. "Good afternoon," the girl said.

"I am looking for a little information," Mason said.

"We sell cigars and cigarettes, chewing gum, candy, newspapers and magazines."

Mason laughed. "Well, don't get me wrong."

"And don't get *me* wrong."

"I'm a tenant in the building," Mason said, "and have been for some time. You're new here, aren't you?"

"Yes, I bought the cigar stand from Mr. Carson. I—Oh, I place you now! You're Perry Mason, the famous lawyer! Excuse me, Mr. Mason. I thought you were . . . well, you know a lot of people think that just because a girl is running a cigar counter she wraps herself up with every package of cigarettes she sells."

Mason smiled. "Pardon *me*. I should have introduced myself first."

"What can I do for you, Mr. Mason?"

"Probably nothing," Mason said. "I wanted a little information, but if you're new here, I'm afraid you won't know the tenants in the building well enough to help me."

"I'm afraid that's right, Mr. Mason. I don't have too good a memory for names and faces. I'm trying to get to know the regular customers. It's quite a job."

Mason said, "There are a couple of relative newcomers here in the building. One of them is named Jefferson, the other Irving."

"Oh, you mean the ones that have that gem importing company?"

"Those are the ones. Know them?"

"I do *now*. We had a lot of excitement here this afternoon, although I didn't know anything about it. It seems their office was broken into and—"

"They were pointed out to you?"

"Yes. One of them—Mr. Jefferson, I believe it was—stopped here for a package of cigarettes and was telling me all about it."

"But you didn't know them before?"

"You mean by sight?"

Mason nodded.

She shook her head. "I'm sorry, I can't help you, Mr. Mason."

"Well, that's all right," Mason told her.

"Why do you ask, Mr. Mason? Are you interested in the case?"

Mason smiled. "Indirectly," he said.

"You're *so* mysterious. I may not have recognized you when you walked up, but I have heard so much about you that I feel I know you very well indeed. What's an indirect interest, Mr. Mason?"

"Nothing worth talking about."

"Well, remember that I'm rather centrally located down here. If I can ever pick up any information for you, all you have to do is to let me know. I'll be glad to co-operate in any way that I can. Perhaps I can't be so efficient now, since I am relatively new here, but I'll get people spotted and . . . well, just remember, if there's *anything* I can do, I'll be glad to."

"Thanks," Mason told her.

"Did you want me to talk with Mr. Jefferson some more? He was quite friendly and chatted away with me while I was waiting on him. I didn't encourage him, but I have a feeling . . . well, you know how those things are, Mr. Mason."

Mason grinned. "You mean that he's lonely and he likes your looks?"

Her laugh showed that she was flustered. "Well, I didn't exactly say that."

"But you feel he could be encouraged?"

"Do you want me to try?"

"Would you like to?"

"Whatever you say, Mr. Mason."

The lawyer handed her a folded twenty dollar bill. "Try and find out just where the manager of the building was when Jefferson and Irving came back from lunch."

"Thank *you*, Mr. Mason. I feel guilty taking this money, because now that you mention the manager of the building I know the answer."

"What is it?"

"They came in while the manager and a young woman were standing watching the elevators. One of the men started to approach the manager as though he wanted to ask him a question, but he saw the manager was preoccupied watching the elevators, so he veered off.

"I didn't think anything about it at the time, but it comes back to me now that those were the two men who were pointed out to me later. I hope that's the information you wanted, Mr. Mason."

"It is, thanks."

"Thank *you*, Mr. Mason. If there's ever anything I can do for you I'd be glad to, and it isn't going to cost you a twenty every time either."

"Thanks," Mason said, "but I never want something for nothing."

"*You* wouldn't," she said, giving him her most dazzling smile.

Mason rode back up in the elevator.

Della Street, in a state of subdued excitement, was waiting to pounce on him as soon as he opened the door of his private office.

"Good heavens!" she said. "We're mixed in it up to our eyebrows."

"Go on," Mason said. "What are we mixed in?"

Della Street produced a small, square tin box.

"What," Mason asked, "do you have there?"

"A great big hunk of semi-dried chewing gum."

"And where did you get it?"

"It was plastered on the underside of the desk where Mae Wallis had been working."

"Let's take a look, Della."

Della Street slid open the lid of the box and showed Mason the chewing gum. "This is just the way it was plastered to the underside of the desk," she said.

"And what did you do?"

"Took an old safety razor blade and cut it off. You can see there is an impression of fingers where she pushed the gum up against the desk."

Mason looked at Della Street somewhat quizzically. "Well," he said, "you *are* becoming the demon detective, Della. So now we have a couple of fingerprints?"

"Exactly."

"Well," Mason told her, "we're hardly going to the police with them, Della."

"No, I suppose not."

"So in that case, since we aren't particularly anxious to co-operate with the police, it would have been just as well if you had destroyed the fingerprints in removing the gum, Della."

"Wait," she told him. "You haven't seen anything yet. You observe that that's a terrific wad of gum, Chief. A girl could hardly have had all that in her mouth at one time."

"You think it was put there in installments?" Mason asked.

"I think it was put there for a purpose," Della Street said. "I thought so as soon as I saw it."

"What purpose?" Mason asked.

Della Street turned the box over on Mason's desk so that the wad of gum fell out on the blotter. "This," she said, "is the side that was against the desk."

Mason looked at the coruscations which gleamed through a few places in the chewing gum. "Good Lord, Della!" he said. "How many are there?"

"I don't know," Della said. "I didn't want to touch it. This is just the way it came from the desk. You can see parts of two really large-sized diamonds there."

Mason studied the wad of chewing gum.

"Now then," he said thoughtfully, "this becomes evidence, Della. We're going to have to be careful that nothing happens to it."

She nodded.

"I take it the gum is hard enough so it will keep all right?" Mason asked.

"It's a little soft on the inside, but now that the air's getting to the top, the gum is hardening rapidly."

Mason took the small tin box, replaced the gum and studied it, tilting the box backwards and forwards so as to get a good view of both the top and bottom sides of the chewing gum. "Two of those fingerprints are remarkably good latents, Della," he said. "The third one isn't so good. It looks more like the side of the finger. But those two impressions are perfect."

Della Street nodded.

"Probably the thumb and the forefinger. Which side of the desk was it on, Della?"

"Over on the right-hand side of the desk."

"Then those are probably the impressions of the right thumb and forefinger."

"So what do we do?" Della Street asked. "Do we now call in the police?"

Mason hesitated a moment, said, "I want to know a little more about what's cooking, Della. You didn't find anything in the restroom?"

Della Street said, "I became a scavenger. I dug down into the container that they use for soiled paper towels—you know, they have a big metal box with a wedge-shaped cover on top that swings back and forth and you can shove towels in from each side."

Mason nodded. "Find anything, Della?"

"Someone had used the receptable to dispose of a lot of love letters, and the disposal must either have been very, very hasty, or else the girl certainly took no precautions to keep anyone who might be interested from getting quite an eyeful. The letters hadn't even been torn through."

"Let's take a look at them," Mason said.

Della Street said, "They were all in one bunch, and I salvaged the whole outfit. Gosh, I'm glad the rush hour is over. I would have felt pretty self-conscious if someone had come in and caught me digging down in that used towel container!"

Mason's nod showed that he was preoccupied as he examined the letters.

"What do you make of them?" Della Street asked.

"Well," Mason said thoughtfully, "either, as you suggested, the person who left them there was in very much of a hurry, or this was a plant and the person wanted to be certain that the letters would be noticed and could be read without any difficulty. In other words, it's almost too good. A girl trying to dispose of letters would hardly have been so careless about dropping them into the used-towel receptacle in one piece—unless it was a plant of some kind?"

"But how about a man?" Della Street asked. "Apparently, the letters were sent to a man and—"

"And they were found in the *ladies'* restroom," Mason pointed out.

"Yes, that's so."

Mason studied one of the letters. "Now, these are rather peculiar, Della. They are written in a whimsical vein. Listen to this:

"My dearest Prince Charming,

"When you rode up on your charger the other night, there were a lot of things I wanted to say to you, but I couldn't think of them until after you had left.

"Somehow the glittering armor and that formidable helmet made you seem so virtuous and righteous that I felt a distant creature from another and more sordid world. . . . You perhaps don't know it, Prince Charming, but you made quite a handsome spectacle, sitting there with the visor of your helmet raised, your horse with his head down, his flanks heaving and sweating from the exertion of carrying you on that last mission to rescue the damsel in distress, the setting sun reflecting from your polished armor . . ."

Mason paused, glanced up at Della Street, and said, "What the devil!"

"Take a look at the signature," Della Street said.

Mason turned over two pages and looked at the signature—"Your faithful and devoted Mae."

"You will notice the spelling," Della Street said. "It's M-A-E."

Mason pursed his lips thoughtfully, said, "Now, all we need, Della, is a murder to put us in a thoroughly untenable position."

"What position?"

"That of withholding important evidence from the police."

"You're not going to tell them anything about Mae Wallis?"

Mason shook his head. "I don't dare to, Della. They wouldn't make even the slightest effort to believe me. You can see the position I'd be in. I'd be trying to explain that while the police were making a search of the building in order to find the woman who had broken into the offices of the South African Gem Importing and Exploration Company, I was sitting innocently in my office; that I had no idea that I should have mentioned the typist who dropped in from nowhere at exactly the right time, who seemed completely terrified, who was supposed to have been sent from Miss Mosher's agency, even though, at the time, I *knew* that she hadn't been sent from Miss Mosher's agency."

"Yes," Della Street said, smiling. "With your connections and reputation, I can see that the police would be at least skeptical."

"Very, very skeptical," Mason said. "And since it's bad for the police to develop habits of skepticism, Della, we'll see that they aren't placed in an embarrassing position."

CHAPTER **4**

IT WAS THREE DAYS LATER WHEN PERRY MASON UNLOCKED THE door of his private office and found Della Street waiting for him, his desk carefully cleaned and for once the pile of mail far to one side.

"Chief," Della Street said in a voice of low urgency, "I've been trying to get you. Sit down and let me talk with you before anyone knows you're in."

Mason hung up his hat in the hat closet, seated himself at the desk, glanced at Della Street quizzically and said, "You're certainly worked up. What gives?"

"We have our murder case."

"What do you mean 'our murder case'?"

"Remember what you said about the diamonds? That we only needed a murder case to make the thing perfect?"

Mason came bolt upright in his chair. "What is it, Della? Give me the low-down."

"No one seems to know what it's all about, but Duane Jefferson of the South African Gem Importing and Exploration Company has been arrested for murder. Walter Irving, the other member of the company, is out there in the outer office waiting for you. There's a cablegram from the South African Gem Importing and Exploration Company sent from South Africa, advising you that they are instructing their local representative to pay you two thousand American dollars as a retainer. They want you to represent Duane Jefferson."

"Murder?" Mason said. "Who the devil is the corpse, Della?"

"I don't know. I don't know very much about it. All I know is about the cablegram that came and the fact that Walter Irving has been in three times to see you. He asked that I notify him just as soon as you arrived, and this last time he decided that he wouldn't even take chances on the delay incident to a telephone call but was going to wait. He wants to see you the minute you come in."

"Send him in, Della. Let's find out what this is all about. Where's that tin box?"

"In the safe."

Mason said, "Where's the desk Mae Wallis was using when she was here?"

"I moved it back into the far corner of the law library."

"Who moved it?"

"I had the janitor and one of his assistants take it in for us."

"How are you on chewing gum, Della?"

"Pretty good. Why?"

Mason said, "Chew some gum, then use it to plaster that wad with the diamonds in it back on the desk in exactly the same place you found it."

"But there'll be a difference in freshness, Chief. That other gum is dry and hard now, and the new gum that I chew will be moist and—"

"And it will dry out if there's a long enough interval," Mason interrupted.

"How long will the interval be?"

"That," Mason told her, "will depend entirely on luck. Send Walter Irving in, Della, and let's see what this is all about."

Della Street nodded and started for the outer office.

"And fix that gum up *right away*," Mason reminded her.

"While Irving is in here?"

Mason nodded.

Della Street went to the outer office and returned with Walter Irving, a well-dressed, heavy-set man who had evidently prepared for the interview by visiting a barber shop. His hair was freshly trimmed, his nails were polished, his face had the smooth pink-and-white appearance which comes from a shave and a massage.

He was about forty-five years old, with reddish-brown, expressionless eyes, and the manner of a man who would show no surprise or emotion if half of the building should suddenly cave in.

"Good morning, Mr. Mason. I guess you don't know me. I've seen you in the elevator and you've been pointed out to me as being the smartest criminal lawyer in the state."

"Thank you," Mason said, shaking hands, and then added dryly, " 'Criminal lawyer' is a popular expression. I prefer to regard myself as a 'trial lawyer.' "

"Well, that's fine," Irving said. "I guess you received a cablegram from my company in South Africa, didn't you?"

"That's right."

"They've authorized me to pay you a retainer for representing my associate, Duane Jefferson."

"That cablegram is a complete mystery to me," Mason said. "What's it all about?"

"I'll come to that in a moment," Irving told him. "I want to get first things first."

"What do you mean?"

"Your fees."

"What about them?"

Irving raised steady eyes to Mason. "Things are different in South Africa."

"Just what are you getting at?"

"Just this," Irving said. "I'm here to protect the interests of my employers, the South African Gem Importing and Exploration Company. It's a big, wealthy company. They want me to turn over a two-thousand-dollar retainer to you. They'd leave it to your discretion as to the balance of the fee. I won't do business that way. On this side of the water, criminal attorneys are inclined to grab all they can get. They—Oh, hell, Mr. Mason, what's the use of beating around the bush? My company has an idea that it's dealing with a barrister in a wig and gown. It doesn't have the faintest idea of how to deal with a criminal lawyer."

"Do you?" Mason asked.

"If I don't I'm sure as hell going to try and find out. I'm protecting my company. How much is it going to cost?"

"You mean the total fee?"

"The total fee."

Mason said, "Tell me about the case, just the general facts and I'll answer your question."

"The facts are utterly cockeyed. Police raided our office. Why, I don't know. They found some diamonds. Those diamonds had been planted. Neither Jefferson nor I had ever seen them before. Our company is just opening up its office here. Some people don't like that."

"What were the diamonds worth?"

"Something like a hundred thousand dollars retail."

"How does murder enter into it?"

"That I don't know."

"Don't you even know who was murdered?"

"A man named Baxter. He's a smuggler."

"Were these his diamonds—the ones the police found in your office?"

"How the hell would *I* know?"

Mason regarded the man for a few seconds, then said, "How the hell would *I* know?"

Irving grinned. "I'm a little touchy this morning."

"So am I. Suppose you start talking."

"All I can tell you for sure is that there's some kind of a frame-up involved. Jefferson never killed anyone. I've known him for years. My gosh, Mr. Mason, look at it this way. Here's a large, exceedingly reputable, ultraconservative company in South Africa. This company has known Duane Jefferson for years. As soon as they hear that he's been arrested, they're willing to put up whatever amount is required in order to secure the very best available representation.

"Mind you, they don't suggest they'll advance Jefferson money to retain counsel. The company itself instructed me to retain the best available counsel for Jefferson."

"And you suggested me?" Mason asked.

"No. I would have, but somebody beat me to it. I got a cable-gram authorizing me to draw a check on our local account in an amount of two thousand dollars and turn that money over to you so you could start taking the necessary legal steps immediately. Now if my company pays your fees, who will your client be?"

"Duane Jefferson."

"Suppose Jefferson tries to get you to do something that isn't in his best interests. What would you do—follow his instructions, or do what was best for him?"

"Why do you ask that question?"

"Duane is trying to protect some woman. He'd let himself get convicted before he'd expose her. He thinks she's wonderful. *I* think she's a clever, two-timing schemer who is out to frame him."

"Who is she?"

"I wish I knew. If I did, I'd have detectives on her trail within the next hour. The trouble is I don't know. I only know there *is* such a woman. She lost her head over Duane. He'll protect her."

"Married?"

"I don't think so. I don't know."

"What about the murder case?"

"It ties in with smuggling. Duane Jefferson sold a batch of diamonds to Munroe Baxter. That was through the South African office. Baxter asked Jefferson to arrange to have the diamonds cut, polished and delivered to our Paris office. Our Paris office didn't know the history of the transaction. It simply made delivery to Baxter on instructions of the South African office. Usually we try to know something about the people with whom we are dealing. Baxter juggled the deal between our two offices in such a way that each office thought the other one had done the investigating.

"Baxter had worked out one hell of a slick scheme. He had faked a perfect background of respectability."

"How did you find out about the smuggling?" Mason asked.

"His female accomplice broke down and confessed."

"Who is she?"

"A girl named Yvonne Manco."

"Tell me about it," Mason said.

"Didn't you read the account about a fellow jumping overboard from a cruise ship and committing suicide a while back?"

"Yes, I did," Mason said. "Wasn't *that* man's name Munroe Baxter?"

"Exactly."

"I knew I'd heard the name somewhere as soon as you mentioned it. How does the murder angle enter into it?"

Irving said, "Here's the general sketch. Yvonne Manco is a very beautiful young woman who sailed on a cruise ship around the world. She was the queen of the cruise. The ship touched at Naples. Yvonne started down the gangplank. She was met by Munroe Baxter, a man who had the appearance of a Frenchman, but the name, citizenship and passport of a United States citizen. You must understand all of these things in order to appreciate the sequence of events."

"Go ahead," Mason said.

"Apparently, Munroe Baxter had at one time been in love with Yvonne Manco. According to the story that was given to the passengers, they had been going together and then the affair had broken up through a misunderstanding.

"Whoever wrote that script did a beautiful job, Mr. Mason."

"It was a script?" Mason asked.

"Hell, yes. It was as phony as a three dollar bill."

"What happened?"

"The passengers naturally were interested. They saw this man burst through the crowd. They saw him embrace Yvonne Manco. They saw her faint in his arms. There was a beautiful romance, the spice of scandal, a page out of this beautiful young woman's past. It was touching; it was pathetic—and naturally, it caused an enormous amount of gossip."

Mason nodded.

"The ship was in Naples for two days. It sailed, and when it sailed Munroe Baxter was pleading with Yvonne Manco to marry him. He was the last man off the ship; then he stood on the pier and wept copiously, shedding crocodile tears."

"Go on," Mason said, interested.

"The ship sailed out into the Mediterranean. It stopped in Genoa. Munroe Baxter met the ship at the dock. Again Yvonne Manco swooned in his arms, again she refused to marry him, again the ship sailed.

"Then came the pay-off. As the ship was off Gibraltar a helicopter hovered overhead. A man descended a rope ladder, dangled precariously from the last rung. The helicopter hovered over the deck of the ship, and Munroe Baxter dropped to the deck by the swimming pool, where Yvonne Manco was disporting herself in the sunlight in a seductive bathing suit."

"Romantic," Mason said.

"And opportune," Irving said dryly. "No one could resist such an impetuous, dramatic courtship. The passengers virtually forced Yvonne to give her consent. The captain married them on the high seas that night. The passengers turned the ship upside down in celebration. It was wonderful stuff."

"Yes, I can imagine," Mason said.

"And, of course," Irving went on, "since Baxter boarded the ship in that dramatic manner, without so much as a toothbrush or an extra handkerchief, how would the customs people suspect that Munroe Baxter was smuggling three hundred thousand dollars' worth of diamonds in a chamois-skin belt around his waist?

"In the face of all that beautiful romance, who would have thought that Yvonne Manco had been Munroe Baxter's mistress for a couple of years, that she was his accomplice in a smuggling plot and that this courtship was all a dramatic hoax?"

"I see," Mason said.

Irving went on, "The stage was all set. Munroe Baxter, in the eyes of the passengers, was a crazy Frenchman, a United States citizen, of course, but one who had acquired all the excitability of the French.

"So, when the ship approached port and Yvonne Manco, dressed to the hilt, danced three times with the good-looking assistant purser, it was only natural that Munroe Baxter should stage a violent scene, threaten to kill himself, break into tears, dash to his stateroom and subsequently leap overboard after a frenzied scene in which Yvonne Manco threatened to divorce him."

"Yes," Mason said, "I remember the newspapers made quite a play of the story."

"It was made to order for press coverage," Irving said. "And who would have thought that the excitable Munroe Baxter carried with him three hundred thousand dollars in diamonds when he jumped overboard, that he was a powerful swimmer who could easily swim to a launch which was opportunely waiting at a prearranged spot, and that later on he and the lovely Yvonne were to share the proceeds of a carefully written, superbly directed scenario, performed very cleverly for the sole purpose of fooling the customs authorities?"

"And it didn't?" Mason asked.

"Oh, but it did! Everything went like clockwork, except for one thing—Munroe Baxter didn't reappear to join Yvonne Manco. She went to the secluded motel which was to be their rendezvous. She waited and waited and waited and waited."

"Perhaps Baxter decided that a whole loaf was better than half a loaf," Mason said.

Irving shook his head. "It seems the lovely Yvonne Manco went to the accomplice who was waiting in the launch. At first, the accomplice told her that Baxter had never showed up. He told her that Baxter must have been seized by cramps while he was swimming underwater."

"Did this take place within the territorial waters of the United States?" Mason asked.

"Right at the approach to Los Angeles Harbor."

"In daylight?"

"No, just before daylight. You see, it was a cruise ship and it was gliding in at the earliest possible hour so the passengers could have a maximum time ashore for sightseeing."

"All right, Baxter was supposed to have drowned," Mason said. "What happened?"

"Well, Yvonne Manco had a horrible suspicion. She thought that the accomplice in the launch might have held Baxter's head underwater and might have taken the money belt.

"Probably, she wouldn't have said anything at all, if it hadn't been for the fact that customs agents were also putting two and two together. They called on the lovely Yvonne Manco to question her about her 'husband' after it appeared that she and her 'husband' had sailed on another cruise ship as man and wife some eighteen months earlier."

"And Yvonne Manco broke down and told them the whole story?" Mason asked.

"Told them the whole story, including the part that it had been Duane Jefferson who had been involved in the sale of the jewels. So police became very much interested in Duane Jefferson, and yesterday afternoon, on an affidavit of Yvonne Manco, a search warrant was issued and police searched the office."

"And recovered a hundred thousand dollars in gems?" Mason asked.

"Recovered a goodly assortment of diamonds," Irving said. "Let us say, perhaps a third of the value of the smuggled shipment."

"And the remaining two-thirds?"

Irving shrugged his shoulders.

"And the identification?" Mason asked.

Again Irving shrugged his shoulders.

"And where were these gems found?"

"Where someone had very cleverly planted them. You may remember the little flurry of excitement when an intruder was discovered in the office—the police asked us to check and see if anything had been taken. It never occurred to us to check *and see if anything had been planted*."

"Where were the diamonds found?"

"In a package fastened to the back of a desk drawer with adhesive tape."

"And what does Duane Jefferson have to say about this?"

"What could he say?" Irving asked. "It was all news to him, just as it was to me."

"You can vouch for these facts?" Mason asked.

"I'll vouch for them. But I can't vouch for Duane's romantic, crazy notions of protecting this girl."

"She was the same girl who entered the office?"

"I think she was. Duane would have a fit and never speak to me again if he knew I ever entertained such a thought. You have to handle him with kid gloves where women are concerned. But if it comes to a showdown, *you're* going to have to drag this girl into it, and Duane Jefferson will cease to co-operate with you as soon as you mention her very existence."

Mason thought the matter over.

"Well?" Irving asked.

"Make out your check for two thousand dollars," Mason told him. "That will be on account of a five-thousand-dollar fee."

"What do you mean a five-thousand-dollar fee?"

"It won't be more than that."

"Including detectives?"

"No. You will have to pay expenses. I'm fixing fees."

"Damn it," Irving exploded. "If that bunch in the home office hadn't mentioned a two-thousand-dollar retainer, I could have got you to handle the whole case for two thousand."

Mason sat quietly facing Irving.

"Well, it's done now, and there's nothing I can do about it," Irving said, taking from his wallet a check already made out to the lawyer. He slid the check across the desk to Perry Mason.

Mason said to Della Street, "Make a receipt, Della, and put on the receipt that this is a retainer on behalf of Duane Jefferson."

"What's the idea?" Irving asked.

"Simply to show that I'm not responsible to you or your company but only to my client."

Irving thought that over.

"Any objections?" Mason asked.

"No. I presume you're intimating that you'd even turn against me if it suited Duane's interests for you to do so."

"I'm more than intimating. I'm telling you."

Irving grinned. "That's okay by me. I'll go further. If at any time things start getting hot, you can count on me to do anything needed to back your play. I'd even consent to play the part of a missing witness."

Mason shook his head. "Don't try to call the plays. Let me do that."

Irving extended his hand. "I just want you to understand my position, Mason."

"And be sure *you* understand *mine*," Mason said.

CHAPTER 5

MASON LOOKED AT DELLA STREET AS WALTER IRVING LEFT THE office.

"Well?" Della Street asked.

Mason said, "I just about had to take the case in self-defense, Della."

"Why?"

"Otherwise, we'd be sitting on top of information in a murder case, we wouldn't have any client whom we would be protecting, and the situation could become rather rugged."

"And as it is now?" she asked.

"Now," he told her, "we have a client whom we can be protecting. An attorney representing a client in a murder case is under no obligation to go to the police and set forth his surmises, suspicions, and conclusions, particularly if he has reason to believe that such a course would be against the best interests of his client."

"But how about the positive evidence?" Della Street asked.

"Evidence of what?"

"Evidence that we harbored a young woman who had gone into that office and planted diamonds."

"We don't *know* she planted diamonds."

"Who had gone into the office then."

"We don't *know* she was the same woman."

"It's a reasonable assumption."

"Suppose she was merely a typist who happened to be in the building. We go to the police with a lot of suspicions, and the police give the story to the newspapers, then she sues for defamation of character."

"I see," Della Street said demurely. "I'm afraid it's hopeless to try and convince you."

"It is."

"And now may I ask you a question, Counselor?"

"What?"

"Do you suppose that it was pure coincidence that you are the attorney retained to represent the interests of Duane Jefferson?"

Mason stroked his chin thoughtfully.

"Well?" she prompted.

"I've thought of that," Mason admitted. "Of course, the fact that I am known as a trial attorney, that I have offices on the same floor of the same building would mean that Irving had had a chance to hear about me and, by the same token, a chance to notify his home office that I would be available."

"But he said he didn't do that. He said somebody beat him to it and he got the cable to turn over the two thousand dollars to you."

Mason nodded.

"Well?" Della Street asked.

"No comment," Mason said.

"So what do we do now?"

"Now," Mason said, "our position is very, very clear, Della. I suggest that you go down to the camera store, tell them that I want to buy a fingerprint camera, and you also might get a studio camera with a ground-glass focusing arrangement. Pick up some lights and we'll see if we can get a photograph of those latent fingerprints on the gum."

"And then?" she asked.

"Then," Mason said, "we'll enlarge the film so that it shows only the fingerprints and not the gum."

"And then?"

"By that time," Mason said, "I hope we have managed to locate the girl who made the fingerprints and find out about things for ourselves. While you're getting the cameras I'll go down to Paul Drake's office and have a chat with him."

"Chief," Della Street asked somewhat apprehensively, "isn't this rather risky?"

Mason's grin was infectious. "Sure it is."

"Hadn't you better forget about other things and protect yourself?"

Mason shook his head. "We're protecting a client, Della. Give me a description of that girl—the best one you can give."

"Well," Della Street said, "I'd place her age at twenty-six or twenty-seven, her height at five feet three inches, her weight at about a hundred and sixteen pounds. She had reddish-brown hair and her eyes were also a reddish-brown—about the same color as her hair, very expressive. She was good-looking, trim and well proportioned."

"Good figure?" Mason asked.

"Perfect."

"How was she dressed?"

"I can remember that quite well, Chief, because she looked stunning. I remember thinking at the time that she looked more like a client than a gal from an employment agency.

"She wore a beautifully tailored gray flannel suit, navy blue kid shoes. Umm, let me see . . . yes, I remember now. There was fine white stitching across the toes of the shoes. She carried a matching envelope purse and white gloves. Now let me think. I am quite sure she didn't wear a hat. As I recall, she had a tortoise-shell band on, and there wasn't a hair out of place.

"She didn't take her jacket off while she was working, so I can't be certain, but I think she had on a pale blue cashmere sweater. She opened just the top button of her jacket, so I can't say for sure about this."

Mason smiled. "You women never miss a thing about another woman, do you, Della? I would say that was remembering *very* well. Would you type it out for me—the description? Use a plain sheet of paper, not my letterhead."

Mason waited until Della Street had finished typing the description, then said, "Okay, Della, go down and get the cameras. Get lots of film, lights, a tripod, and anything we may need. Don't let on what we want to use them for."

"How about the fingerprint camera? Isn't that a giveaway?"

"Tell the proprietor I'm going to have to cross-examine a witness and I want to find out all about how a fingerprint camera works."

Della Street nodded.

Mason took the typed description and walked down the hall to Paul Drake's office. He nodded to the girl at the switchboard. "Paul Drake in?"

"Yes, Mr. Mason. Shall I say you're here?"

"Anybody with him?"

"No."

"Tell him I'm on my way," Mason said, opening the gate in the partition and walking down the long glassed-in runway off which there were numerous cubbyhole offices. He came to the slightly more commodious office marked "Paul Drake, Private," pushed open the door and entered.

"Hi," Drake said. "I was waiting to hear from you."

Mason raised his eyebrows.

"Don't look so innocent," Drake said. "The officials of the South African Gem Importing and Exploration Company have been checking up on you by long-distance telephone. They called the manager of the building and asked him about you."

"Did they ask him about me by name," Mason asked, "or did they ask him to recommend some attorney?"

"No, they had your name. They wanted to know all about you."

"What did he tell them?"

Drake grinned and said, "Your rent's paid up, isn't it?"

"What the devil is this all about, do you know, Paul?"

"All I know is it's a murder rap," Drake said, "and the way the police are acting, someone must have caved in with a confession."

"Sure," Mason said, "a confession that would pass the buck to someone else and take the heat off the person making the so-called confession."

"Could be," Drake said. "What do we do?"

"We get busy."

"On what?"

"First," Mason told him, "I want to find a girl."

"Okay, what do I have to go on?"

Mason handed him Della Street's typewritten description.

"Fine," Drake said. "I can go downstairs, stand on the street corner during the lunch hour and pick you out a hundred girls of this description in ten minutes."

"Take another look," Mason invited. "She's a lot better than average."

"If it was average, I could make it a thousand," Drake said.

"All right," Mason said. "We're going to have to narrow it down."

"How?"

"This girl," Mason said, "is an expert typist. She probably holds down a very good secretarial job somewhere."

"Unless, of course, she *was* an exceedingly fine secretary and then got married," Drake said.

Mason nodded, conceding the point without changing his position. "She also has legal experience," he said.

"How do you know?"

"That's something I'm not at liberty to tell you."

"All right, what do I do?"

Mason said, "Paul, you're going to have to open up a dummy office. You're going to telephone the Association of Legal Secretaries; you're going to put an ad in the bar journal and the newspapers; you're going to ask for a young, attractive typist. Now, I don't *know* that this girl takes shorthand. Therefore, you're going to have to state that a knowledge of shorthand is desirable but not necessary. You're going to offer a salary of two hundred dollars a week—"

"My Lord!" Drake said. "You'll be deluged, Perry. You might just as well ask the whole city to come trooping into your office."

"Wait a minute," Mason told him. "You don't have the sketch yet."

"Well, I certainly hope I don't!"

"Your ad will provide that the girl must pass a typing test in order to get the job. She must be able to copy rapidly and perfectly and at a very high rate of speed—fix a top rate of words per minute.

"Now, the type of girl we want will already have a job somewhere. We've got to get a job that sounds sufficiently attractive so she'll come in to take a look. Therefore, we can't expect her in during office hours. So mention that the office will be open noons and until seven o'clock in the evening."

"And you want me to rent a furnished office?" Drake asked.

"That's right."

Drake said lugubriously, "You'd better make arrangements to replace the carpet when you leave. The one that's there will be worn threadbare by the horde of applicants— How the devil will I know if the right girl comes in?"

"That's what I'm coming to," Mason said. "You're going to start looking these applicants over. You won't find many that can type at the rate specified. Be absolutely hard-boiled with the qualifications. Have a good secretary sitting there, weeding them out. Don't pay any attention to anyone who has to reach for an eraser. The girl I want can make that keyboard sound like a machine gun."

"Okay, then what?"

"When you get girls who qualify on the typing end of the job," Mason said, "give them a personal interview. Look them over carefully to see how they check with this description and tell them you want to see their driving licenses. A girl like that is bound to have a car. That's where the catch comes in."

"How come?"

Mason said, "Sometime this afternoon I'm going to send you over a right thumbprint—that is, a photograph of a thumbprint—perhaps not the best fingerprinting in the world but at least you'll be able to identify it. When you look at their driving licenses, make it a point to be called into another room for something. Get up and excuse yourself. You can say that there's another applicant in there that you have to talk to briefly, or that you have to answer a phone or something. Carry the girl's driving license in there with you, give the thumbprint a quick check. You can eliminate most of them at a glance. Some of them you may have to study a little bit. But if you get the right one, you'll be able to recognize the thumbprint."

"What do I do then?"

"Make a note of the name and address on the driving license. In that way, she won't be able to give you a phony name. And call me at once."

"Anything else?" Drake asked.

"This is what I think," Mason said, "but it's just a hunch. I *think* the girl's first name will be Mae. When you find a girl who answers that general description and can type like a house afire, whose first name is Mae, start checking carefully."

"When will you have that thumbprint?"

"Sometime this afternoon. Her driving license will have the imprint of her right thumb on it."

"Can you tell me what this is all about?" Drake asked.

Mason grinned and shook his head. "It's better if you don't know, Paul."

"One of those things, eh?" Drake asked, his voice showing a singular lack of enthusiasm.

"No," Mason told him, "it isn't. It's just that I'm taking an ounce of prevention."

"With you," Drake told him, "I prefer a *pound* of prevention. If things go wrong, I know there won't be more than an ounce of cure."

CHAPTER 6

MASON SAT IN THE VISITORS' ROOM AT THE JAIL AND LOOKED across at Duane Jefferson.

His client was a tall, composed individual who seemed reserved, unexcited, and somehow very British.

Mason tried to jar the man out of his extraordinary complacency.

"You're charged with murder," he said.

Duane Jefferson observed him coolly. "I would hardly be here otherwise, would I?"

"What do you know about this thing?"

"Virtually nothing. I knew the man, Baxter, in his lifetime—that is, I assume it was the same one."

"How did you know him?"

"He represented himself as a big wholesale dealer. He showed up at the South African office and wanted to buy diamonds. It is against the policy of the company to sell diamonds in the rough, unless, of course, they are industrial diamonds."

"Baxter wanted them in the rough?"

"That's right."

"And he was advised he couldn't have them?"

"Well, of course, we were tactful about it, Mr. Mason. Mr. Baxter gave promise of being an excellent customer, and he was dealing on a cash basis."

"So what was done?"

"We showed him some diamonds that were cut and polished. He didn't want those. He said that the deal he was putting across called for buying diamonds in the rough and carrying them through each step of cutting and polishing. He said he wanted to be able to tell his customers he had personally selected the diamonds just as they came from the fields."

"Why?"

"He didn't say."

"And he wasn't asked?"

"In a British-managed company," Jefferson said, "we try to keep personal questions to a minimum. We don't pry, Mr. Mason."

"So what was done finally?"

"It was arranged that he would select the diamonds, that we would send them to our Paris office, that there they would be cut and polished, and, after they were cut and polished, delivery would be made to Mr. Baxter."

"What were the diamonds worth?"

"Wholesale or retail?"

"Wholesale."

"Very much less than their retail price."

"How much less?"

"I can't tell you."

"Why not?"

"That information is a very closely guarded trade secret, Mr. Mason."

"But I'm your attorney."

"Quite."

"Look here," Mason said, "are you British?"

"No."

"American?"

"Yes."

"How long have you been working for a British company?"

"Five or six years."

"You have become quite British."

"There are certain mannerisms, Mr. Mason, which the trade comes to expect of the representatives of a company such as ours."

"And there are certain mannerisms which an American jury expects to find in an American citizen," Mason told him.

"If a jury should feel you'd cultivated a British manner, you might have reason to regret your accent and cool, impersonal detachment."

Jefferson's lip seemed to curl slightly. "I would have nothing but contempt for a jury that would let personal considerations such as those influence its judgment."

"That would break the jurors' hearts," Mason told him.

Jefferson said, "We may as well understand each other at the outset, Mr. Mason. I govern my actions according to principle. I would rather die than yield in a matter of principle."

"All right," Mason said. "Have it your own way. It's your funeral. Did you see Baxter again?"

"No, sir, I didn't. After that, arrangements were completed through the Paris office."

"Irving?" Mason asked.

"I don't think it was Irving, Mr. Mason. I think it was one of the other representatives."

"You read about the arrival of the cruise ship and Baxter's supposed suicide?"

"I did, indeed, Mr. Mason."

"And did you make any comment to the authorities?"

"Certainly not."

"You knew he was carrying a small fortune in diamonds?"

"I assumed that a small fortune in diamonds had been delivered to him through our Paris office. I had no means, of course, of knowing what he had done with them."

"You didn't make any suggestions to the authorities?"

"Certainly not. Our business dealings are highly confidential."

"But you did discuss his death with your partner, Irving?"

"Not a partner, Mr. Mason. A representative of the company, a personal friend but—"

"All right, your associate," Mason corrected.

"Yes, I discussed it with him."

"Did he have any ideas?"

"None. Except that there were certain suspicious circumstances in connection with the entire situation."

"It occurred to you that the whole thing might have been part of a smuggling plot?"

"I prefer not to amplify that statement, Mr. Mason. I can simply say that there were certain suspicious circumstances in connection with the entire transaction."

"And you discussed those with Irving?"

"As a representative of the company talking to an associate, I did. I would prefer, however, not to go into detail as to what I said. You must remember, Mr. Mason, that I am here not in an individual but a representative capacity."

"You may be in this country in a representative capacity," Mason said, "but don't ever forget that you're here in this jail in a purely individual capacity."

"Oh, quite," Jefferson said.

"I understand police found diamonds in your office," Mason went on.

Jefferson nodded.

"Where did those diamonds come from?"

"Mr. Mason, I haven't the faintest idea. I am in my office approximately six hours out of the twenty-four. I believe the building provides a scrubwoman with a master key. The janitor also has a master key. People come and go through that office. Police even told me that there was someone trying to break into the office, or that someone had broken into the office."

"A girl," Mason said.

"I understand it was a young woman, yes."

"Do you have any idea who this woman was?"

"No. Certainly not!"

"Do you know any young women here in the city?"

Jefferson hesitated.

"Do you?" Mason prodded.

Jefferson met his eyes. "No."

"You're acquainted with *no* young woman?"

"No."

"Would you perhaps be trying to shield someone?"

"Why should I try to shield someone?"

"I am not asking you why at the moment. I am asking you if you are."

"No."

"You understand it could be a very serious matter if you should try to falsify any of the facts?"

"Isn't it a rule of law in this country," Jefferson countered, "that the prosecution must prove the defendant guilty beyond all reasonable doubt?"

Mason nodded.

"They can't do it," Jefferson said confidently.

"You may not have another chance to tell me your story," Mason warned.

"I've told it."

"There is no girl?"

"No."

"Weren't you writing to some young woman here before you left South Africa?"

Again there was a perceptible hesitancy, then Jefferson looked him in the eyes and said, "No."

"Police told you there was some young woman who broke into your office?"

"Someone who opened the door with a key."

"Had you given your key to any woman?"

"No. Certainly not."

Mason said, "Look here, if there's anyone you want protected, tell me the whole story. I'll try to protect that person as far as possible. After all, I'm representing you. I'm trying to do what is for your best interests. Now, don't put yourself in such a position that you're going to have to try to deceive your attorney. Do you understand what that can lead to?"

"I understand."

"And you are protecting no one?"

"No one."

"The district attorney's office feels that it has some evidence against you, otherwise it wouldn't be proceeding in a case of this kind."

"I suppose a district attorney can be mistaken as well as anyone else."

"Better sometimes," Mason said. "You're not being very helpful."

"What help can I give, Mr. Mason? Suppose *you* should walk into your office tomorrow morning and find the police there. Suppose they told you that they had uncovered stolen property in your office. Suppose I should ask you to tell me the entire story. What could you tell me?"

"I'd try to answer your questions."

"I have answered your questions, Mr. Mason."

"I have reason to believe there's some young woman here in the city whom you know."

"There is no one."

Mason got to his feet. "Well," he told the young man, "it's up to you."

"On the contrary, Mr. Mason. I think you'll find that it's up to *you.*"

"You're probably right, at that," Mason told him, and signaled the guard that the interview was over.

CHAPTER 7

MASON UNLOCKED THE DOOR OF HIS PRIVATE OFFICE. DELLA Street looked up from her work. "How did it go, Chief?"

Mason made a gesture of throwing something away.

"Not talking?" Della Street asked.

"Talking," Mason said, "but it doesn't make sense. He's protecting some woman."

"Why?"

"That," Mason said, "is something we're going to have to find out. Get the cameras, Della?"

"Yes. Cameras, lights, films, tripod—everything."

"We're going into the photographic business," Mason said. "Tell Gertie we don't want to be disturbed, no matter what happens."

Della Street started to pick up the connecting telephone to the outer office, then hesitated. "Gertie is going to make something out of *this!*" she said.

Mason frowned thoughtfully. "You have a point there," he said.

"With her romantic disposition, she will get ideas in her head that you'll never get out with a club."

"All right," Mason decided. "Don't let her know I'm in. We'll just go into the law library and—do you think you could help me tilt that desk over on its side, Della?"

"I can try."

"Good. We'll just go in the library, close and lock the door."

"Suppose Gertie should want me for something? Can't we tell her what we're doing so she can—"

Mason shook his head. "I don't want *anyone* to know about this, Della."

Della went through the motions of throwing something in the wastebasket. "There goes my good name," she said.

"You'll need to stay only to help me get the desk over on its side, and you can fix up the lighting. We'll lock the door from the law library to the outer office and leave the door to this office open. You can hear the phone if Gertie rings."

"That's all right," Della Street said, "but suppose she comes in for something?"

"Well, if the door's open," Mason said, "she'll see that we're photographing something."

"Her curiosity is as bad as her romanticism," Della said.

"Does she talk?" Mason asked.

"I wish I knew the answer to that one, Chief. She must talk to that boy friend of hers. You couldn't keep Gertie quiet with a muzzle. I doubt that she talks to anyone else."

"Okay," Mason said, "we'll take a chance. Come on, Della. Let's get that desk on its side and get the floodlights rigged up."

"Here's a chart," Della Street said, "giving all the exposure factors. I told the man at the camera store we wanted to copy some documents. You have to change your exposure factor when you do real close-up photography. He suggested that we use film packs with the camera where you focus on the ground glass. The fingerprint camera is supposed to be a self-contained unit, with lights and every—"

"I understand," Mason interrupted. "I want to get the wad of chewing gum photographed in place on the bottom of the desk, then I want to get close-ups showing the fingerprints. We can get the photographer to enlarge the fingerprints from these photographs in case the fingerprint camera doesn't do a good job."

"The fingerprint camera seems to be pretty near—" She paused suddenly.

Mason laughed. "Foolproof?"

"Well," Della Street said, "that's what the man at the camera store said."

"All right," Mason told her, "let's go. We'll take photographs at different exposures. You have plenty of film packs?"

"Heavens, yes! I figured you'd want to be sure you had the job done, and I got enough film so you can take all the pictures you want at all kinds of different exposures."

"That's fine," Mason told her.

Della Street took one end of the typewriter desk, Mason the other. "We'll have to move it out from the wall," Mason said. "Now tilt it back, Della. It'll be heavy just before it gets to the floor. You think you can—?"

"Good heavens, yes, Chief. It's not heavy."

"The drawers are full of stationery, and that typewriter— We could take some of the things out and lighten it."

"No, no, let's go. It's all right."

They eased the desk back to the floor.

"All right," Mason said, "give me a hand with the lights and the tripod. We'll get this camera set up and focused."

"I have a magnifying glass," Della Street said. "They seem to think that on the critical focusing necessary for close-ups it will help."

"Good girl," Mason told her. "Let's see what we can do. We'll want an unbalanced cross-lighting, and since light varies inversely as the square of the distance, we'll space these lights accordingly."

Mason first took a series of pictures with the fingerprint camera, then got the lights plugged in and adjusted, the studio camera placed on the tripod and properly focused. He used a tape measure to determine the position of the lights, then slipped a filmpack into the camera, regarded the wad of chewing gum thoughtfully.

"That's going to be fine," Della Street said. "How did you know about using unbalanced cross-lighting to bring out the ridges?"

"Cross-examining photographers," Mason said, "plus a study of books on photography. A lawyer has to know a little something about everything. Don't you notice *Photographic Evidence* by Scott over there?" Mason indicated the thick book found in red leather.

"That's right," she said. "I remember seeing you studying that from time to time. You used some of his stuff in that automobile case, didn't you?"

"Uh huh," Mason said. "It's surprising how much there is to know about photography. Now, Della, I'm going to start with this lens at $f11$, taking a photograph at a twenty-fifth of a second. Then we'll take one at a tenth of a second, then one at a second. Then I'll use the cable release and we'll take one at two seconds. Then we'll try $f16$, run through the exposures all over again, then take another batch at $f22$."

"All right," Della Street said. "I'll keep notes of the different exposures."

Mason started taking the pictures, pulling the tabs out of the film pack, tearing them off, dropping them into the wastebasket.

"Oh oh," Della Street said. "There's the phone. That's Gertie calling."

She made a dash for Mason's private office. Mason continued taking pictures.

Della Street was back after a moment. "Walter Irving wants you to call just as soon as you come in."

Mason nodded.

"Gertie asked if you were in yet, and I lied like a trooper," Della Street said.

"Okay, Della. Walter Irving didn't say what he wanted, did he?"

"He said he wanted to know if you'd been able to get any information out of Duane Jefferson about the woman in the case."

Mason said, "As soon as we get finished here, Della, tell Paul Drake I want to put a shadow on Irving."

"You suspect him?"

"Not exactly. The policy of this office is to protect our client and to hell with the rest of them."

"What's the client doing?"

"Sitting tight. Says he knows nothing about the girl who broke into the office, that he doesn't know any girl here, hasn't been corresponding with anyone, and all that."

"You think he has?"

"That wasn't just a casual visit that Mae Wallis paid to their office."

"You've decided she was the girl?"

"Oh, not officially. I'd deny it to the police. But where did the diamonds in the chewing gum come from?"

"Chief, why would *she* plant a hundred thousand dollars' worth of diamonds and then keep a couple of diamonds with her and conceal them in a wad of chewing gum?"

"I can give you *an* answer," Mason said, "but it may not be *the* answer."

"What is it?"

"Suppose she had been given some gems to plant. She must have had them wrapped in tissue paper in her purse. She had to work in a hurry and probably became somewhat alarmed. Something happened to make her suspicious. She realized that she had been detected."

"What makes you say that?"

"Because she roughed up the office, making it appear she was looking *for* something. Otherwise she'd have slipped in, planted the diamonds and left."

"Then you think the diamonds that she put in the chewing gum were ones she had overlooked when she was making the plant?"

"I said it was *an* answer. After she got established as a typist in our office, she had a breathing spell. She opened her purse to make sure she hadn't overlooked anything, and found several of the diamonds. She knew that police were on the job and that there was a good chance she might be picked up, questioned, and perhaps searched. So she fastened the diamonds to the underside of the desk."

"I keep thinking those 'Prince Charming' letters have something to do with it, Chief."

Mason nodded. "So do I. Perhaps she planted the diamonds in the office and at the same time deliberately planted the letters in the restroom."

"She could have done that, all right," Della Street admitted. "There's the phone again."

She gathered her skirts and again sprinted for Mason's private office. Mason continued to take photographs while she answered the phone and returned.

"What is it?" Mason asked.

"I have to announce," she said, "that Gertie is just a little suspicious."

"Yes?" Mason asked.

"Yes. She wants to know why it's taking me so long to answer the phone."

"What did you tell her?"

"Told her I was doing some copy work and I didn't want to stop in the middle of a sentence."

Mason snapped out the floodlights. "All right, Della. We'll quit. We have enough pictures. Tell Paul Drake I want shadows put on Walter Irving."

CHAPTER 8

A FEW MORNINGS LATER MASON WAS SCANNING THE PAPERS on his desk. "Well, I see that the grand jury has now filed an indictment, charging Duane Jefferson with first-degree murder."

"Why the indictment?" Della Street asked.

"The district attorney can proceed against a defendant in either of two ways. He can file a complaint or have someone swear to a complaint. Then the Court holds a preliminary hearing. At that time the defendant can cross-examine the witnesses. If the Court makes an order binding the defendant over, the district attorney then files an information and the case is brought on to trial before a jury.

"However, the district attorney can, if he wishes, present witnesses to the grand jury. The grand jury then returns an indictment, and the transcript of the testimony of the witnesses is delivered to the defendant. In that case, there is no opportunity for counsel for the defense to cross-examine the witnesses until they get to court.

"Now, in this case against Duane Jefferson, the main witness before the grandjury seems to have been Yvonne Manco, who tells a great story about how her lover-boy, Munroe Baxter, was rubbed out by some nasty people who wanted to steal the diamonds he was smuggling. Then there is the testimony of a police officer that a large portion of those diamonds was found in the office occupied by Duane Jefferson."

"Is that testimony sufficient to support an indictment?" Della Street asked.

Mason grinned and said, "It certainly wouldn't be sufficient standing by itself to bring about a conviction in a court of law."

"Do you intend to question the sufficiency of the evidence?"

"Lord, no," Mason said. "For some reason the district attorney is breaking his neck to get a prompt trial, and I'm going to cooperate by every means in my power."

"Wouldn't it be better to stall the thing along a bit until—?"

Mason shook his head.

"Why not, Chief?"

"Well, the rumor is that the district attorney has a surprise witness he's going to throw at us. He's so intent on that he may overlook the fact that there isn't any real *corpus delicti*."

"What do you mean?"

"The body of Munroe Baxter has never been found," Mason said.

"Does it have to be?"

"Not necessarily. The words *corpus delicti*, contrary to popular belief, don't mean the 'body of the victim.' They mean the 'body of the crime.' But it *is* necessary to show that a murder was committed. That can be shown by independent evidence, but of course the *best* evidence is the body of the victim."

"So you're going to have an immediate trial?"

"Just as soon as we can get an open date on the calendar," Mason said. "And with the district attorney and the defense both trying to get the earliest possible trial date, that shouldn't be too difficult. How's Paul Drake coming with his office setup?"

"Chief, you should see that. It's wonderful! There's this ad in all of the papers, advertising for a legally trained secretary who can type like a house afire. The salary to start—to start, mind you—is two hundred dollars a week. It is intimated that the attorney is engaged in cases of international importance and that there may be an opportunity to travel, to meet important personalities. It's a secretary's dream."

"And the office where he's screening applicants?" Mason asked.

"All fitted out with desks, typewriters, law books, plush carpets and an air of quiet dignity which makes it seem that even the janitor must be drawing a salary about equal to that of the ordinary corporation president."

"I hope he hasn't overdone it," Mason said. "I'd better take a look."

"No, it isn't overdone. I can assure you of that. The air of conservatism and respectability envelops the place like a curtain of smog, permeating every nook and cranny of the office. You should see them—stenographers who are applicants come in chewing gum, giggling and willing to take a chance that lightning may strike despite their lack of qualifications. They stand for a few seconds in that office, then quietly remove their gum, look around at the furniture and start talking in whispers."

"How does he weed out the incompetents?" Mason asked.

"There's a battery of typewriters; girls are asked to sit at the typewriters, write out their names and addresses and list their qualifications.

"Of course, a good typist can tell the minute a girl's hands touch the keyboard whether she is really skillful, fairly competent, or just mediocre. Only the girls who can really play a tune on the keyboard get past the first receptionist."

"Well," Mason said, "it's—"

The private, unlisted phone jangled sharply.

"Good Lord," Della Street said, "that must be Paul Drake now. He's the only other one who has that number."

Mason grabbed for the phone. "That means he's got information so hot he doesn't dare to go through the outer switchboard. Hello . . . hello, Paul."

Drake's voice came over the wire. He was talking rapidly but in the hushed tones of one who is trying to keep his voice from being heard in an adjoining room.

"Hello, Perry. Hello, Perry. This is Paul."

"Yes, Paul, go ahead."

"I have your girl."

"You're certain?"

"Yes."

"Who is she?"

"Her name is Mae W. Jordan. She lives at Seven-Nine-Two Cabachon Street. She's employed at the present time in a law office. She doesn't want to give the name. She would have to give two weeks' notice. She wants the job very badly, and, boy, can that girl tickle the typewriter! And it's wonderful typing."

"What does the *W* stand for?" Mason asked. "Wallis?"

"I don't know yet. I'm just giving you a quick flash that we have the girl."

"You know it's the same one?"

"Yes. The thumbprints match. I'm holding her driving license right at the moment."

"How about the address?" Mason asked.

"And the address is okay. It's Seven-Nine-Two Cabachon Street, the same address that's given on her driving license."

"Okay," Mason said. "Now here's what you do, Paul. Tell her that you *think* she can do the job; that you'll have to arrange an appointment with Mr. Big himself for six o'clock tonight. Tell her to return then. Got that?"

"I've got it," Drake said. "Shall I tell her anything else about the job?"

"No," Mason said. "Try and find out what you can. Be interested but not *too* curious."

"You want me to put a shadow on her?"

"Not if you're certain of the address," Mason said.

"Think we should try to find out about the law office where she's working?"

"No," Mason said. "With her name and address we can get everything we need. This girl is smart and sharp, and she may be mixed up in a murder, Paul. She's undoubtedly connected in some way with a diamond-smuggling operation. Too many questions will—"

"I get it," Drake interrupted. "Okay, Perry, I'll fix an appointment for six o'clock and call you back in fifteen or twenty minutes."

"Do better than that," Mason said. "As soon as you've finished with this girl, jump in your car and come up here. There's no use waiting around there any longer. We've found what we were looking for. You can close the office tomorrow. Take your ads out of the papers and tell all other applicants that the job has been filled. Let's start cutting down the expense."

"Okay," Drake said.

Mason hung up the phone and grinned at Della Street. "Well, we have our typist, Della. She's Mae W. Jordan of Seven-Nine-Two Cabachon Street. Make a note of that—and keep the note where no one else can find it."

CHAPTER 9

PAUL DRAKE WAS GRINNING WITH THE SATISFACTION OF A JOB well done as he eased himself into the big overstuffed chair in Perry Mason's office.

"Well, we did it, Perry, but it certainly was starting from scratch and working on slender clues."

Mason flashed Della Street a glance. "It was a nice job, Paul."

"What gave you your lead in the first place?" Drake asked.

"Oh," Mason said with a gesture of dismissal, "it was just a hunch."

"But you had a damn good thumbprint," Drake said.

"Purely fortuitous," Mason observed.

"Well, if you don't want to tell me, I don't suppose you will," Drake said. "I see they've indicted Jefferson."

"That's right."

"The district attorney says there are certain factors in the situation which demand a speedy trial in order to keep evidence from being dissipated."

"Uh huh," Mason said noncommittally.

"You going to stall around and try for delay?"

"Why should I?"

"Well, ordinarily when the D.A. wants something, the attorney for the defense has different ideas."

"This isn't an ordinary case, Paul."

"No, I suppose not."

"What have you found out about Irving?" Mason asked.

Drake pulled a notebook from his pocket. "Full name, Walter Stockton Irving. Been with the Paris branch of the South African Gem Importing and Exploration Company for about seven years. Likes life on the Continent, the broader standards of morality, the more leisurely pace of life. Quite a race horse fan."

"The deuce he is!"

"That's right. Of course, over there it isn't quite the way it is here."

"A gambler?"

"Well, not exactly. He'll get down to Monte Carlo once in a while and do a little plunging, but mostly he likes to get out with a pair of binoculars and a babe on his arm, swinging a cane, enjoying the prerogatives of being a quote gentleman unquote."

"Now that," Mason said, "interests me a lot, Paul."

"I thought it would."

"What's he doing with his time here?"

"Simply waiting for the branch to get ready for business. He's leading a subdued life. Doubtless the murder charge pending against Jefferson is holding him back slightly. He seems to have made one contact."

"Who?" Mason asked.

"A French babe. Marline Chaumont."

"Where?"

"A bungalow out on Ponce de Leon Drive. The number is 8257."

"Does Marline Chaumont live there alone?"

"No. She has a brother she's taking care of."

"What's wrong with the brother?"

"Apparently he's a mental case. He was released from a hospital, so that his sister could take care of him. However, elaborate precautions are being taken to keep the neighbors from knowing anything about it. One of the neighbors suspects, but that's as far as it goes at the present time."

"Violent?" Mason asked.

"No, not at this time. Just harmless. You've heard of prefrontal lobotomy?"

"Yes, sure. That's the treatment they formerly used on the hopelessly violent insane and on criminals. I understand they've more or less discontinued it."

"Turns a man into a vegetable more or less, doesn't it?"

"Well, you can't get doctors to agree on it," Mason said. "But I think it now has generally been discontinued."

"That's the operation this chap had. He's sort of a zombie. I can't find out too much about him. Anyhow, Marline knew your man Irving over in Paris. Probably when Marline is freed of responsibilities and gets dolled up in glad rags she's quite a number."

"How about now?" Mason asked.

"Now she's the devoted sister. That's one thing about those French, Perry. They go to town when they're on the loose, but when they assume responsibilities they *really* assume them."

"How long has she been here?" Mason asked.

"She's been in this country for a year, according to her statements to tradesmen. But we haven't been able to check up. She's new in the neighborhood. She moved into her house there when she knew that her brother was coming home. She was living in an apartment up to that time. An apartment house would be a poor place to have a mental case. Marline knew it, so she got this bungalow."

"Living there alone with her brother?"

"A housekeeper comes in part of the day."

"And Irving has been going there?"

"Uh huh. Twice to my knowledge."

"Trying to get Marline to go out?"

"What he's *trying* to get is a question. Marline seems to be very devoted to her brother and very domesticated. The first time my operative shadowed Irving to the place it was in the afternoon. When Marline came to the door there was an affectionate greeting. Irving went inside, stayed for about an hour, and when he left, seemed to be trying to persuade Marline to come with him. He stood in the doorway talking to her. She smiled but kept shaking her head.

"So Irving went away. He was back that night, went inside the house, and apparently Marline sold him on the idea of brother sitting because Marline went out and was gone for an hour or two."

"How did she go?"

"By bus."

"She doesn't have a car?"

"Apparently not."

"Where did she go?"

"Gosh, Perry! You didn't tell me you wanted me to shadow *her*. Do you want me to?"

"No," Mason said, "I guess not, Paul. But the thing interests me. What's happened since?"

"Well, apparently Irving recognized the futility of trying to woo Marline away from her responsibilities, or else the trouble Jefferson is in is weighing heavily on his shoulders. He's keeping pretty much to himself in his apartment now."

"What apartment?" Mason asked.

"The Alta Loma Apartments."

"Pick up anything about the case, Paul?"

"The D.A. is supposed to be loaded for bear on this one. He's so darned anxious to get at you, he's running around in circles. He's told a couple of friendly reporters that this is the sort of case he's been looking for and waiting for. Perry, are you all right on this case?"

"What do you mean, 'all right'?"

"Are *you* in the clear?"

"Sure."

"You haven't been cutting any corners?"

Mason shook his head.

"The D.A. is acting as though he had you where he wanted you. He's like a kid with a new toy for Christmas—a whole Christmas tree full of new toys."

"I'm glad he's happy," Mason said. "What about this Mae Jordan, Paul?"

"I didn't get a lot more than I told you over the phone, except that she's promised to be there at six tonight."

"She's working?"

"That's right."

"What kind of an impression does she make, Paul?"

"Clean-cut and competent," Drake said. "She has a nice voice, nice personality, very neat in her appearance, knows what she's doing every minute of the time, and she certainly can type. Her shorthand is just about as fast as you'd find anywhere."

"She's happy in her job?"

"Apparently not. I don't know what it's all about, but she wants to get away from her present environment."

"Perhaps a thwarted love affair?"

"Could be."

"Sounds like it," Mason said.

"Well, you can find out tonight," Drake told him.

"When we get her into that office tonight, Paul," Mason said, "don't mention my name. Don't make *any* introductions. Simply state that I am the man for whom she will be working."

"Will she recognize you?" Drake asked.

"I don't think I've ever seen her," Mason said, glancing at Della Street.

"That doesn't necessarily mean anything. Your pictures get in the paper a lot."

"Well, if she recognizes me it won't make any difference," Mason said, "because outside of the first few questions, Paul, I'm not going to be talking to her about a job."

"You mean that she'll know the thing was a plant as soon as you walk in?"

"Well, I hope not quite *that* soon," Mason said. "But she'll know it shortly after I start questioning her. As long as she talks I'm going to let her talk."

"That won't be long," Drake said. "She answers questions, but she doesn't volunteer any information."

"All right," Mason said. "I'll see you a little before six tonight, Paul."

"Now remember," Drake warned, "there may be a little trouble."

"How come?"

"This girl has got her mind all set on a job where she can travel. She wants to get away from everything. The minute you let her know that you were simply locating her as a witness, she's going to resent it."

"What do you think she'll do?" Mason asked.

"She may do anything."

"I'd like that, Paul."

"You would?"

"Yes," Mason said. "I'd like to know just what she does when she's good and angry. Don't kid yourself about this girl, Paul. She's mixed up in something pretty sinister."

"How deep is she mixed up in it?"

"Probably up to her eyebrows," Mason said. "This Marline Chaumont knew Walter Irving in Paris?"

"Apparently so. She was sure glad to see him. When he rang the bell and she came to the door, she took one look, then made a flying leap into his arms. She was all French."

"And Irving doesn't go there any more?"

Drake shook his head.

"What would she do if I went out to talk with her this afternoon?"

"She might talk. She might not."

"Would she tell Irving I'd been there?"

"Probably."

"Well, I'll have to take that chance, Paul. I'm going to call on Marline Chaumont."

"May I suggest that you take me?" Della Street asked.

"As a chaperon or for the purpose of keeping notes on what is said?" Mason asked.

"I can be very effective in both capacities," Della Street observed demurely.

"It's that French background," Drake said, grinning. "It scares the devil out of them, Perry."

CHAPTER **10**

PERRY MASON DROVE SLOWLY ALONG PONCE DE LEON DRIVE.

"That's it," Della Street said. "The one on the left, the white bungalow with the green trim."

Mason drove the car past the house, sizing it up, went to the next intersection, made a U turn, and drove back.

"What are you going to tell her?" Della Street asked.

"It'll depend on how she impresses me."

"And on how we impress her?"

"I suppose so."

"Isn't this somewhat dangerous, Chief?"

"In what way?'"

"She'll be almost certain to tell Irving."

"Tell him what?"

"That you were out checking up on him."

"I'll tell him that myself."

"And then he'll know that you've had people shadowing him."

"If he's known Miss Chaumont in Paris, he won't know just *how* we checked up. I'd like to throw a scare into Mr. Walter Irving. He's too damned sure of himself."

Mason walked up the three steps to the front porch and pushed the bell button.

After a moment the door was opened a cautious three inches. A brass guard chain stretched taut across the opening.

Mason smiled at the pair of bright black eyes which surveyed him from the interior of the house. "We're looking for a Miss Chaumont."

"I am Miss Chaumont."

"Of Paris?"

"*Mais oui.* I have lived in Paris, yes. Now I live here."

"Would you mind if I asked you a few questions?"

"About what?"

"About Paris?"

"I would love to have you ask me questions about Paris."

"It's rather awkward, standing out here and talking through the door," Mason said.

"Monsieur can hear me?"

"Oh, yes."

"And I can hear you."

Mason smiled at her. Now that his eyes were becoming accustomed to the half-light he could see the oval of the face and a portion of a trim figure.

"Were you familiar with the South African Gem Importing and Exploration Company in Paris?"

"Why do you ask me that question?"

"Because I am interested."

"And who are you?"

"My name is Perry Mason. I am a lawyer."

"Oh, *you* are Perry Mason?"

"That's right."

"I have read about you."

"That's interesting."

"What do you want, Mr. Mason?"

"To know if you knew of the company in Paris."

"I have known of the company, yes."

"And you knew some of the people who worked for that company?"

"But of course, Monsieur. One does not become, as you say, familiar with a company, *non*. One can only become familiar with people, with some of the people, yes? With the company, *non*."

"Did you know Walter Irving while you were in Paris?"

"Of course. He was my friend. He is here now."

"You went out with him occasionally in Paris?"

"But yes. Is that wrong?"

"No, no," Mason said. "I am simply trying to get the background. Did you know Duane Jefferson?"

"Duane Jefferson is from the South African office. Him I do not know."

"Did you know anyone from the South African office?"

"Twice, when people would come to visit in Paris, they asked me to help . . . well, what you call, entertain. I put on a daring dress. I act wicked with the eyes. I make of them . . . what you call the visiting fireman, *non?*"

"And who introduced you to these men?"

"My friend, Walter."

"Walter Irving?"

"That is right."

"I would like to find out something about Mr. Irving."

"He is nice. Did he tell you I am here?"

"No. I located you through people who work for me. They have an office in Paris."

"And the Paris office locates me here? Monsieur, it is impossible!"

Mason smiled. "I am here."

"And *I* am here. But . . . well, a man of your position, Monsieur Mason, one does not—how you call it?—contradict."

"What sort of a fellow is Walter Irving?"

"Walter Irving has many friends. He is very nice. He has—how you say?—the too big heart. That big heart, she is always getting him in trouble. He gives you too much . . . the shirt off his back. When he trusts, he trusts, that one. Sometime people, they take advantage of him. You are his friend, Monsieur Mason?"

"I would like to know about him."

"This woman with you is your wife?"

"My secretary."

"Oh, a thousand pardons. You seem . . . well, you seem as one."

"We have worked together for a long time."

"I see. Could I say something to you as the friend of Walter Irving?"

"Why not?"

"This Duane Jefferson," she said. "Watch him."

"What do you mean?"

"I mean he is the one to watch. He is sharp. He is very smooth. He . . . he is filled with crazy ideas in his head."

"What do you know about him?"

"*Know*, Monsieur? I *know* but little. But a woman has intuition. A woman can tell. Walter, I know very well. He is big. He is honest. He is like a dog. He trusts. But Walter likes what you call the show-off, the grandstand. He likes many clothes and to show off the good-looking woman on his arm. He likes crowds. He likes—"

She broke off and laughed. "He is simple, that one, for one who is so smart otherwise. He cares about a girl, that she should make people turn to look when he walks with her. So when I go out with Walter I put on a dress that . . . well, your secretary will know. The curves, yes?"

Della Street nodded.

She laughed very lightly. "Then Walter is very happy. I think, Monsieur Mason, that this Jefferson—"

"But I thought you didn't know Jefferson?"

"I hear people talk, and I listen. At times I have very big ears. And now, Monsieur Mason, you will pardon me, no? I have a brother who is sick in his upstairs. He will get better if he can be kept very quiet and have no excitement. You are nice people, and I would invite you in, but the excitement, no."

"Thank you very much," Mason said. "Does Walter Irving know you are here in the city?"

"Know I am here? Of course he knows. He has located me. He is very eager, that Walter Irving. And he is nice company. If I did not have my brother, I would put on clothes that show the curves and go with him to the night clubs. That he would love. That also I would like. However, I have responsibilities. I have to stay home. But, Monsieur Mason, please . . . you listen to Marline Chaumont. This Duane Jefferson, he is very cold, very polished, and treacherous like a snake."

"And if you see Walter Irving, you will tell him we were here?"

"You wish me not to?"

"I don't know," Mason said. "I am simply checking."

"I will make you the bargain, Monsieur Mason. You do not tell Walter Irving what I have said about Duane Jefferson, and I do not say to Walter Irving anything that you are here. We keep this a little secret between us, no?

"But, Monsieur Mason, please, if this Duane Jefferson has done things that are wrong, you see that he does not pull my friend Walter down with him?"

"You think Jefferson did something wrong?"

"I have heard people talk."

"But his company gives him an excellent reputation. His company feels the utmost confidence in his honor and his integrity."

"I have told you, Monsieur Mason, that companies cannot feel; only the people in the companies. And later on, when the case comes to trial, Monsieur Mason, I shall read the papers with much interest. But you watch closely this Duane Jefferson. Perhaps he will tell you a story that is very fine as stories go when you do not question, but when he gets on the witness stand and finds that he cannot use the cold English manner to hide behind, then perhaps he gets mad, and when he gets mad, poof! Look out!"

"He has a temper?" Mason asked.

"That, Monsieur Mason, I do not know, but I have heard what others say. He is bad when he gets mad. His manner is a mask."

"I thank you," Mason said.

She hesitated a moment, then archly blew him a kiss with the tips of her fingers. The door closed gently but firmly.

CHAPTER 11

PERRY MASON AND PAUL DRAKE LEFT THE ELEVATORS, WALKED down the corridor of the big office building.

"Here's the suite," Drake said, pausing in front of a door which had on its frosted glass only the single word "Enter" and the number 555.

Drake opened the door.

"Well," Mason said, looking around, "you certainly fixed up a place here, Paul."

"Rental of desks and chairs," Drake said. "Rental of typewriters. The rest of it all came with the furnished office."

"I didn't know you could rent places like this," Mason said.

"This building caters to an international clientele," Drake explained. "Occasionally they need a large furnished office for directors' meetings, conferences, and things of that sort. The last time this was rented, which was last week, a big Mexican company had it for a trade conference.

"They expect to lose money on this office, of course, but the international goodwill and the convenience to tenants in the building who have big meetings from time to time are supposed to more than offset the loss. Come on in here, Perry."

Mason led the way into a private office.

"This where the interviews take place?" Mason asked.

"That's right."

"This girl will be here at six o'clock?"

"Right on the dot. I have an idea that girl prides herself on being prompt and efficient."

"That's the way I had her sized up," Mason said.

"You aren't ready to tell me yet how you got a line on her?"

"No."

"Or what she has to do with the case?"

Mason said, "She *may* be the girl who made the surreptitious entry into the offices of the South African Gem Importing Exploration Company."

"I surmised that," Drake said. "It's almost the same description that the police had."

"You have a tape recorder connected?" Mason asked.

"This room is bugged with three microphones," Drake told him. "There's a tape recorder in that closet."

"And what about a receptionist?" Mason asked.

"My receptionist is coming in to—" He broke off as a buzzer sounded. "That means someone's coming in."

Drake got up, went out into the big reception room, came back in a moment with a very attractive young woman.

"Meet Nora Pitts, Perry. She's one of my operatives, working as a receptionist here, and she really knows the ropes."

Miss Pitts, blushing and somewhat flustered, came forward to give Perry Mason her hand.

"I'd been hoping I'd meet you on one of these jobs, Mr. Mason," she said. "Mr. Drake keeps me for the office type of work. Usually I'm on stake-outs. I was beginning to be afraid I was just *never* going to meet you."

"You shouldn't hold out on me like this, Paul," Mason said to the detective.

Drake grinned, looked at his wrist watch, said, "You understand the setup, Nora?"

She nodded.

"Do you know Della Street, my secretary?" Mason asked.

"I know her by sight, yes."

"Well," Mason said, "after this girl has been in here for a few minutes, Miss Street is going to come in. I told her to be here promptly at fifteen minutes past six."

Nora was listening now, her personal reaction at meeting Mason completely subdued by professional concentration.

"What do I do?" she asked.

"I think that this girl will be here by six o'clock, or at least a couple of minutes past six," Mason said. "You send her in as soon as she arrives. I'll start talking with her and questioning her. Della Street will be in at six-fifteen on the dot. We'll hear the buzzer in the office when the door opens and know that she's here, so there'll be no need for you to notify us. Just have Della sit down and wait. I'll buzz for her when I want her sent in."

"Okay," she said.

"You got it, Nora?" Drake asked.

She nodded. "Of course."

Drake looked at his watch. "Well, it's seven minutes to six. She may come in early. Let's go."

Nora Pitts, with a quick smile at Mason, went back to the reception room.

In the office Drake settled down for a smoke, and Mason joined him with a cigarette.

"The newspapers indicate your client is a cold fish," Drake said.

Mason said irritably, "The guy is trying to protect some girl, and we're not going to get his story out of him until after we've got the story out of this girl."

"And you think Mae Jordan is the girl?"

"I don't know. Could be."

"Suppose she is?"

"Then we'll break her down and get her story."

"What do you propose to do then?"

"We'll get a tape recording," Mason said. "Then I'll go down to the jail, tell Jefferson what I have, and tell him to come clean."

"Then what?"

"Then I'll have his story."

"How's the district attorney going to identify those diamonds, Perry?"

"I don't know much about the case, Paul, but I do know a lot about the district attorney. He's been laying for me for years.

"This time he thinks he has me. He must have a pretty good case. But I'm gambling there's a legal point he's overlooked."

"What's the point?"

"The *corpus delicti.*"

"You think he can't prove it?"

"How's he going to prove a murder?" Mason asked. "They've never found Munroe Baxter's body. Now then, I can show the jury, by Hamilton Burger's own witnesses, that Munroe Baxter was a clever actor who planned to fake a suicide in order to smuggle in gems. Why wouldn't he fake a murder in order to keep from splitting the profit with his female accomplice?

"I'll tell the jury that it's almost certain Baxter has some new babe he's stuck on, some oo-la-la dish who is ready, able and willing to take Yvonne Manco's place as his female accomplice.

"What would be more likely than that Baxter would pretend he had been murdered, so that Yvonne Manco wouldn't be looking for him with fire in her eye?"

"Well, of course, when you put it that way," Drake said, "I can see the possibilities."

"All right," Mason grinned, "that's the way I'm going to put it to the jury. Hamilton Burger isn't going to have the smooth, easy sailing he's anticipating. He'll surprise me. I'll concede he must have something that will hit me hard, but after that, we're going to get down to fundamentals. He can hurt me, but I don't think he can do any more than that. I can blast his case out of court."

They smoked in silence for a few minutes, then Mason said, "What time have you got, Paul? I have five minutes *past* six."

"I have six minutes past, myself," Drake said. "What do you suppose has happened?"

"Do you think she's changed her mind?" Mason asked.

"Hell, no! She was too eager."

Mason began to pace the floor, looking from time to time at his watch.

Promptly at six-fifteen the buzzer sounded.

Mason opened the door to the reception room, said, "Hello, Della. Come in."

Della Street entered the private office. "No typist?" she asked.

"No typist," Mason said.

"Suppose it's simply a case of her being delayed or—"

Mason shook his head. "That girl wasn't delayed. She has become suspicious."

"Not while she was here," Drake said positively. "When she left the place, her eyes were shining. She—"

"Sure," Mason said. "But she's smart. She went to the Better Business Bureau or a credit agency and got somebody to call up the office of this building and find out who was renting this office."

"Oh-oh!" Drake exclaimed.

"You mean you left a back trail?" Mason asked.

"I had to, Perry. If she went at it that way, she could have found out this office was being rented by the Drake Detective Agency."

Mason grabbed for his hat. "Come on, Paul. Let's go."

"Want me?" Della Street asked.

Mason hesitated, then said, "You may as well come on, and we'll buy you a dinner afterward."

Mason paused in the big reception office only long enough to tell Nora Pitts to stay on the job until Drake phoned.

"If that girl comes in, hold her," Drake said. "Keep her here and phone the office."

They got in Mason's car. Mason drove to the address on Cabachon Street, which was a narrow-fronted, two-story apartment house.

"Apartment two-eighteen," Drake said.

Mason repeatedly jabbed the button. When there was no answer he rang the bell for the manager.

The door latch clicked open. Drake held the door open. They went in. The manager, a big-boned woman in her sixties, came out to look them over. She studied the group with a cold, practiced eye. "We have no short-term rentals," she said.

Drake said, "I'm an investigator. We're looking for information. We're trying to locate Mae Jordan."

"Oh, yes," the woman said. "Well, Miss Jordan left."

"What do you mean she left?"

"Well, she told me she'd be away for a while and asked me if I'd feed her canary."

"She was going somewhere?"

"I guess so. She seemed in a terrific hurry. She dashed into the apartment and packed a couple of suitcases."

"Was she alone?" Mason asked.

"No. Two men were with her."

"Two men?"

"That's right."

"Did she introduce them?"

"No."

"They went up to the apartment with her?"

"Yes."

"And came down with her?"

"Yes. Each one of them was carrying a suitcase."

"And Miss Jordan didn't tell you how long she'd be gone?"

"No."

"How did she come here? Was it in a car or a taxicab?"

"I didn't see her come, but she left in a private car with these two men. Why? Is there anything wrong?"

Mason exchanged glances with Paul Drake.

"What time was this?" Mason asked.

"About . . . oh, let's see . . . It's been a little over an hour and a half, I guess."

"Thank you," Mason said, and led the way back to the car.

"Well?" Drake asked.

"Start your men going, Paul," Mason said. "Find out where Mae Jordan worked. Get the dope on her. Dig up everything you can. I want that girl."

"What are you going to do with her when you get her?" Drake asked.

"I'm going to slap her with a subpoena, put her on the witness stand, and tear her insides out," Mason said grimly. "How long will it take you to find out where Walter Irving is right now?"

"I'll know as soon as my operatives phone in the next report. I've got two men on the job. Generally, they phone in about once an hour."

"When you locate him, let me know," Mason said. "I'll be in my office."

Della Street smiled at Paul Drake. "Dinner," she said, "has been postponed."

CHAPTER 12

MASON HAD BEEN IN HIS OFFICE LESS THAN TEN MINUTES WHEN the unlisted phone rang. Della Street glanced inquiringly at Mason. The lawyer said, "I'll take it, Della," and picked up the phone.

"Hello, Paul. What is it?"

Drake said, "One of my operatives reported Irving is on his way to this building, and he's hopping mad."

"To *this* building?"

"That's right."

"That leaves three objectives," Mason said. "His office, your office, or mine. If he comes to your office, send him in here."

"If he comes to your office, will you want help?"

"I'll handle it," Mason said.

"My operative says he's really breathing fire. He got a phone call when he was right in the middle of dinner. He never even went back to his table. Just dashed out, grabbed a cab, and gave the address of this building."

"Okay," Mason said. "We'll see what develops."

Mason hung up the telephone and said to Della Street, "Irving is on his way here."

"To see you?"

"Probably."

"So what do we do?"

"Wait for him. The party may be rough."

Five minutes later angry knuckles banged on the door of Mason's private office. "That will be Irving," Mason said. "I'll let him in myself, Della."

Mason got up, strode across the office and jerked the door open.

"Good evening," he said coldly, his face granite hard.

"What the hell are you trying to do?" Irving asked furiously. "Upset the apple cart?"

Mason said, "There are ladies present. Watch your language unless you want to get thrown out."

"Who's going to throw me out?"

"I am."

"You and who else?"

"Just me."

Irving sized him up for a moment. "You're one hell of a lawyer, I'll say that for you."

"All right," Mason told him. "Come in. Sit down. Tell me what's on your mind. And the next time you try to hold out anything on me, you'll be a lot sorrier than you are right now."

"I wasn't holding out on you. I—"

"All right," Mason told him. "Tell me *your* troubles, and then *I'll* tell *you* something."

"You went out to call on Marline Chaumont."

"Of course I did."

"You shouldn't have done it."

"Then why didn't you tell me so?"

"To tell you the truth, I didn't think you could possibly find out anything about her. I still don't know how you did it."

"Well, what's wrong with going to see her?" Mason asked.

"You've kicked your case out of the window, that's all that's wrong with it."

"Go on. Tell me the rest of it."

"I'd been nursing that angle of the case until I could get the evidence we needed. She was pulling this gag of having an invalid brother on her hands so she—"

"That's a gag?" Mason interrupted.

"Don't be any simpler than you have to be," Irving snapped.

"What about her brother?" Mason asked.

"Her brother!" Irving stormed. "Her brother! You poor, simple-minded boob! Her so-called brother is Munroe Baxter."

"Go on," Mason said. "Keep talking."

"Isn't that fact enough to show you what you've done?"

"The fact would be. Your statement isn't."

"Well, I'm telling you."

"You've told me. I don't want your guesses or surmises. I want facts."

"Marline is a smart little babe. She's French. She's chic, and she's a fast thinker. She's been playing around with Munroe Baxter. He likes her better than Yvonne Manco. He was beginning to get tired of Yvonne.

"So when Munroe Baxter took the nose dive, he just kept on diving and came up into the arms of Marline Chaumont. She had a home all prepared for him as the invalid brother who was weak in the upper story."

"Any proof?" Mason asked.

"I was getting proof."

"You've seen Marline?"

"Of course I've seen her. After I got to thinking things over, I made it a point to see her."

"And did you see her brother?"

"I tried to," Irving said, "but she was too smart for me. She had him locked in a back bedroom, and she had the only key. She wanted to go to the all-night bank and transact some business. I told her I'd stay with her brother. She took me up on it.

"After she was gone, I prowled the house. The back bedroom

was locked. I think she'd given him a sedative or something. I could hear him gently snoring. I knocked on the door and tried to wake him up. I wanted to look at him."

"You think he's Munroe Baxter?"

"I know he's Munroe Baxter."

"How do you know it?"

"I don't have to go into that with you."

"The hell you don't!"

Irving shrugged his shoulders. "You've started messing the case up now. Go ahead and finish it."

"All right, I will," Mason said. "I'll put that house under surveillance. I'll—"

"You and your house under surveillance!" Irving exclaimed scornfully. "Marline and her brother got out of there within thirty minutes after you left the place. That house is as cold and dead as a last-year's bird's nest. In case you want to bet, I'll give you ten to one you can't find a fingerprint in the whole damn place."

"Where did they go?" Mason asked.

Irving shrugged his shoulders. "Search me. I went out there. The place was empty. I became suspicious and got a private detective agency to get on the job and find out what had happened. I was eating dinner tonight when the detective phoned. Neighbors had seen a car drive up. A man and a woman got out. The neighbor was looking through the curtains. She recognized you from your pictures. The description of the girl with you checked with that of your secretary here, Miss Street.

"Half an hour after you left, a taxi drove up. Marline sent out four big suitcases and a handbag. Then she and the taxi driver helped a man out to the car. The man was stumbling around as though he was drunk or drugged or both."

"And then?" Mason asked.

"The cab drove away."

"All right," Mason said. "We'll trace that cab."

Irving laughed scornfully. "You must think you're dealing with a bunch of dumb bunnies, Mason."

"Perhaps I am," Mason said.

"Go on and try to trace that couple," he said. "Then you'll find out what a mess you've made of things."

Irving got to his feet.

"How long had you known all this?" Mason asked, his voice ominously calm.

"Not long. I looked Marline up when I came here. She knows everyone in the Paris office. She was our party girl. She always helped in entertaining buyers.

"She's smart. She got wise to the Baxter deal and she put the heat on Baxter.

"As soon as I went out to Marline's place to call on her, I knew something was wrong. She went into a panic at the sight of me. She tried to cover up by being all honey and syrup, but she overdid it. She had to invite me in, but she told me this story about her brother. Then she kept me waiting while she locked him up and knocked him out with a hypo. That evening she left me alone, so I could prowl the house. Baxter was dead to the world. She's a smart one, that girl.

"I was getting ready to really bust this case wide open, and then you had to stick your clumsy hand right in the middle of all the machinery."

Irving started for the door.

"Wait a minute," Mason said. You're not finished yet. You know something more about all—"

"Sure I do," Irving said. "And make no mistake, Mason. What I know I keep to myself from now on. In case you're interested, I'm cabling the company to kiss their two-thousand-dollar retainer goodby and to hire a lawyer who at least has *some* sense."

Irving strode out into the corridor.

Della Street watched the closing door. When it had clicked shut she started for the telephone.

Mason motioned her away. "Remember, it's all taken care of, Della," he said. "Paul Drake has two men shadowing him. We'll know where he goes when he leaves here."

"That's fine," she said. "In that case, you can take me to dinner now."

CHAPTER 13

DELLA STREET LAID THE DECODED CABLEGRAM ON MASON'S DESK
as the lawyer entered the office.

"What's this, Della?" Mason asked, hanging up his hat.

"Cablegram from the South African Gem Importing and Exploration Company."

"Am I fired?"

"Definitely not."

"What does it say?" Mason asked.

"It says you are to continue with the case and to protect the interests of Duane Jefferson, that the company investigated you before you were retained, that it has confidence in you, and that its official representative in this area, and the only one in a position to give orders representing the company, is Duane Jefferson."

"Well," Mason said, "that's something." He took the decoded cablegram and studied it. "It sounds as though they didn't have too much confidence in Walter Irving."

"Of course," she told him, "we don't know what Irving cabled the company."

"We know what he told us he was cabling the company."

"Where does all this leave him?" Della Street asked.

"Out on a limb," Mason said, grinning, and then added, "It also leaves us out on a limb. If we don't get some line on Mae Jordan and Marline Chaumont, we're behind the eight ball."

"Couldn't you get a continuance under the circumstances until—"

Mason shook his head.

"Why not, Chief?"

"For several reasons," Mason said. "One of them is that I assured the district attorney I'd go to trial on the first date we could squeeze in on the trial calendar. The other is that I still think we have more to gain than to lose by getting to trial before the district attorney has had an opportunity to think over the real problem."

"Do you suppose this so-called brother of Marline Chaumont is really Munroe Baxter?"

Mason looked at his watch, said, "Paul Drake should have the answer to that by this time. Get him on the phone, Della. Ask him to come in."

Ten minutes later Paul Drake was laying it on the line.

"This guy Irving is all wet, Perry. Marline Chaumont showed up at the state hospital. She identified herself as the sister of Pierre Chaumont. Pierre had been there for a year. He'd become violent. They'd operated on his brain. After that, he was like a pet dog. He was there because there was no other place for him to be. Authorities were very glad to release Pierre to his sister, Marline. The chance that he is Munroe Baxter is so negligible you can dismiss it.

"In the first place, Marline showed up and got him out of the state hospital more than a month before Baxter's boat was due. At the time Marline was getting him out of the hospital, Munroe Baxter was in Paris."

"Is his real name Pierre Chaumont?"

"The authorities are satisfied it is."

"Who satisfied them?"

"I don't know; Marline, I guess. The guy was going under another name. He'd been a vicious criminal, a psychopath. He consented to having this lobotomy performed, and they did it. It apparently cured him of his homicidal tendencies, but it left him like a zombie. As I understand it, he's in sort of a hypnotic trance. Tell the guy anything, and he does it."

"You checked with the hospital?"

"With everyone. The doctor isn't very happy about the outcome. He said he had hoped for better results, but the guy was a total loss the way he was and anything is an improvement. They were damn glad to get rid of him at the hospital."

"Yes, I can imagine. What else, Paul?"

"Now here's some news that's going to jolt you, Perry."

"Go ahead and jolt."

"Mae Jordan was picked up by investigators from the district attorney's office."

"The hell!" Mason exclaimed.

Drake nodded.

"What are they trying to do? Get a confession of some sort out of her?"

"Nobody knows. Two men showed up at the law office where

she works yesterday afternoon. It took me a while to get the name of that law office, but I finally got it. It's one of the most substantial, conservative firms in town, and it created quite a furor when these two men walked in, identified themselves and said they wanted Mae Jordan.

"They had a talk with her in a private office, then came out and hunted up old man Honcut, who's the senior member of the firm Honcut, Gridley and Billings. They told him that for Mae's own safety they were going to have to keep her out of circulation for a while. She had about three weeks for vacation coming, and they told Honcut she could come back right after the trial."

"She went willingly?" Mason asked.

"Apparently so."

Mason thought that over. "How did they find her, Paul?"

"Simplest thing in the world. They searched Jefferson when they booked him. There was a name and address book. It was all in code. They cracked the code and ran down the names. When they came to this Jordan girl she talked."

"She tried to talk herself out by talking Duane Jefferson in," Mason said grimly. "When that young woman gets on the stand she's going to have a cross-examination she'll remember for a long, long time. What about Irving, Paul? Where did he go after he left here?"

"Now there," Drake said, "I have some more bad news for you."

Mason's face darkened. "That was damn important, Paul. I told you—"

"I know what you *told* me, Perry. Now *I'm* going to tell *you* something about the shadowing business that I've told you a dozen times before and I'll probably tell you a dozen times again. If a smart man knows he's being tailed and doesn't want to be shadowed, there's not much you can do about it. If he's smart, he can give you the slip every time, unless you have four or five operatives all equipped with some means of intercommunication."

"But Irving didn't *know* he was being tailed."

"What makes you think he didn't?"

"Well," Mason said, "he didn't act like it when he came up here to the office."

"He sure acted like it when he left," Drake said. "What did you tell him?"

"Nothing to arouse his suspicions. Specifically, what did he do, Paul?"

"He proceeded to ditch the shadows."

"How?"

"To begin with, he got a taxi. He must have told the taxi driver there was a car following him that he wanted to ditch. The cab driver played it smart. He'd slide up to the traffic signals just as they were changing, then go on through. My man naturally tried to keep up with him, relying on making an explanation to any traffic cop who might stop him.

"Well, a traffic cop stopped him and it happened he was a cop who didn't feel kindly toward private detectives. He got tough, held my man, and gave him a ticket. By that time, Irving was long since gone.

"Usually a cop will give you a break on a deal like that if you have your credentials right handy, show them to him and tell him you're shadowing the car ahead. This chap deliberately held my man up until Irving got away. Not that I think it would have made any difference. Irving knew that he was being tailed, and he'd made up his mind he was going to ditch the tail. When a smart man gets an idea like that in his head, there's nothing you can do about it except roll with the punch and take it."

"So what did you do, Paul?"

"Did the usual things. Put men on his apartment house to pick him up when he got back. Did everything."

"And he hasn't been back?"

Drake shook his head.

"All right. What about the others?"

"Marline Chaumont," Drake said. "You thought it would be easy to locate her."

"You mean you've drawn a blank all the way along the line?" Mason interposed impatiently.

"I found out about Mae Jordan," Drake said.

"And that's all?"

"That's all."

"All right. What about Marline Chaumont? Give me the bad news in bunches."

"It took me a devil of a time to find the taxicab driver who went out to the house," Drake said. "I finally located him. He remembered the occasion well. He took the woman, the man, four suit-cases and a handbag to the airport."

"And then what?" Mason asked.

"Then we draw a blank. We can't find where she left the airport."

"You mean a woman with a man who is hardly able to navigate by himself, with four big suitcases and a handbag, can vanish from the airport?" Mason asked.

"That's right," Drake said. "Just try it sometime, Perry."

"Try what?"

"Covering all of the taxicab drivers who go to the air terminal. Try and get them to tell you whether they picked up a man, a woman, four suitcases and a handbag. People are coming in by plane every few minutes. The place is a regular madhouse."

Mason thought that over. "All right, Paul," he said. "Irving told me we'd get no place, but I thought the four suitcases would do it."

"So did I when you first told me about it," Drake said.

"They went directly to the airport?"

"That's right."

"Paul, they must have gone *somewhere*."

"Sure, they went somewhere," Drake said. "I can tell you where they *didn't* go."

"All right. Where didn't they go?"

"They didn't take any plane that left at about that time of day."

"How do you know?"

"I checked it by the excess baggage. The taxi driver says the suit-cases were heavy. They must have weighed forty pounds each. I checked the departures on the planes."

"You checked them by name, of course?"

Drake's look was withering. "Don't be silly, Perry. That was the first thing. That was simple. Then I checked with the ticket sellers to see if there was a record of tickets sold at that time of day with that amount of excess baggage. There wasn't. Then I checked with the gate men to see if they remembered some woman going through the gate who would need help in getting a man aboard the plane. There was none. I also checked on wheel chairs. No dice. So then I concluded she'd gone to the airport, unloaded, paid off the cab, and had picked up another cab at the airport to come back."

"And you couldn't find that cab?"

"My men are still working on it. But that's like going to some babe wearing a skirt reaching to her knees, a tight sweater, and asking her if she remembered anybody whistling at her yesterday as she walked down the street."

After a moment Mason grinned. "All right, Paul. We're drawing a blank. Now why the devil would the district attorney have Mae Jordan picked up?"

"Because he wanted to question her."

"Then why wouldn't he have let her go after he questioned her?"

"Because he hasn't finished questioning her."

Mason shook his head. "You overlook what happened. She went up to her room, packed—got two suitcases. The district attorney is keeping her in what amounts to custody."

"Why?"

Mason grinned. "Now wait a minute, Paul. That's the question that I asked you. Of course, the only answer is that he wants her as a material witness. But if he does that, it means she must have told a story that has pulled the wool completely over his eyes, and he fell for it hook, line, and sinker."

"You don't think she's a material witness?" Drake asked.

Mason thought the situation over for a minute, then a slow smile spread over his features. "She would be, if she told the truth. I don't think there's any better news that I could have had."

"Why?"

"Because if the district attorney doesn't put her on the stand as a witness, I'll claim that he sabotaged my case by spiriting away *my* witnesses. If he does put her on the stand, I'll make him the sickest district attorney west of Chicago."

"You're going to play into his hands by going to an immediate trial?" Drake asked.

Mason grinned. "Paul, did you ever see a good tug of war?"

Drake thought for a moment, then said, "They used to put them on in the country towns on the Fourth of July."

"And did you ever see the firemen having a tug of war with the police department?"

"I may have. I can't remember. Why?"

"And," Mason went on, "about the time the fire department was all dug in and huffing and puffing, there would be a secret signal from the police department and everybody would give the firemen a lot of slack and they'd go over backwards, and then the police department would give a big yo-heave-ho and pull the whole aggregation right over the dividing line on the seat of their pants."

Drake grinned. "Seems to me I remember something like that, now that you speak of it."

"Well," Mason said, "that is what is known as playing into the hands of the district attorney, Paul. We're going to give him lots of slack. Now, answering your question more specifically—yes, I'm going to an immediate trial. I'm going to go to trial while the D.A. is hypnotized by Mae Jordan's story and before he finds out I know some of the things I know and that he doesn't know."

CHAPTER 14

THE SELECTION OF THE JURY WAS COMPLETED AT TEN-THIRTY on the second day of the trial. Judge Hartley settled back on the bench, anticipating a long, bitterly contested trial.

"Gentlemen," he said, "the jury has been selected and sworn. The prosecution will proceed with its opening statement."

At that moment, Hamilton Burger, the district attorney, who had left the selection of the jury to subordinates, dramatically strode into the courtroom to take charge of the trial personally.

The district attorney bowed to the judge and, almost without pausing, passed the counsel table to stand facing the jury.

"Good morning, ladies and gentlemen of the jury," he said. "I am the district attorney of this county. We expect to show you that the defendant in this case is an employee of the South African Gem Importing and Exploration Company; that through his employment he had reason to know that a man named Munroe Baxter had in his possession a large number of diamonds valued at more than three hundred thousand dollars on the retail market; that the defendant knew Munroe Baxter intended to smuggle those diamonds into this country, and that the defendant murdered Munroe Baxter and took possession of those diamonds. We will introduce witnesses to show premeditation, deliberation and the cunning execution of a diabolical scheme of murder. We will show that a goodly proportion of the diamonds smuggled into the country by Munroe Baxter were found in the possession of the defendant. On the strength of that evidence we shall ask for a verdict of first-degree murder."

And Hamilton Burger, bowing to the jury, turned and stalked back to the counsel table.

Court attachés looked at each other in surprise. It was the shortest opening statement Hamilton Burger had ever made, and no one missed its significance. Hamilton Burger had carefully refrained from disclosing his hand or giving the defense the faintest inkling of how he intended to prove his case.

"My first witness," Hamilton Burger said, "will be Yvonne Manco."

"Come forward, Yvonne Manco," the bailiff called.

Yvonne Manco had evidently been carefully instructed. She came forward, trying her best to look demure. Her neckline was high and her skirt was fully as long as the current styles dictated, but the attempt to make her look at all conservative was as unsuccessful as would have been an attempt to disguise a racing sports car as a family sedan.

Yvonne gave her name and address to the court reporter, then looked innocently at the district attorney—after having flashed a sidelong glance of appraisal at the men on the jury.

Under questioning of the district attorney, Yvonne told the story of her relationship with Munroe Baxter, of the carefully laid plot to smuggle the gems, of the tour aboard the cruise ship, the spurious "whirlwind courtship."

She told of the plot to arrange the fake suicide, her deliberate flirtation with the assistant purser, the scene on the ship, and then finally that early morning plunge into the waters of the bay. She disclosed that she had carried a small compressed air tank in her baggage and that when Baxter went overboard, he was prepared to swim for a long distance underwater.

Hamilton Burger brought out a series of maps and photographs of the cruise ship. He had the witness identify the approximate place where the leap had taken place, both from the deck of the steamer and from its location in the bay.

"You may cross-examine," he said to Perry Mason.

Mason smiled at the witness, who promptly returned his smile, shifted her position slightly and crossed her legs, so that two of the masculine members of the jury hitched forward in their chairs for a better look, while the chins of two of the less attractive women on the jury were conspicuously elevated.

"You go by the name of Yvonne Manco?" Mason asked.

"Yes."

"You have another name?"

"No."

"You were really married to Munroe Baxter, were you not?"

"Yes, but now that I am a widow I choose to keep my maiden name of Yvonne Manco."

"I see," Mason said. "You don't want to bear the name of your husband?"

"It is not that," she said. "Yvonne Manco is my professional name."

"What profession?" Mason asked.

There was a moment's silence, then Hamilton Burger was on his feet. "Your Honor, I object. I object to the manner in which the question is asked. I object to the question. Incompetent, irrelevant, and immaterial."

Judge Hartley stroked his chin thoughtfully. "Well," he said, "under the circumstances I'm going to sustain the objection. However, in view of the answer of the witness— However, the objection is sustained."

"You were, however, married to Munroe Baxter?"

"Yes."

"On shipboard?"

"Yes."

"Before that?"

"No."

"There had been no previous ceremony?"

"No."

"Are you familiar with what is referred to as a common law marriage?"

"Yes."

"Had you ever gone by the name of Mrs. Baxter?"

"Yes."

"Prior to this cruise?"

"Yes."

"As a part of this plot which you and Munroe Baxter hatched up, he was to pretend to be dead. Is that right?"

"Yes."

"With whom did the idea originate? You or Munroe Baxter?"

"With him."

"He was to pretend to jump overboard and be dead, so he could smuggle in some diamonds?"

"Yes. I have told you this."

"In other words," Mason said, "if at any time it should be to his advantage, he was quite willing to pretend to be dead."

"Objected to as calling for the conclusion of the witness as already asked and answered," Hamilton Burger said.

"Sustained," Judge Hartley said.

Mason, having made his point, smiled at the jury. "You knew that you were engaging in a smuggling transaction?" he asked the witness.

"But of course. I am not stupid."

"Exactly," Mason said. "And after this investigation started, you had some contact with the district attorney?"

"Naturally."

"And was it not through the offices of the district attorney that arrangements were made so you could testify in this case, yet be held harmless and not be prosecuted for smuggling?"

"Well, of course—"

"Just a minute, just a minute," Hamilton Burger interrupted. "I want to interpose an objection to that question, Your Honor."

"Go ahead," Judge Hartley ruled.

"It is incompetent, irrelevant and immaterial. It is not proper cross-examination."

"Overruled," Judge Hartley said. "Answer the question."

"Well, of course there was no definite agreement. That would have been . . . unwise."

"Who told you it would be unwise?"

"It was agreed by all that it would be unwise."

"By all, whom do you mean? Whom do you include?"

"Well, the customs people, the district attorney, the detectives, the police, my own lawyer."

"I see," Mason said. "They told you that it would be unwise to have a definite agreement to this effect, but nevertheless they gave you every assurance that if you testified as they wished, you would not be prosecuted on a smuggling charge?"

"Your Honor, I object to the words 'as they wished,'" Hamilton Burger said. "That calls for a conclusion of the witness."

Judge Hartley looked down at the witness.

Mason said, "I'll put it this way, was there any conversation as to what you were to testify to?"

"The truth."

"Who told you that?"

"Mr. Burger, the district attorney."

"And was there some assurance given you that if you so testified, you would be given immunity from the smuggling?"

"If I testified to the *truth?* Yes."

"Before this assurance was given you, you had told these people what the truth was?"

"Yes."

"And that was the same story you have told on the witness stand here?"

"Certainly."

"So that when the district attorney told you to tell the truth, you understood that he meant the same story you have just told here?"

"Yes."

"So then, the assurance that was given you was that if you would tell the story you have now told on the witness stand, you would be given immunity from smuggling."

"That was my understanding."

"So," Mason said, "simply by telling this story you are given immunity from smuggling?"

"Well, not— It was not that . . . not that crude," she said.

The courtroom broke into laughter.

"That," Mason said, "is all."

Hamilton Burger was plainly irritated as the witness left the stand. "My next witness will be Jack Gilly," he said.

Jack Gilly was a slender, shifty-eyed man with high cheekbones, a long, sharp nose, a high forehead, and a pointed chin. He moved with a silence that was almost furtive as he glided up to the witness stand, held up his hand, was sworn, gave his name and address to the court reporter, seated himself, and looked expectantly at the district attorney.

"What's your occupation?" Hamilton Burger asked.

"At the moment?" he asked.

"Well, do you have the same occupation now you had six months ago?"

"Yes."

"What is it?"

"I rent fishing boats."

"Where?"

"At the harbor here."

"Were you acquainted with Munroe Baxter during his lifetime?"

"Just a moment before you answer that question," Mason said to the witness. He turned to Judge Hartley. "I object, Your Honor, on the ground that the question assumes a fact not in evidence. As far as the evidence before this court at the present time is concerned, Munroe Baxter is still alive."

"May I be heard on that, Your Honor?" Hamilton Burger asked.

"Well," Judge Hartley said, hesitating, "it would certainly seem that the logical way to present this case would be first to— However, I'll hear you, Mr. District Attorney."

"If the Court please," Hamilton Burger said, "Munroe Baxter jumped overboard in deep water. He was never seen alive afterward. I have witnesses from the passengers and the crew who will testify that Munroe Baxter ran to the rear of the ship, jumped overboard and vanished in the water. The ship called for a launch to come alongside, the waters were searched and searched carefully. Munroe Baxter never came up."

"Well," Judge Hartley said, "you can't expect this Court to rule on evidence predicated upon an assumption as to what you intend to prove by other witnesses. Moreover, your own witness has testified that this was all part of a scheme on the part of Munroe Baxter to—"

"Yes, yes, I know," Hamilton Burger interrupted. "But schemes can go astray. Many unforeseen things can enter into the picture. Jumping from the deck of a ship is a perilous procedure."

Judge Hartley said, "Counsel will kindly refrain from interrupting the Court. I was about to say, Mr. District Attorney, that the testimony of your own witness indicates this was all part of a planned scheme by which Munroe Baxter intended to appear to commit suicide. In view of the fact that there is a presumption that a man remains alive until he is shown to be dead, the Court feels the objection is well taken."

"Very well, Your Honor, I will reframe the question," Hamilton Burger said. "Mr. Gilly, did you know Munroe Baxter?"

"Yes."

"How well did you know him?"

"I had met him several times."

"Were you acquainted with Yvonne Manco, who has just testified?"

"Yes."

"Directing your attention to the sixth day of June of this year, what was your occupation at that time?"

"I was renting boats."

"And to the fifth day of June, what was your occupation?"

"I was renting boats."

"Did you rent a boat on the fifth of June at an hour nearing seven o'clock in the evening?"

"Yes, sir."

"To whom did you rent that boat?"

"Frankly, I don't know."

"It was to some man you had never seen before?"

"Yes."

"Did the man tell you what he wanted?"

"He said that he had been directed to me because I was—"

"Just a moment," Mason interrupted. "I object to any conversation which did not take place in the presence of the defendant and which is not connected up with the defendant."

"I propose to connect this up with the defendant," Hamilton Burger said.

"Then the connection should be shown before the conversation," Mason said.

Judge Hartley nodded. "The objection is sustained."

"Very well. You rented a boat to this man who was a stranger to you?"

"Yes, sir."

"From what this man said, however, you had reason to rent him the boat?"

"Yes."

"Was money paid you for the boat?"

"Yes."

"And when did the man start out in the boat, that is, when did he take delivery of it?"

"At about five o'clock the next morning."

"What were the circumstances surrounding the delivery of the boat?"

"He stood on the dock with me. I had a pair of powerful night glasses. When I saw the cruise ship coming in the harbor, I said to this man that I could see the cruise ship, and he jumped in the boat and took off."

"Did he start the motor?"

"The motor had been started an hour previously so it would be warm and so everything would be in readiness."

"And what did the man do?"

"He guided the boat away from my dock and out into the channel."

"Just a moment," Mason said. "Your Honor, I move to strike all of this evidence out on the ground that it has not been connected with the defendant in any way."

"I am going to connect it up," Hamilton Burger said, "within the next few questions."

"The Court will reserve a ruling," Judge Hartley said. "It seems to me that these questions are largely preliminary."

"What did *you* do after the boat was rented?" Hamilton Burger asked the witness.

"Well," Gilly said, "I was curious. I wanted to see—"

"Never mind your thoughts or emotions," Hamilton Burger said. "What did you *do?*"

"I walked back to where my car was parked, got in the car and drove out to a place I knew on the waterfront where I could get out on the dock and watch what was going on."

"What do you mean by your words, 'what was going on'?"

"Watch the boat I had rented."

"And what did you see?"

"I saw the cruise ship coming slowly into the harbor."

"And what else did you see?"

"I saw Munroe Baxter jump overboard."

"You know it was Munroe Baxter?"

"Well, I— Of course, I knew it from what happened."

"But did you recognize him?"

"Well . . . it looked like Baxter, but at that distance and in that light I couldn't *swear* to it."

"*Don't* swear to it then," Hamilton Burger snapped. "You saw a man jump overboard?"

"Yes."

"Did that man look like anyone you knew?"

"Yes."

"Who?"

"Munroe Baxter."

"That is, as I understand your testimony, he looked like Munroe Baxter, but you can't definitely swear that it *was* Munroe Baxter. Is that right?"

"That's right."

"Then what happened?"

"I saw people running around on the deck of the cruise ship. I heard voices evidently hailing a launch, and a launch came and cruised around the ship."

"What else happened?"

"I kept my binoculars trained on the boat that I had rented."

"What did you see?"

"There were two men in the boat."

"*Two* men?" Hamilton Burger asked.

"Yes, sir."

"Where did the other man come from, do you know?"

"No, sir, I don't. But I am assuming that he was picked up on one of the docks while I was getting my car."

"That may go out," Hamilton Burger said. "You don't know of your own knowledge where this man came from?"

"No, sir."

"You know only that by the time you reached the point of vantage from which you could see the boat, there were two men in the boat?"

"Yes, sir."

"All right, then what happened?"

"The boat sat there for some time. The second man appeared to be fishing. He was holding a heavy bamboo rod and a line over the side of the boat."

"And then what happened?"

"After quite a while I saw the fishing pole suddenly jerk, as though something very heavy had taken hold of the line."

"And then what?"

"Then I could see a black body partially submerged in the water, apparently hanging onto the fish line."

"And then what did you see?"

"One of the men leaned over the side of the boat. He appeared to be talking—"

"Never mind what he appeared to be doing. What did he do?"

"He leaned over the side of the boat."

"Then what?"

"Then he reached down to the dark object in the water."

"Then what?"

"Then I saw him raise his right arm and lower it rapidly several times. There was a knife in his hand. He was plunging the knife down into the dark thing in the water."

"Then what?"

"Then both men fumbled around with the thing that was in the water; then one of the men lifted a heavy weight of some kind over the side of the boat and tied it to the thing that was in the water."

"Then what?"

"Then they started the motor in the boat, slowly towing the weighted object in the water. I ran back to my automobile, got into it and drove back to my boat pier."

"And what happened then?"

"Then after a couple of hours the man who had rented the boat brought it back."

"Was anyone with him at the time?"

"No, sir, he was alone."

"What did you do?"

"I asked him if he had picked anyone up and he—"

"I object to any conversation which was not in the presence of the defendant," Mason said.

"Just a moment," Hamilton Burger said. "I will withdraw the question until I connect it up. Now, Mr. Gilly, did you recognize the other man who was in the boat with this stranger?"

"Not at the time. I had never seen him before."

"Did you see him subsequently?"

"Yes, sir."

"Who was that man?"

"The defendant."

"You are referring now to Duane Jefferson, the defendant who is seated here in the courtroom?"

"Yes, sir."

"Are you positive of your identification?"

"Just a moment," Mason said. "That's objected to as an attempt on the part of counsel to cross-examine his own witness."

"Overruled," Judge Hartley said. "Answer the question."

"Yes, sir, I am positive."

"You were watching through binoculars?"

"Yes, sir."

"What is the power of those binoculars?"

"Seven by fifty."

"Are they a good pair of binoculars?"

"Yes, sir."

"With coated lenses?"

"Yes, sir."

"You could see the boat clearly enough to distinguish the features of the people who were in the boat?"

"Yes, sir."

"Now then, after the boat was returned to you, did you notice any stains on the boat?"

"Yes, sir."

"What were those stains?"

"Bloodstains that—"

"No, no," Hamilton Burger said. "Just describe the stains. You don't know whether they were blood."

"I know they *looked* like blood."

"Just describe the stains, please," Hamilton Burger insisted, striving to appear virtuous and impartial.

"They were reddish stains, dark reddish stains."

"Where were they?"

"On the outside of the boat, just below the gunwale, and over on the inside of the boat where there had been a spattering or spurting."

"When did you first notice those stains?"

"Just after the boat had been returned to me."

"Were they fresh at that time?"

"Objected to as calling for a conclusion of the witness and no proper foundation laid," Mason said.

"The objection is sustained," Judge Hartley ruled. "Well, how did they appear to you?"

"Same objection."

"Same ruling."

"Look here," Hamilton Burger said, "you have been engaged in the fishing business and in fishing for recreation for some time?"

"Yes, sir."

"During that time you have had occasion to see a lot of blood on boats?"

"Yes, sir."

"And have you been able to judge the relative freshness of the stains by the color of that blood?"

"Yes, sir."

"That's fish blood the witness is being asked about?" Mason interposed.

"Well . . . yes," Hamilton Burger conceded.

"And may I ask the prosecutor if it is his contention that these stains on the boat the witness has described were fish blood?"

"Those were stains of human blood!" Hamilton Burger snapped.

"I submit," Mason said, "that a witness cannot be qualified as an expert on human bloodstains by showing that he has had experience with fish blood."

"The principle is the same," Hamilton Burger said. "The blood assumes the same different shades of color in drying."

"Do I understand the district attorney is now testifying as an expert?" Mason asked.

Judge Hartley smiled. "I think the Court will have to agree with defense counsel, Mr. District Attorney. There must first be a showing as to whether there is a similarity in the appearance of fish blood and human blood *if* you are now trying to qualify this witness as an expert."

"Oh, well," Hamilton Burger said, "I'll get at it in another way by another witness. You are positive as to your identification of this defendant, Mr. Gilly?"

"Yes, sir."

"And he was in the boat at the time you saw this thing—whatever it was—stabbed with a knife?"

"Yes, sir."

"Were these stains you have mentioned on the boat when you rented it?"

"No."

"They were there when the boat was returned?"

"Yes."

"Where is this boat now?" Hamilton Burger asked.

"In the possession of the police."

"When was it taken by the police?"

"About ten days later."

"You mean the sixteenth of June?"

"I believe it was the fifteenth."

"Did you find anything else in that boat, Mr. Gilly?"

"Yes, sir."

"What?"

"A sheath knife with the name 'Duane' engraved on the hilt on one side and the initials 'M.J.' on the other side."

"Where is that knife?"

"The police took it."

"When?"

"At the time they took the boat."

"Would you know that knife if you saw it again?"

"Yes."

Hamilton Burger unwrapped some tissue paper, produced a keen-bladed hunting knife, took it to the witness. "Have you ever seen this knife before?"

"Yes. That's the knife I found in the boat."

"Is it now in the same condition it was then?"

"No, sir. It was blood—I mean, it was stained with something red then, more than it is now."

"Yes, yes, some of those stains were removed at the crime laboratory for analysis," Hamilton Burger said suavely. "You may cross-examine the witness, Mr. Mason. And I now ask the clerk to mark this knife for identification."

Mason smiled at Gilly. "Ever been convicted of a felony, Mr. Gilly?" Mason asked, his voice radiating good feeling.

Hamilton Burger jumped to his feet, apparently preparing to make an objection, then slowly settled back in his chair.

Gilly shifted his watery eyes from Mason's face to the floor.

"Yes, sir."

"How many times?" Mason asked.

"Twice."

"For what?"

"Once for larceny."

"And what was it for the second time?" Mason asked.

"Perjury," Gilly said.

Mason's smile was affable. "How far were you from the boat when you were watching it through your binoculars?"

"About . . . oh, a couple of good city blocks."

"How was the light?"

"It was just after daylight."

"There was fog?"

"Not fog. A sort of mist."

"A cold mist?"

"Yes. It was chilly."

"What did you use to wipe off the lenses of the binoculars—or did you wipe them?"

"I don't think I wiped them."

"And you saw one of these men fishing?"

"Yes, sir. The defendant held the fishing rod."

"And apparently he caught something?"

"A big body caught hold of the line."

"Have you seen people catch big fish before?"

"Yes, sir."

"And sometimes when they have caught sharks you have seen them cut the sharks loose from the line or stab them to death before taking them off the hook?"

"This wasn't a shark."

"I'm asking you a question," Mason said. "Have you seen that?"

"Yes."

"Now, did this thing that was on the fishing line ever come entirely out of the water?"

"No, sir."

"Enough out of the water so you could see what it was?"

"It was almost all underwater all the time."

"You had never seen this man who rented the boat from you before he showed up to rent the boat?"

"No, sir."

"And never saw him again?"

"No, sir."

"Do you know this knife wasn't in the boat when you rented it?"

"Yes."

"When did you first see it?"

"The afternoon of the sixth of June."

"Where?"

"In my boat."

"You had not noticed it before?"

"No."

"Yet you had looked in the boat?"

"Yes."

"And from the time the boat was returned to you until you found the knife, that boat was where anyone could have approached and dropped this knife into it, or tossed it to the bottom of the boat?"

"Well, I guess so. Anyone could have if he'd been snooping around down there."

"And how much rental did this mysterious man give you for the boat?"

"That's objected to as incompetent, irrelevant, and immaterial and not proper cross-examination," Hamilton Burger said.

"Well," Mason said, smiling, "I'll get at it in another way. Do you have an established rental rate for that boat, Mr. Gilly?"

"Yes, sir."

"How much is it?"

"A dollar to a dollar and a half an hour."

"Now then, did this stranger pay you the regular rental rate for the boat?"

"We made a special deal."

"You got *more* than your regular rental rate?"

"Yes, sir."

"How much more?"

"Objected to as not proper cross-examination, calling for facts not in evidence, and incompetent, irrelevant, and immaterial," Hamilton Burger said.

"Overruled," Judge Hartley said.

"How much rental?" Mason asked.

"I can't recall offhand. I think it was fifty dollars," Gilly said, his eyes refusing to meet those of Mason.

"Was that the figure that you asked, or the figure that the man offered?"

"The figure that I asked."

"Are you sure it was fifty dollars?"

"I can't remember too well. He gave me a bonus. I can't recall how much it was."

"Was it more than fifty dollars?"

"It could have been. I didn't count it. I just took the bills he gave me and put them in the locked box where I keep my money."

"You keep your money in the form of cash?"

"Some of it."

"Did you ever count this bonus?"

"I can't remember doing so."

"It could have been more than fifty dollars?"

"I guess so. I don't know."

"Could it have been as much as a thousand dollars?"

"Oh, that's absurd!" Hamilton Burger protested to the Court.

"Overruled," Judge Hartley snapped.

"Was it?" Mason asked.

"I don't know."

"Did you enter it on your books?"

"I don't keep books."

"You don't know then how much cash is in this locked box where you keep your money?"

"Not to the penny."

"To the dollar?"

"No."

"To the hundred dollars?"

"No."

"Have you more than five hundred dollars in that box right now?"

"I don't know."

"More than five thousand dollars?"

"I can't tell."

"You may have?"

"Yes."

"Now, when were you convicted of perjury," Mason asked, "was that your first offense or the second?"

"The second."

Mason smiled. "That's all, Mr. Gilly."

Judge Hartley glanced at the clock. "It appears that it is now time for the noon adjournment. Court will recess until two o'clock. During this time the jurors will not form or express any opinion as to the merits of the case, but will wait until the case is finally submitted before doing so. Nor will the jurors discuss the case among themselves or permit it to be discussed in their presence. The defendant is remanded to custody. Court will recess until two o'clock."

Paul Drake and Della Street, who had been occupying seats which had been reserved for them in the front of the courtroom, came toward Perry Mason.

Mason caught Paul Drake's eye, motioned them back. He turned to his client. "By the way," Mason said, "where *were* you on the night of the fifth and the morning of the sixth of June?"

"In my apartment, in bed and asleep."

"Can you prove it?" Mason asked.

Jefferson said scornfully, "Don't be absurd! I am unmarried, Mr. Mason. I sleep alone. There was no occasion for me to try and show where I was at that time, and there is none now. No one is going to pay any attention to the word of a perjurer and a crook who never saw me in his life before. Who is this scum of the waterfront? This whole thing is preposterous!"

"I'd be inclined to think so, too," Mason told him, "if it wasn't for that air of quiet confidence on the part of the district attorney. Therefore, it becomes very important for me to know exactly where you were on the night of the fifth and the morning of the sixth."

"Well," Jefferson said, "on the night of the fifth . . . that is, on the evening of the fifth I— I see no reason to go into that. On the sixth . . . from midnight on the fifth until eight-thirty on the morning of the sixth I was in my apartment. By nine o'clock on the morning of the sixth I was in my office, and I can *prove* where I was from a little after seven on the morning of the sixth."

"By whom?"

"By my associate, Walter Irving. He joined me for breakfast at seven in my apartment, and after that we went to the office."

"What about that knife?" Mason asked.

"It's mine. It was stolen from a suitcase in my apartment."

"Where did you get it?"

"It was a gift."

"From whom?"

"That has nothing to do with the case, Mr. Mason."

"Who gave it to you?"

"It's none of your business."

"I *have* to know who gave it to you, Jefferson."

"I am conducting my own affairs, Mr. Mason."

"I'm conducting your case."

"Go right ahead. Just don't ask me questions about women, that's all. I don't discuss my female friends with anyone."

"Is there anything you're ashamed of in connection with that gift?"

"Certainly not."

"Then tell me who gave it to you."

"It would be embarrassing to discuss any woman with you, Mr. Mason. That might bring about a situation where you'd feel I was perjuring myself about my relationship with women . . . when I get on the stand and answer questions put by the district attorney."

Mason studied Jefferson's face carefully. "Look here," he said. "Lots of times a weak case on the part of the prosecution is bolstered because the defendant breaks down under cross-examination. Now, I hope this case is never going to reach a point where it will become necessary to put on any defense. But if it does, I've got to be *certain* you're not lying to me."

Jefferson looked at Mason coldly. "I *never* lie to *anyone*," he said, and then turning away from Mason signaled to the officer that he was ready to be taken back to jail.

Della Street and Paul Drake fell in step with Mason as the lawyer started down the aisle.

"What do you make of it?" Mason asked.

"There sure is something fishy about this whole thing," Drake said. "It stinks. It has all the earmarks of a frame-up. How can Burger think people of that sort can put across a deal like this on a man like Duane Jefferson?"

"That," Mason said, "is the thing we're going to have to find out. Anything new?"

"Walter Irving's back."

"The deuce he is! Where has he been?"

"No one knows. He showed up about ten-thirty this morning. He was in court."

"Where?"

"Sitting in a back row, taking everything in."

Mason said, "There's something here that is completely and thoroughly contradictory. The whole case is cockeyed."

"The police have something up their sleeves," Drake said. "They have some terrific surprise. I can't find out what it is. Do you notice that Hamilton Burger seems to remain thoroughly elated?"

"That's the thing that gets me," Mason said. "Burger puts on these witnesses and acts as though he's just laying a preliminary foundation. He doesn't seem to take too much interest in their stories, or whether I attack their characters or their credibility. He's playing along for something big."

"What about Irving?" Drake asked. "Are you going to be in touch with him?"

"Irving and I aren't on friendly terms. The last time he walked out of my office he was mad as a bucking bronco. He cabled his company, trying to get me fired. You haven't found out anything about Marline Chaumont or her brother?"

"I haven't found out where they are," Drake said, "but I think I've found out how they gave me the slip."

"How?" Mason asked. "I'm interested in that."

"It's so damn simple that it makes me mad I didn't get onto it sooner."

"What?"

Drake said, "Marline Chaumont simply took her suitcases and had a porter deposit them in storage lockers. Then she took her brother out to an airport limousine, as though they were *incoming* passengers. She gave a porter the keys for two of the lockers, so two suitcases were brought out. She went in the limousine to a downtown hotel. She and her brother got out and completely vanished."

"Then, of course, she went back and got the other suitcases?" Mason asked.

"Presumably," Drake said, "she got a taxicab after she had her brother safely put away, went out to the airport, picked up the other two suitcases out of the storage lockers, and then rejoined her brother."

Mason said, "We've got to find her, Paul."

"I'm trying, Perry."

"Can't you check hotel registrations? Can't you—?"

"Look, Perry," Drake said, "I've checked every hotel registration that was made at about that time. I've checked with rental agencies for houses that were rented. I've checked with the utilities for connections that were put in at about that time. I've done everything I can think of. I've had girls telephoning the apartment houses to see if anyone made application for apartments. I've even checked the motels to see who registered on that date. I've done everything I can think of."

Mason paused thoughtfully. "Have you checked the car rental agencies, Paul?"

"What do you mean?"

"I mean the drive-yourself automobiles where a person rents an automobile, drives it himself, pays so much a day and so much a mile?"

The expression on Drake's face showed mixed emotions. "She wouldn't— Gosh, no! Good Lord, Perry! Maybe I overlooked a bet!"

Mason said, "Why couldn't she get a drive-yourself automobile, put her stuff in it, go to one of the outlying cities, rent a house there, then drive back with the automobile and—"

"I'd say it was one chance in ten thousand," Drake said, "but I'm not going to overlook it. It's all that's left."

"Okay," Mason said. "Try checking that idea for size, Paul."

CHAPTER 15

PROMPTLY AT TWO O'CLOCK COURT RECONVENED AND JUDGE Hartley said, "Call your next witness, Mr. District Attorney."

Hamilton Burger hesitated a moment, then said, "I will call Mae Wallis Jordan."

Mae Jordan, quiet, demure, taking slow, steady steps, as though steeling herself to a task which she had long anticipated yet which was still extremely distasteful, walked to the witness stand, was sworn, gave her name and address to the court reporter, and seated herself.

Hamilton Burger's voice fairly dripped sympathy. "You are acquainted with the defendant, Duane Jefferson, Miss Jordan?" he asked.

"Yes, sir."

"When did you first get acquainted with him?"

"Do you mean, when did I first see him?"

"When did you first get in touch with him," Hamilton Burger asked, "and how?"

"I first saw him after he came to the city here, but I have been corresponding with him for some time."

"When was the date that you first *saw* him? Do you know?"

"I know very well. He arrived by train. I was there to meet the train."

"On what date?"

"May seventeenth."

"Of this year?"

"Yes, sir."

"Now then, you had had some previous correspondence with the defendant?"

"Yes."

"How had that correspondence started?"

"It started as a . . . as a joke. As a gag."

"In what way?"

"I am interested in photography. In a photographic magazine there was an offer to exchange colored stereo photographs of Africa for stereo photographs of the southwestern desert. I was interested and wrote to the box number in question."

"In South Africa?"

"Well, it was in care of the magazine, but it turned out that the magazine forwarded the mail to the person who had placed the ad in the magazine. That person was—"

"Just a moment," Mason interrupted. "We object to the witness testifying as to her conclusion. *She* doesn't know who put the ad in the magazine. Only the records of the magazine can show that."

"We will show them," Hamilton Burger said cheerfully. "However, Miss Jordan, we'll just skip that at the moment. What happened?"

"Well, I entered into correspondence with the defendant."

"What was the nature of that correspondence generally?" Hamilton Burger asked. And then, turning to Mason, said, "Of course, I can understand that this may be objected to as not being the best evidence, but I am trying to expedite matters."

Mason, smiling, said, "I am always suspicious of one who tries to expedite matters by introducing secondary evidence. The letters themselves would be the best evidence."

"I only want to show the *general* nature of the correspondence," Hamilton Burger said.

"Objected to as not being the best evidence," Mason said, "and that the question calls for a conclusion of the witness."

"Sustained," Judge Hartley said.

"You received letters from South Africa?" Hamilton Burger asked, his voice showing a slight amount of irritation.

"Yes."

"Those letters were signed how?"

"Well . . . in various ways."

"What's that?" Hamilton Burger asked, startled. "I thought that—"

"Never mind what the district attorney thought," Mason said. "Let's have the *facts*."

"How were those letters signed?" Hamilton Burger asked.

"Some of them were signed with the name of the defendant, the first ones were."

"And where are those letters now?"

"They are gone."

"Where?"

"I destroyed them."

"Describe the contents of those letters," Hamilton Burger said unctuously. "Having proved, Your Honor, that the best evidence is no longer available, I am seeking to show by secondary evidence—"

"There seems to be no objection," Judge Hartley said.

"I was going to state," Mason said, "that I would like to ask some questions on cross-examination as to the nature and contents of the letters and the time and manner of their destruction, in order to see whether I wished to object."

"Make your objection first, and then you may ask the questions," Judge Hartley said.

"I object, Your Honor, on the ground that no proper foundation for the introduction of secondary testimony has been laid and on the further ground that it now appears that at least some of these letters did not even bear the name of the defendant. In connection with that objection, I would like to ask a few questions."

"Go ahead," Hamilton Burger invited, smiling slightly.

Mason said, "You said that those letters were signed in various ways. What did you mean by that?"

"Well—" she said, and hesitated.

"Go on," Mason said.

"Well," she said, "some of the letters were signed with various . . . well, gag names."

"Such as what?" Mason asked.

"Daddy Longlegs was one," she said.

There was a ripple of mirth in the courtroom, which subsided as Judge Hartley frowned.

"And others?"

"Various names. You see we . . . we exchanged photographs . . . gag pictures."

"What do you mean by gag pictures?" Mason asked.

"Well, I am a camera fan, and the defendant is, too, and . . . we started corresponding formally at first, and then the correspondence became more personal. I . . . he asked me for a picture, and I . . . for a joke I—"

"Go ahead," Mason said. "What did you do?"

"I had taken a photograph of a very trim spinster who was no longer young, a rather interesting face, however, because it showed a great deal of character. I had a photograph of myself in a bathing suit and I . . . I made a trick enlargement, so that the face of the trim spinster was put on my body, and I sent it to him. I thought that if he was simply being flirtatious, that would stop him."

"Was it a joke, or was it intended to deceive him?" Mason asked.

She flushed and said, "That first picture was intended to deceive him. It was done so cunningly that it would be impossible for him to know that it was a composite picture—at least, I thought it would be impossible."

"And you asked him to send you a picture in return?"

"I did."

"And did you receive a picture?"

"Yes."

"What was it?"

"It was the face of a giraffe wearing glasses, grafted on the photograph of a huge figure of a heavily muscled man. Evidently, the figure of a wrestler or a weight-lifter."

"And in that way," Mason asked, "you knew that he had realized your picture was a composite?"

"Yes."

"And what happened after that?"

"We exchanged various gag pictures. Each one trying to be a little more extreme than the other."

"And the letters?" Mason asked.

"The letters were signed with various names which would sort of fit in with the type of photograph."

"You so signed your letters to him?"

"Yes."

"And he so signed his letters to you?"

"Yes."

Mason made his voice elaborately casual. "He would sign letters to you, I suppose, as 'Your Prince,' or 'Sir Galahad,' or something like that?"

"Yes."

"Prince Charming?"

She gave a quick start. "Yes," she said. "As a matter of fact, at the last he signed *all* of his letters 'Prince Charming.'"

"Where are those letters now?" Mason asked.

"I destroyed his letters."

"And where are the letters that you wrote to him, if you know?"

"I . . . I destroyed them."

Hamilton Burger grinned. "Go right ahead, Mr. Mason. You're doing fine."

"How did you get possession of them?" Mason asked.

"I . . . I went to his office."

"While he was there?" Mason asked.

"I— When I got the letters, he was there, yes."

Mason smiled at the district attorney. "Oh, I think, Your Honor, I have pursued this line of inquiry far enough. I will relinquish the right to any further questioning on the subject of the letters. I insist upon my objection, however. The witness can't swear that these letters ever came from this defendant. They were signed 'Prince Charming' and other names she said were gag names. That's her conclusion."

Judge Hartley turned toward the witness. "These letters were in response to letters mailed by you?"

"Yes, Your Honor."

"And how did you address the letters you mailed?"

"To 'Duane Jefferson, care of the South African Gem Importing and Exploration Company.' "

"At its South African address?"

"Yes, Your Honor."

"You deposited those letters in regular mail channels?"

"Yes, Your Honor."

"And received these letters in reply?"

"Yes, Your Honor."

"The letters showed they were in reply to those mailed by you?"

"Yes, Your Honor."

"And you burned them?"

"Yes, Your Honor."

"The objection is overruled," Judge Hartley said. "You may introduce secondary evidence of their contents, Mr. District Attorney."

Hamilton Burger bowed slightly, turned to the witness. "Tell us what was in those letters which were destroyed," he said.

"Well, the defendant adopted the position that he was lonely and far from the people he knew, that he didn't have any girl friends, and . . . oh, it was all a gag. It's so difficult to explain."

"Go ahead; do the best you can," Hamilton Burger said.

"We adopted the attitude of . . . well, we pretended it was a lonely hearts correspondence. He would write and tell me how very wealthy and virtuous he was and what a good husband he would make, and I would write and tell him how beautiful I was and how— Oh, it's just simply out of the question to try and explain it in cold blood this way!"

"Out of context, so to speak?" Hamilton Burger asked.

"Yes," she said. "That's just it. You have to understand the mood and the background, otherwise you wouldn't be able to get the picture at all. The letters, standing by themselves, would appear to be hopelessly foolish, utterly asinine. That was why I felt I had to have them back in my possession."

"Go ahead," Hamilton Burger said. "What did you do?"

"Well, finally Duane Jefferson wrote me one serious letter. He told me that his company had decided to open a branch office in the United States, that it was to be located here, and that he was to be in charge of it and that he was looking forward to seeing me."

"And what did you do?"

"All of a sudden I was in a terrific panic. It was one thing to carry on a joking correspondence with a man who was thousands of miles away and quite another thing suddenly to meet that man face to face. I was flustered and embarrassed."

"Go on. What did you do?"

"Well, of course, when he arrived—he wired me what train he was coming on, and I was there to meet him and—that was when things began to go wrong."

"In what way?"

"He gave me a sort of brush-off, and *he* wasn't the type of person *I* had anticipated. Of course," she went on hastily, "I know what a little fool I was to get a preconceived notion of a man I'd never seen, but I had built up a very great regard for him. I considered him as a friend and I was terribly disappointed."

"Then what?" Hamilton Burger asked.

"Then I called two or three times on the telephone and talked with him, and I went out with him one night."

"And what happened?"

She all but shuddered. "The man was utterly impossible," she said, glaring down at the defendant. "He was patronizing in a cheap, tawdry way. His manner showed that he had completely mistaken the tone of my correspondence. He regarded me as . . . he treated me as if I were a . . . he showed no respect, no consideration. He had none of the finer feelings."

"And what did *you* do?"

"I told him I wanted my letters back."

"And what did he do?"

She glared at Duane Jefferson. "He told me I could *buy* them back."

"So what did you do?"

"I determined to get those letters back. They were mine, anyway."

"So what did you do?"

"On June fourteenth I went to the office at a time when I knew neither the defendant nor Mr. Irving would normally be there."

"And what did you do?" Hamilton Burger asked.

"I entered the office."

"For what purpose?"

"For the sole purpose of finding the letters I had written."

"You had reason to believe those letters were in the office?"

"Yes. He told me they were in his desk and that I could come and get them at any time after I had complied with his terms."

"What happened?"

"I couldn't find the letters. I looked and I looked, and I pulled open the drawers of the desk and then—"

"Go on," Hamilton Burger said.

"And the door opened," she said.

"And who was in the doorway?"

"The defendant, Duane Jefferson."

"Alone?"

"No. His associate, Walter Irving, was with him."

"What happened?"

"The defendant used vile language. He called me names that I have never been called before."

"And then what?"

"He made a grab for me and—"

"And what did you do?"

"I backed up and tipped over a chair and fell over. Then Mr. Irving grabbed my ankles and held me. The defendant accused me of snooping and I told him I was there only to get my letters."

"Then what?"

"Then he stood for a moment looking at me in apparent surprise, and then said to Mr. Irving, 'Damned if I don't believe she's right!' "

"Then what?"

"Then the phone rang and Irving picked up the receiver, listened for a minute and said, 'Good God! The police!' "

"Go on," Hamilton Burger said.

"So the defendant ran over to a filing cabinet, jerked it open, pulled out a whole package of my letters tied up with string and said, 'Here, you little fool! Here are your letters. Take them and get out! The police are looking for you. Someone saw you break into the place, and the police have been notified. Now, see what a damn fool you are!' "

"What happened?"

"He started pushing me toward the door. Then Mr. Irving pushed something into my hand and said, 'Here, take these. They'll be a reward for keeping your big mouth shut.' "

"And what did you do?"

"As soon as they pushed me out of the door, I made a dash for the women's restroom."

"Go on," Hamilton Burger said.

"And just as I opened the door of the restroom, I saw the defendant and Walter Irving run out of their office and dash to the men's room."

"Then what?"

"I didn't wait to see any more. I dashed into the restroom and unfastened the string on the package of letters I had been given, looked through the contents to see that they were mine, and destroyed them."

"*How* did you destroy them?"

"I put them in the wastepaper receptacle with the used towels, where they would be picked up and incinerated."

"And then what did you do?"

"Then," she said, "I was trapped. I knew the police were coming. I—"

"Go ahead," Hamilton Burger said.

"I had to do something to get out of there."

"And *what* did you do?" Hamilton Burger said, a smile on his face.

"I felt that perhaps the exits might be watched, that I must have been seen by someone who had given the police a good description, so I . . . I looked around for some place to go, and I saw a door which had the sign on it saying, 'Perry Mason, Attorney at Law, Enter.' I'd heard of Perry Mason, of course, and I thought perhaps I could hand him a line, telling him I wanted a divorce or something of that sort, or that I'd been in an automobile accident . . .

just make up a good story, anything to hold his interest. That would enable me to be in his office when the police arrived. I felt I could hold his interest long enough to avoid the police. I wanted to stay there just long enough so I could get out after the police had given up the search. I realize now that it was a crazy idea, but it was the only available avenue of escape. As it happened, Fate played into my hands."

"In what way?"

"It seemed Mr. Mason's secretaries were expecting a typist. They'd telephoned some agency and a typist was supposed to be on her way up. I stood, hesitating, in the doorway for a moment, and the receptionist took me for the typist. She asked me if I was the typist, so of course I told her yes and went to work."

"And," Hamilton Burger said smugly, "you worked in the office of Perry Mason that afternoon?"

"I worked there for some little time, yes."

"And then what?"

"When the coast was clear I made my escape."

"When was that?"

"Well, I was working on a document. I was afraid that if it was finished, Mr. Mason would ring up the secretarial agency to find out what the bill was. I just didn't know what to do. So when there was a good break, I slipped down to the restroom, then to the elevator and went home."

"You have mentioned something that was pushed into your hand. Do you know what that consisted of?"

"Yes."

"What?"

"Diamonds. Two diamonds."

"When did you find out about them?"

"After I'd been working for a few minutes. I'd slipped what had been given me into my handbag. So when I had a good chance I looked. I found two small packets of tissue paper. I removed the paper and found two diamonds.

"I got in a panic. I suddenly realized that if these men should claim the intruder had stolen diamonds from their office, I'd be framed. I wouldn't have any possible defense anyone would believe. So I just had to get rid of these diamonds. I realized right away I'd walked into a trap."

"What did you do?"

"I stuck the diamonds to the underside of the desk, where I was working in Mr. Mason's office."

"How did you stick them to this desk?"

"With chewing gum."

"How much chewing gum?"

"A perfectly terrific amount. I had about twelve sticks in my purse, and I chewed them all up and got a big wad of gum. Then I put the diamonds in the gum and pushed them up against the underside of the desk."

"Where are those diamonds now?"

"As far as *I* know, they're still there."

"Your Honor," Hamilton Burger said, "if the Court please, I suggest that an officer of this court be dispatched to the office of Perry Mason, with instructions to look at the place described by this witness and bring back the wad of chewing gum containing those two diamonds."

Judge Hartley looked at Mason questioningly.

Mason smiled at the judge. "*I* certainly would have no objection, Your Honor."

"Very well," Judge Hartley ruled. "It will be the order of the Court that an officer of this court proceed to take those diamonds and impound them."

"And may they be sent for *immediately*, Your Honor," Hamilton Burger asked, "before . . . well, before something happens to them?"

"And what would happen to them?" Judge Hartley asked.

"Well, now that it is known," Hamilton Burger said, "now that the testimony has come out . . . I . . . well, I would dislike to have anything happen to the evidence."

"So would I," Mason said heartily. "I join the prosecutor's request. I suggest that one of the deputy district attorneys instruct an officer to proceed at once to my office."

"Can you designate the desk that was used by this young lady?" Hamilton Burger asked.

"The desk in question was one that was placed in the law library. It can be found there."

"Very well," the judge ruled. "You may take care of that matter, Mr. District Attorney. Now, go on with your questioning."

Hamilton Burger walked over to the clerk's desk, picked up the knife which had been marked for identification. "I show you a dagger with an eight-inch blade, one side of the hilt being engraved with the word 'Duane,' the other side with the initials *M.J.* I will ask you if you are familiar with that knife."

"I am. It is a knife which I sent the defendant at his South African address as a Christmas present last Christmas. I told him he could use it to protect . . . protect my honor."

The witness began to cry.

"I think," Hamilton Burger said suavely, "that those are all of the questions I have of this witness. You may cross-examine, Mr. Mason."

Mason waited patiently until Mae Jordan had dried her eyes and looked up at him. "You are, I believe, a very fast and accurate typist?"

"I try to be competent."

"And you worked in my office on the afternoon in question?"

"Yes."

"Do you know anything about gems?"

"Not particularly."

"Do you know the difference between a real diamond and an imitation diamond?"

"It didn't take an expert to tell those stones. Those were very high-grade stones. I recognized what they were as soon as I saw them."

"Had you bought those stones from the defendant?" Mason asked.

"What do you mean, had I bought those stones?"

"Did you pay him anything? Give him any consideration?"

"Certainly not," she snapped.

"Did you pay Mr. Irving for those stones?"

"No."

"Then you knew those stones did not belong to you," Mason asked.

"They were given to me."

"Oh, then you thought they were yours?"

"I felt certain I'd walked into a trap. I felt those men would say I'd gone to their office and stolen those diamonds. It would be my word against theirs. I knew they hadn't given me two very valuable diamonds just to keep quiet about having exchanged letters."

"You say *they* gave you the diamonds. Did you receive them from Jefferson or from Irving?"

"From Mr. Irving."

Mason studied the defiant witness for a moment. "You started corresponding with the defendant while he was in South Africa?"

"Yes."

"And wrote him love letters?"

"They were not love letters."

"Did they contain matters which you wouldn't want this jury to see?"

"They were foolish letters, Mr. Mason. Please don't try to put anything in them that wasn't in them."

"I am asking you," Mason said, "as to the nature of the letters."

"They were *very foolish* letters."

"Would you say they were indiscreet?"

"I would say they were indiscreet."

"You wanted them back?"

"I felt . . . well, I felt very foolish about the whole thing."

"So you wanted the letters back?"

"Yes, very badly."

"And, in order to get them back, you were willing to commit a crime?"

"I wanted the letters back."

"Please answer the question. You were willing to commit a crime in order to get the letters back?"

"I don't know that it's a crime to enter an office to get things that belong to me."

"Did you believe it was illegal to use a skeleton key to enter property belonging to another person, so that you can take certain things?"

"I was trying to get possession of property that belonged to me."

"Did you believe that it was illegal to use a skeleton key to open that door?"

"I . . . I didn't consult a lawyer to find out about my rights."

"Where did you get the key which opened the door?"

"I haven't said I had a key."

"You've admitted you entered the office at a time when you knew both Jefferson and Irving would not be there."

"What if I did? I went to get my own property."

"If you had a key which opened the door of that office, where did you get it?"

"Where does one ordinarily get keys?"

"From a locksmith?"

"Perhaps."

"Did you get a key to that office from a locksmith?"

"I will answer no questions about keys."

"And suppose the Court should instruct you that you had to answer such questions?"

"I would refuse on the grounds that any testimony from me relating to the manner in which I entered that office would tend to incriminate me, and therefore I would not have to answer the question."

"I see," Mason said. "But you have already admitted that you entered the office illegally. Therefore, an attempt to exercise your constitutional prerogative would be too late."

"Now, if the Court please," Hamilton Burger said, "I would like to be heard on this point. I have given this question very careful thought. The Court will note that the witness simply stated that she entered the office at a time when the defendant and his associate were absent. She has not stated *how* she entered the office. As far as her testimony is concerned, the door could well have been unlocked; and, inasmuch as this is a public office, where it is expected the public will enter in order to transact business, there would have been nothing illegal about an entrance made in the event the door had been unlocked. Therefore, the witness is in a position, if she so desires, to refuse to testify as to the manner in which she entered that office, on the ground that it might tend to incriminate her."

Judge Hartley frowned. "That's rather an unusual position for a witness called on behalf of the prosecution, Mr. District Attorney."

"It's an unusual case, Your Honor."

"Do you wish to be heard on that point, Mr. Mason?" Judge Hartley asked.

Mason smiled and said, "I would like to ask the witness a few more questions."

"I object to any more cross-examination on this point," Hamilton Burger said, his voice showing exasperation and a trace of apprehension. "The witness has made her position plain. Counsel doesn't dare to cross-examine her about the pertinent facts in the case, so he continually harps upon the one point where this young woman, yielding to her emotions, has put herself in an embarrassing position. He keeps prolonging this moment, as a cat plays with a mouse, hoping thereby to prejudice the jury against this witness. The witness has made her position plain. She refuses to answer questions on this phase of the matter."

Mason smiled. "I have been accused of prolonging this phase of the examination in an attempt to prejudice the jury. I don't want to prejudice the jury. I'd like to get information which the jurors want.

"When the district attorney was prolonging the examination of Mr. Gilly in an attempt to prejudice the jury against the defendant, you didn't hear me screaming. What's sauce for the goose should be sauce for the gander."

Judge Hartley smiled. "The objection is overruled. Go ahead with your questions."

"Will you tell us the name of the person who furnished you with the key that enabled you to get into the office of the South African Gem Importing and Exploration Company?"

"No."

"Why not?"

"Because, if I answered that question, it would tend to incriminate me, and therefore I shall refuse to answer."

"You have discussed this phase of your testimony with the district attorney?"

"Oh, Your Honor," Hamilton Burger said, "this is the same old gambit so frequently pursued by defense attorneys. I will stipulate that this witness has discussed her testimony with me. I would not have put her on the stand unless I knew that her testimony would be pertinent and relevant. The only way I could know what it was, was to talk with her."

Mason kept his eyes on the witness. "You have discussed this phase of your testimony with the district attorney?"

"Yes."

"And have discussed with him what would happen in case you were asked a question concerning the name of the person who furnished you the keys?"

"Yes."

"And told him you would refuse to testify on the ground that it would incriminate you?"

"Yes."

"Did you make that statement to the district attorney, or did he suggest to you that you could refuse to answer the question on that ground?"

"Well, I . . . I . . . of course I know my rights."

"But you have just stated," Mason said, "that you didn't know that it was a crime for you to enter an office to get property that belonged to you."

"Well, I . . . I think there's a nice legal point there. As I now understand it, a public office . . . that is, a place that is intended to be open to the public is different from a private residence. And where property belongs to me—"

Mason smiled. "Then you are *now* taking the position, Miss Jordan, that it was no crime for you to enter that office?"

"No."

"Oh, you are *now* taking the position that it *was* a crime for you to enter that office?"

"I now understand that under the circumstances it— I refuse to answer that question on the ground that the answer may incriminate me."

"In other words, the district attorney suggested to you that you should consider it was a crime, and therefore you could refuse to answer certain questions when I asked them?"

"We discussed it."

"And the suggestion came from the district attorney that it would be well under the circumstances for you to refuse to answer certain questions which I might ask on cross-examination. Is that right?"

"There were certain questions I told him I wouldn't answer."

"And he suggested that you could avoid answering them by claiming immunity on the ground that you couldn't be forced to incriminate yourself?"

"Well, in a way, yes."

"Now then," Mason said, "you had two diamonds with you when you left that office?"

"Yes."

"They didn't belong to you?"

"They were given to me."

"By whom?"

"By Mr. Irving, who told me to take them."

"Did he say *why* you were to take them?"

"He said to take them and keep my big mouth shut."

"And you took them?"

"Yes."

"And you kept your mouth shut?"

"I don't know what you mean by that."

"You didn't tell anyone about the diamonds?"

"Not at that time."

"You knew they were valuable?"

"I'm not simple, Mr. Mason."

"Exactly," Mason said. "You knew they were diamonds and you knew they were valuable?"

"Certainly."

"And you took them?"

"Yes."

"And what did you do with them?"

"I've told you what I did with them. I fastened them to the underside of the desk in your office."

"Why?" Mason asked.

"Because I wanted a place to keep them."

"You could have put them in your purse. You could have put them in your pocket," Mason said.

"I . . . I didn't want to. I didn't want to have to explain how I came by the diamonds."

"To whom?"

"To anybody who might question me."

"To the police?"

"To *anyone* who might question me, Mr. Mason. I felt I had walked into a trap and that I was going to be accused of having stolen two diamonds."

"But you had been given those diamonds?"

"Yes, but I didn't think anyone would believe me when I told them so."

"Then you don't expect the jury to believe your story now?"

"Objected to," Hamilton Burger snapped. "Argumentative."

"Sustained," Judge Hartley said.

"Isn't it a fact," Mason asked, "that someone who gave you a key to the office which you entered illegally and unlawfully, also gave you a package of diamonds which you were to plant in that office in a place where they would subsequently be found by the police?"

"No!"

"Isn't it a fact that you carried those diamonds into the building wrapped up in tissue paper, that you put those diamonds in a package and concealed them in the office, that you were forced to leave hurriedly because you learned the police had been tipped off, and after you got in my office and started to work, you checked through your purse in order to make certain that you had disposed of all of the diamonds and to your horror found that two of the diamonds you were supposed to have planted in that office had been left in your purse, and that, therefore, in a panic, you tried to get rid of those diamonds by the means you have described?"

"Just a moment!" Hamilton Burger shouted. "I object to this on the ground that it assumes facts not in evidence, that it is not proper cross-examination, that there is no foundation for the assumption that—"

"The objection is overruled," Judge Hartley snapped.

"Isn't it a fact," Mason asked, "that you did what I have just outlined?"

"Absolutely not. I took no diamonds with me when I went to that office. I had no diamonds in my possession when I went in."

"But you don't dare to tell us who gave you a key to that office?"

"I refuse to answer questions about that."

"Thank you," Mason said. "I have no further questions."

Mae Jordan left the stand. The jurors watched her with some skepticism.

Hamilton Burger called other witnesses who established technical background—the exact position of the cruise ship in the harbor when Baxter jumped overboard, passengers who had seen Baxter jump and the owner of a launch which had been cruising in the vicinity. He also introduced police experts who had examined the bloodstains on Gilly's boat and bloodstains on the knife and pronounced them to be human blood.

Mason had no cross-examination except for the expert who had examined the bloodstains.

"*When* did you make your examination?" Mason asked.

"June nineteenth."

"At a time when the bloodstains were at least ten days to two weeks old?"

"So I should judge."

"On the boat?"

"Yes."

"On the knife?"

"Yes."

"They could have been older?"

"Yes."

"They could have been a month old?"

"Well, they could have been."

"The only way you have of knowing when those bloodstains got on the boat was from a statement made to you by Jack Gilly?"

"Yes."

"And did you know Jack Gilly had previously been convicted of perjury?"

The witness squirmed.

"Objected to as incompetent, irrelevant, and immaterial and not proper cross-examination," Hamilton Burger said.

"Sustained," Judge Hartley snapped. "Counsel can confine his cross-examination to the bloodstains, the nature of the tests, and the professional competency of the witness."

"That's all," Mason said. "I have no more questions."

Max Dutton, Hamilton Burger's last witness of the afternoon, was distinctly a surprise witness. Dutton testified that he lived in Brussels; he had come by airplane to testify at the request of the district attorney. He was, he testified, an expert on gems. He used a system of making models of gems so that it would be possible to identify any particular stone of sufficient value to make it worth while. He made microscopic measurements of the dimensions, of the angles, of the facets, and of the locations of any flaws. The witness testified he maintained permanent records of his identifications, which facilitated appraisals, insurance recoveries and the identification of stolen stones.

He had, he said, been employed by Munroe Baxter during his lifetime; Munroe Baxter had given him some gems and asked him to arrange for the identification of the larger stones, so that they could be readily identified if necessary.

The witness tried to state what Munroe Baxter had told him—the manner in which he had received the stones—but on objection by Perry Mason the objection was sustained by the Court. However, Hamilton Burger was able to show that the stones came to the witness in a box bearing the imprint of the Paris office of the South African Gem Importing and Exploration Company.

The witness testified that he had selected the larger stones and had made complete charts of those stones, so that they could be identified. He further stated that he had examined a package of stones which had been given him by the police and which he understood had been recovered from the desk of the defendant, and that ten of those stones had proved to be identical to the stones he had so carefully charted.

"Cross-examine," Hamilton Burger said.

"This system that you have worked out for identifying stones takes into consideration every possible identifying mark on the stones?" Mason asked.

"It does."

"It would, therefore, enable anyone to duplicate those stones, would it not?"

"No, sir, it would not. You might cut a stone to size; you might get the angle of the facets exactly the same. But the flaws in the stone would not be in the proper position with relation to the facets."

"It would, however, be possible to make a duplication in the event you could find a stone that had certain flaws?"

"That is very much like asking whether it would be possible to duplicate fingerprints, provided you could find a person who had exactly identical ridges and whorls," the witness said.

"Do you then wish to testify under oath that your system of identifying stones is as accurate as the identification of individuals through the science of fingerprinting?" Mason asked.

The witness hesitated a moment, then said, "Not quite."

"That's all," Mason announced, smiling. "No further questions."

The court took its evening adjournment.

As Mason gathered his papers together Walter Irving pushed his way through the crowd that was leaving the courtroom. He came up to Mason's table. His grin was somewhat sheepish.

"I guess perhaps I owe you an apology," he said.

"You don't owe me anything," Mason told him. "And make no mistake about it, I don't owe you anything."

"You don't owe me anything," Irving said, "but I'm going to make an apology anyway. And I'm further going to tell you that that Jordan girl is a brazen-faced liar. I *think* she broke into that office to plant those diamonds; but regardless of her purpose in getting into the office, there was never any scene such as she testified to. We didn't get back from lunch until after she had done what she wanted to do in that office and had skipped out. We can prove that, and that one fact makes that Jordan girl a damn liar.

"And what's more, I didn't give that Jordan girl any diamonds," Irving said. "I didn't tell her to keep her mouth shut. Now that I've seen her, I remember having seen her at the train. She met Duane and tried to force herself on him. As far as I know, that's the only time in my life I've ever set eyes on her. That girl is playing some deep game, and she's not playing it for herself, Mr. Mason. There's something behind it, something very sinister and something being engineered by powerful interests that have made a dupe of your district attorney."

"I hope so," Mason said. "Where have you been, incidentally?"

"I've been in Mexico. I admit, I underestimated your abilities, but I was trying to give you an opportunity to direct suspicion to me in case you wanted to."

"Well, I haven't wanted to," Mason said, and then added significantly, "yet."

Irving grinned at him. "That's the spirit, Counselor. You can always make a pass at me and confuse the issues as far as the jury is concerned, even if you don't want to be friendly with me. Remember that I'm available as a suspect."

Mason looked into his eyes. "Don't think I'll ever forget it."

Irving's grin was one of pure delight. His reddish-brown eyes met the cold, hard gaze of the lawyer with steady affability. "Now you're cooking with gas! Any time you want me, I'll be available, and I can, of course, give Duane a complete alibi for the morning of the sixth. We had breakfast together a little after seven, got to the office shortly before nine, and he was with me all morning."

"How about the evening of the fifth?" Mason asked.

Irving's eyes shifted.

"Well?" Mason asked.

"Duane was out somewhere."

"Where?"

"With some woman."

"Who?"

Irving shrugged his shoulders.

Mason said, "You can see what's happening here. If the district attorney makes enough of a case so that I have to put the defendant on the stand, there is every possibility that Duane Jefferson's manner, his aloofness, his refusal to answer certain questions, will prejudice his case with the jury."

"I know," Irving said. "I know exactly what you're up against. Before you ever put him on the stand, Mr. Mason, let me talk with him and I'll hammer some sense into his head, even if it does result in his undying enmity forever afterwards. In short, I want you to know that you can count on me all the way through."

"Yes," Mason said, "I understand you sent a most co-operative cablegram to your company in South Africa?"

Irving kept grinning and his eyes remained steady. "That's right," he said. "I asked the company to fire you. I'm sending another one tonight, which will be a lot different. You haven't found Marline Chaumont yet, have you?"

"No," Mason admitted.

Irving lost his grin. "I told you you wouldn't. That's where you loused the case up, Mason. Aside from that, you're doing fine."

And, as though completely assured of Mason's good-will, Walter Irving turned and sauntered out of the courtroom.

CHAPTER 16

BACK IN HIS OFFICE THAT EVENING, MASON PACED THE FLOOR. "Hang it, Paul!" he said to the detective. "Why is Hamilton Burger so completely confident?"

"Well, you jarred him a couple of times this afternoon," Drake said. "He was so mad he was quivering like a bowl of jelly."

"I know he was mad, Paul. He was angry, he was irritated, he was annoyed, but he was still sure of himself.

"Hamilton Burger hates me. He'd love to get me out on a limb over a very deep pool and then saw off the limb. He wouldn't even mind if he got slightly wet from the resulting splash. Now, there's something in this case that we don't know about."

"Well," Drake said, "as far as this case is concerned, what does he have, Perry?"

"So far he doesn't have anything," Mason said. "That's what worries me. Why should he have that much assurance over a case which means nothing. He has a woman adventuress and a smuggler; he has a man who concededly planned to fake a suicide. The man was a strong swimmer. He had an air tank under his clothes. He did exactly what he had planned he was going to do, to wit, jump over the side of the ship and disappear, so that people would think he was dead.

"Then Hamilton Burger brings on the scum of the earth, the sweepings of the waterfront. He uses a man who deliberately rented a boat to be used in an illegal activity, a man who has been twice convicted of felony. His last conviction was for perjury. The jury isn't going to believe that man."

"And what about the girl?" Della Street asked.

"That's different," Mason said. "That girl made a good impression on the jury. Apparently, she was hired to take those gems to the office and plant them. The jury doesn't know that. Those jurors are taking her at face value."

"Figure value," Paul Drake corrected. "Why did you let her off so easy, Perry?"

"Because every time she answered a question she was getting closer to the jury. Those jurors like her, Paul. I'm going to ask to recall her for further cross-examination. When I do that, I want to have the lowdown on her. You're going to put out operatives who will dig up the dirt on her. I want to know everything about her, all about her past, her friends, and before I question her again, I want to know where she got that key which opened the office."

Drake merely nodded.

"Well," Mason said impatiently, "aren't you going to get busy, Paul?"

The detective sat grinning. "I am busy, Perry. I've been busy. This is once I read your mind. I knew what you'd want. The minute that girl got off the stand, I started a whole bunch of men working. I left this unlisted number of yours with my confidential secretary. She may call any minute with some hot stuff."

Mason smiled. "Give yourself a merit badge, Paul. Hang it, there's nothing that gets a lawyer down worse than having to cross-examine a demure girl who has hypnotized the jury. I can't keep shooting blind, Paul. The next time I start sniping at her, I've got to have ammunition that will score dead-center hits.

"Now, here's something else you'll have to do."

"What's that, Perry?"

"Find Munroe Baxter."

"You don't think he's dead?"

"I'm beginning to think Walter Irving was right. I think the supposedly half-witted brother of Marline Chaumont may well be Baxter, despite those hospital records. In a deal of this magnitude we may find a big loophole. If this fellow in the mental hospital was so much of a zombie, what was to prevent Marline Chaumont from identifying him as her brother, getting him out, then farming him out and substituting Munroe Baxter? What are we doing about finding her, Paul?"

"Well, we're making headway, thanks to you," Drake said. "I'm kicking myself for being a stupid fool. You were right about those car rentals, and I sure overlooked a bet there. Two of those car rentals have agencies right there at the airport. In order to rent a car, you have to show your driving license. That means you have to give your right name."

"You mean Marline Chaumont rented a car under her own name?"

"That's right. Showed her driving license, rented the automobile and took it out."

"Her brother was with her?"

"Not at that time. She left the airport by limousine as an incoming passenger, went uptown with her brother and two suitcases, then came back, rented a car, picked up the other two suitcases, drove out, picked up her brother, and then went some place."

"Where?" Mason asked.

"Now, that's something I wish I knew. However, we stand a chance of finding out. The car rental is predicated on the mileage driven, as well as on a per diem charge. The mileage indicator on the car when Marline Chaumont brought it back showed it had been driven sixty-two miles."

Mason thought for a moment, then suddenly snapped his fingers.

"What now?" Drake asked.

"She went out to one of the suburban cities," Mason said. "She's rented a place in one of those suburbs. Now then, she'll want to rent another car, and again she'll have to use her driving license. She was afraid to keep that car she had rented at the airport because she thought we might be checking there."

"We would have been checking within a matter of hours if I'd been on my toes," Drake said ruefully.

"All right," Mason said, "she rented a car there. She was afraid we might trace her, get the license number of the car, have it posted as a hot car and pick her up. So she got rid of that car just as soon as she could. Then she went to one of the outlying towns where they have a car rental agency and signed up for another car. She's had to do it under her own name because of the license angle. Get your men busy, Paul, and cover *all* of the car rental agencies in those outlying towns."

Paul Drake wormed his way out of the chair to stand erect, stretch, say, "Gosh, I'm all in myself. I don't see how you stand a pace like this, Perry."

He went over, picked up the unlisted telephone, said, "Let me call my office and get people started on some of this."

Drake dialed the number, said, "Hello. This is Paul. I want a bunch of men put out to cover all of the outlying towns. I want to check every car rental agency for a car rented by Marline Chaumont. . . . That's right. Everything.

"Now you can— How's that? . . . Wait a minute now," Drake said. "Give that to me slow. I want to make some notes. Who made the report? . . . All right, bring it down here at once. I'm in Mason's office—and get those men started."

Drake hung up the telephone and said, "We've got something, Perry."

"What?"

"We've found out the ace that Hamilton Burger is holding up his sleeve."

"You're sure?"

"Dead sure. One of the detectives who worked on the case knows the angle. He tipped a newspaper reporter off to come and see you get torn to ribbons tomorrow, and the reporter pumped him enough to find out what it was. That reporter is very friendly with one of my men, and we got a tip-off."

"What is it?" Mason asked.

"We'll have all the dope in a minute. They're bringing the report down here," Drake said. "It concerns the woman that Duane Jefferson is trying to protect."

Mason said, "Now, we're getting somewhere, Paul. If I know that information, I don't care what Hamilton Burger thinks he's going to do with it. I'll outgeneral him somehow."

They waited anxiously until knuckles tapped on the door. Drake opened the door, took an envelope from his secretary, said, "You're getting operatives out checking those car rentals?"

"That's already being done, Mr. Drake. I put Davis in charge of it, and he's on the telephone right now."

"Fine," Drake said. "Let's take a look. I'll give you the dope, Perry."

Drake opened the envelope, pulled out the sheets of flimsy, looked through them hastily, then whistled.

"All right," Mason said, "give."

Drake said, "The night of June fifth Jefferson was down at a nightspot with a woman. It was the woman's car. The parking attendant parked the car and some customer scratched a fender. The attendant got records of license numbers and all that. The woman got in a panic, gave the parking attendant twenty bucks, and told him to forget the whole thing.

"Naturally, the attendant had the answer as soon as that happened. She was a married woman. There's no doubt the guy with her was Duane Jefferson."

"Who was she?" Mason asked.

"A woman by the name of Nan Ormsby."

"Okay," Mason said. "Perhaps I can use this. It'll depend on how far the affair has gone."

Drake, who had continued reading the report, suddenly gave another whistle.

"What now?" Mason asked.

"Hold everything," Drake said. "You have as juror number eleven Alonzo Martin Liggett?"

"What about him?" Mason asked.

"He's a close friend of Dan Ormsby. Ormsby is in partnership with his wife. They have a place called "Nan and Dan, Realtors." Nan Ormsby has been having trouble with her husband. She wants a settlement. He doesn't want the kind of a settlement she wants. He hasn't been able to get anything on her, although he's tried.

"Now, with a juror who is friendly to Dan Ormsby, you can see what'll happen."

"Good Lord!" Mason said. "If Hamilton Burger uses that lever—"

"Remember, this tip comes straight from Hamilton Burger's office," Drake said.

Mason sat in frowning concentration.

"How bad is it?" Drake asked.

"It's a perfect setup for a D.A.," Mason said. "If he can force me to put my client on the stand, he can go to town. The jury isn't going to like Duane Jefferson's pseudo-British manner, his snobbishness. You know how they feel about people who get tied up with the British and then become more English than the English, and that's what Jefferson has done. He's cultivated all those mannerisms. So Hamilton Burger will start boring into him—he was breaking up a home, he was out with a married woman—and there's Dan Ormsby's friend sitting on the jury."

"Any way you can beat that, Perry?" Drake asked.

"Two ways," Mason said, "and I don't like either one. I can either base all of my fight on trying to prove that there's been no *corpus delicti*, and keep the case from going to the jury, or, if the judge doesn't agree with me on that, I'll put the defendant on the stand, but confine my direct examination to where he was at five o'clock on the morning of the sixth and roar like the devil if the district attorney tries to examine him as to the night of the fifth. Since I wouldn't have asked him anything about the night of the fifth—only the morning of the sixth—I can claim the D.A. can't examine him as to anything on the night of the fifth."

"He'll have to make a general denial that he committed the crime?" Drake asked.

 - Mason nodded.

"Won't that open up the question of where he was on the night of the fifth when the boat was being rented?"

"The prosecution's case shows that the defendant wasn't seen until the morning of the sixth, after the boat had been rented—that is, that's the prosecution's case so far. We have the testimony of Jack Gilly to that effect."

"Well," Drake said, "I'll go down to my office and start things going. I'll have my men on the job working all night. You'd better get some sleep, Perry."

Mason's nod showed his preoccupation with other thoughts. "I've got to get this thing straight, Paul. I have a sixth sense that's warning me. I guess it's the way Hamilton Burger has been acting. This is one case where I've got to watch every time I put my foot down that I'm not stepping right in the middle of a trap."

"Well," Drake said, "you pace the floor and I'll cover the country, Perry. Between us, we may be in a better position tomorrow morning."

Mason said, "I should have known. Burger has been triumphant, yet his case is a matter of patchwork. It wasn't the strength of his own case that made him triumphant, but the weakness of my case."

"And now that you know, can you detour the pitfalls?" Drake asked.

"I can try," Mason said grimly.

CHAPTER 17

JUDGE HARTLEY CALLED COURT TO ORDER PROMPTLY AT TEN o'clock.

Hamilton Burger said, "I have a couple more questions to ask Mr. Max Dutton, the gem expert."

"Just a moment," Mason said. "If the Court please, I wish to make a motion. I feel that perhaps this motion should be made without the presence of the jury."

Judge Hartley frowned. "I am expecting a motion at the conclusion of the prosecution's case," he said. "Can you not let your motion wait until that time, Mr. Mason? I would like to proceed with the case as rapidly as possible."

"One of my motions can wait," Mason said. "The other one, I think, can properly be made in the presence of the jury. That is a motion to exclude all of the evidence of Mae Jordan on the ground that there is nothing in her testimony which in any way connects the defendant with any crime."

"If the Court please," Hamilton Burger said, "the witness, Dutton, will testify that one of the diamonds which was found on the underside of the desk in Perry Mason's office was one of the identical diamonds which was in the Munroe Baxter collection."

Mason said, "That doesn't connect the defendant, Duane Jefferson, with anything. Jefferson didn't give her those diamonds. Even if we are to take her testimony at face value, even if we are to concede for the sake of this motion that she took those diamonds out of the office instead of going to the office to plant diamonds, the prosecution can't bind the defendant by anything that Walter Irving did."

"It was done in his presence," Hamilton Burger said, "and as a part of a joint enterprise."

"You haven't proven either one of those points," Mason said.

Judge Hartley stroked his chin. "I am inclined to think this motion may be well taken, Mr. District Attorney. The Court has been giving this matter a great deal of thought."

"If the Court please," Hamilton Burger pleaded desperately, "I have a good case here. I have shown that these diamonds were in the possession of Munroe Baxter when he left the ship. These diamonds next show up in the possession of the defendant—"

"Not in the possession of the defendant," Mason corrected.

"In an office to which he had a key," Hamilton Burger snapped.

"The janitor had a key. The scrubwoman had a key. Walter Irving had a key."

"Exactly," Judge Hartley said. "You have to show some act of domination over those diamonds by the defendant before he can be connected with the case. That's a fundamental part of the case."

"But, Your Honor, we *have* shown that act of domination. Two of those diamonds were given to the witness Jordan to compensate her for keeping silent about her letters. We have shown that Munroe Baxter came up and took hold of that towing line which was attached to the heavy fishing rod; that the defendant stabbed him, took the belt containing the diamonds, weighted the body, then towed it away to a point where it could be dropped to the bottom."

Judge Hartley shook his head. "That is a different matter from the motion as to the testimony of Mae Jordan. However, if we are to give every credence to all of the prosecution's testimony and all inferences therefrom, as we must do in considering such a motion, there is probably an inference which will be sufficient to defeat the motion. I'll let the motion be made at this time, and reserve a ruling. Go ahead with your case, Mr. District Attorney."

Hamilton Burger put Max Dutton back on the stand. Dutton testified that one of the gems which had been recovered from the blob of chewing gum that had been found fastened to the underside of Mason's desk was a part of the Baxter collection.

"No questions," Mason said when Hamilton Burger turned Dutton over for cross-examination.

"That," Hamilton Burger announced dramatically and unexpectedly, "finishes the People's case."

Mason said, "At this time, Your Honor, I would like to make a motion without the presence of the jury."

"The jurors will be excused for fifteen minutes," Judge Hartley said, "during which time you will remember the previous admonition of the Court."

When the jurors had filed out of court the judge nodded to Perry Mason. "Proceed with your motion."

"I move that the Court direct and instruct the jury to return a verdict of acquittal," Mason said, "on the ground that no case has been made out which would sustain a conviction, on the ground that there is no evidence tending to show a homicide, no evidence of the *corpus delicti,* and no evidence connecting the defendant with the case."

Judge Hartley said, "I am going to rule against the defense in this case, Mr. Mason. I don't want to preclude you from argument, but the Court has given this matter very careful consideration. Knowing that such a motion would be made, I want to point out to you that while, as a usual thing, proof of the *corpus delicti* includes finding the body, under the law of California that is not necessary. *Corpus delicti* means the body of the crime, not the body of the victim.

"Proof of *corpus delicti* only shows that a crime has been committed. After the crime has been committed, then it is possible to connect the defendant with that crime by proper proof.

"The *corpus delicti,* or the crime itself, like any other fact to be established in court, can be proved by circumstantial as well as direct evidence. There can be reasonable inferences deduced from the factual evidence presented.

"Now then, we have evidence which, I admit, is not very robust, which shows that Munroe Baxter, the purported victim, was carrying certain diamonds in his possession. Presumably he would not have parted from those diamonds without a struggle. Those diamonds were subsequently found under circumstances which at least support an inference that they were under the domination and in the possession of the defendant.

"One of the strongest pieces of evidence in this case is the finding of the bloodstained knife in the boat. I am free to admit that if I were a juror I would not be greatly impressed by the testimony of the witness Gilly, and yet a man who has been convicted of a felony, a man who has been convicted of perjury may well tell the truth.

"We have in this state the case of *People* v. *Cullen,* 37 California 2nd, 614, 234 Pacific 2nd, 1, holding that it is not essential that the body of the victim actually be found in order to support a homicide conviction.

"One of the most interesting cases ever to come before the bar of any country is the case of *Rex* v. *James Camb.* That was, of course, a British case, decided on Monday, April twenty-sixth, nineteen hundred and forty-eight, before the Lord Chief Justice of England.

"That is the famous *Durban Castle* case in which James Camb, a steward aboard the ship, went to the cabin of a young woman passenger. He was recognized in that cabin. The young woman disappeared and was never seen again. There was no evidence, other than circumstantial evidence, of the *corpus delicti,* save the testimony of the defendant himself admitting that he had pushed the body through the porthole but claiming that the woman was dead at the time, that she had died from natural causes and he had merely disposed of the body in that way.

"In this case we have, of course, no admission of that sort. But we do have a showing that the defendant sat in a boat, that some huge body, too big in the normal course of things to be a fish, attached itself to the heavy fishing tackle which the defendant was dangling overboard; that the defendant or the defendant's companion thereupon reached down and stabbed with a knife. A knife was subsequently found in the boat and the knife was smeared with human blood. It was the defendant's knife. I think, under the circumstances, there is enough of a case here to force the defense to meet the charge, and I think that if the jury should convict upon this evidence, the conviction would stand up."

Hamilton Burger smiled and said, "I think that if the Court will bear with us, the Court will presently see that a case of murder has been abundantly proved."

Judge Hartley looked almost suspiciously at the district attorney for a moment, then tightened his lips and said, "Very well. Call the jury."

Mason turned to his client. "This is it, Jefferson," he said. "You're going to have to go on the stand. You have not seen fit to confide in me as your lawyer. You have left me in a position where I have had to undertake the defense of your case with very little assistance from you.

"I think I can prove the witness Mae Jordan lied when she said that you came into the office while she was still there. I have the girl at the cigar counter who will testify that you men did not come in until *after* the manager of the building was standing down at the elevators. I think once we can prove that she lied in one thing, we can prove that she is to be distrusted in her entire testimony. But that young woman has made a very favorable impression on the jury."

Jefferson merely bowed in a coldly formal way. "Very well," he said.

"You have a few seconds now," Mason said. "Do you want to tell me the things that I should know?"

"Certainly," Jefferson said. "I am innocent. That is all you need to know."

"Why the devil won't you confide in me?" Mason asked.

"Because there are certain things that I am not going to tell anyone."

"In case you are interested," Mason said, "I know where you were on the night of June fifth, and furthermore, the district attorney knows it, too."

For a moment Duane Jefferson stiffened, then he turned his face away and said indifferently, "I will answer no questions about the night of June fifth."

"You won't," Mason said, "because I'm not going to ask them on direct examination. Now just remember this one thing: I'm going to ask you where you were during the early morning hours of June sixth. You be *damn* careful that your answer doesn't ever get back of the time limit I am setting. Otherwise, the District Attorney is going to rip you to shreds. Your examination is going to be very, very brief."

"I understand."

"It will be in the nature of a gesture."

"Yes, sir, I understand."

The jury filed into court and took their seats.

"Are you prepared to go on with your case, Mr. Mason?" Judge Hartley asked.

Mason said, "Yes, Your Honor. I won't even bother the Court and the jury by wasting time with an opening statement. I am going to rip this tissue of lies and insinuations wide open. My first witness will be Ann Riddle."

Ann Riddle, the tall, blond girl who operated the cigar stand, came forward.

"Do you remember the occasion of the fourteenth of June of this year?"

"Yes, sir."

"Where were you at that time?"

"I was at the cigar stand in the building where you have your offices."

"Where the South African Gem Importing and Exploration Company also has its offices?"

"Yes, sir."

"You operate the cigar stand in that building?"

"Yes, sir."

"Do you remember an occasion when the manager of the building came down to stand at the elevator with a young woman?"

"Yes, sir."

"Did you see the defendant at that time?"

"Yes, sir. The defendant and Mr. Irving, his associate, were returning from lunch. They—"

"Now just a minute," Mason said. "You don't *know* they were returning from lunch."

"No, sir."

"All right, please confine your statements to what happened."

"Well, they were entering the building. The manager was standing there. One of the men—I think it was Mr. Irving, but I can't remember for sure—started to walk over to the manager of the building, then saw that he was intent upon something else, so he turned away. The two men entered the elevator."

"This was after the alarm had been given about the burglary?" Mason asked.

"Yes, sir."

"You may inquire," Mason said to Hamilton Burger.

Hamilton Burger smiled. "I have no questions."

"I will call the defendant, Duane Jefferson, to the stand," Mason said.

Duane Jefferson, cool and calm, got up and walked slowly to the witness stand. For a moment he didn't look at the jury, then when he did deign to glance at them, it was with an air of superiority bordering on contempt. "The damn fool!" Mason whispered under his breath.

Hamilton Burger tilted back in his swivel chair, he interlaced his fingers back of his head, winked at one of his deputies, and a broad smile suffused his face.

"Did you kill Munroe Baxter?" Mason asked.

"No, sir."

"Did you know that those diamonds were in your office?"

"No, sir."

"Where were you on the morning of the sixth of June? I'll put it this way, where were you from 2:00 A.M. on the sixth of June to noon of that day?"

"During the times mentioned I was in my apartment, sleeping, until a little after seven. Then I had breakfast with my associate, Walter Irving. After breakfast we went to the office."

"Cross-examine," Mason snapped viciously at Hamilton Burger.

Hamilton Burger said, "I will be very brief. I have only a couple of questions, Mr. Jefferson. Have *you* ever been convicted of a felony?"

"I—" Suddenly Jefferson seemed to collapse in the witness chair.

"Have you?" Hamilton Burger thundered.

"I made one mistake in my life," Jefferson said. "I have tried to live it down. I thought I had."

"Did you, indeed?" Hamilton Burger said scornfully. "Where were you convicted, Mr. Jefferson?"

"In New York."

"You served time in Sing Sing?"

"Yes."

"Under the name of Duane Jefferson?"

"No, sir."

"Under what name?"

"Under the name of James Kincaid."

"Exactly," Hamilton Burger said. "You were convicted of larceny by trick and device."

"Yes."

"You posed as an English heir, did you not? And you told—"

"Objected to," Mason said. "Counsel has no right to amplify the admission."

"Sustained."

"Were you, at one time, known as 'Gentleman Jim,' a nickname of the underworld?"

"Objected to," Mason said.

"Sustained."

Hamilton Burger said scornfully, "I will ask no further questions."

As one in a daze, the defendant stumbled from the stand.

Mason said, his lips a hard, white line, "Mr. Walter Irving take the stand."

The bailiff called, "Walter Irving."

When there was no response, the call was taken up in the corridors.

Paul Drake came forward, beckoned to Mason. "He's skipped, Perry. He was sitting near the door. He took it on the lam the minute Burger asked Jefferson about his record. Good Lord! What a mess! What a lousy mess!"

Judge Hartley said not unkindly, "Mr. Irving doesn't seem to be present, Mr. Mason. Was he under subpoena?"

"Yes, Your Honor."

"Do you wish the Court to issue a bench warrant?"

"No, Your Honor," Mason said. "Perhaps Mr. Irving had his reasons for leaving."

"I daresay he did," Hamilton Burger said sarcastically.

"That's the defendant's case," Mason said. "We rest."

It was impossible for Hamilton Burger to keep the gloating triumph out of his voice. "I will," he said, "call only three witnesses on rebuttal. The first is Mrs. Agnes Elmer."

Mrs. Agnes Elmer gave her name and address. She was, she explained, the manager of the apartment house where the defendant, Duane Jefferson, had rented an apartment shortly after his arrival in the city.

"Directing your attention to the early morning of June sixth," Hamilton Burger said, "do you know whether Duane Jefferson was in his apartment?"

"I do."

"Was he in that apartment?"

"He was not."

"Was his bed slept in that night?"

"It was not."

"Cross-examine," Hamilton Burger said.

Mason, recognizing that the short, direct examination was intended to bait a trap into which he must walk on cross-examination, flexed his arms slowly, as though stretching with weariness, said, "How do you fix the date, Mrs. Elmer?"

"A party rang up shortly before midnight on the fifth," Mrs. Elmer said. "It was a woman's voice. She told me it was absolutely imperative that she get in touch with Mr. Jefferson. She said Mr. Jefferson had got her in—"

"Just a minute," Mason interrupted. "I object, Your Honor, to this witness relating any conversations which occurred outside of the presence of the defendant."

"Oh, Your Honor," Hamilton Burger said. "This is plainly admissible. Counsel asked this question himself. He asked her how she fixed the date. She's telling him."

Judge Hartley said, "There may be some technical merit to your contention, Mr. District Attorney, but this is a court of justice, not a place for a legal sparring match. The whole nature of your examination shows you had carefully baited this as a trap for the cross-examiner. I'm going to sustain the objection. You can make your own case by your own witness.

"Now, the Court is going to ask the witness if there is any other way you can fix the date, any way, that is, depending on your own actions."

"Well," the witness said, "I know it was the sixth because that was the day I went to the dentist. I had a terrific toothache that night and couldn't sleep."

"And how do you fix the date that you went to the dentist?" Mason asked.

"From the dentist's appointment book."

"So you don't know of your own knowledge what date you went to the dentist, only the date that is shown in the dentist's book?"

"That's right."

"And the entry of that date in the dentist's book was not made in your own handwriting. In other words, you have used a conversation with the dentist to refresh your memory."

"Well, I asked him what date I came in, and he consulted his records and told me."

"Exactly," Mason said. "But you don't know of your own knowledge how he kept his records."

"Well, he's supposed to keep them—"

Mason smiled. "But *you* have no independent recollection of anything except that it was the night that you had the toothache, is that right?"

"Well, if you'd had that toothache—"

"I'm asking you if that's the only way you can fix the date, that it was the night you had the toothache?"

"Yes."

"And then, at the request of the district attorney, you tried to verify the date?"

"Yes."

"When did the district attorney request that you do that?"

"I don't know. It was late in the month sometime."

"And did you go to the dentist's office, or did you telephone him?"

"I telephoned him."

"And asked him the date when you had your appointment?"

"Yes."

"Aside from that, you wouldn't have been able to tell whether it had been the sixth, the seventh, or the eighth?"

"I suppose not."

"So you have refreshed your recollection by taking the word of someone else. In other words, the testimony you are now giving as to the date is purely hearsay evidence?"

"Oh, Your Honor," Hamilton Burger said, "I think this witness has the right to refresh her recollection by—"

Judge Hartley shook his head. "The witness has testified that she can't remember the date except by fixing it in connection with other circumstances, and those other circumstances which she is using to refresh her recollection depend upon the unsworn testimony of another. Quite plainly hearsay testimony, Mr. District Attorney."

Hamilton Burger bowed. "Very well, Your Honor."

"That's all," Mason said.

"Call Josephine Carter," Burger said.

Josephine Carter was sworn, testified she was a switchboard operator at the apartment house where the defendant had his apartment, that she worked from 10:00 P.M. on the night of the fifth of June until 6:00 A.M. on the morning of June sixth.

"Did you ring the defendant's phone that night?"

"Yes."

"When?"

"Shortly before midnight. I was told it was an emergency and I—"

"Never mind what you were *told*. What did you *do?*"

"I rang the phone."

"Did you get an answer?"

"No. The party who was calling left a message and asked me to keep calling to see that Mr. Jefferson got that message as soon as he came in."

"How often did you continue to ring?"

"Every hour."

"Until when?"

"When I went off duty at six in the morning."

"Did you ever get an answer?"

"No."

"From your desk at the switchboard can you watch the corridor to the elevator, and did you thereafter watch to see if the defendant came in?"

"Yes. I kept watch so as to call to him when he came in."

"He didn't come in while you were on duty?"

"No."

"You're certain?"

"Positive."

"Cross-examine," Burger snapped at Mason.

"How do you know the phone was ringing?" Mason asked smilingly.

"Why I depressed the key."

"Phones get out of order occasionally?"

"Yes."

"Is there any check signal on the board by which you can tell if the phone is ringing?"

"You get a peculiar sound when the phone rings, sort of a hum."

"And if the phone doesn't ring, do you get that hum?"

"I . . . we haven't been troubled that way."

"Do you know of your own knowledge that you fail to get that hum when the phone is not ringing?"

"That's the way the board is supposed to work."

"I'm asking you if you know of your own knowledge?"

"Well, Mr. Mason, I have never been in an apartment where the phone was not ringing and at the same time been downstairs at the switchboard trying to ring that telephone."

"Exactly," Mason said. "That's the point I was trying to make, Miss Carter. That's all."

"Just a moment," Hamilton Burger said. "I have one question on redirect. Did you keep an eye on the persons who went in and out, to see if Mr. Jefferson came in?"

"I did."

"Is your desk so located that you could have seen him when he came in?"

"Yes. Everyone who enters the apartment has to walk down a corridor, and I can see through a glass door into that corridor."

"That's all," Burger said, smiling.

"I have one or two questions on recross-examination," Mason said. "I'll only bother you for a moment, Miss Carter. You have now stated that you kept looking up whenever anyone came in, to see if the defendant came in."

"Yes, sir."

"And you could have seen him if he had come in?"

"Yes, sir. Very easily. From my station at the switchboard I can watch people who come down the corridor."

"So you want the Court and the jury to understand that you are certain the defendant didn't come in during the time you were on duty?"

"Well, he didn't come in from the time I first rang his telephone until I quit ringing it at six o'clock, when I went off duty."

"And what time did you first ring his telephone?"

"It was before midnight, perhaps eleven o'clock, perhaps a little after eleven."

"And then what?"

"Then I rang two or three times between the time of the first call and one o'clock, and then after 1:00 A.M. I made it a point to ring every hour on the hour."

"Just short rings or—"

"No, I rang several long rings each time."

"And after your first ring around midnight you were satisfied the defendant was not in his apartment?"

"Yes, sir."

"And because you were watching the corridor you were satisfied that he couldn't have entered the house and gone to his apartment without your seeing him?"

"Yes, sir."

"Then why," Mason asked, "if you *knew* he wasn't in his apartment and *knew* that he hadn't come in, did you keep on ringing the telephone at hourly intervals?"

The witness looked at Mason, started to say something, stopped, blinked her eyes, said, "Why, I . . . I . . . I don't know. I just did it."

"In other words," Mason said, "you *thought* there was a possibility he might have come in without your seeing him?"

"Well, of course, that *could* have happened."

"Then when you just now told the district attorney that it would have been impossible for the defendant to have come in without your seeing him, you were mistaken?"

"I . . . well, I . . . I had talked it over with the district attorney and . . . well, I thought that's what I was supposed to say."

"Exactly," Mason said, smiling. "Thank you."

Josephine Carter looked at Hamilton Burger to see if there were any more questions, but Hamilton Burger was making a great show of pawing through some papers. "That's all," he snapped gruffly.

Josephine Carter left the witness stand.

"I will now call Ruth Dickey," Hamilton Burger said.

Ruth Dickey came forward, was sworn, and testified that she was and had been on the fourteenth of June an elevator operator in the building where the South African Gem Importing and Exploration Company had its offices.

"Did you see Duane Jefferson, the defendant in this case, on the fourteenth of June a little after noon?"

"Yes, sir."

"When?"

"Well, he and Mr. Irving, his associate, rode down in the elevator with me about ten minutes past twelve. The defendant said he was going to lunch."

"When did they come back?"

"They came back about five minutes to one and rode up in the elevator with me."

"Did anything unusual happen on that day?"

"Yes, sir."

"What?"

"The manager of the building and one of the stenographers got into the elevator with me, and the manager asked me to run right down to the street floor because it was an emergency."

"Was this before or after the defendant and Irving had gone up with you?"

"After."

"You're certain?"

"Yes."

"About how long after?"

"At least five minutes."

"How well do you know the defendant?" Hamilton Burger asked.

"I have talked with him off and on."

"Have you ever been out with him socially?"

She lowered her eyes. "Yes."

"Now, did the defendant make any statements to you with reference to his relationship with Ann Riddle, the young woman who operates the cigar stand?"

"Yes. He said that he and his partner had set her up in business, that she was a lookout for them, but that no one else knew the connection. He said if I'd be nice to him, he could do something for me, too."

"You may cross-examine," Hamilton Burger said.

"You have had other young men take you out from time to time?" Mason asked.

"Well, yes."

"And quite frequently you have had them make rather wild promises about what they could do about setting you up in business if you would only be nice to them?"

She laughed. "I'll say," she said. "You'd be surprised about what some of them say."

"I dare say I would," Mason said. "That's all. Thank you, Miss Dickey."

"That's all our rebuttal," Hamilton Burger said.

Judge Hartley's voice was sympathetic. "I know that it is customary to have a recess before arguments start, but I would like very much to get this case finished today. I think that we can at least start the argument, unless there is some reason for making a motion for a continuance."

Mason, tight-lipped, shook his head. "Let's go ahead with it," he said.

"Very well, Mr. District Attorney, you may make your opening argument."

CHAPTER 18

HAMILTON BURGER'S ARGUMENT TO THE JURY WAS RELATIVELY short. It was completed within an hour after court reconvened following the noon recess. It was a masterpiece of forensic eloquence, of savage triumph, of a bitter, vindictive attack on the defendant and by implication on his attorney.

Mason's argument, which followed, stressed the point that while perjurers and waterfront scum had made an attack on his client, no one had yet shown that Munroe Baxter was murdered. Munroe Baxter, Mason insisted, could show up alive and well at any time, without having contradicted the testimony of any witness.

Hamilton Burger's closing argument was directed to the fact that the Court would instruct the jury that *corpus delicti* could be shown by circumstantial evidence, as well as by direct evidence. It was an argument which took only fifteen minutes.

The Court read instructions to the jurors, who retired to the jury room for their deliberations.

Mason, in the courtroom, his face a cold, hard mask, thoughtfully paced the floor.

Della Street, sitting at the counsel table, gave him her silent sympathy. Paul Drake, who had for once been too depressed even to try to eat, sat with his head in his hands.

Mason glanced at the clock, sighed wearily, ceased his pacing and dropped into a chair.

"Any chance, Perry?" Paul Drake asked.

Mason shook his head. "Not with the evidence in this shape. My client is a dead duck. Any luck with this car rental?"

"No luck at all, Perry. We've covered every car rental agency here and in outlying towns where they have branches."

Mason was thoughtful for a moment. "What about Walter Irving?"

"Irving has flown the coop," Drake said. "He left the courtroom, climbed into a taxicab and vanished. This time my men knew what he was going to try to do, and they were harder to shake. But within an hour he had ditched the shadows. It was a hectic hour."

"How did he do it?"

"It was very simple," Drake said. "Evidently it was part of a prearranged scheme. He had chartered a helicopter that was waiting for him at one of the outlying airports. He drove out there, got in the helicopter and took off."

"Can't you find out what happened? Don't they have to file some sort of a flight plan or—"

"Oh, we know what happened well enough," Drake said. "He chartered the helicopter to take him to the International Airport. Halfway there, he changed his mind and talked the helicopter into landing at the Santa Monica Airport. A rented car was waiting there."

"He's gone?"

"Gone slick and clean. We'll probably pick up his trail later on, but it isn't going to be easy, and by that time it won't do any good."

Mason thought for a moment. Suddenly he sat bolt upright. "Paul," he said, "we've overlooked a bet!"

"What?"

"A person renting a car has to show his driving license?"

"That's right."

"You've been looking for car rentals in the name of Marline Chaumont?"

"That's right."

"All right," Mason said. "Start your men looking for car rentals in the name of Walter Irving. Call your men on the phone. Start a network of them making a search. I want that information, and I want it now."

Drake, seemingly glad to be able to leave the depressing atmosphere of the courtroom, said, "Okay, I'll start right away, Perry."

Shortly before five o'clock a buzzer announced that the jury had reached its verdict. The jury was brought into court and the verdict was read by the foreman.

"We, the jury impaneled to try the above-entitled case, find the defendant guilty of murder in the first degree."

There was no recommendation for life imprisonment or leniency.

Judge Hartley's eyes were sympathetic as he looked at Perry Mason. "Can we agree upon having the Court fix a time for pronouncing sentence?" he asked.

"I would like an early date for hearing a motion for a new trial," Mason said. "I will stipulate that Friday will be satisfactory for presenting a motion for new trial and fixing sentence. We will waive the question of time."

"How about the district attorney's office?" Judge Hartley asked. "Will Friday be satisfactory?"

The deputy district attorney, who sat at the counsel table, said, "Well, Your Honor, I think it will be all right. Mr. Burger is in conference with the press at the moment. He—"

"He asked you to represent the district attorney's office?" Judge Hartley asked.

"Yes, Your Honor."

"Represent it then," Judge Hartley said shortly. "Is Friday satisfactory?"

"Yes, Your Honor."

"Friday morning at ten o'clock," Judge Hartley said. "Court is adjourned. The defendant is remanded to custody."

Reporters, who usually swarmed about Perry Mason asking for a statement, were now closeted with Hamilton Burger. The few spectators who had been interested enough to await the verdict got up and went home. Mason picked up his brief case. Della Street tucked her hand through his arm, gave him a reassuring squeeze. "You warned him, Chief," she said. "Not once, but a dozen times. He had it coming."

Mason merely nodded. Paul Drake, hurrying down the corridor, said, "I've got something, Perry."

"Did you hear the verdict?" Mason asked.

Paul Drake's eyes refused to meet Mason's. "I heard it."

"What have you got?" Mason asked.

"Walter Irving rented an automobile the day that Marline Chaumont disappeared from the airport. Last night he rented another one."

"I thought so," Mason said. "Has he turned back the first automobile?"

"No."

"He keeps the rental paid?"

"Yes."

"We can't get him on the ground of embezzling the automobile, so we can have police looking for it as a 'hot' car?"

"Apparently not."

Mason turned to Della Street. "Della, you have a shorthand book in your purse?"

She nodded.

"All right," Mason said to Paul Drake, "let's go, Paul."

"Where?" Drake asked.

"To see Ann Riddle, the girl who bought the cigar counter in our building," Mason said. "We may be able to get to her before she, too, flies the coop. Hamilton Burger is too busy with the press, decorating himself with floral wreaths, to do much thinking now."

Drake, his voice sympathetic, said, "Gosh, Perry, it's . . . I can imagine how you feel . . . having a client convicted of first-degree murder. It's the first time you've ever had a client convicted in a murder case."

Mason turned to Paul Drake, his eyes were cold and hard. "My client," he said, "hasn't been convicted of anything."

For a moment Drake acted as if his ears had betrayed him, then, at something he saw in Mason's face, he refrained from asking questions.

"Get the address of that girl who bought the cigar stand," Mason said, "and let's go."

CHAPTER 19

MASON, HIS FACE IMPLACABLY DETERMINED, SCORNED THE chair offered him by the frightened blonde.

"You can talk now," he said, "or you can talk later. Whichever you want. If you talk now it may do you some good. If you talk later you're going to be convicted as an accessory in a murder case. Make up your mind."

"I've nothing to say."

Mason said, "Irving and Jefferson went into the building *before* the excitement. When they entered their office, Mae Jordan was there. They caught her. The phone rang. They were warned that the police had been notified that a girl was breaking into the office and that the police were coming up; that the girl who had seen the woman breaking in and the manager of the building were waiting at the elevators. There was only one person who could have given them that information. That was you."

"You have no right to say that."

"I've said it," Mason said, "and I'm saying it again. The next time I say it, it's going to be in open court.

"By tomorrow morning at ten o'clock we'll have torn into your past and will have found out all about the connection between you and Irving. By that time it'll be too late for you to do anything. You've committed perjury. We're putting a tail on you. Now start talking."

Under the impact of Mason's gaze she at first averted her eyes, then restlessly shifted her position in the chair.

"Start talking," Mason said.

"I don't have to answer to you. You're not the police. You—"

"Start talking."

"All right," she said. "I was paid to keep a watch on things, to telephone them if anything suspicious happened. There's nothing unlawful about that."

"It goes deeper than that," Mason said. "You were in on the whole thing. It was their money that put you in the cigar store. What's your connection with this thing?"

"You can't prove any of that. That's a false and slanderous statement. Duane Jefferson never told that little tramp anything like that. If he did, it was false."

"Start talking," Mason said.

She hesitated, then stubbornly shook her head.

Mason motioned to Della Street. "Go over to the telephone, Della. Ring up Homicide Squad. Get Lieutenant Tragg on the line. Tell him I want to talk with him."

Della Street started for the telephone.

"Now wait a minute," the blonde said hurriedly. "You can't—"

"Can't what?" Mason asked as her voice trailed into silence.

"Can't make anything stick on me. You haven't got any proof."

"I'm getting it," Mason told her. "Paul Drake here is an expert detective. He has men on the job right now, men who are concentrating on what you and Irving were doing."

"All right. Suppose my gentleman friend *did* loan me the money to buy a cigar stand. There's nothing wrong with that. I'm over the age of consent. I can do what I damn please."

Mason said, "This is your last chance. Walter Irving is putting out a lot of false clues, shaking off any possible pursuit. Then he'll go to Marline Chaumont. She's in one of the outlying towns. When she and Irving get together, something's going to happen. He must have given you an address where you could reach him in case of any emergency. That will be Marline's hide-out. Where is it?"

She shook her head.

Mason nodded to Della Street. Della Street started putting through the call.

Abruptly the blonde began to cry.

"I want Homicide Department, please," Della Street said into the phone.

The blonde said, "It's in Santa Ana."

"Where?" Mason asked.

She fumbled with her purse, took out an address, handed it to Mason. Mason nodded, and Della Street hung up the telephone.

"Come on," Mason said.

"What do you mean, come on?" the girl said.

"You heard me," Mason told her. "We're not leaving you behind to make any telephone calls. This is too critical for us to botch it up now."

"You can't *make* me go!"

"I can't make you go with *me*, but I can damn sure see that you're locked up in the police station. The only bad thing is that will cost about fifteen minutes. Which do you want?"

She said, "Stop looking at me like that. You frighten me. You—"

"I'm putting it to you cold turkey," Mason said. "Do you want to take a murder rap or not?"

"I—" She hesitated.

"Get your things on," Mason said.

Ann Riddle moved toward the closet.

"Watch her, Della," Mason said. "We don't want her to pick up any weapons."

Ann Riddle put on a light coat, picked up her purse. Paul Drake looked in the purse and made sure there was no weapon in it.

The four of them went down in the elevator, wordlessly got in Mason's car. Mason tooled the car out to the freeway, gathered speed.

CHAPTER 20

THE HOUSE WAS IN A QUIET RESIDENTIAL DISTRICT. A LIGHT WAS on in the living room. A car was parked in the garage. A wet strip on the sidewalk showed that the lawn had recently been sprinkled.

Mason parked the car, jerked open the door, strode up the steps to the porch. Della Street hurried along behind him. Paul Drake kept a hand on the arm of Ann Riddle.

Mason rang the bell.

The door opened half an inch. "Who is it?" a woman's voice asked.

Mason pushed his weight against the door so suddenly that the door was pushed inward.

Marline Chaumont, staggering back, regarded Mason with frightened eyes. "You!" she said.

"We came to get your brother," Mason said.

"My brother is—how you call it?—sick in the upstairs. He has flies in his belfry. He cannot be disturbed. He is asleep."

"Wake him up," Mason said.

"But you cannot do this. My brother he— You are not the law, *non?*"

"No," Mason said. "But we'll have the law here in about five minutes."

Marline Chaumont's face contorted into a spasm of anger. "You!" she spat at the blonde. "You had to pull a double cross!"

"I didn't," Ann Riddle said. "I only—"

"I know what you did, you double-crosser!" Marline Chaumont said. "I spit on you. You stool squab!"

"Never mind that," Mason said. "Where's the man you claim is your brother?"

"But he *is* my brother!"

"Phooey," Mason told her.

"He was taken from the hospital—"

"The man who was taken from the state hospital," Mason said, "isn't related to you any more than I am. You used him only as a prop. I don't know what you've done with him. Put him in a private institution somewhere, I suppose. I want the man who's taken his place, and I want him now."

"You are crazy in the head yourself," Marline Chaumont said. "You have no right to—"

"Take care of her, Paul," Mason said, and started marching down the hall toward the back of the house.

"You'll be killed!" she screamed. "You cannot do this. You—"

Mason tried the doors one at a time. The third door opened into a bedroom. A man, thin and emaciated, was lying on the bed, his hands handcuffed at the wrists.

A big, burly individual who had been reading a magazine got slowly to his feet. "What the hell!" he thundered.

Mason sized him up. "You look like an ex-cop to me," he said.

"What's it to you?" the man asked.

"Probably retired," Mason said. "Hung out your shingle as a private detective. Didn't do so well. Then this job came along."

"Say, what're you talking about?"

"I don't know what story they told *you*," Mason said, "and I don't know whether you're in on it or not, but whatever they told you, the jig's up. I'm Perry Mason, the lawyer."

The man who was handcuffed on the bed turned to Perry Mason. His eyes, dulled with sedatives, seemed to be having some difficulty getting in focus.

"Who are you?" he asked in the thick voice of a sleep talker.

Mason said, "I've come to take you out of here."

The bodyguard said, "This man's a mental case. He's inclined to be violent. He can't be released and he has delusions—"

"I know," Mason said. "His real name is Pierre Chaumont. He keeps thinking he's someone else. He has a delusion that his real name is—"

"Say, how do you know all this?" the bodyguard asked.

Mason said, "They gave you a steady job. A woman handed you a lot of soft soap, and you probably think she's one of the sweetest, most wonderful women on earth. It's time you woke up. As for this man on the bed, he's going with me right now. First we're going to the best doctor we can find, and then . . . well, then we'll get ready to keep a date on Friday morning at ten o'clock.

"You can either be in jail at that time or a free man. Make your choice now. We're separating the men from the boys. If you're in on this thing all the way, you're in a murder case. If you were just hired to act as a guard for a man who is supposed to be a mental case, that's something else. You have your opportunity to make your decision right now. There's a detective downstairs and police are on their way out. They'll be here within a matter of minutes. They'll want to know where you stand. I'm giving you your chance right now, and it's your *last* chance."

The big guard blinked his eyes slowly. "You say this man *isn't* a mental case?"

"Of course he isn't."

"I've seen the papers. He was taken from a state hospital."

"Some other guy was taken from a state hospital," Mason said, "and then they switched patients. This isn't a debating society. Make up your mind."

"You're Perry Mason, the lawyer?"

"That's right."

"Got any identification on you?"

Mason handed the man his card, showed him his driving license. The guard sighed. "Okay," he said. "You win."

CHAPTER 21

THE BAILIFF CALLED COURT TO ORDER.

Hamilton Burger, his face wearing a look of smug satisfaction, beamed about the courtroom.

Judge Hartley said, "This is the time fixed for hearing a motion for new trial and for pronouncing judgment in the case of *People* v. *Duane Jefferson*. Do you wish to be heard, Mr. Mason?"

"Yes, Your Honor," Perry Mason said. "I move for a new trial of the case on the ground that the trial took place in the absence of the defendant."

"What?" Hamilton Burger shouted. "The defendant was present in court every minute of the time! The records so show."

"Will you stand up, Mr. Duane Jefferson?" Mason asked.

The man beside Mason stood up. Another man seated near the middle of the courtroom also stood up. Judge Hartley looked at the man in the courtroom.

"Come forward," Mason said.

"Just a minute," Judge Hartley said. "What's the meaning of this, Mr. Mason?"

"I asked Mr. Jefferson to stand up."

"He's standing up," Hamilton Burger said.

"Exactly," Mason said.

"Who's this other man?" the Court asked. "Is he a witness?"

"He's Duane Jefferson," Mason said.

"Now, just a minute, just a minute," Hamilton Burger said. "What's all this about, what kind of a flimflam is counsel trying to work here? Let's get this thing straight. Here's the defendant standing here within the bar."

"And here's Duane Jefferson coming forward," Mason said. "I am moving for a new trial on the ground that the entire trial of Duane Jefferson for first-degree murder took place in his absence."

"Now just a moment, just a moment!" Hamilton Burger shouted. "I might have known there would be something like this. Counsel can't confuse the issues. It doesn't make any difference now whether this man is Duane Jefferson or whether he's John Doe. He's the man who committed the murder. He's the man who was seen committing the murder. He's the man who was tried for the murder. If he went under the name of Duane Jefferson, that isn't going to stop him from being sentenced for the murder."

"But," Mason said, "some of your evidence was directed against my client, Duane Jefferson."

"*Your* client?" Hamilton Burger said. "That's your client standing next to you."

Mason smiled and shook his head. "*This* is my client," he said, beckoning to the man standing at the gate of the bar to come forward once more. "This is Duane Jefferson. He's the one I was retained to represent by the South African Gem Importing and Exploration Company."

"Well, he's not the one you defended," Hamilton Burger said. "You can't get out of the mess this way."

Mason smiled and said, "I'm defending him now."

"Go ahead and defend him. He isn't accused of anything!"

"And I'm moving for a new trial on the ground that the trial took place in the absence of the defendant."

"This is the defendant standing right here!" Hamilton Burger insisted. "The trial took place in *his* presence. *He's* the one who was convicted. I don't care what you do with this other man, regardless of what his name is."

"Oh, but you introduced evidence consisting of articles belonging to the real Duane Jefferson," Mason said. "That dagger, for instance. The contents of the letters."

"What do you mean?"

"Mae W. Jordan told all about the letters she had received from Duane Jefferson, about the contents of those letters. I moved to strike out her testimony. The motion was denied. The testimony went to the jury about the Daddy Longlegs letters, about the Prince Charming letters, about the gag photographs, about the getting acquainted, and about the dagger."

"Now, just a moment," Judge Hartley said. "The Court will

bear with you for a moment in this matter, Mr. Mason, but the Court is going to resort to stern measures if it appears this is some dramatic presentation of a technicality which you are using to dramatize the issues."

"I'm trying to clarify the issues," Mason said. "What happened is very simple. Duane Jefferson, who is standing there by the mahogany swinging gate which leads to the interior of the bar, is a trusted employee of the South African Gem Importing and Exploration Company. He was sent to this country in the company of Walter Irving of the Paris office to open a branch office. They were to receive half a million dollars' worth of diamonds in the mail.

"Walter Irving, who had been gambling heavily, was deeply involved and knew that very shortly after he had left Paris there would be an audit of the books and his defalcations would be discovered.

"This man, James Kincaid, was groomed to take the place of Duane Jefferson. After the shipment of gems was received, James Kincaid would take the gems and disappear. Walter Irving would duly report an embezzlement by Jefferson and thereafter Jefferson's body would be discovered under such circumstances that it would appear he had committed suicide.

"The trouble was that they couldn't let well enough alone. They knew that Munroe Baxter was smuggling diamonds into the country, and they decided to kill Baxter and get the gems. Actually, Walter Irving had been working with Baxter in connection with the smuggling and for a fee had arranged for the stones to be delivered to Baxter under such circumstances that they could be smuggled into this country.

"The spurious Duane Jefferson didn't need to be clever about it, because he intended to have the shipment of stones in his possession and the real Duane Jefferson's body found, long before the police could make an investigation. However, because of a tax situation, the shipment of gems was delayed, and naturally they couldn't afford to have the spurious Jefferson disappear until the shipment had been received, so that Walter Irving could then report the defalcation to the company. Therefore, the real Duane Jefferson had to be kept alive."

"Your Honor, Your Honor!" Hamilton Burger shouted. "This is simply another one of those wild-eyed, dramatic grandstands for which counsel is so noted. This time his client has been convicted of first-degree murder, and I intend to see to it personally that his client pays the supreme penalty."

Mason pointed to the man standing in the aisle. "This is my client," he said. "This is the man I was retained to represent. I intend to show that his trial took place in his absence. Come forward and be sworn, Mr. Jefferson."

"Your Honor, I object!" Hamilton Burger shouted. "I object to any such procedure. I insist that this defendant is the only defendant before the Court."

Judge Hartley said, "Now, just a moment. I want to get to the bottom of this thing, and I want to find out exactly what counsel's contention is before I start making any rulings. Court will take an adjournment for fifteen minutes while we try to get at the bottom of this thing. I will ask counsel for both sides to meet me in chambers. The defendant, in the meantime, is in custody. He will remain in custody."

Mason grinned.

The tall, gaunt man standing in the aisle turned back toward the audience. Mae Jordan moved toward him. "Hello, Prince Charming," she ventured somewhat dubiously. Jefferson's eyes lit up.

"Hello, Lady Guinevere," he said in a low voice. "I was told you'd be here."

"Prince . . . Prince Charming!"

Mason said, "I'll leave him in your custody, Miss Jordan." Then Mason marched into the judge's chambers.

CHAPTER 22

"WELL?" JUDGE HARTLEY SAID.

"It was quite a plot," Mason explained. "Actually, it was hatched in Paris as soon as Walter Irving knew he was going to be sent over to assist Duane Jefferson in opening the new office. A girl named Marline Chaumont, who had been a Paris party girl for the company and who knew her way around, was in on it. James Kincaid was in on it. They would have gotten away with the whole scheme, if it hadn't been for the fact that they were too eager. They knew that Baxter was planning to smuggle in three hundred thousand dollars' worth of diamonds. Gilly was to have taken the fishing boat out and made the delivery. They persuaded Gilly that Baxter had changed his mind at the last minute because of Gilly's record. He wanted these other men to take the boat out. Gilly was lying when he testified about his rental for the boat. He received twenty-five hundred dollars. That was the agreed price. Marline Chaumont has given me a sworn statement."

"Now just a minute," Judge Hartley said. "Are you now making this statement about the client you're representing in court?"

"I'm not representing him in court," Mason said. "I'm representing the real Duane Jefferson. That's the one I was retained to represent. I would suggest, however, that the Court give this other man an opportunity to get counsel of his own, or appoint counsel to represent him. He, too, is entitled to a new trial."

"He can't get a new trial," Hamilton Burger roared, "even if what you say is true. You defended him and you lost the case."

Mason smiled coldly at Hamilton Burger. "You might have made that stick," he said, "if it hadn't been for the testimony of Mae Jordan about all of her correspondence with Duane Jefferson. That correspondence was with the real Duane Jefferson, not with the man you are trying for murder. You can't convict Duane Jefferson of anything, because he wasn't present during his trial. You can't make the present conviction stick against the defendant now in court, because you used evidence that related to the real Duane Jefferson, not to him.

"What you should have done was to have checked your identification of the man you had under arrest. You were so damned anxious to get something on me that when you found from his fingerprints that he had a record, you let your enthusiasm run away with you.

"You let Mae Jordan testify to a lot of things that had happened between her and the real Duane Jefferson. It never occurred to you to make certain that the man she sent the knife to was the same man you were trying for murder.

"The spurious Jefferson and Irving drugged the real Jefferson shortly after they left Chicago on the train. They stole all of his papers, stole the Jordan letters, stole the knife. It will be up to you to prove that at the next trial—and I'm not going to help you. You can go get the evidence yourself. However, I have Marline Chaumont in my office and I have a sworn statement made by her, which I now hand to the Court, with a copy for the district attorney.

"Just one suggestion, though. If you ever want to tie this case up, you'd better find out who that man was who was in the boat with Kincaid, because it certainly wasn't Irving.

"And now may I ask the Court to relieve me of any responsibility in the matter of the defendant, James Kincaid, who is out there in the courtroom. He tricked me into appearing in court for him by artifice, fraud, and by misrepresenting his identity. My only client is Duane Jefferson."

"I think," Judge Hartley said, "I want to talk with this Duane Jefferson. I suppose you can establish his identity beyond any question, Mr. Mason?"

"His fingerprints were taken in connection with his military service," Mason said.

"That should be good enough evidence," Judge Hartley agreed, smiling. "I'd like to have a talk with him now."

Mason got up, walked to the door of chambers, looked out at the courtroom, and turned back to smile at the judge. "I guess I'll have to interrupt him," Mason said. "He and the witness Mae Jordan are jabbering away like a house afire. There seems to be a sort of common understanding between them. I guess it's because they're both interested in photography."

Judge Hartley's smile had broadened. "Perhaps, Mr. Mason," he suggested tentatively, "Miss Jordan is telling Mr. Jefferson where she got that key."

THE END

The Case of The
Grinning Gorilla

CHAPTER ONE

AT 9:55 ON A MONDAY MORNING, PERRY MASON, CARRYING A BROWN paper package in his hand, scaled his hat in the general direction of the bust of Blackstone which adorned the top of a low sectional bookcase behind his desk.

The hat made two lazy twists, then settled incongruously at a rakish angle on the marble brow of the great jurist.

Della Street, Mason's confidential secretary, who had been at the desk opening mail, applauded.

"Getting to be good," Mason admitted with boyish pride.

"Blackstone," Della observed, "is probably turning over in his grave."

Mason grinned. "He's accustomed to it by this time. For the last fifty years lawyers have been scaling their hats at Blackstone's noble brow. It marks a period of transition, Della."

"What does?"

"The hat-scaling."

"I don't get it."

"A couple of generations ago," Mason told her, "lawyers were stuffy people. They thrust a hand inside their coats while they declaimed oratorically. Busts of Blackstone adorned their offices.

"Then came a new and more flippant generation. Younger lawyers, who inherited the busts of Blackstone with sets of law books and office furniture, resented the stony-faced dignity of the old boy."

"You should be psychoanalyzed," Della Street said. "Blackstone probably means something you're fighting against. What in the world is in the package?"

"Damned if I know," Mason said. "I think I'm fighting stuffy conventionalities. I paid five dollars for it—the package, I mean."

Della Street's voice was a combination of fond indulgence and official exasperation. "I certainly hope you won't try to charge it as an office expense."

3

"But that's what it is—general expense."

"And you don't know what's in it?"

"No. I bought it sight unseen."

"That's a great way for me to try to get along with my book-keeping, making an entry of five dollars for a package that you don't know . . . How in the world did it happen?"

"Well," Perry Mason said, "it was like this . . ." and grinned.

"Go on," Della Street told him, smiling in spite of herself.

"Do you remember Helen Cadmus? Does that mean anything to you?"

"It's an odd name," she said. "It seems to me . . . Oh, wasn't she the girl who committed suicide by jumping from some millionaire's yacht?"

"That's it. Benjamin Addicks, the eccentric millionaire, was cruising on his yacht. Helen Cadmus, who was his secretary, disappeared. The assumption was she had jumped overboard. This package contains . . . well, now let's see what it's marked."

Mason turned it over and read, " 'Private personal belongings, matter of Estate of Helen Cadmus. Public Administrator's Office.' "

Della Street sighed. "Having been your confidential secretary for lo these many years, I sometimes think I know you pretty well, and then something like this happens and I realize that I don't know you at all. Where on earth did you get that, and why did you pay five dollars for it?"

"Every so often the public administrator sells at public auction bits of personal property that have accumulated in his office.

"As it happened, I was down in the vicinity of the courthouse this morning when the auction was taking place. There was quite a bit of lively bidding over packages which were supposed to contain jewelry, rare linens, silverware, and things of that sort. Then they put this package up, and no one bid on it. Well, you know the public administrator. He's a friend of ours so I tipped him the wink and started the bidding with five dollars, and the next thing I knew I was stuck with a package and was out five dollars."

"Well, what's in it?" Della Street asked.

"Let's find out," Mason said.

He opened his pocketknife, cut the string, undid the wrappings, and said, "Well, well, well! We seem to have an English grammar, a dictionary, a couple of books on a shorthand system, some diaries, and a photograph album."

"Five dollars!" Della Street said.

"Well, let's look at the photograph album," Mason said. "Oh-oh, here's a pin-up picture that's worth five bucks of anyone's money."

She came to look over his shoulder.

"If that's a bathing suit," she said, "I . . ."

"Apparently," Mason said, "the suit consists of three squares of cloth skillfully knotted about the curves of a very nice figure—I wonder if that is Helen."

"She wasn't concealing much from the public," Della Street said.

"You can't tell whether it was the public or just some girl friend manipulating a camera and they did it for a stunt. —Oh here's a whole mess of monkey pictures."

"Now I get it," Della Street said. "Remember, Addicks was her boss. He has a collection of monkeys and apes. He's doing some psychological experiments."

Mason nodded and continued to go through the photograph album. He said, "Some pretty good pictures here. Whoever did the photography knew what he was about. They're sharp as a tack."

"What are they?" Della Street asked, opening the four volumes of diary.

"Mostly bathing and yachting pictures," Mason said. "Helen seems to have taken quite a few pictures of monkeys and apes."

"How do you tell the difference between a monkey and an ape?" Della asked.

"One's bigger than the other, I guess," Mason said. "How should I know? Anyway, you can get a good education going through these photographs."

Della Street said, "Listen to this in the diary, Chief."

Mason said, "Go ahead, I'm listening," but he turned the photograph album to the light so that he could study another pin-up picture of Helen Cadmus in a pose guaranteed to attract masculine attention.

Della Street jerked the book of photographs from his hand, said, "You can look at that later. Listen to this."

She read from the diary:

. . . don't know whether I can stand this much longer. Poor Pete seems to realize that something is being done to him and he keeps clinging to me for protection. I don't mind about the others so much, but I do worry about Pete. If they start trying to break down Pete's mind and undermine his nervous system, I'm going to do something about it. That's definite. I've been saving up a little money and I am going to try and buy Pete if Mr. Addicks will sell him. I know that he won't sell him if he has any idea I'm trying to spare Pete from what the others have gone through. I don't know whether the S.P.C.A. will do anything about this or not, but if I can't buy Pete I'm certainly going to do something about it.

"Well," Mason said, "that was evidently quite a household. I wonder what's going on out there now."

"Let's find out," Della Street said.

Mason frowned thoughtfully. "When you come right down to it," he said, "no one knows whether that girl committed suicide or not. As I remember it, her body was never found. She was out on the yacht and they were in a storm somewhere off Catalina Island. Addicks gave her some dictation which she promised to have typed and on his desk by eight o'clock the next morning. The storm kept getting worse and Addicks thought she might have been indisposed. He went to her stateroom to see if she was all right, and found that the bed hadn't been slept in. So they searched the yacht and she was missing. The assumption was that she'd either been swept overboard by a wave or had committed suicide.

"Addicks put the hush-hush on the case. They called it suicide."

The phone rang.

Della Street picked up the receiver, said, "Hello," then, "Just a minute, Gertie. I'll talk with them."

Once more she said, "Hello. This is Della Street, Mr. Mason's confidential secretary. Can you tell me just what it is you want? . . . Who? . . . Oh, I see. . . ."

She listened for nearly a minute, then said, "Just a minute. I'll try and get in touch with Mr. Mason. He's in an important conference at the moment, but if you'll hang on I'll try and get through to him."

"What is it?" Mason asked.

Della Street cupped her hand over the mouthpiece. "The *In-*

quirer," she said. "They want to send a photographer and a reporter up and get some human interest pictures."

"About what?"

"About you buying the Cadmus diaries. It seems that the public administrator, or someone, tipped off one of the courthouse reporters and they think they have an exclusive on it. They want to run it as a human interest story."

"Tell them to come on up," Mason said. "Sure, I'll pose for them. That'll give you a chance to explain it to the income tax people, Della. You can tell them that it was five dollars invested in publicity."

She said, "They seem to think that you may have bought the diaries for a purpose. There's something about a lawsuit by a Mrs. Kempton against Addicks. Do you know anything about it?"

"Never heard of it," Mason said, "but don't let them know that. Be mysterious and enigmatic. That will heighten public interest and give them a good story."

Della Street said into the telephone, "Mr. Mason is in conference at the moment and then has another appointment, but he can give you a few minutes in exactly thirty-five minutes if you can arrange to be here then."

She hung up the telephone. "I was hoping you'd get some of this mail out of the way this morning."

Mason grinned. "Who knows? We might at that. Have Jackson go up to the courthouse, Della, look through the file of actions and find out what the devil the case of Kempton versus Addicks is all about. He can telephone in a report. After all, I don't want to lead with my chin in this interview, but I'd like the newspaper boys to have a good story. They're entitled to it, and one never knows when he may need a friendly newspaper contact."

Della nodded, walked over to the statue of Blackstone and said, "Good morning, Mr. Blackstone. If you don't mind, I'll take off the hat which you're wearing at such a rakish angle. We're expecting newspaper photographers and we want the office to look dignified."

CHAPTER TWO

ON TUESDAY MORNING MASON UNLOCKED THE DOOR OF HIS PRIVATE office, took off his hat and held it poised for a moment as he stared speculatively at the bust of Blackstone.

"Have you seen the newspapers?" Della Street asked.

"Just took a look at the headlines. Why?" Mason slowly lowered the hand holding his hat.

"You should see your photographs in the picture section of the *Inquirer;* and you should see the three dollar bill who's sitting in the office, looking at his watch every fifteen seconds, waiting for you to come in so he can talk to you about the 'package in the Helen Cadmus estate.'"

"So?" Mason asked, crossing over to the coat closet, and making a more conventional disposal of his hat. "What about the three dollar bill?"

Della Street said, "I mean he's as phony as a three dollar bill."

"In what way?"

"His name is Nathan Fallon. He is, and I quote, 'associated' with Mr. Benjamin Addicks, and he claims to be a distant relative of Helen Cadmus. He was deeply shocked that her memoirs had been sold at auction. He is unctuous, mealymouthed, refined, smirking, and he's not accustomed to that sort of an act. He's more accustomed to sticking out his chin at somebody and saying, 'All right, do this or else.'"

"Well, well, well," Mason said. "And Jackson's report on the case of Kempton versus Addicks?"

"Well, you had the general report he made over the telephone yesterday that it was a suit for defamation of character. We now have a copy of the complaint."

She handed Mason a copy of a complaint which had been filed in the clerk's office, and Mason skimmed through it, nodding his head and smiling as he read. "The plot thickens," he observed. "Apparently Mrs. Josephine Kempton was discharged under circumstances which she found highly unsatisfactory. She was unable to secure any explanation from her employer, and, later on, when she tried to get other jobs, she found out that in every instance where the new employer had written Mr. Addicks for reference, letters had been received from Addicks accusing her of theft."

"What's the law on that?" Della Street asked. "Is it a privileged communication?"

"You mean Addicks' letters?"

"Yes."

Mason grinned. "My dear Della. You are presuming upon the prerogatives of attorneys for the defendant in the case of Kempton versus Addicks. As far as the law of the case is concerned, let them fight it out; but as far as the facts of the case are concerned, I find myself very much interested. I am also interested in knowing why Mr. Fallon should be so concerned about the diaries of Helen Cadmus."

"Well, of course," Della Street said, "he doesn't admit that he's interested primarily in the diaries. He simply wants any of the personal effects that were left by the, and again I quote, 'poor unfortunate girl.'"

"Tut-tut-tut!" Mason said.

"Are you going to see Mr. Fallon," she asked, "before he wears out all of the carpet in the reception room pacing the floor?"

"We're going to see him," Mason said, "but Mr. Fallon, who apparently is a stuffed shirt as well as a poor actor, should see us as we really are, Della. He probably has been accustomed to the dignified corporation attorneys who handle Mr. Addicks' affairs and advise him how he can turn income into capital gains for a smaller tax.

"I think it is time Mr. Fallon realizes he is dealing with an entirely different breed of cat."

With which Mason crossed over to the coat closet, took out his hat, carried it over to the bust of Blackstone, and deliberately adjusted it at a rakish angle.

"And now, Della," he said, "you may show in Mr. Nathan Fallon."

Della Street smiled at Mason's whimsical gesture and promptly went to the outer office to return with the man she had described as a three dollar bill.

Nathan Fallon had a high, bulging forehead, a short pug nose, thick-lensed rimless spectacles, a big smiling mouth, and an over-all attitude of ingratiating good fellowship.

There was a bald spot at the back of his head, and the hair had grown thin above the high forehead, but he had let the hair of the intermediate fringe grow as long as possible. By winding this hair around and around and plastering it in position with hairdressing, he had managed to take away much of the shine from the bald spot.

"Mr. Mason!" he said. "Mr. Perry Mason! I can't begin to tell you, sir, the pleasure that I have in meeting you face to face. I have been an admirer of yours for a long time. I have followed the accounts of your courtroom triumphs in the press. I made up my mind early in the game that if I should ever find myself in trouble I would come to your office at once."

"That's fine," Mason said, shaking hands and flashing Della Street a quick wink. "I take it you're in trouble, then?"

"No, no, no, not at all! No, no, my *dear* Mr. Mason! Oh, please do not misunderstand me. No trouble."

"Oh," Mason said. "I did misunderstand you then. Sit down."

Mason seated himself behind the big desk. Della Street moved up to her secretarial desk with notebook poised.

"Oh, my dear Mr. Mason, I wouldn't have conveyed that impression for anything—and your so charming secretary, Miss Street! It is indeed a pleasure to see her in the flesh."

"You're making her sound naked," Mason said.

"Oh, no, no! My *dear* Mr. Mason, please! Please, I beg of you."

Della Street glanced mischievously up from her notebook.

Fallon hurried on with his explanation. "I meant only that I had read about her, that she had been an intangible. Now she has become very very definite, very tangible."

"And," Mason reminded Fallon, "is waiting to take notes as to the nature of your business so she can make out a proper file and keep the office records straight."

"Yes, yes! You'll pardon me, Mr. Mason. I realize, of course, the value of your time. I'm a man who believes in coming right to the point, Mr. Mason."

"Go ahead."

"I am an associate of Benjamin Addicks, and, strangely enough, I am also related to Helen Cadmus."

"Just what's the nature of the relationship?" Mason asked.

"Oh, rather a distant relative. She always called me Uncle. I was instrumental in getting her her position with Benny."

"Benny?" Mason asked.

"I beg your pardon. Benjamin Addicks. We call him Benny."

"I see."

"Poor dear Helen. I can't imagine what possessed her to do the terrible thing she did, and, above all, in the manner in which she did it. If she had been determined to end it all, an overdose of sleeping pills would have been so much more simple, so—well, if I may express myself frankly, Mr. Mason, so much more considerate."

"I presume," Mason said, "that when a girl finds the problems of life too much for her and decides to take her life, she is primarily concerned with her own adventure into eternity."

"Yes, yes, of course. I understand that. The poor thing. I can understand it personally, and yet, Mr. Mason, it couldn't have been planned so that it was more—well, shall I say more inopportune."

"In what way?"

"All of the newspaper notoriety, all of the inconvenience that it caused Benny—Benjamin Addicks, that is. Mr. Addicks was very much attached to her. Just as an employee, you understand, Mr. Mason, just as an employee. He would have done anything possible to alleviate her suffering if he had only known. I think I am in a position to assure you definitely, Mr. Mason, that if the poor girl's troubles were in any way financial, Mr. Addicks would have done almost anything, made almost any concession . . ."

"What were her troubles?" Mason asked.

Fallon threw out pudgy palms in a gesture. "Now there, Mr. Mason, I'm up a tree. I can't tell you. I simply don't know."

"She didn't confide in anyone?"

"Yes, Mr. Mason. Unfortunately she confided in me, and I didn't believe her. I felt it was only the sort of talk that women sometimes indulge in during periods of despondency. She told me that she felt many times that she couldn't continue to bear the great measure of responsibilities that she found life was heaping on her and that she was . . ."

"What sort of responsibilities?"

"She didn't say, Mr. Mason. I'm sorry to admit that I didn't encourage the girl. I—but then that's neither here nor there. The matter is all over and disposed of, and I know how busy you are, Mr.

Mason. I was surprised to read in the press this morning that you had purchased Helen's intimate personal belongings. I had no idea that she had left behind any personal possessions of that nature. As her nearest relative . . ."

"I thought you said you were a distant relative?"

"Relatively distant, Mr. Mason. Ha-ha-ha! I don't mean a pun. I mean that I am a distant relative, but because there are no nearer relatives I sometimes refer to myself as a near relative. That sounds a bit ambiguous, but I'm quite certain you'll understand."

"I don't share your optimism," Mason said. "Now just what do you want?"

"Why, naturally, Mr. Mason, I want the personal belongings, the mementos of poor dear Helen. I understand that you made a bid largely for the purpose of accommodating your friend, the public administrator, and purchased articles that have no real intrinsic value. The bid, I believe, was five dollars."

Mr. Fallon jumped to his feet, extracted a crisp five dollar note from his pocket, and held it tentatively toward Mason. When the lawyer made no move to accept it, he turned somewhat dubiously to Della Street and said, "I suppose you're the one who has charge of financial transactions, Miss Street."

Della Street looked up at Mason questioningly.

The lawyer imperceptibly shook his head.

Fallon stood holding the five dollar bill, looking from one to the other, his face showing his perplexity at being rebuffed.

"But I don't understand," he said. "Am I perhaps failing to make myself clear?"

Mason said, "I bought the package. It contains some diaries, a photograph album and some other personal belongings. I think I have my five dollars' worth."

"Diaries, Mr. Mason?"

"Exactly," Mason said, his eyes holding those of his visitor. "They are rather complete diaries."

"But my dear Mr. Mason, they certainly can't be of any use to you, and, if you'll pardon the expression, I know you don't want to pry into the secrets of a dead girl."

"Why not?" Mason asked.

"Why not?" Fallon exclaimed, shocked. "Why, good heavens, Mr. Mason, why . . . surely you must be joking!"

"Certainly I'm not joking," Mason said. "I make my living by knowing something about law and something about human nature. I stand up in front of juries. I cross-examine witnesses. I have to know a lot more about human nature than the average man."

"Yes, yes, yes. I understand, Mr. Mason. That part, of course, is quite clear."

"You don't get to understand human nature," Mason said, "by listening to what people tell you when they're talking to you."

"You don't?" Fallon asked, surprised.

Mason shook his head. "That's when you see them with their make-up on, with their best foot forward. You learn about human nature by watching people when they don't know they're being watched, by listening to conversations that they don't know are being overheard, by prying into their thoughts whenever you can find what their true thoughts are. You learn about people when you see their souls stripped naked by suffering."

"Really, Mr. Mason, you amaze me."

"For instance, in your case," Mason said, "one doesn't find out all about you, about your motivations, about your ideas and about what you *really* want by listening to what you say."

"I— Mr. Mason, are you accusing me of hypocrisy?"

"I'll ask you," Mason said. "Are you telling me the *entire* truth?"

"Why, certainly! Yes, of course, of course!"

"And you want these diaries only for sentimental reasons?"

"Yes, that's right."

"Then," Mason said, "I'll tell you I want them for a business reason. They help me to understand human nature. So that will terminate the interview, Mr. Fallon, and there's no hard feelings on either side."

"But I don't understand, Mr. Mason."

"I've tried to tell you."

"Do you perchance mean that these things have a substantial monetary value to you?"

"That's right."

"Oh," Fallon said, beaming, "in that case, Mr. Mason, I am fully prepared to meet you on your own ground. I had assumed, as one gentleman to another, the five dollar reimbursement would be all that was required, but if it's a matter of financial bargaining . . ."

"It isn't," Mason said. "I simply happen to desire to retain the property which I purchased."

"Oh, but on a purely financial basis, on a concrete basis, Mr. Mason, I am prepared to approach the subject from an entirely different viewpoint."

"Go ahead and approach it then."

"Well, Mr. Mason, on a basis of money, on a basis of a transaction which means something to you from a monetary standpoint—let me put it this way, you paid five dollars for this property and you expect to receive at least five dollars' worth of benefit from it. Is that right?"

"That's right."

"I may say more than five dollars."

"That's right, a great deal more."

The ingratiating smile abruptly left Fallon's face. He plunged his stubby hand into his inside coat pocket, pulled out a pigskin wallet, opened it, counted out five one-hundred dollar bills and tossed them on Mason's desk.

"All right, Mason," he said, "let's understand each other. There's a profit."

Mason shook his head.

Fallon raised his eyebrows in surprise.

"I'm sorry," Mason said. "That isn't the sort of compensation I'm looking for."

Fallon's stubby fingers moved once more into the pigskin billfold. He tossed out five more one-hundred dollar bills.

"All right, Mason," he said coldly, "there's a thousand. Now let's end this damned farce."

There was no hint of geniality in the man's face now. He was like a poker player pushing chips into the center of the table, watching his antagonist across the table, trying to determine what he was going to do, what cards he held in his hand.

"The diaries are not for sale," Mason said.

"But, Mr. Mason, this is an absurd situation."

"It doesn't seem absurd to me," Mason said. "I bought something because I wanted it. I continue to want it."

"Mr. Mason," Fallon said, "let's understand each other. Let's be definite. I am not prepared to go higher than one thousand dollars. That is, my instructions were to stop there. I feel, however, that—

Mr. Mason, would you care to talk with Benjamin Addicks?"

"What about?"

"About the documents that you have."

Mason shook his head. "There's nothing to talk about."

"I think there is, Mr. Mason. I think that if you would see Mr. Addicks personally you'd realize—well, after all, Mr. Mason, let's quit sparring around and get down to cold, hard business."

"It's your party," Mason told him. "Go ahead and serve the refreshments. I thought you wanted to get the package merely for sentimental reasons and because you were a relative of Helen Cadmus."

"Did you really think that?"

"That's what you told me."

"Good heavens, Mr. Mason, I had to tell you something! You're a lawyer. Surely you recognize an approach that would enable us both to save face?"

"I'm not certain my face is worth saving," Mason said.

"No, no, please don't joke, Mr. Mason! Let's be frank with each other."

"I've been frank with you."

"All right, I'll be frank with you. The disappearance of Helen Cadmus caused a lot of conjecture. Newspaper writers, who make their living from catering to the demands of an audience which is hungry for sensational slop, fairly eat that stuff up. It was necessary for Mr. Addicks to go into seclusion, to take elaborate precautions from being hounded to death by these sensation-mongers.

"Now then, it appears that Helen kept a diary. I don't know how it happened that the investigative officers didn't find out about that."

"The report is," Mason said, "that Addicks used every bit of political influence at his command to see that the investigation consisted of nothing more than a big coat of whitewash hastily applied with a big brush. There was no investigation worthy of the name."

"Oh, I'm sure you can't say that, Mr. Mason. You can't really believe that. Mr. Addicks tried to save himself personal inconvenience but that's all."

Mason grinned.

"All right," Fallon said, "let's be frank. Those diaries turn up. Good Lord, we had no idea they existed at all. Evidently they were found in some box or something that no one knew anything about. The current diary, of course, was . . ."

"Yes?" Mason asked.

Fallon coughed. "I shouldn't have used that expression. It was unfortunate."

"What happened to the current diary?" Mason asked.

Fallon met Mason's eyes. His own eyes were cold, hard, and hostile. "There was none," he said. "She evidently stopped keeping a diary with the last volume that you now have in your possession."

"How much is Addicks willing to pay?" Mason asked.

"I don't know," Fallon said. "He told me to go up to a thousand dollars. We had no idea on earth but what we could probably get them as a matter of courtesy by merely reimbursing you for the cost you had incurred, or, if you had an idea of making a profit, that two or three hundred dollars would represent all that we needed to pay. It is a measure of the impression that you have made on me that when I saw you weren't being fooled by my sentimental act, I went right away to the extreme limit that I was authorized to offer."

"All right," Mason said, "so what do you do now?"

Fallon pushed the hundred dollar bills back into his pigskin billfold, carefully folded the five dollar bill, put that in his pocket, smiled at Mason and said, "I go back for further instructions. Thank you. Good morning!"

He turned abruptly on his heel and marched out of the office.

Mason glanced at Della Street in an unspoken question.

"Well," Della Street said, "I presume that means the end of all office work for today."

"It means the end of all office work for the day. I'll take one of the volumes, you take one, give one to Jackson, give one to Gertie. We read through those diaries. We read every single word. Make notes of anything that's significant and tie the notes in with the page references. Let's find out what's bothering Mr. Benjamin Addicks, preferably before we hear from Mr. Addicks again. What's the last entry in the last volume, Della?"

"I've already checked on that, Chief," she said. "It's about two weeks before the date of her disappearance."

"Gosh, how I wish we had volume number five," Mason said, "but from the inadvertent slip made by Three-Dollar-Bill Fallon, I am certain that Addicks, Fallon, and Company found that diary, put it in a sack, tied a weight on it and dropped it overboard in the deepest part of the channel. All right, Della, let's find out what we have. Cancel all appointments for today, throw that mail off the desk, and let's go to work."

CHAPTER THREE

LATE TUESDAY AFTERNOON, AFTER ALL OF THE REST OF THE OFFICE force had gone home, Perry Mason and Della Street sat in Mason's private office correlating information that had been received from Helen Cadmus' diary.

"Hang it," Mason said, "*I'm* not excluding the possibility of murder."

Della Street said, "Well, I'm almost at the point of excluding the possibility of accident and suicide."

"We haven't any evidence," Mason told her, "that is, nothing tangible."

"It's tangible enough to suit me," Della Street said with feeling. "You read through that diary, Chief, and you get the picture of a darned nice, normal, young girl with a beautiful body, who has ambitions to get into the movies—which I suppose nearly all girls with beautiful bodies have—and a keenly sympathetic, understanding mentality.

"She was fascinated by the force of Benjamin Addicks' character. She resented his treatment of the gorillas and monkeys. She felt that there was some great mystery in connection with his life. The first volume shows a fierce curiosity to find out what that secret is, and then all of a sudden there's no further reference to it.

"Now here's something else, the girl was in love."

"How do you know, Della?"

"Her attitude, the way she wrote in her diary. She had leisure time and she spent it thinking romantic thoughts."

"But she didn't confide those romantic thoughts to her diary," Mason pointed out.

"Not in so many words," Della Street agreed, "but it's all there in between the lines. For some reason she avoided really confiding to her diary, but she unmistakably disclosed her moods. People who are in love talk about the beautiful things of nature, beauty in the spring of the year and in the spring of the heart."

"Della, you're getting poetic!"

"I'm being logical."

"Do you keep a diary yourself?"

Her face flushed furiously. "And, another thing," she went on quickly, "she hated Nathan Fallon."

"Who doesn't?" Mason asked.

"Nathan Fallon."

Mason threw back his head and laughed.

Della smiled and said, "She loved animals and she was strongly attached to this one monkey named Pete. She resented the experiments Benjamin Addicks was conducting with animals."

Mason's eyes narrowed. "Addicks was experimenting along modern lines, trying to make animals neurotic. And he had some peculiar ideas about hypnotism. Apparently he felt that a man could not be put into such a deep hypnotic trance that he would do something that would outrage his higher moral sense, but he felt that gorillas were so closely related to man that they could be hypnotized, and taught to commit a homicide.

"I'm damned if I know what point Addicks was trying to prove. I have a feeling there's something in his past. He may have been in serious trouble, may have committed a crime and felt that he did it under the hypnotic influence of some person."

"It's a nightmarish background for a secretarial job," Della Street said. "Addicks is wealthy, but that doesn't give him any excuse to torture animals."

Mason nodded. "Apparently Helen Cadmus felt the same way at first. Then she seems to have changed. She certainly referred to Addicks with great respect and seemed to feel there was something important back of his experiments."

"And then she was murdered," Della Street said.

"Don't say that, Della. There's no proof."

"Well, I have an intuitive feeling, a very definite feeling she didn't commit suicide."

Mason said, "There's another interesting angle in the volume of the diary that I read. It interests me very much, Della."

"What?"

"This monkey, Pete, that she was so fond of, developed a habit of making off with her little knickknacks, anything that he saw her admiring. Her compact, her lipstick, her earrings—he'd take them and hide them. Apparently his favorite hiding place was a Grecian urn in the reception hall— Della, I have a hunch. Who's the attorney representing Mrs. Josephine Kempton in that suit against Addicks?"

"I'll look it up," Della Street said. "It's in the outer office."

She was gone for about three minutes. When she came back she handed a typed slip of paper to Mason on which had been written, "James Etna, of the firm of Etna, Etna and Douglas."

As Mason consulted the memo, she said, "I'm afraid I led with my chin, Chief."

"What do you mean?"

"When I went out in the outer office the board was clattering away at a great rate, so I plugged in to explain that it was after office hours, that there was no one here to answer the phone, and . . . well, I found myself talking with Mortimer Hershey, the business manager of Benjamin Addicks. He wanted very much to arrange a conference between you and Mr. Addicks."

"What did you tell him?" Mason asked.

"I told him that I would have to get in touch with you and consult your appointment book. Then he explained to me that Mr. Addicks couldn't come to your office because he'd been injured."

"Injured?"

"That's what he said."

"Any more details?"

"That was all. He said that Mr. Addicks was injured and couldn't come to your office, but that he felt it would be very much to your advantage to see Mr. Addicks. I told him that I'd have to try to get in touch with you and call him back."

Mason said, "Just on a chance, Della, put through a call to Etna, Etna and Douglas."

"There won't be anyone there at this hour."

"One of the partners might be working late. After all, Della, you know we work late."

"Darned if we don't," she said. She picked up the telephone, dialed a number, then after a moment said, "May I ask who this is talking? . . . This is Mr. Mason's office, Mr. Perry Mason. . . . That's right, the attorney. . . . Oh, it is? . . . Well, I'm sorry to be bothering you at this hour but Mr. Mason was anxious to get in touch with Mr. James Etna. Just hang on please."

Della Street motioned toward Mason and switched over the connection on her desk telephone. "Another night owl," she said. "*He's* working late on a case."

Mason picked up the telephone, said, "Hello. This is Perry Mason speaking. Is this James Etna?"

"That's right."

"You're attorney for Mrs. Josephine Kempton in a suit against Benjamin Addicks?"

"Yes, sir. That's right."

"I find myself taking an interest in that case," Mason said.

"Whom are you representing?" Etna asked in a coldly cautious tone of voice.

"No one. I'm simply interested in it."

"Well, I'm interested in it myself. Personally I think it's a damned outrage. In fact, it's keeping me from a dinner engagement tonight. The case is scheduled to go to trial day after tomorrow, and I'm trying to dig up a little law on it."

"Would you mind telling me the background of the case?"

"I think it's disclosed by the pleadings," Etna said cautiously.

"I'd like a little more than that."

"Why?"

"Just curiosity, we might say."

"I'm afraid, Mr. Mason, that I can only refer you to the pleadings. Of course, when the case comes to court . . ."

"There's just a chance," Mason said, "that I might be able to give you a little help."

"In what way?"

"I can't tell at the moment, but if you want to tell me anything . . . I wouldn't want you to disclose any confidential communications, but . . ."

"Oh, all right," Etna said. "I can tell you generally what the case is all about. Mrs. Kempton was peremptorily dismissed. She had been in Mr. Addicks' employ for about two and a half years. Addicks gave no reason for dismissing her. Mrs. Kempton was angry when she left. She didn't ask for any letter of recommendation. She was discharged without notice."

"Doesn't she know what the trouble was about?" Mason asked.

"As far as she's concerned there wasn't any trouble."

"Go ahead. What happened after that?"

"Well, she secured employment. Naturally the people wanted to know for whom she'd been working, and Mrs. Kempton told them. She worked for about two weeks. Apparently her services were entirely satisfactory, and then out of a clear sky she was discharged without notice. She couldn't understand it. However, she's a good cook and housekeeper and she got another position right away. Naturally there, too, people wanted to know where she had been working, so she told them and settled down on the job and everything was fine. The people expressed themselves as being very well pleased and then abruptly let her go without a word."

"Go ahead," Mason said.

Etna hesitated.

"Well?" Mason prompted.

"This thing," he said, "is not generally known. I—oh, I guess it's all right to tell you."

"Don't tell me if it isn't all right," Mason said. "I'm not asking for anything confidential."

"Oh, it's going to come out in court," Etna said. "Mrs. Kempton had had some other dealings with our office over an insurance matter. She became suspicious. She came to me and told me what had happened, so I had one of my friends write to Benjamin Addicks stating that a Mrs. Josephine Kempton was in his employ, that he understood one of her last positions had been with Mr. Addicks for something over two years, and asked Mr. Addicks if he could give any information about Mrs. Kempton's character."

"And what happened?" Mason asked.

"Within a week a letter was received from Benjamin Addicks stating curtly that Mrs. Kempton had been discharged on account of dishonesty, that a very valuable diamond ring, to which Mr. Addicks was very much attached, and which was worth in the neighborhood of five thousand dollars, had disappeared; that a platinum watch, which was worth seventeen hundred and fifty dollars, had also disappeared; that the theft had not been brought home to Mrs.

Kempton with sufficient evidence so that she could be prosecuted, but that there had been sufficient evidence so that Addicks had summarily discharged her."

"That's a devil of a letter to write," Mason said.

"Isn't it?"

"And what did you do?"

"Well, just to make assurance doubly sure, I had Mrs. Kempton get a job with friends of mine, people whom I could trust, and where the letter would possibly have more legal significance. The fact that the other letter had been written by someone who hadn't actually employed Mrs. Kempton, you understand, might make a difference in the legal situation."

"I understand."

"So Mrs. Kempton secured a position at two hundred and fifty dollars a month with board and room, a very nice position. The people wrote to Mr. Addicks and received the same type of letter as the other, which, of course, they have retained in their possession, and which they're ready to identify in court."

"And the case comes up day after tomorrow?"

"That's right. I've been trying my damnedest to rush the thing through to trial because it makes a considerable difference to my client. Addicks can clip coupons. My client has to work."

"You've asked Addicks to retract?"

"I did everything I could to bring pressure to bear on Addicks. I don't know whether you know him."

"I don't."

"Well, he's a very obstinate individual. He told me he had evidence that would convince anyone that Mrs. Kempton had made away with the diamond ring and the watch; that he hadn't been sufficiently nasty about it to resort to criminal proceedings, but that if I dragged him into court he'd blast Mrs. Kempton's name forever. He said that if she wanted to get a job without giving him as a reference, it would be all right with him. All she had to do was to lie about where she'd been working, but that when anyone wrote to him and asked him for his opinion about Mrs. Kempton, he was going to give it."

"I suppose," Mason said, "you've looked up the law in regard to privileged communications?"

"That's what I'm digging around in now," Etna said. "There's a

question of privileged communications. Also the question of malice, the question of reasonable grounds for writing such a letter,
and all of that stuff. The law isn't too clear."

"Now I want to ask you one question," Mason said. "Do you
remember reading in the paper about the disappearance of
Addicks' secretary, a girl by the name of Helen Cadmus?"

"I don't remember too much about the newspaper accounts, no,"
Etna said cautiously.

"But you do know something of her disappearance?"

"I know a few things that Mrs. Kempton has told me," Etna said
cautiously.

"Now," Mason said, "you're getting close to what I want. What
did Mrs. Kempton tell you?"

"Why do you want to know?"

"I'm not at liberty at the moment to disclose that information."

"Then I'm not at liberty at the moment to give you any."

"All right, can you tell me about when Mrs. Kempton was discharged with reference to the disappearance of Helen Cadmus?"

Etna said, "Helen Cadmus is supposed to have committed suicide about two days before Mrs. Kempton was discharged. It is our
considered opinion that if—now understand, Mr. Mason, I'm not
making any charges—that if anything had been feloniously taken
from the Addicks' residence, there is much more reason to believe
that Helen Cadmus was responsible than Mrs. Kempton. Now I'll
elaborate that to this extent. The ring and the watch were left in
Mr. Addicks' bedroom. That bedroom was kept locked. Two people had a key to it. One was Mrs. Kempton, and the other was
Helen Cadmus. Mrs. Kempton had to go in in connection with her
duties as housekeeper, and Helen Cadmus had to go into the room
in connection with her secretarial duties. It was actually a suite of
rooms. A bedroom, office, bath, and den. Now that much I can tell
you, Mr. Mason, and that's all I can tell you at the moment."

"Can you give me a number where I can reach you later on tonight?"

"I'll be here for an hour or two. My home number is West
9-7211."

Mason said, "Thanks a lot. You may hear from me later on."

Mason hung up. Della Street raised inquiring eyebrows.

"I presume," he said, "your unspoken question is a desire to know what Mr. James Etna told me."

"My unspoken question," she said, "is a desire to know when we eat."

Mason laughed. "We eat right now, Della, and after we have eaten we're going to drive out and call on Mr. Benjamin Addicks, and see what he has to say, and if perchance—understand now, Della, this is just a shot in the dark, a one chance in a thousand— but if we should find a five thousand dollar ring and a seventeen hundred and fifty dollar platinum watch in the Grecian urn in the reception room, we're going to make a very arrogant and perhaps a sadistic millionaire crawl in a hole and pull the hole in after him."

"That's fine," Della Street said, "but I take it that is not to be done on an empty stomach."

"Definitely not. Where would you like to eat?"

"Where I can get a thick steak with butter and chopped parsley, and if we're going to call on a millionaire I think we should enjoy the luxury of eating some French bread, toasted to a delicious brown, and dusted with shredded garlic."

"By all means," Mason said gravely. "One owes it to one's profession to enjoy the opportunities of the moment. Now if we were making a will for Mr. Addicks, or, if we had been called to consult with him on a business matter, we would naturally have to forego the garlic, Della."

"Oh, naturally," she agreed, her eyes twinkling, "but under the circumstances, and since I have now labored far into the night, you might also buy me a bottle of red Tipo Chianti to go with the steak and garlic bread."

"Well, before you go," Mason said, "you might call up Mr. Mortimer Hershey, and tell him that we will call on Mr. Addicks this evening at nine-thirty."

"Shall I tell him that if he hasn't dined yet, he'd better try a little garlic bread, because under those circumstances he might enjoy our company more?"

"No," Mason told her, "we don't know him that well yet."

"But we will?" she asked.

"Oh, definitely," Mason promised, smiling. "We will, but he wouldn't enjoy our company anyway."

CHAPTER FOUR

PERRY MASON SWUNG HIS CAR TO A POINT WHERE TWO SQUARE PILLARS furnished supports for wrought iron gates which barred a wide graveled driveway.

A watchman, a big deputy sheriff's star pinned on his chest, a five-cell flashlight in his hand, a revolver holstered in a well-filled cartridge belt, stood just behind the gates.

The beam of the flashlight pilloried the occupants of the car. Mason rolled down the window.

"What do *you* want?" the watchman asked.

"The first thing I want," Mason said, "is for you to take the beam of that flashlight out of my eyes."

The flashlight wavered, then went off.

Mason said, "The next thing I want is to see Benjamin Addicks."

"What I want to know," the watchman said, "is whether Benjamin Addicks wants to see you."

"He said he did."

"What's the name?"

"Perry Mason."

"Wait right there," the watchman said. "Now don't get out of the car. Just wait right there until I telephone the house."

He crossed over to a boxed-in telephone which was recessed in one of the square columns of masonry which supported the gates.

"Nice friendly people, aren't they?" Mason said to Della Street.

"Well, perhaps he has to be. This is rather an isolated spot out here, Chief, and, after all, the man's supposed to be wealthy. I presume he could be pestered with prowlers."

The watchman hung up the telephone, and pressed a switch which started the ponderous gates swinging slowly back on well-oiled hinges.

The watchman came up to stand by the car on Mason's side.

"All right," he said, "he's expecting you. Now you follow this gravel driveway all the way. When you come to the stone porch on the house with the big pillars, you drive right up to the stone steps and stop the car. There'll be somebody there to meet you. Leave the car right there. Don't stop before you get there, and don't get off the graveled driveway. Understand?"

"I understand," Mason said, "but I'm not particularly impressed with the cordiality of your welcome. What happens if we should get off the graveled driveway?"

"Plenty would happen."

"Such as what?"

"Well, for one thing you'd find that you'd crossed beams of invisible light, and when you cross one of those beams all hell breaks loose. Sirens scream, floodlights turn on, and the doors of the kennels automatically open. That releases the police dogs. Don't say I didn't warn you. If you want to experiment, go ahead and find out."

The watchman turned away.

Mason said to Della Street, "I guess Mr. Addicks has arranged for ample protection. Anything that he lacks in hospitality he seems to make up in efficiency."

He eased the car into gear and slid through the gates, the tires crunching the gravel on the wide, sweeping driveway which curved through landscaped grounds, which, to the uninitiated eyes, might seem to furnish plenty of opportunities for concealment.

After a few moments the big house loomed in front of them, a solid masonry affair that had its lines softened here and there by bits of ivy clinging to the stone.

Mason said, "All the soft, pleasing architecture of a state prison."

He slid the car to a stop by the steps on the front porch.

A porch light came on to flood the place with brilliance. Somewhere in the back dogs were barking with savage insistence.

Mason switched off the motor and his headlights, opened the car door, and walked around to assist Della from the car. She opened the door and without waiting jumped to the steps leading to the porch and ran lightly up the stairs.

The big front door swung open and Nathan Fallon came out to greet them.

"Welcome to Stonehenge," he said.

"Stonehenge?" Della Street exclaimed.

Fallon said, "That's the name of the place. Rather a huge mansion, Miss Street. It has plenty of room for all of Mr. Addicks' requirements. Room for entertaining, room for working, and room for his animal experimentation."

"Can you tell me just what is the purpose of this animal experimentation that you refer to?" Mason asked.

Nathan Fallon didn't bother any longer to keep up the front of smiling affability. He looked at Mason through his thick-lensed glasses in silent appraisal.

"No," he said.

For a moment there was silence, then Nathan Fallon stepped back to indicate the door. "Won't you come in?" he invited.

They entered a reception hall, which, with its ponderous, powerful architecture, still seemed to carry out the motif of a state prison.

Curtains parted from a doorway on the right, and a tall, slender individual stood there surveying them.

His eyes were slate gray, utterly without expression, and were so large that when he closed his eyelids the process seemed deliberately exaggerated as though one might have been looking at the eyes of an owl. The slow closing of the lids disclosed a distinct convexity of the big eyes, then the lids opened again like the shutters on twin studio cameras perpetuating a photographic image on film.

"Good evening," the man said in a voice that somehow made the simple greeting a matter of slow, deliberate formality.

"This is Mortimer Hershey," Nathan Fallon said, "Mr. Addicks' business manager."

"I take it," Hershey said, "the young lady is Miss Street, and I have the honor to address Mr. Perry Mason."

"That's right."

"Won't you step in here, please."

He ushered them into a room which was a cross between a library and a huge office.

There was a massive table fully fifteen feet long. Comfortable leather directors' chairs were arranged along one side of this table.

Huge as was the table, the very size of the room kept it from dominating the surroundings. Low bookcases ran around three sides of the room. Over these bookcases were oil paintings depicting knights engaged in battle.

Some of these pictures showed armored knights on horseback,

leaning forward, lances set, charging each other. Others portrayed individual knights engaged in hand to hand conflict. Still others showed bodies of armored knights charging against footmen; bowmen drawn up in battle array, releasing arrows from their longbows, arrows which arched heavily in flight, indicating their weight and momentum as they sped toward a group of armored knights; horses screaming in agony or dying among corpses of foot soldiers piled one on the other and armored knights holding shields and swords that were crimson with blood.

Elsewhere around the room were big leather chairs in which a person could settle down into luxurious comfort. There were footstools in front of each of these chairs, and beside each chair was a shaded reading light. The room itself was illuminated by an indirect lighting system.

"Won't you be seated?" Hershey invited, and led the way toward the table, pulling out chairs so that Mason and Della Street could sit on one side, Nathan Fallon and Hershey on the other.

"Now then," Hershey said, smiling with slow deliberation, "I wish to apologize to you, Mr. Mason, on behalf of Mr. Addicks."

"Why?" Mason asked.

"Because you were underestimated."

"You mean Mr. Addicks underestimated me?"

"Fallon did," Hershey said, and turned to look deliberately at Fallon. He raised his lids, lowered them, and raised them again.

There was something in the slow, winking appraisal which seemed deliberately scornful, but Hershey's lips remained in a fixed smile.

He turned back to Mason.

"All right," Mason said, "I've been underestimated, and I've been apologized to. The apology wasn't at all necessary."

"Certainly not."

Mortimer Hershey opened a drawer in the desk. He took out a sheaf of bank notes and slowly, deliberately counted them until he had thirty new, crisp, one hundred dollar bills before him.

"What's that for?" Mason asked.

"The diaries and the photographs," Hershey said.

"And why do you make that offer?"

"Because Mr. Addicks wants them. Of course, Mr. Mason, you understand that Mr. Addicks would never admit that he paid any such sum for the documents, and you would be under no necessity to make any such admission."

"What do you mean?"

"I mean this," Hershey said. "The books of Mr. Addicks would not show that you had been paid three thousand dollars. The books of Mr. Addicks would show that you were reimbursed the amount of five dollars which you paid for the books. The other three thousand dollars would be in the nature of a gift which Mr. Addicks would make you. As such, it would not be subject to income tax. Do I make myself clear?"

"Oh quite," Mason said. "The only thing I don't understand is why Mr. Addicks is so anxious to get hold of the photographs and the diaries."

"There are reasons."

"I think," Mason said, "that I would prefer to discuss the matter with Mr. Addicks. I thought that I was going to see him. That's why I came out here."

"Mr. Addicks begs to be excused. He is indisposed."

Mason shook his head. "I came out here to see Benjamin Addicks. You told me he was indisposed and couldn't come to see me. I told you I'd come out to see him. I want to talk with him."

"If you insist," Hershey said, "I am quite certain that Mr. Addicks would be willing to see you, but, after all, Mr. Mason, I can assure you that this offer is complete and final. Mr. Addicks won't raise it not so much as a red cent. You can either accept it or reject it."

"All right," Mason said promptly. "It's rejected."

"You reject offers rather abruptly," Hershey said.

"Well, if you'd prefer more diplomacy," Mason told him, smiling, "I'll state that in view of the fact that I find the diaries most interesting, and in view of the fact I think they offer a very distinct clue, I do not care to part with them."

"Clue?" Hershey said in cold solemnity.

"A clue," Mason said.

"To what, may I ask?"

"Certainly you may ask," Mason said, "and I won't answer. The answer to that question will be reserved for Mr. Addicks himself."

"You understand, Mr. Mason, that this is going to cause Mr. Addicks some inconvenience, but I'll be very glad to convey your message to him, and I'm quite certain he'll be willing to see you. If you'll wait just a moment, please."

Hershey turned and looked at Fallon.

Nathan Fallon jumped up from the chair as though he had suddenly received an electric shock, and, walking with his distinctive, energetic strides, crossed the room and went through the curtained doorway.

Hershey looked at the three thousand dollars in hundred dollar bills, picked up the money, stacked the bills together in an inviting pile and made a gesture of extending them toward Mason. Mason shook his head.

Hershey opened the drawer in the table, dropped the money back into the drawer, then closed it, put his hands in front of him on the table, interlaced long fingers, and sat silent and motionless.

A moment later the heavy draperies at the far end of the room parted, and a barrel-chested man, leaning heavily on a cane, came hobbling into the room. His face was partially covered by a bandage, and his eyes were concealed behind dark glasses. Nearly all of the right side of the face, and part of the left side, was covered by the bandage. The left side had a bit of gauze held in place by adhesive tape, which failed to conceal evidence of a blue-black beard under the clean-shaven skin.

It was hard to judge the face beneath the bandage, but the jaw seemed heavy, and the low forehead was surmounted by a shock of black hair cut short.

"Mr. Benjamin Addicks," Hershey announced.

Addicks nodded, said, "How do you do? How do you do? Sorry that I'm indisposed."

Followed by Nathan Fallon, he hobbled across the room and extended his hand.

"Mr. Perry Mason," Hershey said.

"Glad to meet you, Mr. Mason. Heard a lot about you. Followed a few of your cases in the newspapers."

"And Miss Street, Mr. Mason's secretary," Hershey went on.

"Good evening, Miss Street. I'm very pleased to meet you. Sorry I'm a little bit banged up. I do animal experimenting, you know, and it's not always conducive to good health."

The bandaged face contorted into a twisted grin.

"One of those damn gorillas," Addicks went on to explain, speaking slowly through the bandage, "caught me a little too close to his cage, grabbed my coat, and before I could slip out of it, jerked me around so he got hold of my arm, and pulled me toward the cage. I flung back and tried to kick loose. He caught my foot and made a grab; caused some pretty deep scratches and bruises on my face. I'll be all right, but I'm not very presentable."

He pulled out a chair and eased himself into it in the manner of a man who is sore and stiff.

"The gorilla," Nathan Fallon explained, "was trying to grab Mr. Addicks' throat. If he'd ever caught it in his powerful fingers he'd have torn the throat right out."

"Now wait a minute," Addicks said impatiently. "You're always jumping at conclusions from insufficient data, Nathan. You're a damned old woman that way. I don't think the gorilla was making a grab for my throat. I'm not too satisfied but what he was just after my necktie."

He turned to Mason and said, "Gorillas are like that. They're eager to get hold of some article of wearing apparel, particularly something that's loose. If you wear a necktie around 'em, they're very apt to reach through the cage and grab you by it—and, of course, if he's developed vicious tendencies, he's a very dangerous animal."

"You deliberately encourage this type of danger?" Mason asked.

"I'm conducting scientific research," Addicks said. "I want to know how deeply the homicidal instincts have been implanted in the minds of the higher primates."

"It would seem," Mason said, "that you were very close to finding out."

"I jerked back instinctively," Addicks said. "Hang it, *I* thought for a minute he was trying to grab my throat, but thinking back on it I can't exclude the possibility that he was merely grabbing for my necktie. They do that, you know, and this one was particularly tricky. They're big animals, but they're quick as a flash, Mason, just as quick as a flash."

"I saw it all," Fallon said, "and there is absolutely no doubt in my mind that he was grabbing for your throat, Benny."

"Well, he certainly gave me a rough time," Addicks admitted. "I sort of surprised him by bringing up my foot and kicking, and bracing against the bars. Then Nathan yelled at him and picked up a club."

Mason said, "It would seem that your experiments are destined to be inconclusive until they reach a point where a gorilla has very definitely killed someone."

Addicks regarded him with cold, watchful eyes, then shrugged his shoulders. "I think you misunderstand what I'm trying to do, Mr. Mason, and, frankly, I see no reason to explain. I'm more interested in learning something about the real explanation of hypnotism than anything else. Some people don't approve. I don't give a damn whether they do or don't. They're my gorillas. I buy 'em, and they're mine."

"I doubt it," Mason said.

"What do you mean by that?"

"You may be able to get physical possession of the gorillas," Mason said, "but morally I don't think a man can really own any living thing. The animal has a right to his own development through the phenomena of life."

"You're a lawyer. I have legal title. You'll have to admit that."

"I was discussing moral ownership, moral responsibilities."

"Give me physical possession of something that's locked behind iron bars in a cage, and give me a bill of sale to it, and you can have all your moral responsibilities. I'll take legal title as far as I'm concerned."

"You wanted to see me about something?" Mason asked.

"I did, but I don't now."

"What changed your mind?"

"You did. You were offered three thousand dollars for those diaries. You turned the offer down. Okay, if that's the way you want it, that's the way we'll play. The offer is withdrawn. The price has gone back to five dollars. Is that clear?"

"That's clear," Mason said. "The money is yours, the diaries are mine."

"Let's understand each other, Mason. You're a smart lawyer. I'm a mean fighter. You give those diaries to the press and start stirring up things about Helen's death, and I'll break you."

Mason got to his feet. "Talk big if you like to impress your employees," he said. "It doesn't tell me anything except that you're scared. Come on, Della. Let's go." They left the room, followed by the three men.

In the hallway, Mason said to Della, "Can you give me a hand for a moment, Della?"

"What do you want now?" Addicks said.

"I want to see what's in that stone urn."

"What makes you think anything's in it?" Addicks asked.

Mason smiled coldly. "The diaries. *My* diaries."

"Nathan, you and Mort lift that urn down. Turn it up. Show Mason there's nothing in it."

They lifted down the big stone urn, deposited it gently on the floor.

Nathan Fallon turned a pocket flashlight down into the dark interior. Immediately it seemed as though the interior of the urn had been illuminated with a thousand scintillating reflections.

"Good heavens!" Fallon said. "That's a big diamond in there, Benny."

"Get it out," Addicks said curtly.

Fallon reached down into the urn, but his arm wouldn't quite get to the bottom. "I'll have to take off my coat," he said, "and I don't know whether I can reach it even then."

"We can turn the urn upside down," Addicks said. "Get hold of it, you fellows. Turn it up. Let's see what the devil's in there."

They grasped the upper edge and bottom of the urn, tilted it over to its side, then slowly lifted. The first thing that came rolling out was a huge diamond ring.

"My solitaire!" Addicks exclaimed.

A platinum watch came slithering down the smooth side of the urn.

Fallon grabbed it.

"Tilt it up a little more," Mason said.

A whole collection of jewelry, coins, a wallet, a card case, a girl's compact, rolled out to the floor.

"Well, I'll be damned!" Addicks said.

Mason said dryly, "The diary indicated that the monkey, Pete, was rather mischievous at times and had developed a tendency to pick up objects, particularly objects which he thought Helen Cadmus prized, and conceal them in this Grecian urn."

"So *that* explains it!" Addicks said.

Mason looked him squarely in the eye. "I believe there is a trial coming up day after tomorrow, the case of Josephine Kempton, who is suing you for defamation of character."

"Oh, that!" Addicks said.

"Ah-hah!" Fallon exclaimed. "*Now* the thing becomes apparent. Now we see why the great Perry Mason interested himself in the diaries of Helen Cadmus. *Now* we begin to get the whole picture, Benny."

Addicks looked at him for a moment, then said, "Shut up."

He turned to Perry Mason. "You're clever. I like clever men. What's your position?"

"I haven't any," Mason said.

Nathan Fallon said, "Don't you get it, Benny?"

Addicks picked up the watch, turned it over and over in his hand. "No, I don't get it, and I doubt like hell if you do."

"This is the thing that Mason has been planning all along. He set an elaborate trap for us," Fallon went on.

"Keep talking," Mason said. "You're doing fine, Fallon. Just watch what you say."

"I don't have to watch what I say," Fallon said angrily. "When you went through this hall the first time you tossed those objects into the stone urn, then you made up a story about a monkey having hidden them."

"I didn't go near the stone urn," Mason said.

"You walked right by it."

"You were standing right here with me at the time."

"I had my back turned. I was leading the way into the other room."

Mason said, "Fallon, I want you to look at me, look me right in the eyes."

Fallon looked at him.

"You're a damn liar," Mason said.

Fallon doubled up his fist, then thought better of it.

"Now wait a minute," Addicks said. "This thing is moving pretty fast. I want to get some more information about this business. Hershey, I have confidence in you. Were you standing where you could see Mason when he walked past this urn?"

"He didn't go near the urn," Hershey said. "He looked at it, but he didn't go near it, and he couldn't have tossed anything in it.

You can see for yourself there's dust all over these things. They've been there a long time."

"That's the trouble with you, Fallon," Addicks said. "You're always putting two and two together and making six, and then trying to sell me on the idea that that's the answer. Dammit, you're going to get us all into trouble. Now sit down and shut up."

The telephone in the entrance hallway rang sharply.

"Now what the devil?" Addicks said, and then to Fallon, "Answer it."

Fallon picked up the telephone, said, "Hello, this is Nathan Fallon. . . . Who is it? . . . Well, Mr. Addicks wasn't expecting him. . . . Just a moment."

"Here's something," Nathan said to Addicks. "Your lawyer, Sidney Hardwick is out there."

"I can't see him," Addicks said. "I'm definitely not going to subject myself to any further nerve strain or have any further visitors tonight. To hell with him. I didn't ask him to come out."

"Well, he says it's important," Fallon said. "What are we going to do? We can't very well turn him away from the gate."

Addicks turned. "Who are you to tell me what I can do and what I can't do, Fallon? I picked you up out of the gutter. Some day I'll toss you back. I told you I wouldn't see Hardwick and I meant it. I don't care *how* important it is."

Addicks hobbled from the room, then came back to stand for a moment in the doorway. "You played your cards damned cleverly, Mason," he said. "Good night."

Mortimer Hershey gave Fallon a meaning look. "You're going to have to take care of Hardwick, Nathan."

Fallon said into the telephone, "Open the gates. Sidney Hardwick can come in any time."

He hung up the phone and said, "I'm going to have to ask you to wait right here a minute, Mr. Mason. I'm sorry I shot my face off the way I did. I'm sorry. I was trying to protect Benny's interests. You see how much thanks I got for it."

Mason, bending over the assortment of objects which had spilled from the urn, said to Della Street, "Make a list of every object that was in this urn, Della."

"Don't touch anything," Fallon warned. "Don't touch a thing there. I'm warning you."

"I'm not touching anything," Mason told him. "I'm looking. Is there any objection to looking?"

Fallon hesitated a moment, then said, "I've said enough. Hardwick will answer all questions now."

He opened the front door. "Well, well, well, Mr. Hardwick. Come on in. Come right on in!"

Hardwick, a tall, bony-faced individual in the middle sixties, with a long nose, sharp chin, bushy eyebrows, keen gray eyes, paused in the doorway to shake hands with Fallon.

He wore glasses from which dangled ostentatiously a black ribbon. There was a hearing aid in his right ear. He said, "How do you do, Nathan? How's Benny this evening?"

"Benny isn't at all well," Nathan said. "He can't see you."

"What?" Hardwick exclaimed in surprise. "Can't see *me*? It's important. I've told him about the complications that have necessitated that his will be . . ."

"A lot of other things are important," Fallon said meaningly, jerking his thumb over to where Perry Mason and Della Street were standing. "We're in a little trouble."

"What do you mean?" Hardwick asked, seeing Mason and Della Street for the first time.

"We're having legal troubles," Nathan Fallon said. "This is Perry Mason."

"Well, bless my soul, so it is," Hardwick said. His face lit up in a smile. He came over and extended a strong bony hand, which gripped Mason's cordially.

"Miss Della Street, my secretary," Mason said.

Hardwick bowed. "So pleased to meet you, Miss Street. Well, well, Mason, what brings *you* here?"

"I came here," Mason said, "at the request of Mr. Addicks, and on an entirely different matter. As Mr. Fallon will explain to you, we have just uncovered evidence indicating that the alleged thefts claimed to have been committed by Mrs. Josephine Kempton, a housekeeper, were actually committed by a monkey."

Hardwick's face instantly lost its smile and became fixed in a look of professional gravity. He turned to Fallon. "How did it happen, Nathan?" he asked.

"Mr. Mason came here to see Hershey and me about another matter. We offered him some financial adjustment."

"What matter?" Hardwick asked, his voice cracking like a whip.

"Those diaries of Helen Cadmus."

"I saw Mason's picture in the paper in connection with those," Hardwick said. "That's another thing I want to see Addicks about."

"We offered him money for them."

"How much?"

"Three thousand."

"What happened?"

"He turned it down."

Hardwick frowned, turned to Mason. "Really, Counselor, I would have anticipated you'd have been glad to turn those diaries over in return for what you paid for them."

"If they'd acted halfway decent, I'd have given them the diaries," Mason said. "But they were scared stiff. I thought I'd see what it was that was frightening them."

"Just the thought of publicity," Hershey said.

Mason's smile was coldly skeptical, a silent contradiction of Hershey's words.

Hershey closed his eyes.

"Go ahead," Hardwick said.

Nathan Fallon supplied the information. "From reading those diaries, Mason got the idea of looking in the stone urn here in the reception hallway. You can see for yourself what we found in it. There it is on the floor. Benny has the diamond ring, but there's the platinum watch, a girl's compact, some other jewelry, a billfold that probably is pretty well filled with cash. In fact, I think that's *my* billfold."

Hardwick walked over to look down at the assortment of stuff on the floor.

"I can tell you in a minute about the billfold," Fallon said.

He stooped over, picked up the billfold, opened it, smiled and showed Hardwick the identification card in the front of the billfold.

"Well," he said, "that's it. I've been missing it for some time."

"How much money is in it?" Hardwick asked.

"Thirty-two dollars when I lost it," Fallon said. He unfolded the leather so that he could peer inside of the billfold, said, "That's right," and hurriedly dropped it into his pocket.

"Better count it and see if there's any missing," Mason suggested.

Fallon looked at him coldly. "It's all there."

Hardwick said, "This complicates the situation. Mason, what's your interest in this?"

"I'm interested."

"I understand, but in what way? Who has retained you?"

"No one," Mason said and then added, "As yet."

"Well, now," Hardwick said, "that poses, of course, an interesting question. Under the circumstances I would suggest that Mr. Addicks retain you to assist me in handling this case which is coming up the day after tomorrow, a case in which, of course, it may be possible—however, I think I'll discuss the legal aspects with you *after* you have been retained."

"I'm sorry," Mason said, "but I'm not open to a retainer from Mr. Addicks."

"Are you giving me to understand then that you're retained by Mrs. Kempton?"

"Not exactly," Mason said. "I do happen to know something about the suit, and I have discussed it with her attorney."

"All right," Hardwick said, "let's be fair about this, Mr. Mason. Don't tell Mrs. Kempton or her lawyers anything about this until we have had a chance to effect a settlement."

Mason smiled and shook his head.

"You mean you're going to them with the information?"

"I mean I'm going to tell James Etna of Etna, Etna and Douglas, about the entry in the diary, and I'm going to tell him about what we found."

"It won't do a particle of good," Hardwick said. "It may do harm."

Mason shrugged his shoulders.

"Let's look at the thing from a cold, legal standpoint," Hardwick went on. "There are two instances in which one person may accuse another person of crime with no liability on the part of the person making the accusation. One of them is in the event the person actually is guilty of the crime. The law of slander and libel in this country is different from what it is in many countries. Here the truth is always a defense to a statement which might otherwise be libelous or slanderous."

"Thank you for telling me the law," Mason said.

Hardwick smiled. "I'm not *telling* you the law. I'm pointing out

a legal situation. The second class of case, Mr. Mason, is a privileged communication.

"Now let's suppose Mr. Addicks accused Josephine Kempton of
crime. He has two defenses. In the event she was guilty of crime,
he can plead the truth, and that's a complete defense. In the event
she wasn't guilty of crime but he said she was, all he needs to do is
to show that the communication was privileged. In other words,
that he was acting in good faith in giving information to a person who had a legitimate interest in the matter. That completely
disposes of any question of defamation."

Mason stretched his arms, yawned, and said, "I never like to
argue legal points unless I'm paid for it. So far no one has retained
me, and I somehow don't think anyone is going to."

Hardwick said, "Of course, Mr. Mason, circumstances have put
you in rather a peculiar position. Am I to understand that you first
suspected the articles in question might have been concealed in
this stone urn because of entries in the diary of Helen Cadmus?"

"That's right."

"Those entries were in her handwriting?"

"Frankly, Counselor, I don't know."

"Of course, such entries wouldn't be evidence of anything,"
Hardwick said. "They couldn't be introduced in court. It's merely
something that Helen Cadmus has written. They could have been
self-serving declarations."

"In what way?" Mason asked.

"She *could* have taken these things herself and concealed them in
the urn and then gone to the trouble of making this entry in the
diary so that in the event she was ever involved in any way, she
could refer to the entry as supporting her statement that the
monkey had been concealing things here. Surely, Mason, you don't
need to have me point out to you that this would be a self-
serving declaration?"

Mason said, "I don't think I need to have you point out anything to me."

Hardwick turned to Nathan Fallon. "I think we had better go
into conference with Mr. Addicks at once."

"He told me to tell you he wouldn't see you," Fallon said ob-
stinately. "He's been hurt. Yesterday he was almost killed by a
gorilla that he'd been training. I saw the whole thing."

Hardwick frowned. "Well, Nathan, I think we won't need to detain Mr. Mason and Miss Street any longer. I take it they were just leaving."

"That's right."

"Good night," Hardwick said abruptly, shaking hands with Mason and bowing once more to Della Street.

Fallon said, "I'll telephone the gateman so that he'll let you out, Mr. Mason. I think it's only fair to warn you to keep driving at a steady pace right on down the driveway and through the gate. Don't stop and, above all, don't get out of the car. Good night."

"Good night," Mason said.

CHAPTER FIVE

PERRY MASON EASED HIS CAR THROUGH THE BIG IRON GATES. THE watchman stood suspiciously alert. The moment the car had passed through the stone portals, the heavy, wrought iron gates swung ponderously on their hinges, clanged shut, and an iron bar dropped into place.

Mason stepped on the throttle.

"Well, that's that," Della Street said.

"Quite a bit of action for one evening," Mason said.

"What do we do now?"

"We do several things," Mason told her. "One of the things is that we try to get hold of James Etna. Let's hope he's still up. There's a drugstore with a phone booth down here about half a mile, as I remember."

Mason put the car into speed.

"Did you notice the peculiar, musty odor in that house?" Della Street asked. "It was something that . . . I can't place it, and yet it gave me the creeps."

"The odor of a zoo," Mason said. "Animals are confined in cages."

"It makes goose pimples," she said, laughing.

"It's a creepy place," Mason told her. "I'd like to know a lot more about Benjamin Addicks, but, after all, it's no skin off our nose, Della. We'll do James Etna a good turn and let it go at that."

He drove to the drugstore. Della Street called James Etna's residence, talked for a minute, then nodded to Mason and said, "It's all right, they haven't gone to bed yet. I've talked with his wife. He just got in from the office."

She said into the transmitter, "This is Mr. Mason's secretary, Mr. Etna. Just hold on a moment, please."

She got up from the stool. Mason slid into position in the telephone booth, and said, "I'm sorry to bother you at this hour of the night, Etna, but there were some rather peculiar developments. As a matter of fact, Addicks' attorneys are going to be in touch with you trying to effect a compromise, and I thought that in view of your courtesies extended earlier in the evening I should let you know what happened."

"Addicks won't compromise," Etna said, his voice weary from the strain of his long night session at the office. "He's one of those obstinate chaps who will fight just as long as he has anything to fight with, and that's going to be a long time. He swears he has never paid out a nickel by way of compromising lawsuits yet, and he doesn't intend to."

"He'll pay out a nickel now," Mason told him. "As a matter of fact, Sidney Hardwick is probably going to call you within the next few minutes, or at least as soon as you open the office in the morning, and start talking compromise."

"What happened?"

"They found the platinum watch and the big diamond solitaire which Addicks thought Mrs. Kempton had stolen."

"The devil they did!" Etna exclaimed jubilantly over the telephone.

"That's right."

"Where were they and how did they happen to find them?"

"As a matter of fact," Mason said, "I found them."

"*You* did?"

"That's right. I was running through these Helen Cadmus diaries, and I noticed that she referred to a hiding place where one of the more mischievous monkeys had a habit of putting trinkets, particularly trinkets in which he thought Helen Cadmus was interested. So I went out to see Addicks at his suggestion, and told him I thought it would be a good plan to look in this hiding place."

"Where was it?"

"A stone urn in the hallway."

"Well, well, well!" Etna exclaimed. "That certainly puts a new face on the situation. As a matter of fact, Mason, that was what bothered me about the case. I couldn't be absolutely certain of my client. I thought she was honest, but, after all, the evidence in the case, that is, the evidence indicating that she might have taken the articles in question, was entirely in the control of the opposite side. You know how that is. They might have introduced any amount of circumstantial evidence which would have shown that Addicks had at least a reasonable ground for believing that she had taken the objects. Then I'd have been on the defensive all through the case."

"Of course," Mason pointed out, "there's another legal hurdle. As Hardwick tried to tell me, the situation is not exactly changed in its legal implications. The fact that the articles have been found doesn't affect his defense that it's a privileged communication, and . . ."

Etna laughed gleefully. "Let him try to pull all those technicalities," he said. "If I'm not on the defensive, I can smash through their defense. I'll reduce the case to its simplest form, Mason. A hard-working woman does her best to give satisfaction to a millionaire. The millionaire discharges her abruptly and without any reason. Thereafter he accuses her of dishonesty and blackens her reputation and prevents her from obtaining a livelihood because he claims she stole a very valuable diamond ring and a platinum watch. Then he finds the platinum watch and the diamond ring right there in his own house, where they had been all the time. My client is without funds, and hasn't been able to get work, and Addicks is a multimillionaire. Now you figure how that's going to look to a jury. I don't give a damn how many technicalities they raise now. They're hooked, and hooked good."

"Well, I thought I'd let you know," Mason said.

"Look here, Mason, that's mighty fine of you. Now, of course, I assume that you want to be associated in the case. I haven't as yet made definite arrangements in regard to a fee, but, of course, this information that you have given is . . ."

"Wait a minute," Mason told him, "don't get me wrong. I don't want to be associated in the case. I'm simply giving you this information as a matter of friendly accommodation."

"Well—well, what *do* you want?"

"Nothing," Mason said, "except that after the settlement has been completed I'd like to have Mrs. Josephine Kempton drop in at my office for a visit."

"A visit?"

"That's right," Mason said. "I'm interested in the strange death of Helen Cadmus, and the circumstances under which it happened. I'd like to know just a little something about the setup there."

"Mrs. Kempton will be in your office at any time you say," Etna told him.

"How about ten o'clock tomorrow morning?"

"She'll be there, and I'll be there with her. I want to shake hands and tell you how much I appreciate the information you've given me, Mr. Mason. Good night."

"Good night," Mason said.

CHAPTER SIX

DELLA STREET SAID, "OUR TEN O'CLOCK APPOINTMENT IS HERE, CHIEF."

Mason looked up from the papers on his desk. "Mrs. Kempton?"

"That's right. Mrs. Josephine Kempton, and her attorney, James Etna."

"How do they look to you, Della?"

"Mrs. Kempton is something of an enigma. She's spare, somewhere around fifty, and rather poker-faced I would say. You gather that life hasn't been kind to her, and she's had to adjust herself to take things philosophically."

"And Etna?"

"He's just a good, active, young lawyer. He's an admirer of yours and makes no secret of the fact that the chance to meet you is one of the big thrills of his life."

"Well, let's get them in," Mason said, "and see what they have to say."

Della Street went into the outer office and returned with the visitors.

James Etna, a man in the middle thirties, came rushing forward to grasp Mason's hand. "Mr. Mason, I can't begin to tell you how much this means to me. I want to tell you that I think what you did last night was one of the most splendid things, one of the finest things— I have found out a lot about it since I talked with you."

"Well, I'm glad I was able to be of some help," Mason said. "And I take it this is Mrs. Kempton."

Mrs. Kempton smiled, a tired, patient smile, extended her hand and said, "How do you do, Mr. Mason?"

"Do you know what happened?" Etna went on, bubbling with enthusiasm. "You hadn't any more than hung up your phone when Hardwick telephoned. He told me that he wanted to apologize for putting through a call at that hour, but that he was going to be busy in the morning and he felt that the information he had was important enough so that it would be of interest to me."

"Indeed," Mason said.

"That's right, and then he offered me five thousand dollars to settle the case—five thousand dollars."

"Did you take it?" Mason asked tonelessly, conscious of the presence of Etna's client.

"Do I look silly?" Etna said. "Yesterday afternoon I'd have settled the case for fifteen hundred dollars. In fact, I'd have settled the case if he'd promised not to write any more letters accusing my client of dishonesty, but last night, knowing what I knew, I wouldn't have accepted the first offer they made if it had been five hundred thousand dollars."

"Good boy," Mason said. "What happened after that?"

"Well, then there was a lot of hemming and hawing over the telephone, and he increased his offer to seventy-five hundred dollars."

"What did you do?"

"I refused."

"Then what?"

"Then he asked me point blank if I had heard from you."

"What did you tell him?"

"Told him the truth. I told him, yes, I'd heard from Mr. Mason, that Mr. Mason had promised me that if he found out anything that would be of interest in the case he'd let me know, that he had certainly found out something of interest and that he had let me know."

"So then what?"

"Then Hardwick said, 'Very well. I don't think Mr. Mason had any right interfering in this case. I think it was a matter that, to put it plainly, was none of his damn business, but in view of the circumstances and since he already has made this interference, and since my client desires to be fair, I am offering you twenty thousand dollars. That's our top limit, and that's all there is to it. Otherwise we'll sit tight on the fact that the communication was a privileged communication made in good faith.' "

"And what did you do?" Mason asked.

"I sank my teeth into that offer," Etna said. "I told him that we'd take it."

"Good boy," Mason said. "I have an idea that Hardwick was probably telling you the truth and that *was* their final offer."

"That's the way I figured it. Of course, there's a lot of law involved. There's the question of good faith, absence or presence of malice, a privileged communication, and all of that."

"But, as you pointed out last night, when you come right down to a showdown," Mason said, "when a multimillionaire, who is rolling in money and is able to indulge in all of his hobbies, proceeds to take it upon himself to persecute a working woman who is trying to make her way in the world—well, you know how a jury would have looked at it."

"I sure do, and what's more, so did Hardwick. I think I could have secured a bigger verdict out of a jury, but it might have been set aside and a new trial granted, and—well, we're satisfied with twenty thousand dollars, aren't we, Josephine?"

Mrs. Kempton smiled her patient, tired smile, but she was looking at Perry Mason rather than the lawyer. "Very, very much satisfied," she said.

"I thought I'd let you know," Etna said, "that I have charged Josephine five thousand dollars and she is keeping the fifteen thousand."

"That's fine," Mason said.

"And I want to pay *you* some of that fifteen thousand," Mrs.

Kempton said. "I feel that I should. If it hadn't been for you, Mr. Mason . . ."

Mason shook his head.

"But you did a lot of work in the case. You dug through those diaries and worked out a theory, and . . ."

"No, please sit down," Mason told her. "Let's get informal and friendly right away. I don't want a dime from either one of you. I'm glad that you were able to make a good settlement. I think your lawyer made a very fine settlement. I agree with Mr. Etna that while you might have recovered more from a jury, that once Addicks had been brought into court he'd have fought the thing all the way through to the highest court in the land. After all, the thing that bothered him more than anything else was being ridiculed in the press and placed in the position of a wealthy man who had tried to make it impossible for a working woman to make a living."

"That's the way I felt about it," Etna said.

"Now," Mason said, "you can do something for me, Mrs. Kempton."

"Anything in the world."

"I want to know something about Helen Cadmus."

"Well, she was a little—I don't know how to describe it."

"Go ahead, do the best you can. Do I gather that she was peculiar?"

"She'd had some terrific heartbreak in her life, I know that."

"How long did you work out there with her?"

"Somewhere around two years I guess it was."

"And your employment was terminated very shortly after she disappeared?"

"Two days later."

"Was there anything in the termination of your employment that had anything to do with Helen Cadmus or her disappearance?"

Mrs. Kempton shook her head. "He fired me for stealing."

"Think back," Mason said. "Let's try and get this thing straightened out. After all, it's rather a coincidence that . . ."

"No," she said. "Mr. Addicks was terribly upset about Helen. I think he was fond of Helen, and I think that . . ."

"Now wait a minute," Mason said, "you say he was fond of Helen. Do you think that there was anything . . . ?"

"Well—I don't know. There was the relationship of employer and employee, and then a friendship on top of that. I don't think—Benjamin Addicks isn't an emotional type."

"Well, let's talk about Helen first."

"Helen was very decorative and she knew it. She was very, very proud of her figure. She liked to be photographed and she liked to look at herself in the mirror. I know. There was a full-length mirror in her room, and several times I've noticed that she—well, she was proud of her figure."

"What about the mirror?" Mason said.

"She stood in front of it and looked at herself quite frequently."

"How do you know?"

"I'd open the door and come in and she'd be there."

"You mean that she was fond of clothes, that she was looking at herself in the mirror and the way she wore clothes?"

Mrs. Kempton smiled. "All the clothes she had on you could have covered with a postage stamp."

"Nude?" Mason asked.

"Not nude. Those bathing suits. She loved to take two or three squares of material and knot them around so that they'd make a cute, clever bathing suit. Of course, it wouldn't have stood any swimming, and it wouldn't have stood any great amount of wear and tear."

"Did she wear those on the yacht?"

"Occasionally."

"When there were mixed gatherings?"

"Well, people she knew. She wasn't—I'll put it this way, there wasn't anything modest about Helen. She was a frank sort of a girl, and I know that she loved to be out in the sunlight. She had a body that was one of the most beautiful bronzed bodies you've ever seen. She'd tanned herself until she was just, well, just a beautiful bronze."

"Except, of course, where the bathing suit came?" Mason asked.

"That was the thing that annoyed her more than anything else, having white streaks on her body. No, Mr. Mason, she had a sun-bathing place on the roof, and she would sunbathe in the nude. She wanted her body to have a uniform tan. I think she was even more proud of her tan than she was of her—well, of her curves. And her curves were all right and were all in the right places."

"Wouldn't it be unusual for a girl like that to have committed suicide?"

"Very unusual."

"Where were you when the suicide took place?"

"I was on the yacht."

"On that cruise?"

"Yes."

"I'd like to know something about that. What can you tell me?"

"I'll tell you all I can. Mr. Addicks wanted to go over to Catalina. He nearly always took Helen with him on his trips, and very often he took me."

"Who took care of the house while you were gone?"

"We had quite a staff of servants that came in by the day. I had over-all charge and supervision. I also had supervision of keeping things up on the yacht, and, believe me, that's a job, Mr. Mason. You can have all the sailors in the world to keep the thing ship-shape outside, but things on the inside, the staterooms and the—well, cleaning up, cleaning out the ash trays, getting rid of all the mess that they'd have in the big room after they'd been out on a cruise. Cigars and cigarette stubs, glasses, empty whisky bottles, all of that. It was quite a chore."

"Did anyone help you?"

"No. I handled that by myself. Of course, you understand that even a big yacht is more or less crowded, and there isn't room to carry a large staff of servants, particularly women servants. The men can bunk together up in the front of the boat, but with the women it's different. We had to have rooms of our own."

"All right, let's get back to what happened that day."

"Mr. Addicks wanted to go to Catalina. He telephoned down and had the yacht all ready. He expected that we'd take off about two o'clock in the afternoon, but he was delayed with some important business matters that came up, and we didn't get down there until about five o'clock. By that time one of those sudden, terrific wind-storms had come up. There was a storm warning out for small craft, but Mr. Addicks went out anyway."

"And then what happened?"

"Well, it was quite a storm. We finally had to heave to and just take it. We didn't get into Catalina until the next morning."

"Now how did you go down to the yacht? In automobiles?"

"Yes."

"You went down with Mr. Addicks?"

"Yes."

"And Helen went down with him?"

"No, she left about—oh, I don't know, about an hour before. She drove the sport convertible down and went aboard. She had some typing to do. That was what had caused the delay in the first place. Some business matter had come up, and Mr. Addicks dictated a lot of stuff to her. I believe there were some agreements and some confidential letters that went with them."

"Go on."

"Well, she went down to the yacht. Mr. Addicks stayed behind to gather up some more stuff, then he and I went down together."

"Were there any guests?"

"No. There were some people we were going to pick up in Catalina, but there was only the crew, Helen and me."

"When did you last see Helen?"

"That afternoon—now wait a minute, I didn't *see* her. On the way down Mr. Addicks decided there were some corrections he wanted to make in the letter or agreement, or whatever it was he'd given her, so as soon as we went aboard he went directly to her stateroom. He was dictating in there for—oh, I don't know, I guess half an hour."

"How do you know he was dictating?"

"Oh, I could hear him. Helen's stateroom was next to mine. We shared a bath between the rooms. I remember I went to the bathroom to wash up, and I heard Mr. Addicks dictating, and evidently he wasn't relying on shorthand but was dictating directly to the typewriter because I'd hear him dictating and could hear Helen pounding away on the typewriter."

"Then what happened?"

"There's an inner and an outer harbor. We started out, but it was terribly rough outside, so Mr. Addicks put in at the outer harbor, and we waited for the wind and sea to go down. They didn't go down.

"Mr. Addicks telephoned his friends in Catalina. Their time over there was limited. Mr. Addicks' yacht was a big seagoing affair that could sail around the world, so he decided to put out and go over at half speed."

"How long did he dictate?"

"I guess until it got too rough for Helen to type. It was terrible."

"You heard him dictating after you put out?"

"Oh yes."

"For how long?"

"I can't tell. I'm a poor sailor. I went to sleep."

"To sleep?" Mason asked.

"Yes. I have some stuff that I take when it's going to be rough, and it works pretty well, but it makes me terribly sleepy. I . . ."

"You didn't have any dinner that night?"

"Dinner? Heavens, no! I began to feel miserable and then the medicine took hold and I went to sleep and I don't think I woke up until around midnight. It was pretty bad then. I took some more medicine, and went to sleep, and about, oh, I don't know, about seven or eight o'clock in the morning I woke up and found it was calm. We were coming into the island then."

"And then what happened?"

"Well, it was shortly after that we discovered Helen was missing. Mr. Addicks went down to her stateroom and—well, I guess you know the rest. The bed hadn't been slept in."

"She could have been accidentally washed overboard?" Mason asked.

"She *could* have, yes."

"She could perhaps have been standing out on deck?"

"She *could* have, but it was rough and we were making heavy weather of it until we hove to. I was down in my room myself, but I talked with some of the sailors afterwards. I guess we were taking a bit of water over the decks. It can get terribly rough out there in the channel."

"All right," Mason said, "Helen kept a diary. You knew that?"
"Yes."

"Now then," Mason said, "I have four volumes of that diary. Volume number five is missing. Volume number five would have started in about two weeks prior to Helen's disappearance. That is, volume four ends exactly two weeks before her death. Do you think she gave up keeping her diary?"

"No, I'm sure she didn't. She had a brief case. She used to carry that diary with her all the time. I remember that I remonstrated with her a couple of times."

"Why? What was wrong with keeping a diary?"

"It's all right if a body just puts in a few things about where they are and what they're doing and things of that sort, but Helen just pored over her diary, she put in hours on it. Hours when she should have been out with other people."

"That's the point," Mason said, "that's what I want to know about. What friends did she have?"

"Mr. Mason, I don't think she had any."

"Then what was the idea of keeping herself so beautiful, and getting that beautiful sun tan?"

"She was ambitious. She wanted to go to Hollywood and become an actress, and she thought that sooner or later there would be an opportunity through some of the connections she would make through Mr. Addicks."

"Was Addicks friendly with the Hollywood crowd?"

"No, that's the trouble. He wasn't. He was in a position where he could have been, but Mr. Addicks—I don't like to talk about a former employer, Mr. Mason, but Mr. Addicks is very, very unsocial. I think his life became dominated by—well, I suppose you know about his brother."

"What about him?"

"He committed a murder."

"Where?"

"In some foreign country. I think it was Australia."

"And was executed?"

"I presume he was. All I know is that he committed murder and that Mr. Addicks was very, very much attached to his brother, and apparently Mr. Addicks has . . . well, if you ask me, I think Mr. Addicks is afraid."

"Afraid of what?"

"Afraid of himself. Afraid that there's some sort of a curse in the family, some kind of a homicidal complex that he has—the same thing that his brother had. I think he's trying to find out something about that."

"And so he experiments with monkeys and apes."

"Mostly gorillas. He says gorillas are the closest to man in their psychological reasoning; that chimpanzees are friendly and all of that, but he is interested in the lowland gorilla."

"And they're kept in cages?"

"That's right. Of course, you have to have very strong cages for them because . . ."

"And there's a trainer?"

"There are several trainers, and one psychologist who . . ."

"Where do all those people live?" Mason asked. "Who does their housekeeping? Who cooks for them?"

"They live in their homes. They work in a completely separate house that faces the back street. They come and go as they please. They're not permitted to have the run of the grounds at all. They can come to the main house through a corridor, but only if they're sent for."

"Who takes care of the gorillas at night?"

"No one. They're caged in strong, heavily barred cages."

"What would happen if there'd be a fire at night?"

"That'd be just too bad. If you want to bring that up, what would happen if there was a fire in the daytime? You can't just open a cage of a gorilla and say, 'Come on out.'"

Mason thought that over.

"Those gorillas are mean?"

"I guess so. I only petted one of the smaller ones. He loves me. Some like people, some don't. Some of the experiments were for the purpose of confusing them. They'd be trained to take food from a box when a bell rang. At other times they'd get an electric shock when they tried it. Then the trainers would change the signals all around—something about a confused orientation they called it. I didn't like it. Neither did Helen."

"Well," Mason said, "I couldn't help but be interested on account of the diary. Thanks a lot."

Mrs. Kempton said, "Helen kept herself to herself, Mr. Mason. She had a consuming, driving ambition. She was willing to sacrifice everything to that, and, of course, somewhere in the back of her life there was an unfortunate love affair."

"Did she tell you about that?"

"Good heavens, no. She didn't need to. You could see as plain as day what she was doing."

"What was she doing?"

"She'd evidently been jilted by someone who—well, sometimes I had the idea it was someone who fancied that he was a little bit above her in life, a little bit superior to her. Helen seemed to have dedicated her whole life to showing him that she could make a success, and the only thing that she had that she could make an outstanding success of was—well, something like pictures. She was really beautiful."

"So I gather," Mason said. "I have some photographs of her. Who took them, do you know?"

"Mr. Addicks, I suppose. He was always snapping people with a camera, and on the whole he took some pretty good pictures."

"He had a camera on the yacht?"

"He had cameras on the yacht, he had cameras in the house, he had cameras everywhere. He had a whole bunch of cameras of different sorts."

"All this about Helen's love affair, how did you get this information?"

"By putting two and two together. She was a good looking, normal girl, but she didn't seem eager to go out. She worked, she wrote in her diary, she took sunbaths. She even had a quartz light for the cloudy, rainy days."

"That was her whole life?"

"That and her work. Of course, she had no real office hours. She was on call whenever anything turned up, and she went with Mr. Addicks, of course, whenever he went anywhere."

"Was that frequent?"

"Oh yes. He had lots of irons in the fire. There'd be a phone call on some mining deal or other and he'd be running around, throwing things into a car, and then he'd be off—sometimes with Hershey, sometimes with Fallon, sometimes just by himself—with Helen, of course. She went on all of his trips."

"There's one more question before you go. Do you feel that there was anything really strange about Helen's death?"

"Of course there was."

"I mean, do you feel that she didn't commit suicide?"

"That she could have been washed overboard accidentally?"

"I'm asking you," Mason said.

She said, "Mr. Mason, I'm never going to say anything that would make it difficult for anyone. I know all too well how rumors can get started and how much they can do to ruin a person's whole career, but—well, if I'd been the police I wouldn't have quit that easy."

"And why not?"

"Because—well, I know, I just absolutely know Helen didn't commit suicide, and I know that somebody took her diary and threw it overboard."

"How do you know that?"

"Because her diary was missing, and I know that she would have kept it with her."

"How do you know it was missing?"

"I had the job of going through Helen's room afterwards and tidying it up and getting the things together for the public administrator. He went in there with me and we went through everything. He put all of her clothes and personal things in one box, and all of her books in another."

"She left no relatives?"

"No one could find out a thing in the world about her, where she came from or anything."

"Nathan Fallon claims that he's a distant relative," Mason said.

"Nathan Fallon does?" she asked in incredulous surprise.

Mason nodded.

"She hated the ground he walked on. He was no more related to her than—than he was to those apes out in the cages."

"You don't think she had perhaps known him before she got the position and . . . ?"

"You mean that she owed her position to him?"

"In a way, yes."

"Good heavens, no. She hated Nathan Fallon."

"How do you feel about him?"

"I don't like to hate people."

"But you don't like him?"

"Definitely not."

"Did Fallon try to be attentive to . . . ?"

"Try to be attentive to her? Of course he did. He couldn't keep his hands off of her at first—and then she slapped him into his place. He's one of those men who go around pawing and slapping and nudging, and letting his hand rest on your arm, then on your shoulder, and then he'll start patting you on the knee. When he has a chance he'll slip an arm around you, but it's never still. He's —the man is just unclean somehow. You want to spit in his face."

"Well, I think that gives me all the information I wanted," Mason said. "I was primarily interested in finding out about the missing diary."

"Well, I—I've done a lot of wondering about that myself. She *could* have taken it with her when she went overboard."

"Anything else you've been wondering about?"

"Yes."

"Such as what?"

"Well," she said, "that important document that she was doing for Mr. Addicks. I've often wondered about that, and about what happened to it."

"What do you mean?"

"It wasn't in her stateroom, and I don't think Addicks took it with him when he left her stateroom. Of course he could have, but I doubt it. I think she was supposed to have finished the typing the next morning. They called off work when the storm got bad."

"Well, let's suppose her death wasn't suicide, and let's suppose it wasn't accidental," Mason said.

She looked at him steadily. "That leaves murder."

"That leaves murder."

Her face remained absolutely expressionless. Her lips were clamped together.

"You're not saying anything," Mason told her.

"And I'm not going to say anything."

Mason got to his feet and shook hands with her. "Well, I'm glad to have been of some service, and I'm glad you made your compromise, Mrs. Kempton."

James Etna grabbed Mason's hand and pumped his arm up and down. "I can't ever thank you enough both on behalf of my client and for myself. I—well, I just can't begin to tell you how much it has meant to both of us."

"Quite all right," Mason said. "I was glad to do it for you."

"Well, you've certainly been nice."

"By the way," Mrs. Kempton said, "I missed some things out there myself. Would you mind telling me what was found in that collection of stuff in the urn, if you know? Was there a pearl earring that matches this?"

She held out an earring and Della Street nodded emphatically.

"There was the mate to that earring," she said. "I remember noticing it particularly, and noticing the way the pearls were put together in a little cluster."

"Oh, thank you," Mrs. Kempton said. "I'm so glad! My mother had those earrings and—well, I felt terrible when one of them was missing. I . . ."

"Did you report that it was missing?" Mason asked.

"No."

"Why?"

"Well, I thought—I don't know. Live and let live is my motto, and I didn't want to do anything that was going to upset things."

"You thought you had lost it?"

"I knew I hadn't lost it, because they had both of them been in my jewel case, and when I went to put them on just one of them was left."

"So you thought someone had taken it?"

"Well, I—I didn't know."

"And you didn't say anything?"

"No."

"Well," Mason said, "it was in the bunch of stuff that was there in the urn. I remember seeing a pearl earring, and Miss Street seems quite positive it's the mate to that one."

"I *am* positive," Della said.

"Thank you so much," Mrs. Kempton said, and gave them the benefit of her patient, quiet smile.

James Etna looked as though he wanted to shake hands all over again. "This is one of the most interesting experiences I've ever had, Mr. Mason. I've been looking forward to meeting you, and to think that you would help me out in a case of this sort—it means a lot, Mr. Mason. I appreciate it."

"Glad to do whatever I could," Mason said.

They left the office. Della Street looked at Perry Mason.

"Well?" she asked.

"This little playmate of ours," Mason told her.

"You mean Fate?"

Mason nodded.

"What's Fate doing now?"

"I think," he said, "that there was some reason why I was attracted to those diaries of Helen Cadmus."

"All right," she said, "Fate wanted you to do Mrs. Josephine Kempton a good turn, and you've done it. If you ask me, I'll bet that five thousand dollar fee meant a lot to that young lawyer."

"Probably so," Mason said, "but I still don't think we have the answer."

"I don't see why not. You've cleared everything up and—oh, I see, you're thinking about the disappearance of Helen Cadmus?"

"I'm thinking about the disappearance of Helen Cadmus."

"You don't think it was suicide?"

Mason said, "I can't get over a feeling in the back of my mind that it could have been murder."

"Good heavens, Chief, there's only one person who could have murdered her, and that was Benjamin Addicks."

"Or her friend Nathan Fallon," Mason said. "Don't forget him."

"And," Della Street said, and paused.

"Yes," Mason said, smiling, "go ahead."

Della Street shook her head.

Mason's smile broadened.

"Oh, all right," she said. "I hate myself for even entertaining the thought, but if you're starting to figure out a murder case—well, you can't overlook the woman who had the adjoining stateroom, who had an opportunity to enter Helen's stateroom at any time by going through the bathroom, who said she had taken medicine that had drugged her all night—good Lord, Chief, what a horrid, nasty mind I'm getting, working for a cynical lawyer!"

"What a fine, logical mind you're getting," Mason corrected.

"Chief! You don't suspect her?"

"In a murder case," Mason said, "one suspects everyone."

"But you don't know it's a murder case."

"No," Mason said, "and sometimes I wonder if I wasn't supposed to find out. I wonder somehow if people don't leave behind them a sort of telepathic thought that can attach itself to someone's mind."

"Or if you're a spiritist," Della Street said, "you can think that perhaps Helen Cadmus, knowing your ability to ferret out the truth in a case, had been giving you a sub-conscious urge, perhaps . . ."

"Quit it," Mason said, grinning, "or I'll be going to see a medium."

"Well," Della Street said seriously, "under the circumstances, it would be interesting to see what a medium would say."

"I think a good deal of that is mental telepathy," Mason said. "She might read my mind and confuse the issues."

"She couldn't confuse them any more than you've confused me," Della Street said. "You've given me the creeps. There's something about that . . . well, I don't know, now that you mention it, there's something about that woman."

"You mean Mrs. Kempton?"

"Yes."

"Rather a peculiar type," Mason said, "but not an unusual type. You see them quite frequently, particularly persons who are house-keepers. Those are the people who, because of death, divorce or some other reason, have lost their own homes and yet are interested in making a home. So they hire out to make a home for someone else, and in doing it . . . well, naturally they have to repress a lot of their own feelings, so you get that general atmosphere of re-pression and . . ."

Della Street shivered. "I wish I hadn't thought of it. I'm getting a prickly, cold feeling all the way up my spine.

"All right, let's quit thinking of it," Mason said, "and go to work."

CHAPTER SEVEN

MASON AND DELLA STREET, WORKING LATE IN THE OFFICE THAT NIGHT, were interrupted by the constant buzzing of the switchboard in the outer office.

"I thought we'd shut that off," Mason said.

"It still buzzes," she said. "You can hear it."

"Someone certainly is optimistic," Mason said. "That board's been buzzing away at intervals for the last five minutes. Go see who it is, Della."

"I don't know who could possibly think you'd be at the office at this time of night."

"Well, you remember what happened with James Etna. We took a chance and—see who it is, Della."

Della plugged into the switchboard, said, "Hello," frowned, said, "Yes . . . Who? . . . Oh yes, Mrs. Kempton."

She motioned to catch the attention of Perry Mason and pointed to the telephone.

Mason gently picked up the receiver from his telephone so he could listen in on the conversation.

Mrs. Kempton's voice, coming over the line, sounded almost hysterical. "I can't get Mr. Etna. I'm in a terrible situation! I don't know what to do. I have to see someone. I want—oh, I want Mr. Mason *so* desperately! I've tried and tried and tried and someone must help me. I don't know what's happening here. I'm in an awful predicament."

"Where are you?" Della Street asked.

"I'm out at Stonehenge. Out at Benjamin Addicks' place, and something terrible has happened."

"You're where?"

"At Stonehenge. At Mr. Addicks' place."

Mason cut in on the conversation.

"This is Perry Mason, Mrs. Kempton. Now can you tell me what the trouble is?"

"Not over the telephone, Mr. Mason. It's terrible. I need help."

"I suggest you call the police, Mrs. Kempton."

"No, no, no, not the police. Not until I've seen a lawyer. I simply have to see a lawyer. I tried to get Mr. Etna so that he could get you. You're the one I want. Mr. Mason, I have money to pay you with, thanks to you. I simply *must* see you."

"You can't leave there?"

"I don't want—there's something here that—that's what I want to see you about. I need your advice."

"How did you happen to go out there?"

"Mr. Mason, please! I can't explain over the telephone. Oh, if you could *only* come out here. *Please* come out, Mr. Mason. I can assure you it's the most important thing I ever asked of anybody in my whole life. I'm going absolutely crazy."

"All right," Mason said. "I'll come out. Now where's Mr. Addicks?"

"Mr. Mason," she said, ignoring the question, "please do exactly as I say. The front entrance of the house is on Olive Street. There's a barred gate and a watchman there, but there's a back entrance on Rose Street that is used by the people who work with the animals. That entrance doesn't have a watchman. There's a locked door. I'm going to try to be at that door. It'll take you about fifteen minutes to get out here, Mr. Mason. Please hurry just as fast as you can. Can you start now?"

"I'll start now," Mason said. "You meet me at the back door. That's on Rose Street, as I understand."

"On Rose Street, exactly opposite the place on Olive Street where the big iron gates are located. It's just a plain looking structure like a garage. The door has the number 546 on it. That's all there is. Just that door with the number 546, and it's on Rose Street. You go there and turn the knob of the door. I'll be there, waiting—if I can make it and if you hurry."

"Is there any reason why you might not be able to make it?" Mason asked.

"Yes," she said, and abruptly hung up.

Mason clicked the receiver a couple of times, then glanced at Della Street, who had left the other telephone to come and stand beside him.

"Think she was cut off, Della?"

"I think she hung up, Chief."

"Well," Mason said, "evidently the situation out there has come to a head."

"But, Chief, what in the world would she be doing out there? She's made a settlement with Addicks."

"She may have been trying to blackmail him for the murder of Helen Cadmus," Mason said. "You know, she's rather a peculiar individual. She certainly was listening intently to everything we said about Helen Cadmus and her diaries."

"Well," Della Street said, "let's go. We can talk it over on the road and . . ."

"Where do you get that 'we' stuff?" Mason asked. "This may be a little rugged, Della."

"Don't think you're going to leave me behind now," she said. "I'm a rugged girl. Come on, let's go."

She flew around the office, switching out lights, grabbed her hat, thrust it on her head, handed Mason his hat, and jerked open the exit door.

"I'll run down the hall and get the elevator up here," she said, and flashed past Mason to run on tiptoes down the long, echoing corridor of the building.

By the time Perry Mason had arrived at the elevator, Della Street had the cage waiting at the floor.

"Good girl," Mason said.

The night janitor, on duty at the elevator, said, "You folks look as though you're going some place in a hurry."

"We are," Mason told him.

The janitor dropped the cage to the ground floor while Mason was scrawling his signature in the book, showing the time of departure from his office.

They ran across to the parking place, jumped into Mason's car, and Mason gunned the motor into life, waved at the parking attendant, and tore out through the back of the parking lot into the alley so fast the tires sent up a squeal of protest.

Mason slowed the car just enough to keep it under control as he came to the end of the alley, made an abrupt right turn into the street and pressed the accelerator almost to the floor board.

He slipped through the first intersection on an amber light, just skimmed a red signal at the next.

"If we should have to stop and do a lot of explaining to a traffic officer," Della Street said, "it's going to delay us."

"I know," Mason told her, "but I have a hunch this is really urgent."

"And," Della Street pointed out, "if we don't get there in one piece, we might as well not have started."

"That also is true," Mason said dryly.

"Chief, are you going to go at this thing blind?"

"What do you mean?"

"Just take her as a client in case she's—well, you know what I mean?"

"In case we find a body out there?" Mason said.

"Yes."

"I don't know," Mason told her. "There's something peculiar about Josephine Kempton. I don't know what it is. You have the impression all the time you're talking with her that she's very much interested in finding out what you're thinking, but that she has no intention of letting you know what she's thinking. It's like playing stud poker. You have the feeling that she has a pretty good idea of what your hole card is, but you don't know anything about hers, and somehow you have the uneasy feeling that it may be an ace."

"She could get you into trouble in case you became impulsive."

"I know," Mason admitted. "That's why I want to size up the situation before I decide what to do. There's something about this case, Della, the whole thing, that has aroused my curiosity."

"For your information," she told him dryly, "that was a boulevard stop back there."

"I know," Mason said, "but I didn't see any cars coming, and I saw no reason to comply with an empty legal formality."

Della Street settled back in the cushions of the car, placed a neatly shod foot against the dash so as to brace herself against sudden stops, and said, "I think probably that last remark is a very complete index to your character."

As they approached Stonehenge Mason said, "I'm just going to take a quick swing around the front of the house, Della."

"The watchman will see you."

"I'm not going to stop in the parking place. I'm just going to drive by long enough to give it a once-over and see what the front of the house looks like."

"You can't see it from the road, can you?"

"I think we can get glimpses of it."

The lawyer drove his car down Olive Street, slowed slightly as he came to the parking place by the side of the road and the two massive square stone columns.

The heavy iron gates were closed.

"I don't see anything of the watchman," Della Street said.

"If I stopped the car I have an idea he'd pop into sight," Mason said, driving rapidly to the intersection and turning to the right.

Halfway down the side street there was a place where it was possible to get an unobstructed view of the entire north gable of the house.

"The place is lit up like a church," Della Street said.

Mason slowed the car to a stop.

"A ten foot, heavy-meshed fence all around the place," he said. "It breaks into a Y at the top, with barbed wire on both sides of the Y. That means there's an overhang so you can't climb in or climb out. Mr. Addicks certainly does value his privacy."

"Doesn't he—Chief, look! Look up there!"

"Where?"

"That upper window in the gable. See the man—he's pushing his way out of the window and . . ."

"That's not a man," Mason said. "That's a gorilla."

They sat in spellbound silence while the oblong of light framed the massive body of the huge gorilla. The animal stretched forth a long, groping arm, then made a leap for the branches of a shade tree. A moment later he was slithering down the shade tree, and, within a matter of seconds after that, floodlights blazed on all over the yard, sirens began to scream a warning, and the barking of dogs reached a crescendo of excitement.

"*Now* what?" Della Street asked.

"Evidently our gorilla slid down to the ground," Mason said, "and crossed a beam of invisible light. He's set in motion an electrical apparatus which turns on floodlights all over the place, starts sirens going and releases the police dogs. Now we'll see what's going to happen."

He sat watching for a second or two, then suddenly put the car into gear.

Della looked at him in surprise. "Chief, you're not going to try to get to the house now?"

He nodded.

"Hadn't we better wait and see what developments are?"

"Perhaps we'd better get there before some of these developments take place," Mason said.

He spun the car into Rose Street.

The high, wire fence, with the barbed-wire Y at the top, angled back from the road, leaving a cemented parking place in front of a row of garages. A two-story building sat back some twenty feet from the road, leaving ample space for parking and turning automobiles.

On the door of this two-story building the numbers 546 were plainly legible.

Mason stopped the car in front of the door, jumped out and pushed his finger against a bell button.

He could hear the sound of an electric bell in the interior, but waited in vain for any indication that anyone had heard the summons.

"Chief," Della Street said apprehensively, "she said she'd meet us here. If she doesn't—well, that's all there is to it. We can call the police, or . . ."

Mason shook his head and pressed the bell button again. "Something's happened," he said, "something that upset her plans. At least one of those big gorillas is loose."

"Chief, they could tear you in two. The way that big animal loomed against the oblong of light and then jumped out into space to grab the tree limb . . ."

She broke off, shuddering.

"I know," Mason said. "It gives you the creeps, but there's something definitely wrong here. Mrs. Kempton had real panic in her voice."

"Well, apparently no one's going to answer the bell. She must have gone somewhere."

Mason tried the door.

"It's unlocked," he said.

"Chief, don't."

"You wait in the car," Mason told her. "If I'm not back here in five minutes, drive to the nearest telephone and notify the police."

"No, no. I'm going in with you. I . . ."

"You wait in the car," Mason told her. "You have five minutes . . ."

"Chief, I'm going in there with you."

"You can't help any. You can't do a thing."

"Perhaps not, but it would be a lot better than sitting out here in the car wait . . ."

"No," Mason interrupted. "*You're* going to wait in the car. At the end of five minutes call the police. If I'm not out in five minutes don't wait for me, don't hesitate. Just drive that car to the nearest telephone and get the police."

"If you're not back in five minutes it wouldn't do any good to call the Army," she said. "You know it and I know it."

"You wait in the car," Mason told her.

"You're just trying to keep me out of danger," she protested.

"That's an order," Mason told her, and, opening the door, he went inside, slamming it shut behind him. There was a bolt on the inside of the door and he slid it into place, just in case Della Street should decide to ignore his instructions and try to follow him.

Here the peculiar, fetid smell of animal occupancy was accentuated. It was as though he had stepped into a zoo.

He walked down a short corridor toward an open door and entered an office equipped with desks, filing cabinets and typewriters. There were a dozen or so graphs on the wall.

Mason crossed this office, opened a door and found himself in a long, concrete corridor, on one side of which was a long row of cages.

In these cages were gorillas, chimpanzees, monkeys, all apparently in a state of great excitement.

Every light in the place seemed to be on and the whole corridor was flooded with brilliance.

Far down at the end of the corridor he saw that two of the big iron gates were swung open.

Hesitating for a long instant, he then walked down the corridor, keeping his steps as uniform as possible, his eyes straight ahead, trying above all else not to show any fear.

Monkeys chattered at him in shrill excitement. A gorilla clapped his hands as the lawyer walked by. The explosive sound was like that of a machine gun ripping into action.

With effort, Mason continued to walk steadily, controlling every outward manifestation of his nerves.

He was directly abreast of a big cage with heavy iron bars across the door, when, with a demoniacal cry, a huge gorilla that had been at the far corner of the cage sprang toward him, hurling against the bars of the cage with an impact which made even the floor shake. A moment later a long, hairy arm came snaking through the bars, trying to grab the lawyer.

He jumped back. The stubby fingers of the huge gorilla scraped down his coat, tried for a hold and failed.

He flattened against the wall. The huge animal glared at him ferociously, and then, suddenly dropping from the bars of the cage, bared his fangs and began to beat a tattoo on his chest.

Pressing against the wall, Mason edged his way on past.

The big gorilla made another grab. This time his hand was inches short of reaching Mason's garment.

Then apparently the gorilla started laughing. Mason stared in fascination at the black body, the black face, the sardonic eyes, and the huge red mouth that opened up, baring fangs in a great engulf-ing grin.

Mason said, "Old boy, I don't know whether you're playing games with me and tried to frighten me, or whether you wanted to grab me and tear me into my component parts, but I'm just not taking any chances."

The gorilla continued to beat his chest.

Beyond this cage was a cage containing an animal which Mason took to be a chimpanzee, then a cage of monkeys, and then the two empty cages with swinging doors that were wide open.

He had the uneasy feeling that it had been only a few moments earlier that the huge animals had made their escape, and in all probability had entered the main house through the door which Mason could see swinging ajar at the end of the corridor.

He looked at his watch. It had been but a little over a minute since he had left Della Street at the door.

Mason pushed back the door. As he had surmised, this door led directly into the main house, with its rich deep carpets on the floor, a crystal chandelier hanging from the ceiling, a flight of winding stairs leading up to a second floor.

Mason hesitated, debated whether to turn back.

"Hello!" he called.

Even to his own ears his voice seemed to lack assurance.

Suddenly from the second floor came a terrific pounding, a se-ries of blows struck with indescribable rapidity, a pounding that seemed to shake the entire house.

Mason called out, "Mrs. Kempton, are you all right?"

The pounding ceased.

"Mrs. Kempton!" he called. "Oh, Mrs. Kempton!"

Again the pounding was renewed, this time seeming to be closer, nearer to the head of the stairs.

He ran up the stairs two at a time.

The stairs led to an upper corridor. Looking down this corridor, Mason learned the cause of the noise. A big gorilla was hanging onto the top edge of an open door, his long left arm extended. His two feet and the other hand were beating a violent tattoo on the floor of the hallway.

As he saw Mason, the gorilla released his hold on the door,

ceased pounding and came running toward the lawyer with a peculiar shambling gait.

Mason stood stock-still.

The gorilla continued to advance.

Mason looked apprehensively back over his shoulder, realized
that before he could get halfway down the staircase the gorilla
would overtake him.

Mason stretched forth his arm, holding up his hand with the palm
outward.

The gorilla came to a stop, stood upright, beat his chest rapidly
with both hands until the whole hallway reverberated with hollow,
drumlike sounds.

Mason took a slow step backwards, groping behind him with his
hand for the edge of the iron balustrade.

The gorilla abruptly ceased to beat his chest, watched Mason as
a cat might watch a mouse.

The lawyer's groping hand encountered not the iron balustrade
but the knob of a door. He twisted the knob. The door, which was
unlocked, opened inward. He slipped through the door, abruptly
closed it, and, searching frantically for a lock, found a heavy bolt
which he shot into place.

There was complete, utter silence from the hallway.

Mason found that he was in a big room equipped as a combined
bedroom and office. Behind a screen he could see the foot of a bed
and on the bed he was able to glimpse a man's foot.

There was a big desk, a couple of filing cases, a round cannon
ball safe, shelves containing books, paintings on the walls, some
framed photographs, and half a dozen large chairs.

Mason started around the big desk, and as he did so stopped
short as he saw the body of a woman crumpled on the floor, lying
slightly on one side, her head bent backwards, her left hand
clenched, her right hand on the carpet with the fingers extended.

Light shining down on the woman's face left no doubt of her
identity. It was Mrs. Kempton.

Mason ran around the screen to the bed.

A man lay face down on the bed, sprawled out.

The handle of a big carving knife protruded from his back. The
knife had been driven in to the hilt, and blood had spread out

over the bedspread, blood had spurted up onto the wall, and, as Mason looked closer, he saw another jagged wound on the side of the man's neck.

There was no need to take the man's pulse. He was obviously dead.

Mason turned back toward the place where Mrs. Kempton was lying.

As he did so the whole room rocked under the impact of a terrific weight which was hurled against the door.

Then, for a moment, there was silence. A framed painting on the corridor wall, which had been pushed out by the impact, thudded back into place.

There was a half-second of silence, and then suddenly the impact against the door was renewed. This time the door crashed from its hinges and exploded inward into the room.

Standing in the doorway, glowering at Mason was the big gorilla the lawyer had seen at the end of the corridor.

Mason tried using his voice. "Just a minute, boy," he said. "Steady. Take it easy now."

The gorilla stood perfectly motionless, looking directly at Mason. The bulk of the big desk prevented the animal from seeing Mrs. Kempton sprawled on the floor, just as it had prevented Mason from seeing her.

It was a tense moment. Mason could hear the pounding of his own heart, could see the gorilla watching him with keen eyes that took in every move, every detail of Mason's appearance.

"Take it easy, boy," Mason said.

The gorilla moved forward, putting one of its feet on the smashed, splintered doorway, then abruptly withdrawing it as though thinking better of it. The animal's long arms were thrust forward, the knuckles of the left forearm resting lightly on the splintered doorway, the right arm clinging to the wrecked door-jamb.

Mason tried to hold the animal with his eyes.

For a long moment neither moved.

Mason started talking, striving to keep his voice natural. "I don't know what the devil to say to you under the circumstances," Mason said, addressing the gorilla. "I don't know what I'm supposed to do. I have an idea that if I advance I'm going to get killed, and if I retreat I'm sure I'll get killed. If I stand here without doing anything, I'm simply building up a tension and . . ."

Abruptly Mason became conscious of Mrs. Kempton's voice from the floor, a voice that was weak but edged with urgency.

"Don't look at him, Mr. Mason," she warned. "Crouch down on the floor and start doing something, anything. Take some coins from your pocket, a knife, a watch, anything that glitters. Start arranging them in patterns."

Mason, with his eyes still on the gorilla, said over his shoulder, "Are you all right? I was afraid you . . ."

"Never mind about me, do as I say. Hurry!"

Mason heard Mrs. Kempton stir behind him, struggling to a sitting position.

Mason had some loose coins in his right-hand trouser pocket. He pulled them out and started arranging them in a haphazard design on the floor, bending over the coins in complete concentration.

After a moment Mason was conscious that the gorilla had moved another step forward, sensed that the animal was peering down at the coins Mason was arranging with such careful precision.

Mrs. Kempton managed to get to a sitting position, then to her knees. "Haven't you something else?" she asked. "A gold pencil, a watch? Anything."

Mason unbuckled his wrist watch, placed it on the floor in the center of the circle of coins, noticing as he did so that it was now exactly five and one half minutes since he had left Della Street at the doorway. If she had followed instructions she should now be headed for a telephone, calling the police.

"Now then," Mrs. Kempton said, "back away slowly, keeping your eyes on the coins. Don't look at the gorilla. Back away. Back away slowly. When you do that he'll come forward and try to find out what you were doing. He'll be curious. He'll start playing with the objects you've left on the floor—I hope."

Mason straightened to his feet.

"Don't look at the gorilla," she warned.

Mason continued to stare down at the assortment of coins, the gold-plated pencil, and the wrist watch on the floor.

"Keep backing away," she said. "Back away slowly over toward me."

Mason followed instructions.

He felt her hand on his arm, felt her weight for a moment as she used his arm as support to pull herself to her feet.

The gorilla, his eyes fastened on the assortment of objects on the floor, moved forward and bent down over the coins just as Mason had done.

"Quick," she said, "but don't run. Walk quietly, firmly, and with a great deal of assurance. Leave him there with that problem to puzzle over. Come quickly."

Mason said, "What's happened? What . . . ?"

"I don't know. Let's get out of here first. Our lives are in danger. That gorilla is dangerous. If he ever thinks we're afraid of him, if he ever thinks we're running away from him—oh, please, come!"

"There's a dead man on the bed," Mason said.

"I know," she told him. "Benjamin Addicks. He's been stabbed."

"Who stabbed him?"

"Don't talk now. Just follow me, please."

She led the way around the bed to a bathroom. "In here, quick."

She closed and locked that door, opened a door at the other end of the bathroom which opened on a communicating bedroom.

"Hurry," she said.

She was running now, leading the way.

Mason kept pace with her.

"Will that gorilla . . . ?"

"Heaven knows what that gorilla will do," she said. "You can't tell what's going to happen. Gorillas are unpredictable anyway, and these animals have been subjected to psychiatric experiments. They're nervously unstable."

"What in the world are *you* doing here?"

"I'll tell you later on."

She had crossed the room now and stood listening at a door. She opened this door, put her head out, glanced quickly from side to side, said in a whisper, "I think the coast is clear. We're going to have to cross this corridor and go down the stairs to the front reception room—I think you'd better take off your shoes."

Mason slipped his shoes off and was aware that Mrs. Kempton also had removed her shoes while she was talking.

"We'll run," she said, "but we don't want them to know we're running. If they hear the sound of running feet, if there's any sign of panic—it's going to be too bad."

She stepped out into the corridor. Mason was at her side. Together they reached the winding staircase which led down to the reception hallway where Mason had been given his first glimpse of the interior of the house.

Abruptly Mason realized that for some time now he had been conscious of a background of noise, which now resolved itself into the steady wailing of sirens, an almost hysterical barking of police dogs. Suddenly the barking rose to a crescendo, and then abruptly ceased in a chorus of yelps, the sound being similar to that made by a dog that has been hit a glancing blow by an automobile.

"What's that?" Mason asked.

"I tell you I don't know," she said. "We've got to get out of here! We've *got* to get out of here!"

She led the way down the stairs, across the reception corridor. Mason moved toward the front door.

"No, no, not that way," she said.

She crossed through another room, through a dining room, a serving pantry, a kitchen, said, "We've got to take a chance on this. This is a doorway that leads to the zoo. Heaven knows whether any of those animals are back."

She opened the door.

Mason stepped past her into the corridor, saw that the doors on the vacant cages were still swung open. Apparently no animals were loose in the corridor.

"Come on," Mason said, and led the way at a run.

"Watch out for that gorilla," she warned.

They paused to put on their shoes. Mason veered over so that he was brushing against the wall.

Once more, as he passed the cage, the gorilla flung himself in a savage leap that was arrested by the bars of the cage.

Even the walls of the corridor shook at the impact of that body as it hurtled against the door.

Mason looked back over his shoulder to see that Mrs. Kempton was keeping against the wall.

The gorilla's long, hairy arms shot through the bars in the cage, groped in savage fury, missed them by a matter of inches.

Out in the yard the dogs began barking as though they had something treed. The sirens were sounding a continual scream of noise.

Mason opened the door, looked out, said, "Let's make a run for it."

They emerged on Rose Street. The night air seemed pure and sweet in their nostrils in contrast to the animal odors of the corridor with its closely packed cages.

Behind them was the blaze of light from the battery of floodlights which now illuminated every inch of the grounds. One of the dogs yelped in pain, then there was another round of excited barking.

Mason surveyed the street. Since he had left his wrist watch for the gorilla to play with he had no means of knowing how long it had been since Della had gone for the police.

"We may run into someone," he said, "so let's try to act like passers-by who have been attracted by the commotion. We'll walk rapidly, but try not to run.

"Now, tell me what happened."

"Well," she said, "it's a long story. There's one matter on which I need the help of a lawyer at once, and . . ."

"Who killed Addicks?" Mason interrupted impatiently.

She quickened her pace.

"Hold it," Mason ordered. "Who killed . . . ?"

He broke off as a police car swung around the corner, two red spotlights throwing blood-red beams ahead of the car.

The headlights etched Mason and Mrs. Kempton into brilliance, then a huge searchlight pilloried them in a glare.

A siren screamed at them.

Mrs. Kempton looked at Mason in dismay.

"Stand still," Mason said.

A voice from the police car shouted, "Get 'em up!"

Mason elevated his hands.

The police car slowed almost to a stop, drew up alongside. Mason could see the reflection of lights from the blued steel of weapons.

"What the devil's coming off here?" a voice asked.

"I wish *I* knew," Mason told them.

"Well, you should know. You were legging it away from the house just as fast as you could make it."

Mason said, "Any time you are sufficiently satisfied that I am unarmed, I'll reach into my pocket, bring out my billfold and show you that I am an attorney at law, and that I am the one who summoned the police."

"By gosh, it's Perry Mason!" another voice in the police car said. "You've been in that house, Mason?"

"I have been in that house," Mason said. "I wish to report a dead man lying on a bed in a bedroom on the second floor. He has quite evidently been stabbed, and from the position of the wounds and the manner in which the handle of the knife is sticking from his back, I would say definitely that it was not suicide. Now then, I've made my report."

The searchlight was clicked off. One of the officers said, "Who's that with you?"

"Her name is Josephine Kempton," Mason said. "She's a client of mine, and I'll do the talking."

"Let's not start that angle."

"It's started," Mason told him.

"What has she got to conceal?"

"As far as I know, nothing."

"Why doesn't she tell her story then?"

"Because," Mason said, "she happens to have certain rights. I want an opportunity to talk with her privately and in detail before I know what she should say and what she shouldn't say. I might further point out that if I were the only one involved I would endeavor to ascertain the facts in the situation and make a statement which would clarify her position. However, as it happens, I am only one of two counsel."

"Who's the other one?"

"James Etna of Etna, Etna and Douglas."

"Where's he?"

"That," Mason said, "is something we don't know, something we've been trying to find out."

"All right, get in the back of this car," the officer said. "There'll be another car here in a minute. If this woman isn't going to talk, she's going to be held as a material witness. You know that."

"That's quite all right," Mason said. "You know your business, and I know mine. Hold her as a witness if you want to. She'll talk when I tell her to. I'll tell her to when I know what she has to say."

One of the officers opened the back door of the automobile. "Get in there in the back seat," he ordered. "How the devil do you get into this house? The front gate seems to be barred, and . . ."

"You get in by driving along this street to a door bearing the number 546. You want to be pretty careful when you go in because there are some gorillas loose in the place and they look as though they might be belligerent."

"Isn't this the devil of an assignment," one officer complained to the other one. "Where's car nineteen?"

"Here it comes."

Another police car swung in at the opposite entrance of Rose Street, and came toward them, its siren, which had been screaming in a crescendo, was now lowering to a grumbling wail.

"All right," the driver said. "I guess I go in with nineteen. You stay here and keep an eye on these people. You'd better hand me that machine gun. This gorilla hunting is something I don't like."

Mason turned to Mrs. Josephine Kempton. "You heard what I said?" he inquired in a low voice.

"Yes."

"Do you understand you're not to talk to anybody until you have talked to me, until I have had a chance to get your whole story? You understand that?"

"Yes."

"Can you follow those instructions? Can you keep from making any statement?"

"Certainly."

Chapter Eight

Police cars continued to converge on the place. officers made reports through two-way radio telephones, and a couple of squad cars came screaming to the scene.

Della Street parked Mason's car on a side street, and came running frantically down the alley.

Mason started to get out of the police car.

"Sit right still, buddy," the man who had been left in charge warned him.

"That's my secretary," Mason said. "I instructed her to call the police. Get her attention."

The officer seemed dubious for a moment, then manipulated a switch which flashed the red spotlight on and off.

Mason, thrusting his head out of the car window, shouted, "Della, here we are, over here! Della! It's all right!"

Della Street turned her head for a moment trying to get the direction of the voice, then seeing and correctly interpreting the flashing spotlight once more broke into a run and came up calling, "Chief, Chief, where are you?"

"Here, Della. It's all right."

"You this man's secretary?" the officer asked.

"Yes."

"She called the police," Mason said. "She's the one who put in the call."

"That right?" the officer asked.

"That's right," Della said. "Who's that in there with you? Oh, Mrs. Kempton. Good heavens, Chief, whatever happened? I was never so frightened in my life. I waited there for the five minutes, just as you told me to, but, believe me, I was watching the second hand on my watch, and I had the motor running, and the very second the five minutes were up I was on my way. It seemed as though I'd never get to a telephone."

Mason said, "Don't worry, Della. There seems to have been quite a bit of trouble inside the house. I don't really know all that did happen. The doors of some of the cages were opened. Apparently some gorillas made their escape and were prowling through the house. I tried to get back to tell you what was going on, but one of the gorillas didn't seem to want to be too friendly—or perhaps I should say he wanted to be more friendly."

"But what caused all of the commotion? What caused all this . . . ?"

"Apparently," Mason said, "there are burglar alarms and . . ."

"You'd better get in and sit down, ma'am," the officer interposed. "If you're the one who called the police, we'll want to get a statement from you. You'd better wait right here."

"My car's parked down on the side street," Della said. "I jumped out in such a hurry I didn't take the key out of the lock. I'm afraid I left the motor running."

"Let it run," the officer told her.

"I could go down and shut it off and . . ."

"And again you *could* stay right here," the officer said.

Mason said, "Apparently, Della, Mr. Benjamin Addicks has been murdered. The police naturally want to find out all they can about the circumstances surrounding his death."

"Oh-oh!" Della Street said.

Mason opened the car door. "Get in and sit down."

"Good evening, Miss Street," Mrs. Kempton said.

"Good evening. What are *you* . . . ?"

She broke off as Mason's knee nudged her leg.

"Go on," the officer said. "What were you going to say?"

Della Street said demurely, "I was just going to ask her what she was doing about transportation back to town. I was going to tell her that I was driving Mr. Mason's car, and that we'd take her back to town."

"You don't need to worry a bit about that," the officer said. "Her transportation back to town is all taken care of. So's Mr. Mason's transportation, and so's yours."

The loud-speaker said, "Calling car seven, car seven."

The officer leaned forward, pushed a switch and said, "Car seven reporting. Go ahead."

"You reported a homicide at the Addicks place?"

"That's right. I got it from two people we picked up who were just leaving the house. One of them's Perry Mason, the lawyer. He says Benjamin Addicks has been murdered.

"Now then, there's a woman with him, Josephine Kempton, and just now Mr. Mason's secretary showed up. Mr. Mason claims that she telephoned the police. What do I do?"

The officer leaned over and pressed a button.

"Car seven, in response to your inquiry, as soon as you have been rejoined by your fellow officer drive the car with Mr. Mason, Mrs. Kempton and Mr. Mason's secretary to headquarters. Under no circumstances let them leave the car. Don't let them communicate with anyone else. Don't let them hide anything. We are giving instructions to your fellow officer to join you at once. That is all."

The officer flipped a switch, turned his head back to Mason and said, "Okay, you heard those instructions."

"I certainly feel," Mason said, "that I should be given an opportunity to drive my own car to headquarters so that it will be there. I'll follow you or go directly ahead of you along any streets you . . ."

"You'll sit right there," the officer said. "There's something funny about this business. You know damn well what caused those instructions from headquarters."

"What?" Mason asked innocently.

"Somebody made a telephone call from inside that house and reported something. Whatever it was, it was something that made . . . here comes my partner."

The door leading to the zoo opened and a uniformed officer came running toward the car.

The officer who was guarding the three people in the back seat pressed the starter button and brought the motor to life, moved over to the side.

The other officer jerked open the car door and jumped in behind the steering wheel.

"Headquarters came on with instructions for us, and . . ."

"I know," the driver said, slamming the car into gear. "They want these people up at headquarters just as quick as we can get them there. Start the siren, Mike, and keep her going."

"I left Mr. Mason's car parked with the motor running," Della Street said.

No one paid the slightest attention to her.

The police car swept down Rose Street, turned to the right, and Della Street, looking back through the rear window of the car, said, "Oh dear, I've left the headlights on too."

The man at the wheel concentrated on driving. The other officer started watching the side streets. The needle on the speedometer passed forty, went past fifty, up to sixty, then settled down at around seventy miles an hour as they hit a through boulevard.

Mason settled back and said, "Relax. Relax and enjoy it."

"Relax!" Josephine Kempton said through clenched teeth. "In the name of heaven, why?"

"You," Mason told her, "should be more familiar with Chinese proverbs."

CHAPTER NINE

PERRY MASON SAT IN A SMALL WITNESS ROOM AT POLICE HEADQUARTERS. Half a dozen battered chairs lined the wall. There was a scarred oak table in the center of the room, bearing the traces of cigarette burns along the edges. A water cooler, with a container of paper cups, was at one end of the room. Aside from the chairs, the table, the water container, a wastebasket and two battered spittoons, the room was entirely bare.

Mason shifted his position in one of the uncomfortable chairs, stretched out his long legs, crossed the ankles, and glanced significantly at the place where his wrist watch should have been, then hastily lowered his bare wrist.

The uniformed officer who sat there, stolidly puffing away at a cigar, said, "It won't be long now. Take it easy."

Mason said angrily, "I don't like being treated this way."

"I suppose you don't."

"You'd think we had committed the murder."

"You could have, couldn't you? There wasn't anyone else in the house."

"Oh, bunk!" Mason said.

There was silence for several seconds.

"This business of putting my secretary in one room, me in another, my client in a third, holding us all where we can't get in touch with each other—that's cheap theatrical stuff as far as I'm concerned."

"Well," the officer said, puffing away at the cigar, "it's orders as far as I'm concerned. What do you think of the Giants?"

"Doing all right," Mason said.

"Uh-huh. The Dodgers is quite a team."

"Uh-huh," Mason said.

The officer smoked with that air of complete detachment which indicated that the only hour on the clock which meant anything to him was the time at which he would be off duty. Aside from that he took things as they came. He had been instructed to sit in this room with Perry Mason and keep him from communicating with anyone, and he was making himself as comfortable as possible while he was carrying out his orders.

"Who's the mastermind that gave these orders?" Mason asked.

The officer hesitated a moment, turned the cigar in his mouth, inspected the end of it to make certain it was drawing evenly, and said, "Sergeant Holcomb."

"Well," Mason said, "my time's valuable. My automobile is out there with the motor running and the lights on."

"No, it isn't."

"What do you mean?"

"It's right downstairs. You don't need to tell anybody I told you, but you can quit worrying about your automobile."

"That's fine," Mason said. "I'll drive it home then."

The officer grinned.

"Good Lord!" Mason said. "You don't mean they're going to impound that for evidence too."

"The boys are going over it," the officer told him. "Maybe they'll be done by the time you get out of here. Maybe they won't."

Mason said angrily, "That's what I get for instructing my secretary to call the police."

"No," the officer said, "that's what you get for finding so damn many bodies. You get around too much. According to the way the Sarge thinks about it, you should stay in your office and let people come to you. You always get out on the firing line some place, and seem to have a knack for being around about the time somebody gets bumped off.

"You know, when it comes to pennant winning I like a team that has the old power house. You get fellows that can bunch their hits and that's what counts. Funny the way some teams are like that. Some just scatter their hits all through the game; and then you can take a power house gang that's playing along just ordinary base-ball, and all of a sudden somebody sparks a play, and the next thing you know the whole team is going crazy, batting pitchers out of the box, slamming balls all over the diamond. They bring in a fistful of runs and then they settle down. They can afford to. They've got the game won."

Mason said wearily, "Runs are what win a ball game."

"You said it, buddy. Now you take the Giants. Ever since Durocher got in there the team is like a unit. You can figure everything is teamwork. They'll play machine-precision baseball until something happens to give them a break, and then they pounce on that break like nobody's business. They . . ."

The door opened.

A tall, affable, good looking man in plain clothes, stood on the threshold smiling at Perry Mason.

Mason got up out of his chair and said, "Well, well, Lieutenant Tragg himself. This is a pleasure. I thought I was going to have a session with Sergeant Holcomb's bullnecked stupidity."

Lieutenant Tragg shook hands. "You shouldn't run down one officer to a brother officer, Mason," he said. "Sergeant Holcomb is busy interviewing—others."

"I hope he isn't using his tact and diplomacy on Della Street," Mason said.

Lieutenant Tragg walked over the table and sat down.

"All right, Mason," he said, "what's the story?"

The door opened. A plain-clothes man with a shorthand notebook came in, sat down at the table, opened the notebook, took a fountain pen from his pocket, unscrewed the cap, shifted his position in the chair as though trying to get his hips and elbows in just the right place, then nodded to Lieutenant Tragg.

"You can begin at the beginning," Lieutenant Tragg said to Mason.

"In the beginning," Mason said, "Della Street and I were in my office. The switchboard kept clattering away. It's rather annoying. Ordinarily we wouldn't answer calls at night, and ordinarily we wouldn't have any calls. But we took the call. Someone asked us to go out to Benjamin Addicks' place."

"Someone?" Tragg said.

"That's right."

"Who was the someone?"

"I didn't recognize the voice myself," Mason said, "not well enough to swear to it."

"Well, you've got your opinion, haven't you?"

"I thought you wanted evidence."

"Are you going to be difficult, Mason?"

"No, just cautious."

"All right, I'll put it to you straight. Was it Mrs. Kempton on the line?"

"I don't know."

"Did the voice say it was Mrs. Kempton?"

"I can't tell you."

"What do you mean, you can't tell me? Don't you know what the voice said?"

"Yes, but I haven't had a chance to talk with my client."

"How long has she been your client?"

"There again," Mason said, "we get into a matter which I would like to talk over with my client before I discuss it with the police. If you'll give me an opportunity for a five or ten minute private talk with my client, I can save us both a lot of time."

"We might surprise you by doing just that," Tragg said casually, as though conceding a minor point. "So you went out to the Addicks place. What did you find when you got out there, Mason?"

"A door."

"Good heavens, you astound me! And what did you do when you found the door?"

"I rang the bell. Nobody answered. I tried the door. It was open. I looked inside. I didn't like what I . . ."

"Yes. Go on," Tragg said as Mason hesitated.

"I didn't like the setup," Mason said.

"So what?"

"So I told Della Street that if I wasn't back in five minutes to call the police. I didn't get back in five minutes, and she called the police."

"Why didn't you get back?"

"I was busy."

"Doing what?"

"Playing tag with a bunch of gorillas who seemed to want to play a little rough, and finding bodies."

"Where was the body when you found it?"

"I presume exactly where it was when you found it. Lying face down on a bed."

"Face down?"

"Well, the body was lying on its stomach, but the head had been turned slightly to one side so you could see the man's profile. There was a wound in the neck, and a knife was sticking out of the back, pretty nearly between the shoulders, just a little to the left side of the backbone, I would say."

"And where was Mrs. Kempton when you found her?"

"Lying on the floor."

"Doing what?"

"Breathing, and that's all."

"Then what?"

"Then we left the house and the police picked us up."

"I'd like a little more," Tragg said.

Mason shrugged his shoulders.

Tragg pushed back the chair, grinned at the officer, said, "Take Mr. Mason into the room where Mrs. Kempton is being held. Tell the officer in charge that I want them left alone. I want them given an opportunity to have a ten minute conversation that is absolutely private. Then Mason can come back."

"Thank you," Mason said.

"Not at all. It's a pleasure," Tragg told him.

The officer escorted Mason across a corridor, into another room where Mrs. Kempton was seated in a chair with an officer on guard.

Mason said rapidly, "Lieutenant Tragg has arranged that we are to have a ten or fifteen minute conversation in private, Mrs. Kempton."

"Oh, I'm so glad."

Mason looked at the officer.

"In private."

The officer in the room received a nod by way of signal, got up and walked out through the door.

As soon as the door closed Mason whipped a fountain pen from his pocket, pulled out a notebook and said, "Now, Mrs. Kempton, just try to relax and tell me exactly what happened."

He put the notebook down on the table and wrote, "There's undoubtedly a microphone in this room. Tell me that you're too nervous to talk."

Mrs. Kempton said, "Oh, I couldn't—I couldn't tell you much now, Mr. Mason. I'm too terribly nervous."

"You've talked with the police?" Mason asked.

"No."

"Well, you must have told them something."

"I told them you were my lawyer."

"What else?"

"I told them if they wanted any statement from me they could get it from my lawyer."

"Well, that's fine," Mason said. "However, we can discuss matters now and then I'll know what to tell the police. Although perhaps —well, if you're nervous we'll try and go at it gradually."

Mason wrote on the notebook, "Tell me that you don't want to make any statement until James Etna is here with me."

Mrs. Kempton cleared her throat and said, "Well, I *would* like to tell you exactly what happened—as far as I know, Mr. Mason."

"That's right," Mason said. "Of course you can only tell what you know, and only as much as you know."

"But, after all, I have another lawyer, James Etna. I don't know why we couldn't get him. I wouldn't want to tell you and then tell him all over again. I think I'd better wait, Mr. Mason, until I can get Mr. Etna and then I can tell both of you everything that I know, which isn't much—and, of course, I'm terribly nervous now."

"Well," Mason said, putting the notebook and fountain pen in his pocket, "if that's the way you feel, Mrs. Kempton, I'm not going to try to urge you. I would only suggest that you regain your composure as soon as possible. I want you to tell us what happened so that we can make a statement to the police and to the press. I think the police are entitled to a statement at the earliest possible moment, and, of course, it's always a bad thing when you adopt the position with the press that you won't make any statement at all."

"They haven't let me see the press yet—or, rather, they haven't let the press see me."

"They probably will," Mason said affably, stretching and yawning. "However, you can tell them that as soon as we've had a joint conference with James Etna, we'll release a statement of some sort to the press."

"Thank you."

They were silent for a few seconds.

Abruptly the door opened, and the officer said to Mason, "Come on back. Lieutenant Tragg wants to see you."

Mason said, "I haven't been here more than three minutes. I was to have a ten or fifteen minute conference."

"That's all right. The Lieutenant wants to see you."

The officer who had been guarding Mrs. Kempton, and who was standing in the corridor, entered the room and sat down.

Mason made a reassuring gesture to Mrs. Kempton, followed the other officer back to the room where Lieutenant Tragg was waiting.

"You take anything out of that house?" Lieutenant Tragg asked.

"What house?"

"That Addicks house, Stonehenge."

Mason shook his head.

"Well," Tragg said, "we've got to make sure. It's just a formality. You don't have any objections, do you?"

"Certainly I have objections."

Tragg said, "Don't be difficult, Mason. You know as well as I do that if you make objections to being searched we'll simply book you as a material witness, and when we book you we'll take all your things away from you and put them in an envelope, and put you in a nice quiet cell and . . ."

"Okay," Mason said. "Go ahead."

Tragg ran his fingers quickly over Mason's clothes and said, "Take everything out of your pockets and put them in a pile on the table, Mason."

Mason said, "Ordinarily I'd tell you to go to hell, Lieutenant, but because I've got a lot of work to do tonight, and want to get this over with, I'll be agreeable."

"That's fine," Tragg said.

"And," Mason went on, "because I have nothing to hide."

Mason took the notebook from his pocket.

Tragg grabbed it.

Mason tried to retrieve it, but was too late.

Tragg grinned and said, "This is what I wanted, Mason."

"You have no right reading my personal notes," Mason said.

Tragg riffled through the notebook, came to the page on which Mason had written his instructions to Mrs. Kempton, tore that page out of the book, said, "Hell, I knew you wouldn't walk into anything like that, but this will establish my point with the guy who thought it was a swell idea."

Mason said, "You have no right to take that page out of my notebook."

"I know, I know," Tragg said. "Go into court and get an order and we'll give it back. Why are you so afraid to let your client talk?"

"Because I don't know what she's going to say."

"All right," Tragg said. "Now I'm going to tell you something Mason, something for your own good."

"What?" Mason asked.

"There's some evidence against Mrs. Kempton. She's going to be kept here all night and perhaps tomorrow."

"On what charge?"

Tragg grinned.

"You put a charge against her," Mason said, "or I'll slam a writ of *habeas corpus* on you."

Tragg said, "Go ahead, and slam the writ of *habeas corpus* on us, Mason, then we may charge her and we may turn her loose. Until you get a writ she's going to be right with us. And I'm going to warn you not to get tied up with her too much and too deep until you know what her story is. Actually, Mason, she and Benjamin Addicks were the only two people in that house. One of those persons was stabbed to death. Now where does that leave your client?"

Mason said, "If you'd give me a chance to hear her story I'd . . ."

"I gave you your chance," Tragg said. "You wouldn't let her talk."

"Sure," Mason told him. "With a microphone right back of that table and seventeen detectives sitting there listening at the other end of the wire."

"Well, what did you expect?" Tragg asked.

"Just that," Mason said.

"Then you weren't disappointed. I have some other news for you. Your car's ready. Della Street's waiting there for you. Go on back to your office. If you want, get out a writ of *habeas corpus*. You may have trouble finding a judge at night and it'll be tomorrow morning before you can get a writ and have it served. Give me a ring tomorrow morning and I may save you the trouble."

"And in the meantime?" Mason asked.

"In the meantime Mrs. Kempton stays with us."

Chapter Ten

MASON WALKED OVER TO THE PLACE WHERE HIS CAR WAS PARKED IN the police garage. Della Street, who was sitting in the driver's seat, waved her hand at him, and started the motor.

Mason moved over to the right-hand side of the car, opened the door and slid in beside her.

Della Street eased the car into motion, driving out of the police garage and into traffic on the cross street with all of the sure competency of the skilled driver.

She kept her attention on the traffic while she said to Perry Mason over her shoulder, "Did they try any funny stuff?"

"All they could think of," Mason said. "What did they do with you?"

She said, "I talked. I told them my story and they knew it was right because they checked up on the time of the telephone call, and the place. They went over the car looking for fingerprints and trying to find bloodstains. Then they let me go. But I knew they were going to try something with you and Mrs. Kempton. Did she talk?"

"No. She sat tight. They put us together in a room that was all bugged up."

Della merely nodded, jockeyed the car into position at a stop light, and held herself in readiness to beat the line of traffic to the crossing.

Mason studied her with an affectionate smile. "It isn't going to hurt anything if one of those cars gets ahead of us, Della."

"It'll hurt my feelings," she said. "That fellow in the gray sedan has been trying to push me over and hog the traffic for the last block."

She shifted her position slightly, her skirt up over her knees so as to give her freedom of leg action, her left foot on the brake, her right on the throttle.

The signal changed.

Della Street's reactions were instantaneous. The car leaped forward and shot across the intersection. The gray sedan tried to keep up, failed, and sullenly dropped behind.

"Where to?" Della Street asked. "The office?"

Mason said, "The nearest telephone, and then we eat. There's a drugstore with two phone booths around the corner here."

Della Street whipped the car around the corner.

Mason shook his head sadly. "And you object to my driving."

"It seems different when I'm doing it," she admitted sheepishly.

"It is different," Mason told her.

She parked the car, joined Mason in the phone booth.

"First James Etna and then Paul Drake, Della," Mason told her.

Della Street's swiftly competent fingers dialed the number, and a moment later she said, "Just a moment, Mr. Etna. Mr. Mason wants to talk with you."

She passed the telephone across to Mason, and Mason said, "Hello, Etna. Mrs. Kempton has been trying to get you. There have been complications in . . ."

"I heard about it," Etna said. "There was a bulletin on the radio. I was at a friend's house. My wife and I came home at once and I've been trying everywhere I could think of to locate you."

"You didn't call the right place," Mason said.

"Where?"

"Police headquarters."

"Oh-oh!" Etna said.

"Our client, Mrs. Josephine Kempton, is being held at headquarters tonight."

"What charge?"

"No charge."

"Do you want to get a writ of *habeas corpus?*"

"I don't think it would do any good. They'll turn her loose tomorrow anyway, unless she tells them something tonight, and I don't think she will."

Etna said, "I may be able to find out something about what the score is, Mason. Can you tell me just briefly about it?"

"She rang me," Mason said, "and told me she couldn't get you, that she needed a lawyer at once. She was out at Stonehenge. So my secretary and I drove out there. She agreed to have the door on the back street opened for us. The door was open, but she was lying unconscious on the floor of an upper bedroom, and the body of Benjamin Addicks was lying face down on the bed. He'd been stabbed several times, and the handle of a big carving knife was protruding from his back."

"I understand the animals were loose and that the place had been wrecked," Etna said.

"I wouldn't say it had been wrecked, but there's a lot of commotion going on out there."

"What do you think about letting her tell her story?"

Mason said, "I never let a client tell a story to the police unless I know what that story is."

"You're the doctor," Etna told him.

"I'm not the doctor," Mason said. "I'm associate counsel."

"No you're not. You're in charge of the whole thing—in case there is anything. I don't feel competent to handle a case of that kind. Frankly, I'm quite certain there's something in connection with the case that we don't know anything about, and it may be something that's rather disquieting. What was Mrs. Kempton doing out at Stonehenge?"

"That's what the police want to know."

"She didn't tell you?"

"No. Actually she didn't have the opportunity."

"I have some contacts with newspapermen, and I think I can find out something of what's going on. Suppose I get in touch with you, at say nine o'clock in the morning."

"That's fine," Mason said.

"All right, I'll be at your office at nine o'clock. I think I'll have some information."

"And," Mason said, "if they haven't turned Mrs. Kempton loose by that time we'll get a writ of *habeas corpus*."

Mason hung up the phone, waited a moment, then dialed the private, unlisted number of Paul Drake, head of the Drake Detective Agency.

When he had Paul Drake on the line, Mason said, "Paul, I have a job for you, an emergency job."

"Why the devil is it your cases always break at night?" Drake asked irritably.

"They don't, *always*," Mason told him.

"Well, I can always count on a sleepless night whenever I get a phone call from you. Just what am I supposed to do?"

Mason said, "You're supposed to find out everything about the late Benjamin Addicks."

"The *late* Benjamin Addicks?"

"That's right. Somebody pushed a carving knife down between his shoulder blades some time this evening, and the police are holding a client of mine, a Josephine Kempton, for questioning."

"What do you want to know about Addicks?"

"Everything."

"What do you want to know about the murder?"

"Everything."

Drake said sarcastically, "I suppose you want me to have it all ready by nine o'clock tomorrow morning."

"You're wrong," Mason told him. "I want it by eight-thirty," and hung up.

CHAPTER ELEVEN

PROMPTLY AT 8:30 MASON STOPPED BY THE DRAKE DETECTIVE AGENCY, which had offices on the same floor as Mason's law offices.

"Paul in?" he asked the girl at the switchboard.

"He's in," she said, "and waiting for you, Mr. Mason."

"Okay," Mason said, "tell him to come on down to my office. I have an appointment at nine, and Della Street said she was going to be there at eight-thirty."

Mason went on down to his office and found Della Street waiting.

"Hello, Della. Been here long?"

"About ten minutes."

"You had a pretty hard day yesterday."

"I had? You're the one who had a hard day, playing tag with gorillas. Did you have nightmares?"

Mason grinned. "I didn't have nightmares, but I had the devil of a time getting to sleep. There's something about those gorillas— they give you something to think of when they start looking at you and beating themselves on the chest."

"I'll say. Is Paul Drake coming in?"

"Uh-huh. I stopped in and left word. See if you can get Homicide on the line for me, Della. We'll put it up to Lieutenant Tragg and find out what he wants to do."

Della Street rang police headquarters and found that Lieutenant Tragg was not in his office.

"Try Sergeant Holcomb," Mason said.

"You know how he hates you," Della Street warned.

"That's all right," Mason told her. "We'll see what Holcomb has to say. I want information."

A moment later Della Street nodded. Mason picked up the telephone.

"Hello," Mason said, "I wanted to get some information about a client of mine, Sergeant."

"What do you want?"

Mason said, "I want to know whether I'm going to have to get a writ of *habeas corpus* on Josephine Kempton, or whether you're going to turn her loose."

"She's loose."

"She is? I haven't heard anything of it."

"Well, you will. She was released about half an hour ago. I tried your office and got no answer. You don't have your residence telephone listed in the book. You're exclusive. Mrs. Kempton didn't know where it was, and I didn't know where it was. Her other attorney, James Etna, had a phone listed. I telephoned him. He said he wanted to come by and pick her up."

"So you released her," Mason said.

"That's right."

"Then she's no longer under suspicion?"

"Who said she ever was under suspicion?"

"All right," Mason said wearily, "I guess that's that."

He hung up.

Della Street raised her eyebrows.

"Holcomb says she's been released," Mason reported.

Paul Drake gave his code knock at the door.

Della Street opened the door.

"You guys," Paul Drake said, "fresh as daisies, aren't you? Had a nice sleep, I suppose. Look at me. I'm groggy. Filled with equal parts of coffee and information."

"That's fine," Mason told him. "Sit down. Keep the coffee, give us the information."

Paul Drake, a tall, cadaverous, solemn-looking individual, whose eyes had been trained by years of poker-faced observation to show no flicker of expression, assumed his favorite position in the big, overstuffed, leather chair, his long legs hanging over one rounded chair arm, the other arm supporting his back.

He yawned prodigiously, pulled a notebook from his pocket and said, "I suppose you want me to begin at the beginning."

"That's right."

"Benjamin Addicks," Paul Drake said in a drawl, "said to be fifty-two years old. He's supposed to have a younger brother, Herman Addicks, forty-six. The two were inseparable. They didn't have any great amount of formal education, came of a poor family.

"Herman dropped out of sight. Benjamin claimed he didn't have any idea where Herman was. That may have been true. Rumor is that Herman got in a fight and killed someone, and . . ."

"Snap out of it, Paul," Mason interrupted sharply. "You're a detective. What do you care about all the rumor stuff. I want facts. What do you know?"

Drake said, "Actually, Perry, not a damned thing. Addicks is a millionaire. He goes for mining deals in a big way. He's been here for sixteen years. Before that no one knows a damn thing about him, where he came from, when or how he got his money."

Mason said incredulously, "You mean his banks don't know?"

"I mean no one knows. He always refused to answer any question. He'd say, 'I am asking for no credit at any time. I buy and sell in hard cash.'"

"But, good heavens, Paul, how about the income tax people?"

"He told them he had amnesia. The first thing he remembered was being here, waking up in a hotel with about two thousand dollars on him."

"Did they believe any such yarn as that, Paul?"

"Certainly not. They managed to get his fingerprints. Up to that time he'd never been printed. The FBI has no record on him."

"Can you make an estimate of how much he's worth?"

"Probably two or three million dollars net. He has an enormous income and he has stuff spread around so that it's pretty hard to get an accurate estimate. Anyway, he was sufficiently well fixed so that he could do anything he wanted."

"And what did he want to do?" Mason asked.

"There's the rub," Drake said. "You know, Perry, if it came right down to a showdown, there's a two or three million dollar estate there, and he undoubtedly left a will. That will could probably be attacked on the grounds that Benjamin Addicks was of unsound mind."

"Because of the experiments with apes and gorillas?" Mason asked.

"I think it goes deeper than that," Drake said. "I think that Benjamin Addicks was afraid of himself. Personally, I think he wanted to kill somebody, or I think he had killed somebody."

"What makes you think so?"

"Because he was trying desperately to prove that homicidal impulses are an inherent part of man's instinctive equipment. He claimed that civilization might cause those impulses to lie dormant, particularly in the case of a child reared in an atmosphere of security. In a keenly competitive existence he claimed that the urge to kill was an inherent part of the natural instincts of man. He also claimed a man could be hypnotized, could commit murder while he was unaware of what he was doing, and, on awakening from the hypnotic trance, have no knowledge of what he had done —perhaps no memory."

"In other words, he could have been laying an elaborate plan for defending himself against an old murder charge," Mason said.

"Or a new one," Drake commented.

"But surely, Paul, such a prominent personality must have had people trying to check—why, with a history like that, a black-mailer would work for years trying to find the man's secret."

"Sure," Drake said. "The government spent some time on it— even a question of citizenship. Everyone got nowhere. It's surprising what a man can get away with when he says 'I can't remember anything about my past life so I have dismissed it from my mind. After all, the present is the thing, and therefore that's all I'm interested in.'"

"So he spent a fortune trying to demonstrate his theories," Mason said.

"That's right—trying to build up his defense."

"Naturally," Mason went on, "he could hardly start experimenting with men in order to bring out his ideas."

"That's it. He acquired apes and gorillas, trying to teach them to kill, trying to get them hypnotized so they'd obey suggestions."

"How did he go about it?"

"Lots of ways. He had a couple of trainers out there and a psychologist who was willing to ride along with him. I've talked with the psychologist, a man by the name of Blevins, Alan Blevins."

"Where was Blevins last night?" Mason asked.

"Sitting at home."

"He wasn't out at Stonehenge?"

"Everyone connected with the monkey and ape experiments was fired about a week ago," Drake said. "Addicks just cleaned out the whole outfit."

"Why?"

"He said that his experiments had been proven successful."

"What was he doing particularly?"

"Well, that's what I'm getting at. This Blevins can give you quite a picture, Perry. Of course, Blevins wasn't very co-operative. I had to get in touch with him about three o'clock this morning and tell him it was an emergency and all of that stuff."

"Well," Mason said, "if a gorilla didn't murder Addicks, the district attorney is going to have a devil of a time proving who did—but you must have been able to get something on Addicks, Paul."

"Sure. I have a fistful of stuff here. I've merely been telling you the stuff I *didn't* have.

"His lawyer, Sidney Hardwick, knows something about Addicks' background, how much I can't tell, and he won't tell.

"Addicks made a stake in gold mining, turned to oil. He has accounts in a dozen banks, and he does a lot of business on a strictly cash basis.

"The income tax department doesn't like it. They are after him all the time. His business manager, Mortimer Hershey, can make figures run up hill or jump over hurdles.

"Nathan Fallon, a lesser light, has been having trouble with Addicks. Evidently Fallon isn't above a little cut and kickback once in a while."

"Better check on Fallon's whereabouts last night, Paul," Mason said.

Paul Drake looked at the lawyer scornfully. "What the hell do you think *I* was doing all night?" he asked. "I've been trying to find out all the police know, which wasn't much at first. Nathan Fallon was in Las Vegas, Nevada—and I mean he *was* there, every minute. Hershey was in Santa Barbara. I'm checking him, and so are the police."

"Anything else that's important, Paul?"

"Lots of it. Now here's something I can't figure. Addicks didn't trust anyone in his business deals. He had secrets from Fallon and Hershey."

"Can you blame him?" Mason asked.

"No."

"What sort of secrets, Paul?"

"Well, for instance, Addicks would disappear. One of the members of the yacht crew told me that. He was sore at Addicks because Addicks fired him.

"He said lots of times when Addicks was supposed to be cruising, he'd actually get aboard, then get off at the last minute and have the yacht cruise around when he wasn't aboard.

"The yacht had a ship to shore phone, and Addicks would telephone the yacht's captain and give him instructions as to where to sail and all that. Then they'd anchor at Catalina, and first thing anyone would know there would be Addicks, pretending he'd been aboard all the time, shut up in his stateroom, working."

Mason pursed his lips. "Who was in on it, Paul?"

"Just the captain, and the captain's as close-mouthed as a clam."

Mason thought that over, then said suddenly, "All right, Paul, he was calling long distance. He must have placed his calls collect.

"Here's what you do. By hook or crook get hold of the telephone bills on that ship's telephone, start tracing the numbers that he called from. Let's find out where he was when he was hiding from both Fallon and Hershey—do you suppose it was a woman, Paul?"

"Apparently he didn't have any," Drake said, "but he certainly was a great boy for cash transactions, and my own idea is he was slipping something over on the income tax department."

"You've got some photos of him?"

"Oh, sure."

"Well, check on those phone bills and see what you can find out."

"All right," Drake said. "Now here's another thing. He . . .'"

Drake was interrupted by a low, insistent knock at the door.

Della Street opened the door a crack, looked out, then pulled the door back and said, "Good morning. You folks are a little early."

Etna and Josephine Kempton walked through the doorway.

Mason introduced them to Paul Drake, said to Etna, "How's everything coming?"

"Coming fine," Etna said triumphantly. "We're sitting pretty, Mason."

Mrs. Kempton nodded and beamed. "They couldn't have been nicer to me."

Mason's eyes narrowed. "What sort of a story did you tell them?" he asked suspiciously.

"I didn't tell them anything. I did just as you instructed me."

Mason studied her face for a few moments, then abruptly said to Paul Drake, "I'm sorry, Paul, but we're going to have to ask you to leave. It's not that we don't trust your discretion, but it has been held that a client who has a discussion with her attorney in the presence of a third person waives the benefit of the statutory provisions making such conversation absolutely confidential—Della, of course, as my secretary, is included within the scope of the statute, but you aren't."

"That's fine," Drake said. "Maybe I can get myself a little breakfast. I'm so damned tired of coffee and ham sandwiches bolted in between telephone calls. I'll go down and have a real meal off a table."

Drake left the room.

Mason turned to Etna and Mrs. Kempton. "Sit down," he said. "Now, Mrs. Kempton, I want the truth, the whole truth, and nothing but the truth."

"I told you the truth."

Mason shook his head.

"Mr. Mason," she said indignantly, "do you think I would lie?"

Mason said, "I know the police. I know how they work. You were alone in that house with a murdered man. You refuse to tell anyone what you know, and yet you claim that the police turned you loose."

"That's right. They did. They even sent up to my room and got clothes for me."

"How's that?" Mason asked.

"Well, they told me that it was necessary to have my clothes gone over carefully by a laboratory man, that they always did that in cases where a witness had been present at a murder, that it was a matter of routine. They said it would be tomorrow sometime before I could have my clothes back, and that there was no need of waiting there if I didn't want to, that they'd send the matron up to my room and she could get the clothes for me if I'd tell her what I wanted to wear."

"They did that?"

"Yes."

"You gave them a key to your room?"

"It was in my envelope—they take everything away from you and put it in an envelope."

"And you signed something saying it would be all right for her to go in the room?"

"That's right."

"Then what happened?"

"Then they brought me my clothes. Everyone was just as nice as pie. They told me they were sorry they had had to hold me, that they had now found out all about who murdered Mr. Addicks and that I was absolutely in the clear."

"Who told you that?"

"The matron."

"Then what did you do?"

"Well," she said, "they asked me what I wanted to do, and I told them I wanted to call you."

"When was that?"

"That was early this morning."

"Go ahead."

"It seems that no one knew how to reach you before you came to the office, but Mr. Etna had a phone in his residence. I knew that he'd be up so I told them it would be all right to call him."

"And he came and got you?" Mason asked.

"That's right."

Mason looked at Etna. Etna nodded.

"From the detention cells?" Mason asked.

"Well, not exactly," Etna said. "I picked her up in the garage downstairs."

"The garage?"

"Yes."

"What garage?"

"The police garage, where they . . ."

"That's where they drove us in last night," Mrs. Kempton interrupted. "You'll remember there was a storage garage back of the place where they let us out. Well, I didn't want to bother anyone, so I told police that I'd just go on down to the garage and wait there, that they could tell Mr. Etna to come there and get me."

"So you were waiting there?"

"Yes, right where they took us last night, where we got out of the car."

Mason turned to Etna. "You couldn't drive in there?" he asked.

"No, but I left my car outside, and went to the door and motioned to Mrs. Kempton, and she came running out. Why? Does it make any difference?"

"That's what I want to know," Mason said.

"I don't get it," Etna said.

Mason said, "Mrs. Kempton, you're leaving out something."

"What do you mean?"

"You're leaving out something significant, some fact that . . ."

She interrupted him to shake her head in positive negation. "I'm telling you everything, Mr. Mason."

"And Mr. Etna drove you directly here?" Mason asked.

"He took me to my apartment first. I stopped there for five or ten minutes, then we drove here."

"She has a couple of questions she wants to ask you," Etna said.

Mrs. Kempton nodded. "Mr. Mason, when a man dies what happens to his bank account—I mean any checks that are outstanding?"

Mason said, "Checks are no good after a man dies. His bank account is frozen. As soon as the bank is notified of his death it stops payment on all checks."

"But suppose a man had a cashier's check?"

"A cashier's check," Mason said, "is a check given by a bank. Banks don't die."

"And if it—well, I'm just wondering . . ."

"Why are you wondering?" Mason asked.

"Oh, on account of the way Mr. Addicks did business. You know, Mr. Mason, he worked on a cash basis a lot. He juggled things around, and I know he used to do business with cash and with cashier's checks. He'd buy cashier's checks from different banks and then endorse them."

"And you're wondering if his endorsement on a cashier's check would invalidate the cashier's check in case he died before the check was cashed?"

"That's right."

"Why?"

"Just so I can get the picture straight in my own mind."

Mason said, "The cashier's check would be paid—but right now I want to know what happened out there at that house."

"Well," she said, "I'm going to tell you the truth, and I'm going to tell you the whole truth, and then you can tell me what to do. I hardly dare to say a word to anyone because what I have to say sounds so . . ."

"What have you told the newspapermen?" Mason interrupted.

"Nothing."

"Did they talk with you?"

"No. The police told me they'd turn me loose early this morning so that the newspapers wouldn't know anything about it. That would give me a chance to get myself adjusted."

Mason said in an aside to Etna, "This thing gets more and more cockeyed every minute."

"Oh, the police *can* be considerate," Etna said.

"Sure they can," Mason said, "but they're not going to antagonize every newspaper reporter in order to do it."

"They did it this time."

"Damned if they didn't," Mason said in an undertone. "Go ahead, Mrs. Kempton. Tell us what happened. How did you happen to go out to Stonehenge in the first place?"

"Mr. Addicks telephoned me."

"Where did his call reach you?"

"At my room."

"How did he get your number?"

"That I don't know."

"What did he say?"

"He said that he wanted to see me."

"Did he tell you what about?"

"He said he wanted to apologize in person for the great wrong that he had done me. He said he had something important to tell me."

"Did you tell Mr. Etna about the conversation?"

"No. Mr. Addicks told me to say nothing to anyone, but to come out to his house at six o'clock."

"At six?"

"Yes. He said he had some important appointments that would keep him busy until six, and then he had some appointments at six-forty-five. So I was to be there exactly at the stroke of six."

"Were you?"

"Yes."

"How did you get in?"

"I went around to the door at 546 Rose Street."

"It was open?"

"No, it was locked."

"How did you get in?"

"I had my key."

"You mean you've been keeping a key all this time . . . ?"

"Well, I had a key and I was never asked to turn it in."

"Did Addicks know that?"

"He asked me if I had my key, and I told him yes. He said that was fine, to come right in the back way, and go up to his offices on the second floor—why, what's wrong with that, Mr. Mason? I've done that hundreds of times when I was working there."

"That was when you were working there," Mason said. "This is different."

"Well, good heavens, I couldn't expect a busy man like Mr. Addicks to come all the way down the stairs and across that corridor just to let me in, when I had a key and knew the way."

"There was no one else to let you in?"

"No. He was alone in the house."

"Did he tell you that when he telephoned?"

"Yes."

Mason said, "You recognized his voice?"

"Oh yes. Of course, he laughed about the way he had to mumble with that bandage on."

"What time was it he called you?"

"About two-thirty in the afternoon."

"You went out there?"

"Yes. I took the bus that got me to the Olive Street intersection at exactly five-fifty. You see, I know the bus schedules from having been out there so much."

Mason said, "Hang it, I'm jumpy about this thing. Let me hit the high spots. Was he alive when you got there?"

"Yes."

"What did he say to you?"

"That's just the point. He didn't have a chance to say anything. He was killed just as I entered the . . ."

"Who killed him?"

"A gorilla."

Mason said, "Come, come, Mrs. Kempton. Let's be practical."

"Mr. Mason, please don't doubt what I'm telling you. I'm telling you the absolute truth. I saw it with my own eyes. Mr. Addicks was lying on the bed and this gorilla plunged a knife into him several times."

"Which gorilla was it?"

"Mr. Mason, I can't swear which gorilla it was. It was one of the three large ones, but I don't know which. You see it wasn't normal —the gorilla killed him while it was in a hypnotic trance."

Mason regarded her with thoughtful eyes.

"You don't believe me, do you, Mr. Mason?"

Mason said, "Even if I did, a jury wouldn't."

"Well, I don't know why not," she flared. "After all, that's what Mr. Addicks had been trying to do for years and years. He was trying to get a gorilla that he could hypnotize, and . . ."

"All right," Mason said. "It's your story. Let's not waste time arguing. I want to know what happened."

"Well, I entered the room. At first I couldn't see Mr. Addicks. I called out his name, and then I saw him lying there on the bed. He looked as though he might be asleep, and this gorilla came from around the corner by the bathroom. It was hypnotized, Mr. Mason."

"You've said that twice. How do you know?"

"The expression of the eyes. The gorilla grinned at me and moved over to the bed with that peculiar shambling walk, and—it was grinning all the time, as if it enjoyed turning the tables on the man who had tortured it."

"What did you do?"

"I screamed, and I fainted."

"Did you know there were gorillas loose in the house?" Mason asked. "Were any of the animals loose when you went along that walk past the cages?"

"No, everything was shipshape. Two big gorillas were in one of the cages that were opened later, and the friendly gorilla in the other."

Mason said, "Then somebody turned those gorillas loose between the time you . . ."

"The gorilla did that."

"Which one?"

"The gorilla that killed Mr. Addicks."

"How do you know?"

"Why, I know, Mr. Mason. You can't be around them very long without knowing how they work. Those cages had bar locks that could be worked from the outside, and the minute one gorilla got loose, why, he'd open the other cages. That's one of the first things he'd do."

"Go on," Mason said.

She said, "Well, I fainted. I came to and one of the friendly little gorillas, who has always liked me, was sitting down beside me. He was making little whimpering noises of sympathy, and he licked my face with his tongue. I think that's what wakened me out of my faint."

"Were you frightened?" Mason asked.

"Not particularly. I recognized this gorilla as soon as I opened my eyes."

"Then what?"

"Then," she said, "I spoke to him, and he was tickled to death to see that I was all right. He patted my cheek and ran his hands over my hair, and was just as pleased as he could be."

"Then what?"

"Then I got up and looked around, and I could see that Mr. Addicks was dead. I could see the knife sticking out of his back. So I went to the telephone and tried to get Mr. Etna, and I couldn't get him. I tried and tried to get you and couldn't get you, and I was just desperate when Miss Street finally answered the telephone."

"Why didn't you call for the police?"

"Because I didn't know what to do, Mr. Mason. I didn't know but what you'd tell me to get out of the house and not let anyone know I'd been there. But—well, I just didn't know what to do."

"And where was this big gorilla all this time?"

She said, "One of the first things I did was to lock every door leading into Mr. Addicks' suite of rooms upstairs."

"How about your friendly gorilla?"

"Oh, I left him in there. He was perfectly safe. He was just like a child. He was so glad to see me I couldn't get him away. He'd clap his hands and . . ."

"Go on," Mason said.

"Well," she said, "I told you that I'd meet you down at the door at 546 Rose Street. I didn't hardly dare to go out in the corridor, but after a while I decided it would be all right—that was about the time that I was expecting you. So I gently unlocked the door to the corridor and looked out. Everything was quiet, so I sneaked out into the hallway and—well, I guess something hit me. I remember seeing all kinds of shooting stars, and the next thing I knew, I was lying there on the floor with consciousness coming back to me, and then I saw you standing there facing the gorilla, and as soon as I saw that gorilla I knew you were going to have trouble."

"Why?"

"Because that gorilla was one of the really bad ones. He was really dangerous. You couldn't tell what he'd do. I guess he must have smashed the door down or something, because I remember seeing the broken door, and I think it was the sound of some terrific crash that helped me to regain consciousness."

"Go ahead," Mason said.

"You know all the rest. I knew we were in terrible danger, and I —well, I told you what to do."

Mason said, "This is the screwiest, most cockeyed story I have ever heard in my life."

"I'm sorry, Mr. Mason. It's the truth."

"The whole truth?"

"The whole truth, so help me."

Mason got up and began to pace the floor. After a moment he

said, "I suppose there's one chance in a hundred that it could be the truth. But whoever knocked you out would have then carried you back to the room. I look at you while you're talking and you sound almost convincing. Then I look away and I can't believe my ears."

"Mr. Mason, are you doubting my word?"

"Yes," Mason said.

She became angry. "I've told you *exactly* what happened."

"Well," Mason said, "when you stop to figure the environment out there, I suppose that you *could* say perhaps there was one chance in eight or ten the story *might* be the truth, but who's going to believe it? A jury won't, a judge won't, the newspapers won't."

"I don't see why anyone should disbelieve it. After all, Mr. Addicks had been deliberately training those gorillas to do just that thing. He'd been trying to hypnotize them and give them homicidal impulses and . . ."

"It's completely crazy," Mason said.

"There's nothing crazy about it!" she flared at him. "If you ask me, Mr. Addicks had something terrible in his past. He was always afraid that he was going to be charged with a murder. I think that it was a murder that had been committed in some foreign country, and I think Mr. Addicks was going to claim that he had been hypnotized by someone, and that gradually the hypnotic influence had worn off but that he had never regained his memory."

Mason walked over to stand by the window. "Yes," he said slowly, "when you look at the case in the light of the undisputed facts you can see that—but, good Lord, fancy trying to put up a defense like that in a courtroom and in front of a jury."

"Don't worry. You won't have to," she said. "The police have found out about that gorilla because they turned me loose and apologized for holding me. I don't see what *you're* worrying about a jury for, Mr. Mason. I'm not going to be charged with anything."

"And there's the craziest thing of the whole business," Mason said. "You're alone in a house where a man is murdered. If you'd told this story and signed a written statement they might have turned you loose while they made an investigation—you didn't tell them this story, did you?"

"I didn't tell them anything."

"Well, don't," Mason warned. "Keep your lips closed until I can find some way of checking this thing. Hang it all, when you stop to figure the thing in the light of the facts it probably is all right, but it's such a crazy story to try to make anyone believe."

"But it had to be that way, Mr. Mason. There was no one in the house except Mr. Addicks, myself and the gorillas."

"Exactly," Mason said, "and there's no reason why a shrewd person, who knew the way Mr. Addicks had been training his animals, couldn't have plunged a knife into him while he was asleep, and then claimed that he'd been killed by a gorilla."

"But what possible motive would I have for doing that?"

"That," Mason said, "is what gets me. I can't understand what possible motive you had for going out there without talking with James Etna or calling me."

"I suppose I should have done so, but Mr. Addicks asked me to say nothing to anyone."

Mason was on the point of saying something else when knuckles banged on the door with booming authority.

"Open up, Mason," Sergeant Holcomb's voice ordered. "This is the police."

Mason nodded to Della Street. She opened the door.

Sergeant Holcomb, smiling triumphantly, said, "Well, well, Mason, this is the case we've been waiting for. This is the one we *really* want. Come on, Mrs. Kempton. You're going with us."

"Going with you?" she said. "Why, you've just turned me loose."

"We sure did," Holcomb agreed. "And now you're going back with us, and this time the charge is first-degree murder."

Holcomb and two other officers pushed their way into the office, took Mrs. Kempton by the arms, and, before she could protest, snapped handcuffs on her.

"See you in church, Mason," Holcomb said.

"Just a moment," Mason said, getting between the officers and the door. "Have you got a warrant for the arrest of this woman?"

"Right here," Holcomb said, pulling a folded paper from his pocket.

Mason stepped forward.

The two officers gave him the shoulder, pushing him away from the door. Sergeant Holcomb rushed Mrs. Kempton into the corridor.

Mason gained the door.

An officer pushed him back. "Go get a writ if you want," he said, "but don't try to interfere with officers in the performance of their duties."

The other officer and Sergeant Holcomb hurried Mrs. Kempton down the corridor.

"You're damn right I'll get a writ," Mason said angrily.

"That's the spirit," the officer grinned. "Get a couple of 'em."

Mason said to Etna: "Go check the records, slap a writ on them if they aren't in order, Jim."

Etna nodded, and started toward the elevators.

"Take the stairs," Mason said as he turned back to the office. "Quick, Della, help me search this place for a microphone. If they've been listening in on a confidential communication made to an attorney by a client, we'll show them something they've never even thought of."

Mason and Della Street frantically searched the office.

At the end of an hour they admitted themselves baffled. They had looked in every nook and corner, behind every picture. They had moved furniture, raised the rug, inspected every inch of the walls.

"Well?" Della Street asked.

Mason said, "I don't get it. They've got something that we don't know about."

"What could it be?"

"I'm hanged if I know."

"Do you suppose she'll tell the police the same story she told us?"

"I hope not," Mason said.

The lawyer walked over to the window, stood moodily looking down at the traffic of the busy city street.

Suddenly he turned. "Della," he said, "there's such a thing as becoming *too* skeptical."

"What do you mean?"

"Mrs. Kempton tells us a story that sounds weird and bizarre and therefore we immediately reject it."

"You mean she might have told the truth?"

"There's one other possibility."

"What?"

Mason said, "Let's look at it this way, Della. Suppose you wanted to kill Benjamin Addicks and suppose you wanted to have it appear that someone else had done it and that you weren't guilty."

"Well?" she asked.

"So," Mason said, "you would get Josephine Kempton into the house. You would get her to tell a story that absolutely no jury on earth would believe. Then you'd go ahead and kill Benjamin Addicks and be pretty certain that Josephine Kempton would be convicted."

"But how on earth would you get her to tell any such story?" Della Street asked.

"Look at the whole thing," Mason said. "Look at it from a cold-blooded, analytical standpoint. What about Mrs. Kempton's story?"

"It sounds crazy," Della Street said promptly. "It sounds like—like a nightmare."

"And that," Mason said, "is probably *exactly* what it is."

"What do you mean by that, Chief?"

"Look at the facts in the case," Mason said. "Addicks has employed people around him who have been trying to use hypnotism on animals, particularly gorillas."

"Well?"

"Mrs. Kempton has two periods of blackout. The first time she thought she had fainted. The second time she thinks someone hit her on the head."

"Go on," Della Street said.

Mason said, "Suppose someone put Mrs. Kempton in a hypnotic trance, and while she was in that hypnotic trance he told her this story that she was to believe when she regained consciousness."

Della Street's eyes widened. "Chief," she said, "I bet that's it! That would account for the whole thing, and . . ." Suddenly the eager enthusiasm left her manner, her voice trailed away into silence.

"Go ahead," Mason said.

"But," Della Street said dubiously, "you couldn't get any jury to believe that hypnotism story any more than you could get them to believe the gorilla story."

"Not with the evidence presently available," Mason said, "but this is just the beginning of the case."

"Could a woman be hypnotized and have a synthetic nightmare

of that sort implanted on her consciousness so that it would be remembered as an actual experience when she wakened?"

"I think so," Mason said. "I'm going to check. After all, hypnotism is a subject I know very little about. But all of that still doesn't explain how it happened the police were so triumphantly certain of themselves when they came and arrested Mrs. Kempton. They must have uncovered something. We'll know a lot more within the next day or two. There are a lot of angles to this case we still don't know about."

"Perhaps even a few curves," Della Street said demurely.

CHAPTER TWELVE

SHORTLY BEFORE NOON DELLA STREET'S TELEPHONE RANG. SHE ANswered it, said, "Yes . . . oh yes . . . just a moment. I'll see."

She turned to Perry Mason and said, "Sidney Hardwick of Hardwick, Carson and Redding."

Mason nodded.

"Yes, Mr. Mason is here. He'll talk with Mr. Hardwick. Put your party on, please."

Mason picked up the telephone, said, "Hello, Mason speaking. . . . Hello, Mr. Hardwick."

Hardwick said, "Mr. Mason, I'm in rather a peculiar position. I'd like to have a conference with you and Mr. James Etna."

"When?" Mason asked.

"At your earliest convenience."

"Where?"

"At any place you want. At your office if you wish."

"What about?"

"It's about a matter that puzzles me, and, very frankly, Mr. Mason, it may be of some possible advantage or some possible disadvantage to your client, Josephine Kempton. I am assuming that you're anxious to get information concerning her connection with the case, and I'm anxious to get some information from you gentlemen."

"How soon?" Mason asked.

"Just as soon as you conveniently can arrange it."

Mason said, "Be over here in fifteen minutes. I'll have Etna here."

He hung up the phone, said to Della Street, "Get James Etna on the phone, Della, and tell him that we have an important conference with Hardwick. Tell him to come right over."

Della Street nodded.

Mason said, "I'll be back by the time Etna gets here," and walked down the corridor to Paul Drake's office.

"Drake in?" Mason asked the switchboard operator.

She nodded and said, "Go right on in, Mr. Mason. He's alone. I'll tell him you're coming."

"Thanks," Mason said, opened the gate in the low partition which walled off the small reception room, and walked down the long corridor to Drake's office.

Drake was hanging up the phone just as Mason entered.

"Hello," Mason said. "Anything new?"

"I'm digging away," Drake said, "getting a lot of material but I haven't correlated it yet. It's a lot of miscellaneous odds and ends."

Mason said, "Sidney Hardwick, who was Benjamin Addicks' attorney in his lifetime, and who presumably is representing the estate, is coming over right away to see me. I can tell from the way he's acting that there's something on his mind, something that is bothering him to beat the devil. Any idea what it is?"

Drake shook his head. "Not yet I haven't. Give me another two or three hours and I'll probably find out."

"Give me fifteen minutes and I'll find out," Mason said, grinning.

Drake said, "A preliminary test shows that Addicks had .32 percent of alcohol in his blood when he was killed. That was enough to put him into a deep sleep. There is evidence indicating he had previously had an even greater concentration of blood alcohol.

"I don't need to educate you on the mathematics of alcoholism, Perry, but generally the confused stage of intoxication starts with around .15 percent of alcohol in the blood. At .3 percent to .4 percent the subject is really and truly drunk, that is, stuporous, staggering drunk.

"Now Benjamin Addicks had .32 percent of alcohol in his blood. The police know exactly when Mrs. Kempton arrived at the house. They've been able to check with the driver of the bus. She was actually on the bus she claimed to have taken.

"It's a cinch that Addicks at that point was too intoxicated to think clearly. Apparently he'd been drinking right up to the time that he lay down on the bed and passed out. Blood alcohol decreases at the rate of .02 to .04 percent per hour after absorption."

"What caused him to start a drinking spree like that, Paul?"

"Damned if I know. It must have been something important."

"Find out anything about those telephone bills?" Mason asked.

"Not yet, but I'll have that information within an hour. I'm arranging to get copies of all the telephone bills."

"How are you doing that, Paul?"

"I'd rather not tell you. I'm sticking my neck out a little. The point is that I'm getting them."

"As soon as you get some information, let me know. Now tell me about this Alan Blevins. Is he a hypnotist?"

"I'll say he is, a darn good one. Incidentally, he doubts if a gorilla can be hypnotized by ordinary methods. That is, he claimed he had induced the equivalent of a hypnotic state in a gorilla, but when he had done that there was no way to make suggestions direct to the subconscious mind. With a human being you do it by speech. With a gorilla you have no bridge from your mind to his. The animal merely sleeps. There's hardly any way of telling whether it's a hypnotically induced sleep or a natural sleep."

"Blevins had been discharged?"

"Yes."

"Some words?"

"I gathered there was no ill feeling. Nathan Fallon brought him the bad news. Addicks even refused to discuss the matter. The whole crew were fired at once."

"So Blevins hated Addicks?"

"Could have."

"Find out where he was last night," Mason said.

"I already have," Drake said. "He is a bachelor. His wife divorced him two years ago. He said he was home, that he watched television and then went to bed."

"No corroboration?"

"Just his word, so far. Want me to check it further?"

"I sure do. Why did his wife divorce him, Paul?"

"Mental cruelty. She alleged he was always hypnotizing her, trying to use her as a subject, making her ridiculous and all of that."

"Find out more about it," Mason said. "Locate her, Paul. I want to talk with her."

Drake made a note.

"Anything else?"

"Guess that's all. I'll get on back and see what Hardwick wants. He should be about due."

"One other thing," Drake said. "Blevins tells me he taught Addicks how to hypnotize."

"Why?"

"Addicks wanted him to."

Mason said, "Paul, I want all this stuff verified. I'm going to put on a defense in this case that will make history, but first I have to know what really happened out there."

"Can't Josephine Kempton tell you?" Drake asked.

"No."

"Why not?"

"Confidentially, I don't think she knows."

Drake said disgustedly, "Oh, for Pete's sake, Perry! Don't put on one of those defenses where the dame says, 'We were sitting there with the carving knife, and then, all of a sudden, everything went black to me, and when I regained my senses he was lying there on the bed, perfectly still, and I cried, "Speak to me, Benny! Speak to me!"'"

Mason grinned. "It's not like that at all, Paul, and yet it is. Get all the dope on Blevins—find his ex-wife. I'm going over to talk with Hardwick—see you later, Paul."

Mason walked back to his office. Della Street said, "James Etna is on his way over. He seems terribly worked up."

The telephone rang. Della Street picked up the receiver, said, "Hello," and then to Mason, "That's Mr. Etna now."

"Tell him to come on in," Mason said, "and tell Gertie to bring Mr. Hardwick in just as soon as Hardwick arrives at the office."

Della Street hung up the telephone, went out and escorted Etna into the office.

Etna, showing considerable emotion, said, "Mr. Mason, can you tell me what in the world has got into the police?"

Mason shook his head. "They certainly seem to feel they've slipped over a fast one."

Etna said, "It was almost as though they had some means of knowing what had been said . . ."

Mason grinned. "You're not telling me anything," he said. "Della Street and I took this office to pieces, trying to find a microphone. We thought perhaps they'd managed to listen in on our client's story. How about the writ? Did you get it?"

"No. I found it wouldn't do any good."

"You mean she's charged?"

"That's right. First-degree murder. They'd already filed and that was a regular warrant of arrest."

"Something happened to make them feel mighty confident all of a sudden," Mason said.

"Of course, it's an unusual story," Etna ventured.

"You can say that all over again."

"What do you make of it?" Etna asked.

"Her story?"

"Yes."

"I'm not thinking yet."

"What will happen when she tells that to a jury?"

"You mean *if* she tells it to a jury."

"She'll have to get on the stand sooner or later."

Mason grinned. "Let's make it later then, Etna."

"You don't think a jury will believe the story?"

"Do you?"

"Well," Etna said, "hang it, Mason, I do and I don't."

Mason continued to smile.

"Of course, when you take into consideration the entire background out there, the thing sounds reasonable. Here was a millionaire who had been experimenting with hypnotism. He'd been trying to hypnotize gorillas, and apparently trying to instill them with homicidal impulses. It was only natural that sooner or later he should have some measure of success, and then it's only logical to suppose that he might be the first victim."

Mason said, "Go ahead, Jim. You're trying to sell yourself on her story. You're making an argument to yourself as though you were a jury."

"Well, why not?"

Mason said, "When a lawyer has to argue with himself to try to talk himself into believing a client's story, it's a damn sight better to keep anyone else from ever hearing that story."

"I suppose you're right," Etna said with a weak smile. "I hadn't realized exactly what was happening in my own mind, but now that you mention it I guess I have been trying very hard, and not too successfully, to make myself believe a story that—well, hang it, I still don't know just where I stand on it. The story sounds crazy until I consider all the background, and then it's almost logical."

Mason said, "We'll know a lot more in a few days, Jim."

Etna said, "I can't help but think that I've let you in for something."

Mason shook his head. "It's okay. I've been in worse spots than this."

"That brings us back to a question of why the police acted as they did. Wasn't it rather unusual?"

"Unusual!" Mason exclaimed. "It was unique."

The phone rang. Della Street picked up the receiver, nodded to Mason and said, "It's Hardwick."

"We'll postpone this discussion a while," Mason said to Etna. "Let's put up a bold front as far as Hardwick is concerned. We'll be all smiles and optimism—all right, Della, show him in."

Della Street held the door open and said, "Mr. Hardwick."

Sidney Hardwick, apparently very much concerned about something, said, "Good morning, gentlemen, good morning. I hope I haven't disrupted your entire day, Mr. Mason—and you too, Mr. Etna."

"Not at all," Mason said. "Sit down. What can we do for you?"

Hardwick sat down, adjusted the glasses on his nose, pulled the black ribbon back over his ear, adjusted his hearing aid, and said, "Let's please understand each other at the outset. I know that you two people are in many ways in an adverse position to me. You are, I believe, representing Josephine Kempton?"

"I believe so," Mason said. "That is, I think we will be representing her."

"Both of you?" Hardwick asked.

James Etna shifted his position slightly, then said, "Yes, I guess so."

"Now then," Hardwick went on, "I represented Benjamin Addicks during his lifetime. I know more about him than any living man. I drew a will for him some months ago. That will was in accordance with Mr. Addicks' wishes *at that time*."

"You have reason to believe his wishes changed?"

Hardwick cleared his throat. "Both his wishes *and* his will."

Mason said, "You have something to tell us and something you want to ask us. Why not put it on the line?"

Hardwick smiled. "I'm afraid that I'm not a very good poker player."

"You're not playing poker," Mason told him. "You're engaged in a consultation where we're all of us putting certain cards on the table. Now suppose you start putting down as many cards as you want to disclose, and then we'll see what we can do."

"Very well. There is a situation here that is most unusual, a situation that is in some ways very much in favor of your client. I felt that you should know it, Mr. Mason, before you—well, perhaps before you decided you wouldn't represent her."

"Go ahead," Mason said. "We're listening."

Hardwick said, "You called on Benjamin Addicks Tuesday night. Your call upset him. When you found the ring and the watch—well, it was a jolt to Addicks' self-respect and to his self-assurance. He completely changed his mind about what he wanted to do in his will.

"That night, before he went to bed, somewhere around eleven-thirty, he called in Nathan Fallon and Mortimer Hershey for a conference. He said, 'Gentlemen, I have been a fool. I have been self-righteous. I have been arbitrary in my judgments of my fellow men. I am sorry. I am going to try to make what atonement I can. I have here a will which I have drawn up entirely in my own hand-writing. I am putting this will in an envelope. I am giving it to you. I want you gentlemen to seal the envelope and sign your names on the back of it, and place that envelope in a safe place. If anything should happen to me within the next few days I want you to see that Mr. Sidney Hardwick has this will.'"

"Within the next few days?" Mason asked. "Was he then anticipating something . . . ?"

"No, no, nothing like that. It seems that what he had in mind was to make another appointment with me and have his will, this holographic will, reduced to a more conventional form and duly signed in the presence of witnesses. He was making this holographic will as something in the nature of a stopgap so that in case anything *did* happen to him he wouldn't be bound by the old will that he had made."

Mason nodded, said, "You went out there that night to have him make a new will?"

"That's right. He was, however, too upset to see me. I couldn't understand it at the time. In the light of subsequent developments I can put the whole picture together.

"You had jarred the man's self-assurance, Mr. Mason. And I can assure you he was a hard man to jar, a very hard man.

"Now then," Hardwick went on, "I probably have no right to do this, but I am going to read you a portion of the holographic will that Mr. Addicks made, a will that I am going to offer for probate. I think there are some things in here which are of the greatest importance to you gentlemen, and particularly to your client."

"Go ahead," Mason said, glancing significantly at Della Street so that she would be certain to include the quotation from the will in her shorthand notes.

Hardwick unfolded a paper and read:

I, Benjamin Addicks, make this my last will and testament entirely in my own handwriting, in a spirit of abject humility. I have been arbitrary. I have been self-righteous. I have been too prone to judge my fellow men. I particularly regret the circumstances that alienated me from my brother, Herman.

I have had a very great emotional shock tonight. Mrs. Josephine Kempton, a former employee, whom I had more or less directly accused of theft, is absolutely innocent. The valuable objects which I had thought she had stolen have been discovered under such circumstances that it is quite apparent that they were stolen by a mischievous monkey, and that I alone am responsible for the actions of this monkey.

I therefore make my last will and testament as follows: To Josephine Kempton, my former housekeeper, I leave my heartfelt apologies and the sum of fifty thousand dollars. To Mortimer Hershey, my business manager, who has, incidentally, been well paid for his services, I leave the sum of ten thousand dollars. To Nathan Fallon, who, I think, has been grossly overpaid, and who at times has been completely disloyal to my interests, I leave the sum of one dollar and my admonition to him that the prime requisite of an employee is absolute, unswerving loyalty. I trust that this admonition will stand him in good stead in whatever position he may next occupy in his new employment.

I appoint my bank, the Seaboard Mechanics National Trust Company, as executor of this my last will, and direct that all legal matters in connection with the probate of the estate shall be in the hands of Sidney Hardwick of the firm of Hardwick, Carson and Redding.

Hardwick glanced up from the paper and said, "There you are, gentlemen. The will was dated Tuesday evening, and it is entirely in the handwriting of Benjamin Addicks, and is signed by him."

Mason said, "That undoubtedly throws a new light on the situation. I notice that you said you were going to read a *portion* of the will."

Hardwick smiled. "That's right. There are several other bequests to former employees and a residuary clause leaving all the balance of the estate to his brother."

"His brother's last name is Addicks?" Mason asked.

"It is not."

"May I ask what it is?"

"It will be disclosed later."

"How did his former will dispose of his property?"

Hardwick merely smiled.

"I'll put it this way," Mason said, "was Mrs. Kempton mentioned in that will?"

"No. She definitely was not."

"So that Addicks apparently tried to make atonement," Mason said musingly.

"I felt you should know that," Hardwick said. "It strengthens the position of your client, and it might be valuable information for you gentlemen to have in fixing your compensation. In other words, I felt you might be embarrassed if you fixed a definite fee for your services and then found your client had fifty thousand dollars you knew nothing about."

"Thanks," Mason said. "Now what do *you* want?"

Hardwick said, "I want to talk with your client, Josephine Kempton. I want to talk with her alone. I want to talk with her on a matter which is absolutely confidential."

"I take it," Mason said, "that you are indicating that you don't wish us to be present?"

"I want to talk with her in absolute confidence."

Mason glanced at James Etna.

"It's all right by me," Etna said. "I certainly feel very grateful and . . ."

"I don't," Mason said.

"What?" Hardwick exclaimed.

Mason grinned. "I don't feel *that* grateful."

"I certainly have given you information . . ."

"Sure," Mason said, "you've given us information that helps in fixing fees. We're grateful. I'd do anything for you I could, personally. But our client is in a different position. I'm not going to start writing any blank checks on my client's account until I know what it is you're after."

"I can assure you, Mr. Mason, that it's a matter which has absolutely nothing to do with the case in which your client is now involved. It is a matter that must remain highly confidential. In fact, Mrs. Kempton herself will not know what it is I am trying to clear up."

Mason shook his head. "I want to know what you're gunning for before I let any client of mine move onto the target range."

"She's not going to get hurt."

"That," Mason said, "is something on which she's entitled to the benefit of legal advice, legal advice that is completely and solely to her best interests."

"I'm afraid, Mr. Mason, that you're putting too high a price on your offer."

Mason smiled and said, "You put a high enough price on reading us the provisions of the will."

Hardwick said, "All right, suppose you would have learned the provisions anyway after the will had been filed for probate. Having them in advance may make several thousand dollars difference to you gentlemen personally."

"We're grateful," Mason said. "But we advise our clients for their best interests, not ours."

"I don't think my request is unreasonable," Hardwick said.

"What do you want to talk with Mrs. Kempton about?"

"I am not at liberty to tell you."

"All right, then," Mason said, "*I'll* tell *you*, and we'll see how close I come to it."

"*You'll* tell *me?*" Hardwick asked in surprise.

"That's right," Mason said. "You want to ask Josephine Kempton about the murder of Helen Cadmus."

"The *murder* of Helen Cadmus?" Hardwick echoed.

"That's right, the murder. You have reason to believe that someone tossed Helen Cadmus overboard from that yacht. You have some information that we don't have. You also have some problem that bothers you in connection with the estate. When I know more about why you're interested I'll give you a better answer."

Hardwick cleared his throat with a loud harrumph, took off his glasses, polished them vigorously, adjusted them back on his nose.

"How right am I?" Mason asked.

"You're simply guessing," Hardwick said.

"Sure I'm guessing, but I'm guessing pretty close to the truth, am I not?"

"Let us suppose for the sake of the argument that you are. Where does that leave us?"

"That's what I'm trying to find out."

"Frankly, I am concerned over a disquieting possibility which may have some serious effect on the fortunes of your client."

"You surely aren't going to toy around with a theory that Josephine Kempton murdered Helen Cadmus?"

"I didn't make any such accusation."

"You didn't put it in words," Mason said, "but that's the thought you're trying to scare us with—the way someone pulls out a jumping jack and shakes it in front of a kid's nose."

"I merely want you to realize the necessity of having your client co-operate with me."

Mason said, "We certainly don't intend to stand by and have you saddle a murder on our client."

"I'm not going to saddle a murder on her if she co-operates. I promise you gentlemen I will never breathe a word of anything I learn to the police. After all, gentlemen," Hardwick went on, "there is no reason for us to assume a position of antagonism. There are two things I want, and . . ."

"*Two* things?" Mason interrupted.

"Exactly."

"I thought you only wanted one."

"You didn't wait for me to finish. I want to have a private talk with your client, and I want those Helen Cadmus diaries."

Mason shook his head.

"In return for which," Hardwick went on, "you could count on my entire co-operation at every stage of the case."

Mason said, "To hell with all this mealymouthed diplomacy. To get down to brass tacks, you're here to blackmail us. You want the Cadmus diaries and you want to get Mrs. Kempton to pull a chestnut out of the fire for you. If she doesn't do it, you're going to try to pin the Cadmus murder on her."

"Mr. Mason!"

"And," Mason went on, "you're trying to shake down the wrong people."

"Mr. Mason, I am only telling you the two things you can do which will be of the greatest advantage to your client. After all, you know I can get what I want by going to the police—and then the whole thing would be in the public press."

"That's right," Mason said. "The police can inquire about anything they damn please, and the press can publish anything they damn please, and we can advise our client not to answer any questions."

Hardwick got to his feet. "I'll now tell you gentlemen something else," he said. "I have received a cablegram from Benjamin Addicks' brother in Australia."

"That's nice."

"I cabled the only address that I had as soon as I was advised of Benjamin's death and a cablegram of condolence was received. Then, as soon as I knew about the will, I cabled him giving him general terse summary of the terms."

"And you've received a reply from him," Mason said, "suggesting that you are to contest the payment of any money to Josephine Kempton because she is guilty of the murder, and therefore under the law cannot take anything from the estate regardless of what provisions are in the will."

"I haven't as yet received any such cablegram. I have received a cablegram instructing me to file the will for probate, and to use my best judgment in representing his interests."

"Well, you will receive such a cablegram," Mason said, "and in the event you don't receive it, as a lawyer who is interested in protecting the interests of his client, you'll call his attention to that provision of the law and suggest that if Josephine Kempton should be convicted of murder, he'll profit to the tune of fifty thousand dollars."

"For certain considerations my client might be willing to forego raising the point."

"You'll tell him he has a right to take that fact into consideration?"

"What would *you* do if *you* were an attorney in my position?" Hardwick asked.

"I'd tell him, of course," Mason said. "Now then, I'll ask you one. What would you do if you were an attorney representing Josephine Kempton, and some attorney who manifestly wanted to see her convicted of the murder of Benjamin Addicks, wanted to question her in private to see if he couldn't find some grounds for pinning another murder on her?"

Hardwick said, "If I were *certain* of my premise, which you aren't, I'd decide what was for the client's best interests and advise her accordingly."

Mason said, "You can either put all your cards on the table or go to hell."

"You've gotten tough with the wrong man," Hardwick said, coldly. "I'm not going to hell—but your client is—now."

He stalked out of the office.

"Good heavens," Etna said, "you certainly told him off, Mr. Mason."

Mason's eyes narrowed. "He told us something that was to our advantage—and he's suspecting something we don't even know about yet."

"Of course," Etna said, "he has a lot of background information we don't have, and that gives him a terrific advantage."

"All right," Mason said, "let him try and keep it. It's a race now. We're off to a bad start, but we move fast."

He turned to Della Street. "Get me Paul Drake on the line, Della."

When Della Street nodded, Mason took the telephone, said, "Paul, I'm in a rat race. I want some fast action. Helen Cadmus knew more about Benjamin Addicks than any other person except Addicks' own lawyer.

"She knew something that's worrying this lawyer. I want to know what it was. Benjamin Addicks apparently was a bachelor. He was along in middle age, but he was stocky, vigorous, virile. I want to find the woman. . . . How the hell do I know what woman? *The* woman. And when you get the numbers on those phone calls that went through to the yacht, check the numbers and if any are the numbers of hotels or auto courts, rush operatives out there with photographs and see if Addicks was shacked up with some babe."

Mason slammed up the phone.

James Etna said, "Aren't you rather jumping at conclusions, Mason? Everyone says Addicks had no women in his life."

Mason grinned. "Just because some people are liars, Jim, is no reason why we should be fools."

CHAPTER THIRTEEN

GERTIE CLOSED AND LOCKED THE DOOR TO THE ENTRANCE ROOM promptly at 5:00. By 5:30 Della had the outgoing mail arranged in a pile, and Gertie helped her with stamping the envelopes. Then Gertie went home.

Della Street walked into Mason's private office.

"Tired, Della?"

"Not particularly. How about you?"

Mason smiled. "I've been reading diaries until I'm dizzy. Can you take some more?"

"Yes. What is it?"

"We've got to find out what's in those Cadmus diaries."

"But we've done that."

"No, we haven't. We've read the lines. Now we have to see what's written between and behind the lines."

A knock sounded on the door of the outer office, a long peremptory knock.

"Shall I see who it is?" she asked.

Mason shook his head. "Let it go, Della. We've had enough emergency stuff and enough after-hours work."

She sat down at her secretarial desk. Mason came over to place his hip on a corner of the desk. He put his hand over hers. "Nice to have you around," he said.

"Nice to be around," she told him, smiling up at him.

The knock on the outer door became a steady tattoo.

Mason said, "Whoever's trying to get in that outer office seems to be pretty certain someone's here, Della. That's a continued, persistent knocking. Better see who it is."

Della Street hurried through to the outer office, opened the door. Mason heard her exchange a few words, then she came back with a late edition of the afternoon paper. On the paper had been written, "Mr. Mason. Compliments of Sidney Hardwick. I want you to see that I am a fast worker."

Della Street once more sat down at her secretarial desk. Mason leaned over her shoulder as she spread the afternoon paper out on the desk.

Headlines across three columns at the top of the paper screamed:

POLICE HINT POSSIBILITY SECOND MURDER
AUTHORITIES INTERROGATE SUSPECT IN ADDICKS' MURDER
ON DISAPPEARANCE OF ATTRACTIVE SECRETARY

"Why, the nerve of him," Della Street said, "the . . ."

"That's all right," Mason said, "let's take a look and see how far he's gone, Della."

Together they read the article, an article which stated that police were now making inquiries of Mrs. Josephine Kempton concerning the mysterious death of Helen Cadmus, the attractive secretary who was supposed to have jumped overboard from Benjamin Addicks' palatial private yacht in a storm-tossed sea some months earlier.

That death, the newspaper pointed out, has been treated by the authorities either as a suicide or as an accident, but with the murder of Benjamin Addicks authorities had reopened the entire files surrounding the death of Helen Cadmus.

The article went on to say:

> The district attorney pointed out that Josephine Kempton, who is at present under arrest as a suspect in the murder of Benjamin Addicks, shared connecting staterooms on the Addicks yacht with the attractive secretary. Helen Cadmus mysteriously disappeared during the night of a wild storm off the coast of Catalina Island. Mrs. Kempton swore that she had taken a seasick remedy which had made her drowsy and had gone to bed and gone to sleep.
>
> While that statement was taken at its face value at the time, the district attorney declared that, in the light of more recent developments, investigation into the death of Helen Cadmus is being reopened. "We are," he said, "making no accusations or insinuations at the present time because we are not in a position to make any. We simply feel that in the interests of justice the death of Helen Cadmus which, at the time, was taken as a tragic accident in a storm, *may* have had more sinister implications.
>
> "All I can say is that we are making an investigation, and that we have interrogated Mrs. Kempton as to her knowledge of what transpired on the night Helen Cadmus disappeared, and that Mrs. Kempton has refused to give us anything more than the time of day.
>
> "I care to make no other statement."

Mason's jaw clamped, his eyes were cold and angry.

"Well," Della Street said, "Hardwick was as good as his word."

"No better certainly," Mason said. "All right, Della. Wait here for a minute. I'll go see Paul Drake. We're in a shooting war, and I hope he has some ammunition for us."

"You want me to give him a ring?" Della Street asked.

"No," Mason said. "I'll go on down to his office and see what's cooking. In the meantime, Della, ring up the newspapers and tell them that if they'll send representatives over here I'll make a statement about the Addicks murder case."

"Do you want me to wait until you've seen Paul before . . . ?"

Mason shook his head.

"You mean if Paul doesn't have anything you'll make a straight denial and . . . ?"

Mason said, "A straight denial, Della, won't buy us anything in this situation. We're going to have to put Hardwick and his side of the case on the defensive. I'll need something spectacular. If Paul Drake has the ammunition I'll shoot it. If he doesn't, I'll shoot blanks, but those blanks will make so much noise the other side will start running for cover. You put through the calls, Della, and hold the fort. I'll be back as soon as I can get in touch with Paul."

Mason went out through the exit door from his office into the corridor, walked down to the offices of the Drake Detective Agency, jerked open the door, caught the eye of the receptionist at the switchboard, and said, "Is Paul in?"

She smiled. "He insists he's *all* in."

"That's fine," Mason told her, glancing vaguely at a blonde who was waiting. "Tell him I'm on my way."

Mason opened the gate in the long corridor leading to Paul Drake's office, and found Drake holding his ear to a telephone, sorting out papers while carrying on a conversation with one of his men.

Drake motioned for Mason to sit down, and after a moment the detective said into the telephone, "All right. Get her to write her name on the back of the photographs so that it will make an absolute identification. She probably won't care to make an affidavit as yet, but tie her up so she can't back out. Be sure she identifies the photographs."

Drake hung up, gave Mason a tired smile, and said, "Your hunch paid off, Perry."

"What?"

"Getting the telephone numbers from which Addicks placed his collect calls to the yacht, and . . ."

"You mean you've tied him up with a woman?"

"That's right."

"Woman or women?"

"Apparently it's the same woman in both instances—Helen Cadmus."

Mason whistled.

"That's about all there is to it. On a couple of occasions when the yacht got into port along about nine or ten o'clock in the evening, Addicks started back from the beach and yet didn't get in until the next morning. When Addicks hadn't taken Nathan Fallon, Mortimer Hershey, or Josephine Kempton along, there was nobody to make a check between the house and the yacht, and find out when the yacht did get in. I checked on the yacht's log.

"A couple of times when Addicks started out on the yacht and then got off in Catalina, and sent the yacht cruising, he called the captain to give instructions. Those telephone calls were from these same two motels.

"I haven't checked on the dates as yet, but there's no question but what that's where the calls came from, and in one of the motels the woman who runs the place is very definite in her identification. She identifies the photographs of Benjamin Addicks and that of Helen Cadmus."

"How did he register?" Mason asked.

"He used a fictitious name, naturally."

"They want license numbers of cars," Mason said. "Did he . . . ?"

"Yes, he gave the license number of his Cadillac."

Mason thought that over. His eyes narrowed.

"Did you notice a blonde out in the office when you came in?" Drake asked.

"Yes, what about her?"

"I was going to call you. I asked her to wait a few minutes. She's Mrs. Blevins, the wife of the animal psychologist. I got her to come to my office because . . ."

"Let's get her in," Mason said. "I want to talk with her. Now listen, Paul, very definitely I don't want any slip-up on this thing. I want your men to get this angle tied up tight. What alias did Addicks use?"

"In both instances it was Barnwell. He was registered under the name of B. F. Barnwell."

"What was Benjamin Addicks' middle name, Paul?"

"I don't know."

Mason snapped his fingers and said, "I bet you a dime it was Franklin. Benjamin Franklin Addicks."

"Well?" Drake asked.

"B. F. Barnwell would naturally be the way he'd register. He'd keep his first two initials B. F. Now look, Paul, Addicks had a lot of mining interests. He was in Nevada a lot. I want you to get your men started checking everything they can find in Nevada. I want you to find if there are any registrations in motor courts for B. F. Barnwell. And, while you're about it, just for the fun of the thing, check the vital statistics. But find out everything you can about Barnwell."

Drake said, "You're going to have one hell of a bill on this, Perry. I've got men . . ."

"That's all right," Mason interrupted. "I'm in the middle of a fight, and something big is involved. I don't know what it is. Apparently there's nothing in those Helen Cadmus diaries, and yet everyone who has any connection with Addicks wants to get those diaries by one means or another. The only thing that I can think of is that I find nothing in the diaries because I've read them. The other people haven't read them and are therefore assuming there's something important in them because there's something important that *should* be in them—all right, Paul, let's get Mrs. Blevins in here."

Drake said into the telephone, "Send Mrs. Blevins in," then stretched back, rubbed his eyes with his knuckles, yawned prodigiously, said, "Gosh, Perry, I'm all in. I've been sitting here at the end of this telephone night and day . . ."

Mason said reassuringly, "We're getting toward the end of it now, Paul. We're striking pay dirt."

"I don't know what good that stuff's going to do," Drake told him. "The guy plays house with his secretary—an idea not exactly original with him. It *has* been done, you know. You have to admit she was a mighty darned good looking girl . . ."

"I know, I know," Mason interrupted, "but we're getting a lead on something."

"Well, pretty quick," Drake said, "I'm going to fall right forward on my face and . . ."

The door opened and Mrs. Blevins, a blonde about twenty-seven years old, with big blue eyes, stood in the doorway.

Her clothes made no effort to minimize her figure. She not only had a good one but seemed quite conscious of the fact.

"Hello," she said to Perry Mason. "You're Mr. Mason. I saw you come in. I smiled but I guess you didn't notice me. I'm Fern Blevins, Alan Blevins' ex-wife. And you're Mr. Drake."

Mason bowed, smiled, and Mrs. Blevins came toward him to extend her hand.

Drake said to Mason, "You talk, or do I?"

"I will," Mason said. "Please sit down, Mrs. Blevins. We're going to be frightfully inquisitive."

She shifted her blue eyes momentarily, said, "What if I don't choose to answer?"

"You don't have to," Mason told her. "We're interested in your divorce."

"Oh that!" she said, with relief apparent in her voice. "I was afraid you were *really* going to get personal."

"What we're primarily after," Mason said, smiling, "is in finding out everything that went on in the house where Addicks lived."

"Stonehenge you mean?"

"Yes."

"I guess a lot went on there."

"Did you ever stay there with your husband?"

"Good heavens, no. *He* never stayed there. He worked there, that's all—although sometimes he didn't get home until pretty late at night."

"I notice that you allege mental cruelty in your complaint," Mason said.

"That was as good as anything."

"Can you tell us some of the details, some of the things that didn't appear in the complaint?"

She said, "Alan was quite a bit older than I."

"You were his second wife?"

"Yes."

"Go ahead."

She said, "He—well, I guess we got tired of each other, and—I got tired of being a human guinea pig."

Mason glanced significantly at Paul Drake, and said, "Do you mean he hypnotized you, Mrs. Blevins?"

"I'll say he hypnotized me. I think he must have had me under some sort of hypnotic influence when I married him."

"Lots of people feel that way," Mason said. "Can you tell us any details?"

"She said, "I was working as a secretary and I did some work for him on a paper that he was writing. Well, of course, you know hypnotism is something that fascinates people. I became very much interested and asked him about hypnotism, and he—well, he seemed very nice. Those were the days of courtship. Everything he did was nice."

"Go on," Mason said.

"I don't know how to describe it. You get starry-eyed and every minute that you're with a man is just like heaven. Then you marry him, and in place of being happy you find that you're terribly fed up with the whole thing. The glamour vanishes, and you see the man as a very ordinary individual. Moreover, he's a jealous, possessive individual who keeps prying into your secrets and he starts making all sorts of accusations."

"You kept on working after you were married?" Mason asked.

"Yes."

"For your husband?"

"No. I had a regular job. I stayed with it."

"Can you tell us a little more about being a guinea pig?"

"Well, when he told me about hypnotism, he asked me if I'd like to be hypnotized. He was looking right at me, and I had the most delicious feeling of submission. I felt that I'd do anything for him. I wanted to show my confidence in him, and I told him that I'd be perfectly willing."

"And then what?"

She said, "I don't remember."

"What do you mean by that?"

She said, "It's one of those things that a hypnotist can do to you. He can hypnotize you and tell you that you won't remember anything about what you did while you were under a hypnotic influence. I've seen Alan do it dozens of times to people. He'll make them do the craziest things and say the craziest things, and then he'll tell them to wake up without remembering anything that they had done, and not to remember even about being hypnotized."

"And it was like that with you?"

She nodded. "I was looking at him and saying, 'Well, go ahead, Alan, hypnotize me—' and then he told me that he'd already hynotized me, and I thought it was just a joke until I happened to notice my wrist watch and realized that either someone had set my watch ahead forty-five minutes, or there were about forty-five minutes that I couldn't account for."

"Then what?" Mason asked.

"Then he kept looking at me in a peculiar way, and after about five minutes i had the most absolutely insane impulse to—to do something."

"What?" Mason asked.

She shook her head and said, "It was a crazy thing, but anyhow I did it, and—well, I know now what had happened."

"What?"

"It was a post-hypnotic suggestion," she said. "That's the way hypnotists work. They get you under their domination and they cannot only make you do things but they'll give you something to do as a post-hypnotic suggestion—that is, they'll tell you to wake up and not remember you've been hypnotized, and then five or ten minutes after you wake up, you'll do some crazy thing. That's the way it was with me."

"Go on," Mason said.

"After a while we got married."

"The hypnotism kept up?"

"It kept up, Mr. Mason, a lot more often than I realized."

"What do you mean by that?"

"I'd find myself doing things that were the result of post-hypnotic suggestions. There's some of that I don't want to go into."

Mason, watching her, said, "We'd like very much to have your co-operation, Mrs. Blevins. We'd be willing to pay you for any inconvenience that . . ."

"That's what Mr. Drake told me, but there are some things that money can't buy."

"Could you give us a hint?" Mason asked.

She hesitated.

Mason smiled and said, "You were already married to the man and . . ."

"Oh, all right," she blurted. "I was a fool. I kept letting Alan hypnotize me. I'd have a headache and he would put me to sleep and I'd wake up in a minute or two and the headache would be all gone, and I'd feel just wonderful, completely relaxed. Sometimes when I was nervous and couldn't sleep, he'd give me a brief hypnotic treatment with a post-hypnotic suggestion. Then I'd become so sleepy that I simply couldn't hold my head up and—well, that's the way it would happen.

"Then, as I told you, things got to the point where the glamour wore off and—well, I was working and—I don't know how to tell you this."

Mason said, "There was another man?"

"Alan thinks there was."

"Was there?"

"Alan thinks there was," she repeated tonelessly.

"Go on," Mason said, "what happened?"

"Well, one night Alan was working, and I had a sudden crazy desire to put down in writing a lot of things about my private life, things that ordinarily I wouldn't ever tell anyone about. I wanted to put those things in writing and hide the paper in the back of a drawer under a collection of photographs—I just couldn't keep from it. I wrote out a lot of things about my private life and about what had happened and put it there under the photographs in the drawer."

"And then?" Mason prompted.

"The next morning I suddenly realized what a crazy thing I'd done and I wanted to get that paper and burn it up. I went to the drawer and—well, you know the answer, the paper was gone."

"You mean it had been a post-hypnotic suggestion?"

"That's right. I didn't even know that he'd hypnotized me. I still don't know when he had hypnotized me, but he had left that post-hypnotic suggestion in my mind. So then I knew that he had the paper, and the stuff in there was evidence that he could have used against me."

"In a divorce case?"

Her face flushed. "Yes."

"What did you do?"

"I was so darned mad I believe I could have killed him, but I was smart by that time. There are some games two people can play. I didn't let on that I knew a thing in the world about the paper being gone. I waited about two days and then I started searching that house. I took one day to stay home from work and, believe me, I went through that house from top to bottom. I finally found the paper."

"Where?"

She laughed. "He was smart. He'd taken up one corner of the carpet, pulled it back and slid the paper in under the corner."

"So what did you do with the paper?"

"I destroyed it, and then I walked right out of that house and went to a lawyer and filed suit for a divorce. I never went back and I never let Alan get in a position where he could clap those steel-gray eyes on me again."

"He could hypnotize you quickly?"

"Apparently all he had to do was to snap his fingers and I'd be under the influence."

"Go on," Mason said.

"Well, Alan thought that he had me. He thought that I couldn't do a thing, but then when he went to look for his evidence it was gone and—well, I'd sued him for mental cruelty and there were a lot of things that he didn't want to have come out, so—well, I got my decree."

"And remarried?" Mason asked.

She colored a bit and said, "Not yet. My decree isn't final."

"When will it be final?"

"In another week."

"And then you're going to remarry?"

"Yes."

"To a man you've known for some time?"

"Yes."

"He's not a hypnotist, I take it," Mason said, smiling.

"You can bet money on that, Mr. Mason."

Mason opened his wallet, took out four fifty-dollar bills, and said, "Here's two hundred dollars, Mrs. Blevins, that will pay you for your time and compensate you for any inconvenience. Those might help on your trousseau."

She accepted the money, folded it, placed it in her purse, looked up at Mason with eyes that were filled with gratitude.

"Mr. Mason, that's—well, that's just fine of you."

"We certainly appreciate your frankness," Mason said. "Now could you tell us whether Alan ever hypnotized you and made you think something had happened that didn't?"

"Oh, yes. That was one of his pet stunts. He'd hypnotize a person and give him a long song and dance about what had happened, and tell the person to wake up and not to think about the thing for an hour or two hours, but gradually to absorb the narrative into his memory as an actual experience, and then after two hours, as a post-hypnotic suggestion, to start telling about it."

"And people would do that?"

"Some of them would. Of course, you can't hypnotize everyone, Mr. Mason, and . . ."

"I understand. Now do you know whether he ever hypnotized Josephine Kempton, Mr. Addicks' housekeeper?"

"I think he did. I once heard him mention something he had done with her by way of demonstrating a point to Mr. Addicks."

"Do you know anything else that might help us?" Mason asked.

"No."

"Well, thanks a lot. I don't think we need to detain you any longer right now, Mrs. Blevins, but we may want to talk with you again later."

"Any time," she said, "any time after four o'clock. You can call me and I'll come in any time. Mr. Drake has my number."

"Thank you," Mason said.

She rose from the chair, started for the door, then suddenly detoured to take Perry Mason's hand in both of hers. "You're sweet," she said. "Here's something that may be of help. Addicks wasn't his real name. I know that Alan managed to hypnotize him once and learned that his real name was Barnwell. If there's anything else, you just let me know."

Her eyes were grateful as she gave Mason a very cordial smile. Then she opened the door and went out, swinging into the corridor with a saucy flip of her skirts.

"Do you any good?" Drake asked.

Mason grinned at him and said, "Paul, the last few minutes have *really* done things for me. Start your boys working in Nevada, then go on home, take a good hot bath, crawl into bed and get some sleep."

"You mean that?" Drake asked in surprise.

"Sure I mean it," Mason said and hurried out of Drake's office.

Mason opened the door of his private office.

Della Street, who had been standing by his desk, arranging some papers, looked up as he entered.

Mason reached her in two swift strides, put his arms around her, picked her off the floor, whirled her around, and then held her to him. "Baby," he said, "we've struck pay dirt."

She looked up at him somewhat wistfully. "All of which, I presume, accounts for this sudden display of enthusiasm."

"It isn't enthusiasm," Mason said, hugging her to him, "it's affection."

"Well," she said, "it *must* have been important information."

"Get the newspapers?" Mason asked.

"Yes. Reporters are on their way up here. I told them it was hot, and they're coming up fast."

"Good girl," Mason said, and looked down into her eyes.

She put her hands on his shoulders, her face tilted up. Mason bent forward tenderly.

Her lips clung to his for a long moment, then she suddenly was pushing him away, grabbing a Kleenex from her purse and wiping the lipstick off his lips.

"Chief," she exclaimed, "have you forgotten that a bunch of observant, keen-eyed newspaper reporters are due to burst in here at any minute?"

Mason smiled, patted her shoulder and said, "It's okay, Della. We're going to give them something that will jolt Mr. Sidney Hardwick right back on the heels of his shoes."

"Good. I hope you do it. How's my mouth? Am I smeared? Oh, you wouldn't know anyway!"

"I can see anything a keen-eyed reporter can," Mason said.

She laughed, went to the mirror, adjusted her lips for a moment, and then said, "There's someone at the door to the outer office now."

"I'll see the reporters out there," Mason said.

He followed her to the outer office, greeted two reporters who had arrived simultaneously. While he was passing cigarettes a third arrived, and then a fourth.

"What's the big news?" one of the reporters asked. "I hope it's good. We certainly broke our necks getting over here. Your secretary intimated it was red hot."

"It is red hot," Mason said.

"What is it?"

"You have the information about the holographic will that Benjamin Addicks left?"

"Hell, yes. I hope you didn't think *that* was news. Hardwick, Carson and Redding released information about that two hours ago. It's in the late edition."

"That's fine," Mason said. "The will's no good."

"What do you mean, it's no good?"

"Just what I said," Mason told him. "He didn't make provisions for his wife."

"His wife? Benjamin Addicks was a bachelor."

"That's what some people would like to have you think."

"You mean he wasn't?"

Mason shook his head.

"What the devil?— Don't kid us, Mason. Good Lord, Benjamin Addicks was an important figure. He was nutty as a fruit cake and he was all goofy over this idea of the gorilla experimentation, but, after all, the guy was prominent. If he had married anyone the newspapers would have played it up. Not too big, but at least they would have played it up. Everything the guy did was news on account of his money and on account of his private zoo of gorillas."

"You're forgetting that there's a big gap in his biographical data," Mason said. "The man was married."

"Where did he get married?"

"Here and there."

"Come on, come on, give us the low-down."

"Benjamin Addicks," Mason said, "lived with a woman as his wife."

"Where did he live with her?"

"In the house with him a part of the time."

"Are you going to claim that Josephine Kempton . . .?"

"Not so fast," Mason said. "The wife was Helen Cadmus. I'll give you fellows the addresses of some motels where they registered as man and wife, and I can tell you there's been an absolute photographic identification. You can take a picture of Helen Cadmus and check on it if you want to."

"Aw, forget it," one of the men said. "He was playing around with his secretary. That doesn't mean he was married to her or that it makes the will invalid."

Mason grinned. "You fellows are good investigators. Go look up these things. Look up the fact that the registrations at auto courts show that the parties were registered as Mr. and Mrs. B. F. Barnwell."

"Barnwell?"

"That's right."

"Well," one of the reporters said, "that's your answer right there. In order to have a common-law marriage it's necessary to show . . ."

"Who's talking about a common-law marriage?" Mason asked.

"You are, aren't you? And I understand there isn't any such thing in this state anyway. Even if they were, a man would have to use his right name, and . . ."

"What was Addicks' right name?" Mason asked.

"Why, Addicks, of course."

"Was it?"

"Why, of course. He—say, wait a minute, where did you get that name of Barnwell?"

Mason merely smiled.

"What about common-law marriage?" one of the men asked.

"In some states it's recognized," Mason said, "and in others it isn't. But where a man travels with a woman as his wife he may well find himself in a state that recognizes common-law marriage.

"But what you fellows may be overlooking is that right here in this state when two people live together as husband and wife there's a disputable presumption of marriage. That's a rule of evidence, a legal presumption."

The reporters exchanged glances.

Mason opened a book, placed it on the desk. "There it is, Subdivision 30 of Section 1963 of the Code of Civil Procedure."

"But how about the will?" one of the reporters asked.

"He didn't mention Helen Cadmus. If they lived together as husband and wife there is an evidentiary *prima facie* presumption of marriage. He doesn't mention her in his will. Therefore the will is open to attack."

"But he didn't have to mention Helen Cadmus. She was dead."

"Who told you so?"

"I suppose you think she just walked on the water. Come on, give us some facts if you want us to publish anything."

"I don't give a damn whether you publish anything or not," Mason said, "but Helen Cadmus didn't commit suicide."

"You mean she was murdered?"

"She wasn't murdered."

"What the devil *do* you mean?"

Mason said, "I mean that for reasons that suited Benjamin Addicks and Helen Cadmus, she decided to disappear. You can draw your own conclusions."

There was a stunned silence for a moment.

"You mean she took time out to have a baby?" one of the men asked.

Mason shrugged his shoulders and said, "After all, I've only been in this case for a few hours, but I'm constantly receiving new information which I am correlating and checking. I thought that you fellows would like to start from scratch on this and . . ."

"Start from scratch is right. If you've got anything to hang this theory on, it's going to make headlines. Gosh, what a sob story, what a sensation!"

"All right," Mason said, "use your own judgment. Who saw Helen Cadmus aboard the yacht the night of the storm? Who saw Helen Cadmus after the boat pulled out?"

"Crew members, didn't they?"

"Name one," Mason said. "The only person who actually saw her was Benjamin Addicks."

"And Josephine Kempton."

"Not Mrs. Kempton," Mason said. "She heard the clack of a typewriter in the other stateroom. The typewriter kept clacking away. Anyone could have pounded a typewriter—Addicks, for instance. Mrs. Kempton had taken a dose of sleeping medicine and she went to sleep. When she wakened in the morning there was this story about Helen Cadmus having disappeared."

"You got anything to pin that on?" one of the reporters asked.

"Sure," Mason said. "I have the diaries of Helen Cadmus, remember."

"And what does she say about having a baby?"

"I'll show you a passage," Mason said.

He picked up the diary, opened it to a page which Della Street had located and which he had marked with a bookmark. "Here it is. In the handwriting of Helen Cadmus:

> I told B. the news today. At first he was very much upset, and then as he began to think it over I realized everything was going to be all right. He's going to be very proud of him.

The newspapermen studied the page very carefully.

"Say," one of the men said, "let's have these diaries. We can go over them in your law library and perhaps we can find things that . . ."

Mason shook his head. "That's it, boys. That's the lead for your story."

"That isn't a story. That's just a theory with a little stuff to go on. We can't publish that."

"The hell you can't!" Mason said. "How much proof did you have as basis for an accusation that Josephine Kempton had murdered Helen Cadmus?"

"We didn't say she'd murdered Helen Cadmus. We said the authorities were making inquiries."

"That's right," Mason said. "Now you can assure your readers that on the strength of this entry in the diary, the Drake Detective Agency has dozens of operatives out combing this section of the country trying to establish my theory that the passage in the diary means something definite. And if you go back and reopen the Helen Cadmus case you'll find that there wasn't a single member of the crew that saw Helen Cadmus after the boat left port.

"Furthermore, and this is the important thing, no one knows the nature of the confidential work that she was supposed to be doing for Benjamin Addicks. Addicks said that he left her typing the pages in her stateroom. Later on he was asked if he had received the typewritten documents, and he said, of course not, that the last time he had seen her was when she was transcribing the notes—now, get that straight. If she had been committing suicide she wouldn't have taken the typewritten notes with her when she jumped overboard. If she had been intending to commit suicide she wouldn't have typed out her notes. She'd simply have jumped and left the notes without being transcribed in her shorthand book. From the minute I started investigating this case I became very much interested in finding out just what had happened to the dictation Addicks had given her on the night she disappeared.

"There were photographs of the stateroom which she was supposed to have occupied on that last night out of port. Now you fellows study the photographs of that stateroom and you'll notice two or three peculiar things.

"A typewriter has been set up on a table all right, and some paper has been spread around, but I've yet to hear that anyone found a shorthand notebook with any notes in it that hadn't been transcribed, and I've yet to find anyone who would admit that there was any typewritten document found in the stateroom.

"But the thing that interests me is what you can see in this picture. It's a photograph taken after the yacht arrived in Catalina, and shows the stateroom occupied by Helen Cadmus. The door of the connecting bathroom is open, and you can see a portion of the interior of the stateroom occupied by Josephine Kempton on the other side. Now do you fellows notice anything peculiar?"

The newspaper reporters studied the photograph carefully.

Mason said, "The towels on one rack have been used. Those are the towels nearest the door of the stateroom occupied by Josephine Kempton. The towels by the door of the stateroom occupied by Helen Cadmus haven't been used. Do you think she'd have boarded the yacht, have taken dictation, have done a lot of typing, and never so much as washed her hands, never so much as unfolded a towel?"

One of the men gave a low whistle, then said to Perry Mason, "Say, you're a pretty good detective yourself."

Mason grinned. "All right, you fellows have a head start on the police. It would be nice if you boys could find Helen Cadmus yourselves. And if you find that what I think is true, well—you'll have something that's a damn sight more valuable than the empty accusation of an interested party.

"I don't know just how badly your city editors would like to have an exclusive interview with Helen Cadmus, and the true story of her supposed suicide, but I presume the fellow who turned it in could write his own ticket for a while, particularly if he signed her up for an exclusive.

"That's why I'm giving all of you an even break. Here are the names of two motels where they registered as Mr. and Mrs. B. F. Barnwell, and here are some photographs so you won't waste time digging into your morgues."

"Barnwell," one of the men said meditatively. "Say, the fellow Hardwick had a cablegram from Herman Barnwell. He . . ."

The reporter abruptly ceased talking. For a moment the reporters stood there, then one of them lunged for the door.

That started a four-man stampede, everyone making a dash down the corridor.

Mason grinned at Della Street. "Tomorrow morning we can send Mr. Sidney Hardwick copies of the papers, and tell him we're fast workers ourselves."

CHAPTER FOURTEEN

"WELL," DELLA STREET SAID WHEN THE LAST SOUNDS OF RUNNING FEET had died down. "You certainly took a button and sewed a vest on it!"

Mason grinned.

"Chief, are you safe in doing that?"

"What do you mean, safe?"

"My gosh, you've got the girl having a baby and being the common-law wife of Benjamin Addicks. Good heavens, suppose she should be alive?"

"Well?"

"Couldn't she take action against you?"

"In that event," Mason said, "the heat would be off of Josephine Kempton. We're never going to get anywhere by denials and evasions, and being on the defensive. This is a case where we're going to have to carry the fight to the other man."

"But you do have an obligation to be limited by the real facts in the case."

"That's right," Mason said. "Now let's look at the facts for a minute. Quite evidently they were living together. I think they were in love.

"From the time I first began to check through the Helen Cadmus diaries I have been impressed by two things. One of them is that no member of the crew specifically mentioned seeing Helen Cadmus aboard the yacht after they got down to the outer harbor. The other one is that you can't explain what became of the papers she had been typing. Either she took them to Benjamin Addicks, in which event Benjamin Addicks' story to the police was false; or else they were left in the stateroom, in which event someone surreptitiously removed them.

"A professional stenographer doesn't like to type well enough to type an important document, then clutch it in her hand and jump overboard."

"Suppose she was accidentally washed overboard?"

"Waves weren't coming over the ship that bad, Della. It was a rough, choppy night, and there was water being shipped now and then, and quite a bit of spray, but it wasn't one of those all-out storms where solid water comes crashing over the deck every so often and might sweep a girl off her feet."

"Well, you certainly started something."

"I aimed to," Mason said.

"Now what do we do?"

Mason said, "You go home and I settle down for another spell of good, hard work."

"What kind of work?"

"I'm going to study those diaries particularly with reference to the two known dates when she was staying in the motels. I'm certain there must be between-the-line references that will enable me to get some sort of a clue, and when I get that clue I'm going to study the rest of the dates."

Della Street said, "Move over. I'm with you all the way."

"No, you go on home and get some rest."

"Fiddlesticks! I'm going to see this thing through."

"Well, if you insist, go get something to eat."

"What are *you* going to do about food?"

"Oh, I'll have some coffee and a cheeseburger sent up from the lunch counter downstairs."

"Make it two," she said. "Let's start."

Mason happily surrendered. "All right. Della, do you suppose a girl could write diaries the way Helen Cadmus did, be in love with her boss and not have something that would show that love creep into the diary?"

"A lot depends on the nature of the romance. I think a woman who was really in love would naturally be cautious about putting anything in writing that her lover didn't want. On the other hand, there is always a tendency for a woman in love to confide to her diary."

Mason said, "What I want to do is look for a code. She had some sort of a code word or expression that she would use to show that she had been with the man she loved."

"Provided she really loved him," Della Street said.

"I like Helen Cadmus from what I've learned to know about her from her diaries," Mason said. "She was a frank, wholesome, square shooting sort of girl, and a very loyal one, I believe. We have a couple of dates, Della. Let's look up those and study the entries carefully."

Della Street said, "If he really loved her why didn't he marry her?"

"That, of course," Mason said, "is part of the mystery in the case. You wouldn't want a case that didn't have a mystery, would you?"

She smiled and shook her head.

"Well," Mason said, "let's start exploring."

Mason carefully read and reread the entry under the date of the first registration in the motel.

Della Street came to look over his shoulder and for a moment they read in silence.

Suddenly she laughed.

"What's the matter?" Mason asked.

"You're looking under the date at which they registered at the motel."

"Well?" Mason asked.

"It's the wrong date," she said. "She wouldn't have had anything to confide in her diary until she got back the next day. The diary shows that they had just returned from a yacht trip on that day. Now probably it was when they were driving home that Addicks suggested. . ."

"A good point well taken," Mason said. "I guess my sense of romance is snowed under with business considerations. To the legal mind a date is a date. All right, let's look at the next day."

They read the next day's entry and Della Street's right forefinger immediately dropped down to a sentence on the page in the diary.

"There it is, Chief. Just as plain as can be."

Mason read the sentence. " 'They say happiness is where you find it, which is okay by me. I'm willing to ride along and certainly won't try to force the issue as long as there isn't any.' "

"Good Lord," Mason said. "I read this myself. This was the volume that I checked over, Della, and at the time I didn't appreciate the significance of it."

"Well, there it is all right," Della Street said. "It relates to what happened the night before. Evidently that wasn't the first time. She was perfectly willing to ride along and be happy *as long as there wasn't any issue.*"

"All right," Mason said, "let's turn over to that other volume, Della. Let's see if we can find something of importance before the entry announcing its great event to Addicks."

Della Street brought the book over and placed it on the table.

"Draw up a chair and sit down," Mason invited.

"No thanks. I'm doing fine this way. I want to be where I can look right down on the page."

She held her cheek close to Mason's, and, after a moment, Mason reached out and circled her waist with his right arm, drawing her closer.

"Well, there it is," the lawyer said, indicating a passage in the book. "Now that we have the code, it's easy. Listen to this. 'I still don't want to force the issue but now it has to be faced.' "

"That was her code," Della Street said.

Mason pushed back his chair, arose, turned Della so that she was facing him, said, "We've got work to do."

"What?"

"We've got to find her."

"You don't think she jumped overboard?"

Mason shook his head.

"She could have."

"I know she could have," Mason said, "but I don't think she did."

"Suppose that Addicks had told her that he'd marry her if—well, if it became necessary, and she went to him and told him that —good Lord, Chief, people murder women under circumstances like that."

"I know," Mason said, "that's a chance we've got to take, but somehow—I don't know. I don't know what Benjamin Addicks' reason was for not marrying the girl in the first place."

"Perhaps he didn't want to."

"That could be," Mason said.

"And he had the perfect opportunity for a crime," Della Street said. "It was a wild night out in the channel. There was a high wind blowing, screaming through the rigging of the ship, waves were crashing against the bow, a scream would hardly have been noticed. Benjamin Addicks enticed her out to the deck in the rear of the yacht. He perhaps pointed out something to her. Perhaps he said, 'Is that a light over there, Helen?' She braced herself against the rail to look. He suddenly stooped down, grabbed her feet and gave a big heave."

"That's swell," Mason said. "You sound as though you'd planned it all yourself, Della."

"Well, I don't know what's so absurd about it," she said. "It seems the logical development as far as I'm concerned."

"It would be a logical development if it weren't for one fact."

"What's that?"

"Your premise is wrong."

"I don't get it."

He said, "You surmised that Addicks was playing around."

"Well, what's to indicate that he wasn't?"

"The fact that he's a millionaire," Mason said, "the fact that he went to those motels and registered under his *own* name, and registered the girl as his wife.

"You can see what that did. It put him absolutely in her power. She could have cracked the whip over him at any time she wanted to."

"Perhaps she did, and that's why he grabbed her ankles and hoisted her overboard."

Mason shook his head and said, "Come on, Della, we've found one of the answers we want. We're going to have a real meal. Then we're going to get in touch with Drake's office, comb through the diaries and try to find some clue.

"Don't forget one significant fact. Whenever Benjamin Addicks wanted to have some free time he'd pretend to be on the yacht when he wasn't. What more natural than for him to plan a disappearance for Helen Cadmus the same way?"

"But why, Chief? Why go to all that trouble? She could simply have announced she was quitting her job, gone away and had her baby and that's all there'd have been to it."

"I know," Mason said. "There was a reason. There had to be a reason. There's a reason for everything. I think Addicks was afraid."

"Afraid?"

"Yes, afraid something might happen to a woman he loved, and a child he wanted to love. Let's go eat."

CHAPTER FIFTEEN

PERRY MASON AND DELLA STREET FINISHED THE LAST OF THEIR CHINESE dinner.

"Want an almond cake?" Mason asked.

She shook her head and said, "I like the more delicate flavor of those rice flour cookies, those fortune cakes."

"That's fine," Mason told her. "We'll finish up with tea and fortune cakes. Bring us a bowl of them," he instructed the waiter.

The Chinese shuffled off, letting the green curtain fall back in the doorway of the booth.

"You know," Della Street said, "I'm getting the most peculiar hunch. I have a feeling that we're running on a hot scent. I feel tingly."

Mason nodded. "We're going to have to work fast," he said. "There isn't a lot of time."

The Chinese waiter brought back a big pot of tea. "Best kind," he said. "*Ooh loong cha.*"

He gave them fresh teacups and a bowl of rice cakes.

Mason extended the bowl to Della Street. She took one, broke it open, read the fortune, smiled, folded the little printed slip of paper and started to put it in her purse.

"Hey, wait a minute," Mason said.

She shook her head.

"Why, Della," Perry Mason said, "you don't ordinarily keep things from me."

"This one I have to."

"Why?"

"I'm sorry, Chief." She colored furiously. "It wouldn't have been so bad if I'd passed it over to you right at the time, but now it would be—out of the question."

She opened her purse, took out a coin purse and placed the folded slip of paper with its printed message inside.

Mason broke open a cake while Della Street poured tea.

"What's yours?" Della asked.

Mason abruptly folded the fortune and started to put it into his side pocket.

Della Street laughed. "I caught you that time," she said. "You haven't even read it yet."

Mason grinned, unfolded the slip of rice paper, read the printed message, then passed it across to Della Street.

The message read:

"To reach your goal, remember that courage is the only antidote for danger."

"Well," Mason said, "I guess we'd better telephone Drake's office and see if they've uncovered anything."

"Chief, somehow I—do you feel that there's anything to these fortunes?"

Mason laughed. "Of course not, Della. They have them printed by the hundred. They're inserted in the cakes and the cakes are baked so that when you break the cake the fortune is inside of it. I don't know how many different fortunes there are. Probably not over a hundred or so."

"Have you ever received a duplicate in any of the cakes you've eaten?"

"Come to think of it," Mason said, "I don't know that I have. I haven't given it a great deal of thought."

"Do you believe in Fate?"

Mason said, "The Chinese do to this extent. They'll put a hundred different messages in a hundred different fortune cakes. They feel that the one you pick out was really intended for you. That's the way most of their fortunetelling works. Sometimes you shake fortune sticks in a bowl until one drops out."

She said, "I have a feeling that your fortune has a really personal message to you."

Mason laughed. "What you're really trying to say, Della, is that you hope the fortune *you* picked out has a personal message to *you*."

Her face became a fiery red.

"Oh, I'm sorry," Mason said, quickly and impulsively reaching out to place his hand over hers. "I was only kidding, Della. I didn't want you to take me seriously—although," he added, "I thought your psychology was a bit obvious."

"Well, I didn't," she said. "Do you want me to call Paul Drake's office?"

"Sit there and drink your tea," Mason said, "and get over being angry, Della. I'll go call Paul Drake."

"I'm not angry. I—I'm . . ."

"Well, your face flushed up," Mason said.

Abruptly she averted her eyes, said, "All right, go ahead. Call Paul Drake. You have his number."

Mason went to the public phone, dropped a coin and dialed the number of Drake's office.

When Drake's switchboard operator answered, Mason said, "This is Perry Mason. I'm wondering if Paul Drake . . ."

"Just a moment," the voice at the other end of the line interrupted with crisp efficiency.

Mason heard the click of a connection, heard the operative's voice saying, "Mr. Mason for you, Mr. Drake," and Drake exclaimed, "Good for you! Where did you get him?"

"I didn't. He called in. He . . ."

"Hello, hello, Perry, Perry!" Drake said excitedly.

"Okay, Paul, what is it? I thought you were asleep. Have you struck pay dirt?"

"Struck pay dirt by the ton," Drake said. "Jeepers, what a hunch you had. You'd better play the races tomorrow and mortgage the family fortune."

"Go on, Paul, what is it?"

"B. F. Barnwell and Helen Cadmus were married in a little Nevada town that no one would ordinarily check up on. A little place where a person would hardly think to look, a place north and east of Las Vegas on the road to Ely."

"Okay," Mason said. "Give me the dope, Paul."

"Got a pencil there?"

"Just a minute. I'll get Della. Hang on."

Mason left the receiver off the hook, hurried back to the booth, beckoned to Della Street. "Get your pencil and notebook, Della."

Della pushed back the carved teakwood chair, ran to the telephone, opened her purse, hurriedly pulled out a shorthand notebook, hooked one strap of the purse over her left wrist, held the receiver to her ear and said, "Go ahead, Paul."

Her pencil, flying over the page of the shorthand notebook, made a series of pothooks, then a figure and a name.

"That all?" she asked. "All right, the boss wants to speak with you."

She turned away from the telephone. Mason grabbed the receiver, said, "Yes, Paul?"

"I've given the dope to Della, Perry. I've got the thing sewed up. The main thing is that after the marriage was performed, the Justice of the Peace wanted to know where he should send the documents after all the red tape had been complied with, and there was a moment's silence, then the woman said, 'Send them to Mrs. B. F. Barnwell.' She gave an address, a little California town up on the edge of the desert."

"That's all?"

"That's all."

"Della has the dope?"

"Della has it. Now, for the love of Mike, Perry, don't expect me to go tearing up there and . . ."

"I don't," Mason said. "Here's what I want you to do, Paul."

"What?" Drake asked in a weary voice.

"Go take a good hot bath," Mason said. "Finish up with a cool shower, crawl into bed and sleep just as long as you can, because when I wake you up you're going to have to go to work."

Drake said wearily, "Is that music to my ears? I'd just started to go home when that message from Nevada came in. The elevator operator said you folks had just gone out for chow. I've been calling all the restaurants where you usually eat."

"I'm sorry," Mason said. "I intended to call your office but I didn't think you'd get anything this soon. I thought you were asleep. Be seeing you, Paul."

Mason hung up the telephone, grabbed Della Street's arm, said, "Come on, Della, we're on our way."

He ran toward the cashier's booth at the head of the stairs, pulled a ten dollar bill from his wallet, threw it on the counter and said to the Chinese cashier, "We haven't time to wait for a statement. There's ten dollars. Leave the waiter a dollar tip . . ."

"Must have waiter's check," the calm, unperturbed Oriental said.

Exasperated, Mason threw one of his professional cards on the desk, picked up the ten dollar bill, pulled a fifty dollar bill from his pocket, and slammed it down on the desk. "All right, you don't trust me. I trust you. You give the waiter a dollar tip, and I'll come in sometime tomorrow or the next day and pick up the change. Until then—good-by."

He reached for Della's wrist, and they went pell-mell down the flight of stairs to the street.

Mason ran to where his car was parked.

"All right, Della," he said. "Hang on."

He unlocked the car. Della Street jerked the car door open, jumped in, slammed the door shut behind her, reached across the seat back of the steering wheel to unlock the door on the driver's side.

Mason slid in behind the steering wheel, stepped on the starter, then, easing the car away from the curb, began to open the throttle.

At the second intersection Della Street said, "And *you* object to *my* driving!"

"This time," Mason told her, "we're *really* in a hurry."

"So I gathered," Della Street said.

They picked their way through the more congested traffic of the city, hit a freeway and were soon spinning along with the needle of the speedometer indicating seventy miles an hour.

Twice Della Street glanced at Perry Mason, but seeing the fierce concentration of his face knew that his busy mind was working ahead, planning moves even as he crowded the car along.

Twenty minutes later they were out in the open and Mason sent the speedometer up into the eighties.

"What will happen if you get caught?" Della Street said.

"Darned if I know," Mason said. "We'll have to find out. Keep an eye on the road behind, Della."

"At this rate of speed you'll overtake some traffic officer who's cruising along about sixty-five," she said.

"That's a chance we have to take. I'm watching the license numbers of the cars ahead. You help me keep an eye on the road behind."

Three hours later Mason slowed the car to read a sign at a crossroad and then turned to the right.

Della Street said, "From the looks of this place they roll up the sidewalks at seven o'clock. You're not going to find anyone up this time of night."

"We'll get them up," Mason said.

Della Street said, "There's the place. It's a motel, Chief, and there's no one up."

"We'll get someone up."

Mason rang the bell at the office, and after a few minutes a man, rubbing sleep from his eyes, shuffled to the door. "Sorry," he said, "we're full up. Can't you see that sign *No Vacancies?* You're . . ."

Mason said, "Here's five dollars."

"I tell you we're full up. I couldn't let you have a place if . . ."

"I don't want a place," Mason said. "I simply want to know what cabin is occupied by Mrs. Barnwell."

"Mrs. B? She's in number eleven, but she's gone to bed."

"Thanks," Mason said. "Buy yourself a bottle of hooch, and I'm sorry we woke you up."

Mason and Della Street walked rapidly down a little cement walk which bordered the patio parking place surrounded by stucco cottages.

"Here's our cottage," Mason said.

He looked for a bell. There was none. He tried to open the screen door. It was latched on the inside.

Mason tapped his knuckles on the door.

A woman's voice, sharp with alarm, said, "Who is it, please?"

"A message," Mason said, "a very important message."

"I'm sorry. I'll have to know who you are. I . . ."

"Turn on the light," Mason said. "It's a message. It has to do with the validity of a marriage ceremony performed in Nevada. Now are you interested?"

A light clicked on inside.

"Just a minute," the feminine voice said.

A moment later the outer door was opened. A vague, shadowy figure of a young woman bundled in a loose wrapper stood in the doorway. The screen remained latched.

"All right. What is it please?" she said.

Mason, holding a fountain pen flashlight in his right hand, pressed the button. The beam shone through the screen in the door, full in the woman's face.

She jerked back and said sharply, "Don't do that!"

Mason said, "I've found out what I wanted to know, Miss Cadmus."

"Mrs. Barnwell, please."

"I want to talk with you about that."

"Well, I don't want to talk with you about anything," she said sharply, and started to close the door.

"I think you do," Mason told her. "If you don't talk with me now, you'll have to talk with the newspaper reporters two hours from now."

"The newspaper reporters?"

"Yes."

"How did they—how could they locate me?"

"Through me," Mason said.

A masculine voice edged with irritation came from the adjoining cottage. "Oh, pipe down! Hire a hall or go get a woman that feels sociable. Don't stand out there and argue. I want to sleep!"

Mason stood quietly at the screen door, waiting.

The figure in the doorway remained motionless for a matter of seconds, then a hand reached out and snapped off the hook.

"Won't you come in?" she invited. "And please try not to wake the baby."

Mason held the door open for Della Street and followed her into the cabin.

Mason carefully closed the door behind them.

"Who are you?" the woman asked.

The cottage was a spacious, comfortable affair. The small sitting room was comfortably furnished, with good rugs on the floor, and they could see through the door to a bedroom containing a double bed and a crib.

Mason said, "I'm Perry Mason, the lawyer. This is Della Street, my secretary. I'm going to put the cards on the table with you. I'm one of the attorneys representing Josephine Kempton. She's charged with the murder of Benjamin Addicks—your husband."

The woman sat with tight-lipped hostility. "Keep talking."

Mason said, "My connection with the case is purely fortuitous. I bought your diaries and . . ."

"I read about it in the papers. What did you want with them? Were you trying some kind of legalized blackmail? Did you think I'd be foolish enough to put anything in them that . . . ?"

"You put things in them that you didn't know you'd put in them," Mason said. "That is, you put things in that you didn't think other people would find out."

"Such as what?"

"Why do you think I'm here?"

"I don't know. I want to find out."

"And how do you think I got here?"

"That I can't understand. I took elaborate precautions."

"I know you did," Mason said. "The point I'm making is that there was more in those diaries than you had realized. Now then, I want your story."

"Well, you won't get it."

"I think I will," Mason said confidently.

"What makes you think so?"

"Because," Mason said, "I have all the damaging parts of the story. I know the motels where you stayed with Benjamin Addicks. I know the entries in your diary to the effect that you were going to take happiness where you found it, and that you wouldn't force the issue as long as there wasn't any. And then, when you found out there was going to be an issue, you had to face the situation and you put that in your diary.

"I know what happened aboard the yacht. I know that you and Addicks fixed it up so you would pull the wool over the eyes of everyone and make it appear you had committed suicide. I *don't* know why he took all those elaborate precautions. That's what I'd like to find out."

"If you're so smart, go ahead and find out."

"I know," Mason said, "that you were married in Nevada. I know that you directed that the documents solemnizing the marriage should be mailed to you at this address. I know that Addicks' real name was Barnwell.

"Now then, I can make some guesses. They aren't the type of guesses that you might like to have me make. I can communicate my guesses to the newspapers. They've been after me for an interview."

"Go ahead and give them one."

"I have already given them an interview in which I have pointed out that because of certain entries in your diary I felt that you had communicated to Mr. Addicks that he was about to become a father. I have already told them about motels where you stayed with Mr. Addicks, registered as husband and wife, and I have witnesses who have identified your picture. The newspapers have that story. They're going to break out with it tomorrow morning."

"Why did you have to do that to me?" she asked.

"I didn't do it to you," Mason said. "I'm a lawyer. I'm engaged in a case where I had to get at the facts. I didn't make the facts. I didn't cut the pattern. I only discovered the facts."

"And then you had to blab them to the press."

"I did it because it was the thing to do. There was a reason why Mr. Addicks couldn't marry you. What was it?"

"I don't know why I should tell you."

"I don't know why you shouldn't."

She hesitated for a moment, then said, "Just what is your interest in this?"

"I'm trying to find out the truth."

"And you're representing Josephine Kempton?"

"Yes."

"All right," she said bitterly. "If you want the truth about *her*, I'll give you all the truth about her. She killed him!"

"You mean she killed Benjamin Addicks?"

"Of course she killed him. She wanted to kill me more than she wanted to kill him. That's one of the reasons that Benny decided we'd make it appear that—well, that I was already dead."

"It seems to me," Mason said, "that's an unduly complicated way of trying to find a solution to a simple problem."

"The problem wasn't simple."

"Why didn't he clear up that marriage problem with his first wife?" Mason asked, his casual manner masking the fact that he was taking a shot in the dark.

"Because he couldn't."

"Why?"

She shrugged her shoulders, said, "Suppose you do the talking for a while?"

Mason said, "All right. I'm a lawyer. The only possible solution that I can think of why Mr. Addicks wouldn't have acknowledged you publicly as his wife is that he didn't have the legal right to do so, and the only reason I can think of why he didn't have the legal right to make you his wife is that he had another wife living, a wife who had perhaps thrown the hooks into him for alimony, and who had refused to give him a divorce."

She shook her head.

"Not right?" Mason asked.

She said bitterly, "The newspapers have given him a lot of publicity from time to time. They've published his picture plenty of times. You haven't heard anyone come forward and say that she was his wife. You haven't learned of any prior marriage."

"That's one of the things that puzzles me," Mason admitted reluctantly.

She said, "It puzzled me, but I cared enough about him to ride along and take things the way they came."

"You cared that much for him?" Della Street asked.

She regarded Della Street speculatively and said, "He was good to me. I was willing to let it ride along on any kind of a basis that he wanted as long as—as long as it only affected the two of us."

"I still don't get the story," Mason said.

"You're not going to get it."

Mason glanced at Della Street, said, "For some reason the man didn't feel he was at liberty to marry, and yet when it became necessary for him to marry in order to give his child a name, and to give you some measure of protection he went ahead and married. But before he did that he went through an elaborate rigmarole to make everyone think that you were dead. That must have meant that he—oh-oh, I believe I have it."

"What is it, Chief?" Della Street asked.

"He felt that any woman whom he married would be in the greatest danger."

"But why?" Della Street asked.

Mason held up his hand. "First," he said, elevating his forefinger, "he didn't feel that he was legally free to marry. Second, he felt that any woman in whom he took a serious interest would be in great danger. That spells a certain pattern to me, Della—as a lawyer."

"I don't get it, Chief."

Mason looked at the woman in the wrapper. "Perhaps Helen can tell us."

"And perhaps Helen won't."

"All right," Mason said, "let's make a stab at it, Della. At some stage in his life Addicks had married. That marriage had never been dissolved by death or by any decree of divorce. Now why not?"

Della Street shook her head. "There isn't any reason. If he'd married he'd have been divorced. No matter what it cost him he'd have bought his way out of that and got into the clear. He might have been very cautious about taking a second adventure in the field of matrimony, but he certainly would have secured his legal freedom."

"If he could have," Mason said.

"What do you mean, if he could have?"

"There's one legal situation, one very interesting legal situation under which he might not have been able to accomplish what he wanted."

"What?" Della Street asked.

Mason said, "In many states it is impossible to divorce a woman who has been adjudged insane.

"Now then, suppose that Benjamin Addicks had married. Suppose that woman had been adjudged insane. Addicks' hands were tied. And furthermore, suppose that woman developed a form of insanity that would make her dangerous, that would—I think we're getting somewhere, Della."

Mason inclined his head slightly toward the woman in the wrapper.

She was having trouble with her face. A spasm of grief contorted it, then she suddenly said angrily, "Damn you! What are you? A mind reader? Do you have to go prying into peoples' lives and . . . ?"

"I think," Mason said, "you'd better tell me about it, Helen."

She said, "I went through ten thousand hells. You have no idea what it meant."

"Who is this woman?" Mason asked. "Where is she confined?"

"That's just the point," Helen said. "She isn't confined. She escaped. She's at large. She's a homicidal maniac. Do you see what that means?"

Mason narrowed his eyes in thoughtful concentration.

"She's absolutely, utterly insane. She's jealous. She traced Benny and blackmailed him. She told him that if he ever married or tried to marry she'd kill the woman. And she meant it. My marriage to Benny isn't any good legally."

"Then why go through the marriage ceremony?"

"For what it might be worth to give the child a name."

"Where's the first wife?"

"No one knows."

"Why wasn't she kept confined somewhere?"

"You can't keep her confined anywhere. She escaped every time she was locked up. That's why Ben had to keep his affairs in such shape that he could give her cash quickly. The woman is utterly, ferociously mad. She'd kill him and she'd love to kill me."

"She didn't kill him?"

"No, Josephine Kempton did that—but if you've told the newspapers about my marriage, or even if she thinks I am the mother of Benny's child, she'll hunt me out and kill me. She's diabolically ingenious and utterly vindictive.

"You see, she's still insane as far as the law's concerned. There wasn't a thing Benjamin Addicks could do. An action for divorce wouldn't lie, and he couldn't even clarify their property matters. And if he tried to do anything, it would necessarily have disclosed his true name and his true past."

"What about his past?"

"He killed a man."

"I thought that was his brother."

"No. There was some garbled gossip to that effect. Benny kept track of Herman, but Herman thought Benny was dead."

"Did your husband actually kill a man?"

"He claimed he didn't really know. He never told me the details. When I learned how he felt I never asked for them."

"But his wife kept in touch with him?" Mason asked.

"Certainly."

"How?"

"The phone would ring. It would be a call from a pay station. It would be her voice. She'd direct him to put a certain amount of money in the form of cash in a package and leave the package at a certain place. It was all done as mysteriously as though she had been getting ransom for kidnaping."

"And Addicks had some messenger he could trust who delivered the money?"

"Yes."

"Certainly he didn't dare to put you in that situation."

"No. It was Mortimer Hershey who did that. Sometimes it was Nathan Fallon."

"Did they know what they were doing?"

"I don't know, Mr. Mason. I don't think they did. Benny was so afraid of being blackmailed. Heavens, I'm telling you this whole story and I had no intention of doing it, but I've been so lonely, and then—now Benny's gone. He's all I had to tie to and . . ."

"Now wait a minute," Mason said, "let's control the emotions for a little while, Mrs. Barnwell. Let's get down to brass tacks on this thing. What about Josephine Kempton? Did she know about you and Mr. Addicks?"

"She suspected."

"You read about the supposedly stolen property being discovered?"

"Yes, I did. I certainly should have guessed the correct solution myself. Good Lord, I had all the facts available. It just never occurred to me to suspect a monkey. That little mischievous devil! And I'm so fond of him, too—but he's a devil."

"Where's the monkey now?" Mason asked.

"He's—he's being taken care of. Don't worry, he'll have a home."

"Do you think Josephine Kempton is telling the truth about . . . ?"

"She never told the truth about anything in her life. She's a congenital liar. She's a plotter, a sneak, a vicious, backbiting, nasty-minded woman, and she killed Benjamin Addicks. I know it just as well as I know I'm sitting here."

Mason said, "How do you know it?"

"I don't know it by any evidence, but I'm absolutely certain that's the case."

Mason said, "You don't want to be interviewed by the newspaper reporters, do you?"

"No."

"All right," Mason told her, "start packing."

"What do you mean?"

Mason said, "I'm going to put you in a place where you're safe for the time being. You were crazy to think that you couldn't be found in a place of this sort. You left a broad enough trail to . . ."

"I guess I did at that," she said, "but I was—well, I was emotionally upset and—and, frankly, it never occurred to me that in a show-down Benny really would marry me. I thought he'd support the child—I don't know, I thought he might be proud of him."

"Of him?"

"Yes. He's a fine strapping boy," she said. "He's going to have all of Benny's intelligence, and if I have anything to do with it, and I think I'll have a lot to do with it, he's not going to have any of Benny's phobias—you see, Mr. Mason, Benny made a big mistake. He ran away. When a man starts running away from things in life he builds up a whole chain of complexes and fear.

"My son isn't going to be like that. He's going to face things squarely!"

"All right," Mason told her. "I'll do what I can to help."

"Just what are you going to do? What can you do?"

Mason said, "You're going to pack up. Della Street is going to take you and your child to another motel. Della Street is going to register in that motel. You're going to be her sister. You're not going to use the name Addicks. You're not going to use the name Barnwell."

Mason looked at his watch. "You probably have fifteen or twenty minutes. I wouldn't push my luck any more than that. Della will help you pack."

"When you come right down to it, Mr. Mason, why shouldn't I come out in the open right now? I have suddenly realized that I'm starting to do the same thing Benny did. I'd be running away . . ."

Mason interrupted sharply, "There's a difference between retreating until you can fight at the right time and at the right place and just running away.

"There's a crazy woman who wants to kill your child. It's all right to be courageous, but let's find out more about this woman before we take chances on that young life it's your duty to protect."

She hesitated for a moment, then took some clothes, went to the bathroom, said, "Let me dress," and closed the door.

"Chief," Della Street said, "do you dare to hide her?"

"I have to hide her, Della."

"Why?"

"Because if the newspapers get hold of that story of hers that Mrs. Kempton killed Benjamin Addicks, it will set off a chain reaction of adverse public sentiment. I don't dare take that chance."

"But isn't it a crime to conceal a witness?"

"What is she a witness to?"

"Well, all of the things that she's told you."

"She's told me a lot about the disappearance of Helen Cadmus," Mason said, "and she's told me a lot of stuff that she heard from Benjamin Addicks about Addicks' past life, but that doesn't mean she's a witness to those things. She could talk to a newspaper reporter but she couldn't talk to a jury. She isn't a witness unless she can testify to something. The thing we're investigating at the present time is the murder of Benjamin Addicks. She can't testify to a damn thing in that."

"Just the same, if the police find out . . ."

Mason grinned. "Remember what the fortune cake said, Della —courage is the only antidote for danger."

CHAPTER SIXTEEN

Perry Mason's interview with the newspaper reporters brought instant response.

Sidney Hardwick, as the attorney who had represented Benjamin Addicks during his lifetime, and as attorney for the executor of the estate, promptly denounced Mason's interview as "sheer wishful thinking, an attempt to cloud the issues, a fevered imagination desperately seeking some way of escape for a desperate client."

District Attorney Hamilton Burger characterized it more sharply. "An attempt to squirm out from under by blackening the reputation of a dead girl who is no longer able to defend herself. A dastardly, despicable, last-minute attempt conceived in deceit, born in desperation, and ultimately destined to crucify his client."

Mason, with the newspapers tucked under his arm, walked into court to attend the preliminary hearing in the case of People versus Josephine Kempton.

James Etna, moving up alongside, said in a low voice, "I think we won't have any trouble getting a continuance, Mr. Mason."

"Who wants a continuance?" Mason asked.

"Good heavens, we don't want to go to trial the way things are now, do we?"

"We may not want to go to trial," Mason said, "but I'm perfectly willing to hear what they have to say by way of evidence in a pre- liminary hearing."

"Well, you're the boss," Etna told him. "I know that the district attorney really wants a continuance, but, of course, he wants the defendant to ask for it."

Judge Mundy took his place on the bench. The court was called to order.

"People versus Kempton," Judge Mundy called.

"The defense is ready," Mason said.

District Attorney Burger's face showed surprised irritation. "I had understood that the defendant wanted a continuance, and the prosecution was prepared to stipulate that a continuance would be granted."

"I don't know what gave you that understanding," Mason said.

"I received that understanding from a conversation with someone who had been talking with James Etna, your associate counsel."

"Did you indeed?" Mason told him. "Just who was this person and what did he say?"

"I prefer not to divulge the source of my information."

Mason said, "I have made no request for a continuance and I'm quite certain Mr. Etna didn't."

"I didn't say that he made a request for a continuance."

"The defense is entitled to proceed if it wishes," Judge Mundy ruled.

"We're prepared to go ahead," Hamilton Burger said sullenly.
"Very well, proceed."

Burger called one of the radio officers who had answered the call to Stonehenge as his first witness. The officer described conditions as he had found them, told about the night watchman running around with a gun, the dogs having a gorilla up a tree, two more gorillas roaming loose in the house, about the cages, the discovery of the body in the upstairs room, the resulting trouble that ensued in trying to corral the huge gorillas.

Finally, with the aid of two experts from the zoo, some drugged fruit, and by utilizing the combined services of the police and fire departments, the apes were returned to their cages shortly before daylight.

"Cross-examine," the district attorney said.

Mason smiled.

"No questions."

Burger called one of the radio officers who had seen Mason and Mrs. Kempton, as he expressed it, "fleeing down Rose Street." Later on they were joined by Della Street. He had, he stated, advised them that they would have to go to headquarters for questioning.

"Cross-examine," Burger said.

Mason said, "I believe I understood you to state that the defendant and I were fleeing down Rose Street."

"Yes, sir, that's what I said."

"And you put us in an automobile?"

"Yes, sir."

"How did you know we were fleeing?"

"I could tell it by your manner, the high speed at which you were walking, the way you were looking back."

"I see," Mason said. "Now then, shortly after you placed us in the automobile you fled to police headquarters, didn't you?"

"I did what?"

"You fled to police headquarters."

"I *took* you to police headquarters."

"You left behind you the scene of pandemonium, the elements of danger. You left behind you the house with the gorillas running loose, the dogs barking, the sirens sounding."

"I did that because I was under orders."

"But you fled, didn't you?"

"I did not."

"You were leaving the scene of all this commotion?"

"I had to leave it to get you to police headquarters."

"And yet, despite the fact that you weren't fleeing, you did look back over your shoulder several times, didn't you?"

"Well, I glanced in the rear view mirror two or three times and . . ."

"And did you look back over your shoulder?"

"I believe I may have done so—very briefly."

"Certainly," Mason said. "It would necessarily have been quite briefly because you were driving a car, but you did look back over your shoulder several times."

"Oh, perhaps I did. I'll say I did."

"You don't remember?"

"I don't remember definitely."

"Yet you'll state that, to quote your exact words, 'I'll say I did.'"

"That's right. I'll concede you the point."

"You're now ready to swear that you did? You're testifying that you did?"

"Yes!" The witness shouted.

"Your Honor," Hamilton Burger protested to Judge Mundy, "I think this has been asked and answered a dozen times."

"I'm inclined to think so," the judge said.

"I just wanted to get it straight," Mason said. "I wanted Your Honor to understand the attitude of this witness. He has no recollection of having turned around and looked back over his shoulder, but he is willing to say that he did do so simply because he might have done so. He is now swearing positively that he did something of which he has no real recollection. It shows the attitude of the witness."

"I told you I'd say that I *did* turn and look over my shoulder."

"But you don't have any recollection of having done so."

"All right," the officer said belligerently, "I now have a recollection of having done so."

"When did that definite recollection come to you?"

"Just now."

"Then when you testified under oath that you had no definite recollection of having looked back, you hadn't thought of it?"

"That's right."

"So you answered that question without thinking?"

"Yes."

"In other words, you talk faster than you think?"

"I don't know."

"And why did you look back if you weren't fleeing?" Mason asked.

"Simply a matter of curiosity. When you hear a commotion like that and know that apes are running around, it's only natural to turn back and see what's happening as you leave the scene."

"Then, as I now understand your testimony," Mason said, "there was nothing that would indicate that the defendant and I were fleeing from the place."

"I've said there was."

"What?"

"You were turning back and looking over your shoulder—now, wait a minute. You were doing it different from the way I was doing it."

"How do you know?"

"Well, I could tell from the way you acted that something was wrong."

"You could tell something was wrong as soon as you got close enough to hear the sirens, couldn't you?"

"Yes."

"So," Mason said, "you want the court to understand that while it is only perfectly natural for *you* to look back and see what is happening when you are leaving a scene of that sort, when the defendant and I do it, it is evidence of flight."

"There was something in your attitude."

"What?"

"I've already described it."

Mason held up his left hand, extended one forefinger. "First," he said, "you said we were walking rapidly. Two, you said that we kept looking back over our shoulders. Now what else did we do?"

"That's all. That's enough."

"All right, when you left the place," Mason said, "you were driving rapidly, weren't you?"

"That's different."

"Were you or weren't you?"

"Yes."

"And," Mason said, "you looked back over your shoulder repeatedly, did you not?"

"Yes."

"You know that you did?"

"Yes."

"You now have an independent recollection of having done it?"

"Yes."

"But you didn't have that recollection when you first testified?"

"Of course I did."

"Then," Mason said, "you were trying to keep from admitting it."

"I saw the trap you were laying for me. I'm not as dumb as all that."

"Thank you," Mason said. "I merely wanted the court to see your attitude. That's all."

Hamilton Burger conferred briefly with his trial deputy, a bright young lawyer named Ginsberg, who, during the past few months, had won a series of spectacular courtroom victories, and as a result had been placed in charge of the trial deputies who handled preliminary examinations.

Hamilton Burger's presence as consultant to his trial deputy was a tribute to Mason's skill as a dangerous antagonist.

Following the whispered conference, Ginsberg called the matron of the jail.

The matron testified that she had received the defendant, Josephine Kempton, in the female wing of the institution, that she had taken Mrs. Kempton's clothes from her, had given her a temporary uniform, and had delivered the clothes to Philip Groton, the police toxicologist and technician.

"Now then," Ginsberg asked, "did you make any examination of the defendant's body?"

"I did. Yes, sir."

"In what way?"

"She stripped to the skin and took a shower. I inspected every inch of her body."

"What were you looking for?"

"Scratches, cuts, any bruises or marks of violence."

"Did you find any?"

"Mr. Ginsberg, there was absolutely no place on her body where the skin had been broken."

"May I ask the reason for this examination?" James Etna inquired.

"You just listen and you'll find the reason for it," Ginsberg said belligerently.

"Gentlemen, gentlemen," Judge Mundy said, "let's conform to the proprieties. Does Counsel wish to interpose an objection?"

"I was trying to save the time," Etna said angrily, "but in view of the circumstances I will object on the ground that this is incompetent, irrelevant and immaterial."

"We propose to connect it up, Your Honor," Ginsberg said, "with our next witness."

"Very well, proceed."

"That is all. Cross-examine."

Mason said to Etna, "You cross-examine her, Jim."

Etna said, "Why did you take her clothes away?"

"I was instructed to do so."

"You knew that until she had been formally charged you could only hold her as . . . ?"

"I followed instructions," the matron said. "That's what I'm there for. If you want to argue the law, argue it with the district attorney."

"You mean you received instructions from the district attorney?"

"From his office, yes."

"And what became of these clothes that you took away from her and which were turned over to Philip Groton?"

"If you'll wait until our next witness is called, that question will be answered," Ginsberg said.

"Very well," Etna said. "That's all."

"Call Philip Groton," Ginsberg said.

Philip Groton, a tall, thin, studious-looking individual, with high cheekbones, and thick-lensed glasses which seemed to reflect the light so that at times one saw only a blank face with two reflecting ovals where the eyes should be, took the stand and qualified himself as an expert toxicologist, chemist and technical investigator.

"You received certain garments from the matron who has just testified?" Hamilton Burger asked.

"I did. Yes, sir."

"Did you make an examination of those garments?"

"Yes, sir."

"Did you find anything unusual on those garments?"

"I did."

"What did you find?"

"Human blood."

"You have those garments with you?"

"I do. Yes, sir."

"I ask that they be introduced in evidence."

"No objection," Mason said.

The garments were introduced in evidence.

"Cross-examine," Hamilton Burger said.

"You state this was human blood on the garments?" Mason asked.

"Yes, sir."

"How do you know?"

"I performed a precipitin test."

"Now when you perform that test you don't ordinarily test the blood for the purpose of finding whether the blood comes from any particular animal, do you? As I understand it, you have a test solution which will give a reaction to human blood, and will give no reaction to animal blood. Therefore you simply test a bloodstain for the purpose of determining whether it is human blood or animal blood. If it is animal blood you ordinarily don't bother to classify it. If you get a positive reaction you then know it is human blood. Is that right?"

"Yes, sir."

"Is that test infallible?"

"That test is infallible."

Mason said, "I should like to cross-examine Mr. Groton a little more on his qualifications as an expert witness, but I'll confess to the Court that I am not at the moment prepared to pursue the line of questioning that I want. I intend to check on a certain bit of information before completing the cross-examination."

"Is there any objection on the part of Counsel to having this phase of the cross-examination postponed?" Judge Mundy asked the prosecutor.

"None whatever," Hamilton Burger said, waving his hand with a gesture of complete assurance. "We will be glad to have Mr. Perry Mason or anyone else cross-examine Mr. Groton as to his qualifications for an entire day if he so desires, and at any time he so desires."

"Very well, Mr. Groton, you may step down, and will be recalled later for that phase of your cross-examination. Who's your next witness?"

Burger, a sudden note of triumph in his voice, called the other officer who had been in the car that had taken Mason, the defendant, Josephine Kempton, and Della Street to police headquarters. He described how the three had been seated in the back seat, the fact that he had turned and kept his eye on them most of the time.

"After you arrived at police headquarters, what was done with the car?" Burger asked.

"It was put back into service."

"Who occupied that car?"

"My partner and I."

"And what time did you go off duty?"

"At four o'clock in the morning."

"What was done then?"

"I—well, I realized that I hadn't checked the cushions on the back seat, something that we ordinarily do when we have suspects in the car who are not handcuffed. So my partner and I raised the back seat, and as we did so we found a document underneath the cushions of the back seat."

"Generally, what was that document?"

"It was a cashier's check for twenty-five thousand dollars that was payable to Benjamin Addicks, and it had on the back of the check an endorsement 'Pay to the order of Josephine Kempton,' and beneath that was a signature purporting to be that of Benjamin Addicks."

"Did you make some identifying mark upon that check?"

"I did. Yes, sir."

"What did you do?"

"I put my initials in pencil on the upper left-hand corner on the back of the check."

"Would you know that cashier's check if you saw it again?"

"I would. Yes, sir."

"I show you a check and ask you if this is it."

"That is it."

"I ask that it be introduced in evidence," Burger said.

"No objections," Mason said promptly, forestalling any attempt on Etna's part to interpose a technical objection.

Burger then called a handwriting expert who stated that the signature of Benjamin Addicks on the back of the check was a palpable forgery, that an attempt had been made to follow the general characteristics of Addicks' signature, but it was quite apparent that the signature was a forgery.

"Cross-examine," Burger said.

Mason said, "That cashier's check was given you by the district attorney?"

"Yes, sir."

"And the district attorney also gave you certain samples of Addicks' handwriting, certain exemplars that were concededly in his handwriting?"

"Yes, sir."

"What else did the district attorney give you?"

"What do you mean?"

"He gave you some samples of the defendant's handwriting, didn't he?"

"Well, yes."

"And he told you that he wanted you to see if you could detect characteristics in the signature, which you have pronounced a forgery, which would show that it had been made by the defendant?"

"Well, not in exactly those words, but he did give me some samples of the defendant's handwriting."

"And did he tell you for what purpose those were given to you?"

"I believe he did generally."

"And what was that purpose?"

"About what you have stated, Mr. Mason."

"Now then," Mason said, "you had to report to the district attorney that the defendant did not make that forgery, that she was not the one who had forged the signature of Benjamin Addicks, didn't you?"

"Well, no, sir. I told the district attorney that there wasn't enough evidence to tell; that I could be positive that it was not a signature of Benjamin Addicks, but that I felt certain it was a tracery."

"What do you mean by a tracery?"

"Someone had held a genuine signature of Benjamin Addicks against a source of strong light, perhaps a ground glass illuminated with a powerful electric bulb, or perhaps just a common, ordinary window, then the cashier's check had been placed over that signature so that the signature of Benjamin Addicks came through from the other side, and the forger had traced that signature."

"How could you tell it was a tracery?"

"It's a very easy distinction to make, Mr. Mason. A person signing his name uses firm, fast strokes. The lines are quick, so that any small tremor is spread over quite a length of line.

"In tracing a signature the hand moves slowly. The microscope shows the spacing of the tremors. That is true in this case."

"But you couldn't tell who had done this tracery?"

"No, sir."

"You had no way of connecting the forgery with the defendant?"

"I think the next witness will do that," and the handwriting expert smiled dryly.

Hamilton Burger threw back his head and laughed. Evidently he had left this trap for Mason to walk into, and now he was in rare good humor.

"No further questions," Mason said.

Hamilton Burger, knowing now that he was springing a surprise on the defense, exuded self-assurance.

"Mr. Howard Denny, will you take the stand, please," he purred.

Howard Denny came forward and was sworn.

"What's your occupation?"

"I am a fingerprint expert, and a deputy sheriff."

"A full-time deputy sheriff?"

"Yes, sir."

"Now then, I am going to call your attention to this cashier's check which has been introduced as a People's exhibit, and ask you if you ever saw this particular check before."

"Yes, sir."

"Where and when?"

"A representative of the police force called my attention to this about four-thirty in the morning."

"What morning?"

"Last Thursday, the night that Mr. Addicks was murdered—now

wait a minute, actually he was murdered on Wednesday night. This was early Thursday morning."

"And when the police officer called your attention to this cashier's check, did he ask you to do something in connection with it?"

"Yes, sir."

"What?"

"To test a latent fingerprint that was on the check."

"Can you show us where that latent fingerprint is?"

"Yes, sir. It is very faintly outlined, but it is a fingerprint. I ascertained that it was the print of the middle finger of the right hand of the defendant, Josephine Kempton."

"That is not an ordinary latent print such as you customarily develop by powders?"

"No, sir. That print is outlined on the check in a substance that I would say is blood."

"Now then, what did you do with reference to this check?"

"After I had tested the check and identified the fingerprint, the check was put back behind the cushions of the car approximately where I understood it had been found."

"And then what happened?"

"Then the defendant was released from custody."

"When?"

"That was around eight o'clock, I would say, on Thursday morning."

"And where were you?"

"With five other witnesses, I was concealed on a balcony where we could watch what happened."

"And what did happen?"

"At the defendant's request, she was . . ."

Etna said, "Oh, I object to the witness testifying about all of this hearsay."

Mason gently tugged at Etna's coattails as a signal for him to sit down.

"We won't be technical, Your Honor," Mason interposed. "I don't think there's any question on earth but what the defendant did request to be released at the police garage where Mr. Etna could pick her up. We certainly don't want to do anything that's going to interfere with getting the actual evidence before the court."

Judge Mundy nodded approvingly.

Etna slowly sat down.

Mason whispered to him, "This is their bombshell. They thought we'd be blown up. Don't let the prosecutors think it means a thing. If it doesn't bother us, then they'll begin to worry, thinking we have some countermove, and will be tempted to show all their hand. After all, that's all we can expect to do at a preliminary hearing of this kind—get them to show everything they have so they don't save a surprise for us when they come to trial before a jury."

"Go right ahead," Hamilton Burger said to the witness.

"Well, as soon as she thought she was alone, she checked over the police cars that were parked there in order to find the car in which she had been taken to the police station. Those cars all had numbers on them and—well, she was looking for car seven."

Judge Mundy interrupted and said, "I appreciate the attitude of the defense in this case, but, after all, Mr. Denny, you're testifying to a lot of conclusions. Just testify to what you saw."

"Well," Denny said, "by arrangement, two men were left where she could see them. Then those two men were called to other parts of the garage, so that as far as the defendant could see there was no one watching her."

"Then what happened?" Burger asked.

"She walked to two of the parked cars, looking at the numbers. When she came to the third car, which happened to be number seven, the car in which she had been taken to police headquarters, she opened the door, raised the cushion and took out this cashier's check."

"How did you know it was this check she took out? Did you see it?"

"It was folded. I could see it was a piece of paper."

"How did you know it was the cashier's check?"

"I'd inspected the car ten minutes before she was released. At that time the cashier's check was between the seat cushions and the back of the car. As soon as the defendant left the garage, in the company of five other witnesses I returned and inspected the car. The check was gone."

"Had the car been out of your sight in the meantime?"

"No, sir. We had kept an eye on that car every minute of the time."

"You may cross-examine," Burger said.

Mason yawned, glanced at the clock, said, "No questions."

"What!" Burger exclaimed in surprise.

"No questions," Mason said.

"That's all," Judge Mundy said. "Do you have any more witnesses, Mr. Burger?"

Burger, apparently considerably nonplussed, glanced at Mason. Etna leaned forward to whisper to him, but Mason warned him back with a gentle kick under the table.

Mason's attitude showed that he apparently considered the evidence of but minor importance.

Judge Mundy looked at the unperturbed defense counsel, then at Hamilton Burger, who was now holding a frantic whispered conference with Ginsberg.

"Your next witness, Mr. District Attorney," Judge Mundy said.

"Call Frank Cummings."

Cummings testified that he was a deputy sheriff, and was also a brother of the matron at the jail. On Thursday morning he had accompanied the matron to the apartment of Josephine Kempton. The matron let herself in with a key that had been obtained from Mrs. Kempton, and the matron then picked out certain clothes which she was to take back to the defendant. The witness, Cummings, had thereupon bored a small hole in the transom over the door, had donned a pair of coveralls and placed a stepladder in the outer corridor. When the defendant arrived at the apartment house on being released from jail, the witness was working on the stepladder, apparently repairing some wiring in the corridor. As soon as the defendant had entered the apartment and had closed and locked the door from the inside, the witness had moved the stepladder over to the door and mounted the steps so that he could peer through the hole in the transom. He had then seen the defendant raise her skirt, take a folded piece of paper from the top of her stocking, go to a bookcase, open a book and place the open book on the table. She had then fastened the check to a page in the book by means of Scotch tape, and then had replaced the book in the bookcase.

The witness stated he immediately got back down the stepladder, moved the stepladder to the far end of the corridor, and waited until the defendant had emerged from her apartment. He had then re-entered the apartment, opened the book to the page in question and taken out the paper.

"What was that paper?" Hamilon Burger asked.

The witness grinned. "It was this cashier's check for twenty-five thousand dollars, which has been introduced in evidence."

"Cross-examine," Burger said.

Mason regarded the man with a tolerant smile.

"*You* had no authorization to enter the apartment either the first or the second time, did you?"

"No, sir."

"Where did you get the key with which you entered the apartment the second time?"

"I had a duplicate key made."

"You knew you had no right to search that apartment without either a search warrant or permission from the owner?"

The witness glanced at Hamilton Burger, said, "I hadn't thought of it at the time."

"You can think of it now, can't you?"

"Yes, sir."

"Actually you had studied the law in regard to searches before you became a deputy sheriff, hadn't you?"

"Yes, sir."

"And you knew that what you were doing was illegal?"

"If you want to put it that way, yes."

"I want to put it that way," Mason said. "That's all. I have no further questions of this witness."

The next witness was an officer of the zoo, who stated that he had been called to Stonehenge; that he had arrived on the night of the murder and had found three gorillas at liberty; that he had previously visited the place on several occasions to check with Benjamin Addicks on his experiments with the gorillas; that he was familiar with the number of gorillas and their general characteristics; that under his supervision the gorillas had been returned to their cages; that then he had checked these gorillas for blood spatters; that he had found none.

"Cross-examine," Burger said.

"What do you mean by blood spatters?"

"I mean that their coats were very carefully checked for the purpose of seeing whether there were any drops of blood."

"Why was that done?"

"It was done at the request of the district attorney."

"In order to save time," Hamilton Burger said, "I would state to the Court and Counsel that my next witness, a pathologist, will show that the nature of the wounds which were inflicted upon Benjamin Addicks was such that there would necessarily have been a considerable spurting of blood from the first wound in the neck, which was also a fatal wound, and that whoever inflicted that wound must have been spattered with human blood."

"Oh, I see," Mason said. "Go right ahead."

"I'm finished," Burger said. "You may cross-examine."

"There was no evidence of blood upon any of these gorillas?"

"None. Not on the coats—now just a moment, one of the gorillas had certain blood splotches, not droplets but splotches, which had come from a cut in the gorilla's foot. Evidently he had cut his foot upon a sharp piece of glass."

"How do you know?"

"Because there was a piece of glass, a segment, in the form of a sliver, embedded in the gorilla's foot."

"What became of that piece of glass?"

"Oh, it was just an ordinary piece of glass. I don't know what was done with it."

"Who extracted it?"

"I did."

"You extracted it from the gorilla's foot?"

"Yes."

"Was it painful?"

"The gorilla was asleep at the time. In order to assist in their capture they were given fruit containing a powerful sedative. I found the gorillas in a highly excited condition. The very savage police dogs had been making quite a commotion. The gorillas were all quite excited. The sounds of the sirens, barking of the dogs, and the unusual noises incident to the change in environment, and the fact that they knew they were violating the discipline of the place . . ."

"How did they know that?" Mason asked.

"Because they had been liberated from their cages. A gorilla has a very high order of intelligence. He knows when he's supposed to be in a cage, and he knows when he gets out under circumstances that make his exit a contravention of the disciplinary procedure."

"That's all," Mason said.

Burger said, "We will now call Mortimer Hershey as our witness."

Hershey took the witness stand, was sworn, and testified that for some two weeks prior to the murder, Benjamin Addicks had been planning a big business deal; that the details of this deal were locked entirely within the mind of his employer; that the witness knew some of the details but nothing whatever about the consideration; that Addicks customarily kept matters of consideration and price entirely to himself.

Late on the Tuesday evening preceding the murder, Addicks had called Nathan Fallon and Mortimer Hershey into a conference. He had told them he wanted to make a new will, that he intended to have it solemnized in proper legal form, or, as he expressed it, "with all the legal trimmings," at a later date, but in the meantime, since he wanted to be certain that his house was in order, he had made this new will.

"Did he tell you the terms of the will?"

"No, sir. He did not, other than to state that he felt he had been guilty of misjudging Josephine Kempton, and that in view of the dramatic disclosures indicating her innocence he wanted to make some atonement to her."

"Was there any conversation between you as to the nature of this atonement?"

"Just that he wanted to make it."

"Aside from that did he tell you what was in the will?"

"No, sir. He did not. He simply told us that he wanted us to notice that he had executed this will; that it was all in his handwriting; that he wanted me to put it in a safe place with his other papers.

"He placed the will in an envelope, sealed it, and asked Mr. Fallon and me to write our names on the outside."

"Which you did?"

"Yes, sir."

"Both of you did that?"

"Yes, sir."

"Then what happened?"

"Wednesday we started out on a round of—well, it was not out of the usual, it was a round of collection."

"Just what do you mean by that?"

"Cashier's checks had been issued to Mr. Addicks. Other checks had been issued to me, and some to Nathan Fallon. We took those checks to outlying communities where we had banking connections and had the checks reduced to cash."

"How much money did you have when you returned Wednesday evening?"

"I didn't return that evening. I was with friends in Santa Barbara. I was advised of Mr. Addicks' death at about seven o'clock Thursday morning. I drove immediately to Stonehenge and got in touch with the authorities, and then with Mr. Addicks' attorneys, Hardwick, Carson and Redding."

"And you had collected some money on some of those checks?"

"I had something over eighty-five thousand dollars."

"In cash?"

"Yes, sir."

"And you turned that money in to Mr. Hardwick?"

"Yes, sir."

"I think you may cross-examine," Hamilton Burger said, and then, by way of explanation to the Court, "I am calling these witnesses, Your Honor, simply so the Court can have the complete background."

"Very well," Judge Mundy said.

Mason smiled at Hershey and said, "Am I to understand, Mr. Hershey, that your trip for the purpose of raising funds was not at all unusual?"

"That's correct."

"Mr. Addicks, during his lifetime, frequently sent you out on such trips?"

"He did. Yes, sir."

"What became of the cash?"

"I think that in nearly every transaction Mr. Addicks had, that is, every major transaction, the consideration which was mentioned in the documents was probably incorrect."

"In what way was it incorrect?"

"I think the consideration was larger."

"And then what happened?"

"Well, I believe that there was a cash rebate made to Mr. Addicks, but I am not certain."

"We're willing to stipulate," Hamilton Burger said, "that Mr. Addicks was carrying on a rather complicated business which, as it turned out, was highly irregular."

"Can you explain what you mean a little more clearly?" Mason asked the witness.

"Well, if Mr. Addicks was buying some oil properties for a hundred thousand dollars, he would recite in the agreement that the consideration was fifty thousand dollars to be paid at a later date, and two hundred and fifty thousand dollars in cash, or a total price of three hundred thousand dollars."

"But the three hundred thousand dollars wouldn't be paid?"

"Well, now, of course, I'm talking about a purely hypothetical case."

"I understand. Go ahead."

"It would have been customary in such a deal to have paid perhaps fifty thousand dollars in cash, and that, with the fifty thousand dollars to be paid at a later date, would make the hundred thousand dollars."

"But the agreement would show a three hundred thousand dollar consideration? Is that right?"

"Yes, sir."

"What was the purpose of that?"

"I don't know, sir, except that in making trades he was able to produce agreements showing larger considerations than had been paid."

"But what about the income tax of the other party to the contract?"

"I think, sir, that their books only showed one hundred thousand, although the written agreements would show a different figure. However, very infrequently was there any trouble due to the discrepancy."

"In other words, to put it in plain language, Benjamin Addicks was trying to beat the income tax?"

Hershey hesitated, then said, "I think not, Mr. Mason. I, myself, thought so at first. Later, I came to the conclusion there was another explanation."

"What was it?"

"I think Mr. Addicks had at one time been married. I think that wife was living and not divorced. I think that under the law of this state all of the tremendous property interests Mr. Addicks was acquiring could have been declared community property if this woman who was his wife had been so minded.

"So Mr. Addicks fixed things so his books showed only a relatively small profit. In that way he could have questioned the amount of community property as compared with his separate property."

"That's all," Mason said.

"My next witness is Nathan Fallon," Burger said.

Nathan Fallon testified similarly to the testimony given by Hershey, except that it was apparent Fallon had only a feeling of deep resentment toward his deceased employer.

"Where were you on the night of the murder?"

"Las Vegas, Nevada."

"And what were you doing there?"

"Arranging to juggle some bank funds around so that Mr. Addicks could confuse the issues and beat the income tax."

"Do you know of your own knowledge that he was doing that to beat the income tax?"

The witness hesitated.

"Do you?"

"No, sir."

"What you have stated is merely a surmise then?"

"Well, when a man starts juggling cash around the way he did, there's bound to be a reason for it."

"Exactly," Hamilton Burger said. "And so, since if you were doing it, it would be for the purpose of confusing the issues for income tax purposes, you have assumed that was the reason Benjamin Addicks was doing it?"

"Are you," Mason asked, "trying to cross-examine your own witness?"

"Well," Hamilton Burger said, "perhaps the comment was extraneous, but after all Mr. Addicks is not here to defend himself."

"Well," Nathan Fallon said conversationally to Hamilton Burger, "perhaps *you* can give *me* a better reason."

The crowd in the courtroom broke into laughter and even Judge Mundy smiled.

"Mr. Addicks did not take you into his confidence?"

"Mr. Addicks didn't like me. I didn't like Mr. Addicks. I think that my employment would have been terminated within a short time had it not been for Mr. Addicks' death."

"You left Stonehenge on Wednesday, the day of the murder?"

"Yes, sir."

"At about what time?"

"I caught a plane for Las Vegas, Nevada, at two o'clock in the afternoon."

"You had instructions as to what you were to do in Las Vegas, Nevada?"

"Yes, sir. I was to return with a hundred and fifty thousand dollars in cash."

"You did that?"

"No, sir. I did not."

"Why?"

"Because I didn't care to carry that much cash with me unless I had a specific authorization. When I heard of Mr. Addicks' death I took my cash to the bank and made another deposit to the account of Benjamin Addicks. I notified Mr. Addicks' attorneys over the telephone what I intended to do."

"And Mr. Hershey left Stonehenge before you did?"

"No, sir. We left at the same time. Mr. Hershey drove me to the airport, and then he drove to Santa Barbara."

"Who was in Stonehenge when you left?"

"Benjamin Addicks."

"Who else?"

"No one else."

"Wasn't that rather unusual?"

"Yes, sir. That was very unusual."

"Cross-examine," Hamilton Burger said to Perry Mason.

"Why was it unusual, Mr. Fallon?"

"Because usually the animals required a caretaker, and the house required a supervising housekeeper and several servants who came in by the day."

"But the house was unoccupied save for Mr. Addicks when you left?"

"That is right. Several days earlier Mr. Addicks had become dissatisfied with the manner in which the part of the place that we referred to as the zoo was being kept up. He discharged all of the persons who had the animals in charge."

"Who was attending to feeding, cleaning the cages, and things of that sort after the trainers were discharged?"

"We were," Fallon said with obvious disgust. "That was one of the things that brought about friction between my employer and me. I wasn't hired for that sort of work."

"And was Mr. Hershey helping you?"

"Mr. Hershey and Benjamin Addicks. The three of us."

"And what about servants for the housekeeping?"

"There were no servants. There was no housekeeping."

"Were there any accidents because of this program?"

"Yes, sir."

"What?"

"Mr. Addicks was attacked by one of the gorillas, who pushed an arm through the bars, grabbed Addicks by his coat, and jerked him up to the cage. I shouted and beat against the bars of the cage with a scraper which I was using to clean out the cage, and Mr. Addicks flung himself back and kicked his way loose."

"Any injuries?"

"Yes, sir. He had a badly wrenched leg, and he had some cuts and lacerations on his face."

"When was this?"

"Monday morning."

"That's all," Mason said. "No further questions."

Hamilton Burger called a photographer to the stand who introduced photographs of the body lying on the bed, showing the manner in which blood had spurted from the neck wound over the wall and the carpet. There were also photographs of the face of Mr. Addicks, showing the injuries which had been inflicted by the gorilla.

"Cross-examine," Hamilton Burger said.

"I notice that there are two different photographs of the face of the dead man," Mason said. "One of them shows a very appreciable growth of stubble, and in the other the face is clean-shaven."

"One of them was taken before the body was removed to the

mortuary, and the other a short time after the autopsy. The under-
taker shaved the face of the body in preparing the body for the
funeral."

"So you took pictures showing the features of the body, and then
were sent back to take more pictures? Is that right?"

"Yes, sir."

"Why were you sent back?"

"I don't know."

"But you were instructed to go to the mortuary and get some
photographs which would show the features?"

"—Yes."

"Clean-shaven?"

"Yes."

"For purposes of identification?"

"I don't know for what purpose. I was sent to get 'em and I got
'em."

"Thank you," Mason said, smiling. "That's all."

"That's our case, Your Honor," Hamilton Burger said.

Mason said, "I call Your Honor's attention to the fact that I
wanted to look up one point and ask some more questions on cross-
examination. I need a little more opportunity for research upon
one technical point, and would like to confer with my associate. It
is approaching the hour of the afternoon adjournment. Would it
be possible for the Court to continue the case until tomorrow morning at ten o'clock?"

Judge Mundy shook his head. "You've had ample opportunity to
prepare your case, Mr. Mason. The district attorney offered to stipulate to a continuance when the case was called. You didn't want
it. You wanted to go ahead with the case. The Court isn't going to
let you try it piecemeal. I'll take a recess for fifteen minutes so you
may have opportunity to confer.

"The Court will now take a fifteen-minute recess."

Judge Mundy walked to his chambers.

Mason turned to where Mrs. Kempton was seated, the matron a
few feet away.

"I'm sorry," Mrs. Kempton whispered to him. "I tried to be
smart and it backfired. Put me on the stand and I'll tell the real
truth and clear everything up."

"Clear it up here and now. Were you lying to me?"

"Only about the cashier's check, and I didn't really lie about that. I merely held out on you."

"All right, where did that check come from?"

"From the little table by Mr. Addicks' bed. He was asleep, and he'd been drinking. The check was there, all made out to me. I knew at once he had been intending to give it to me . . ."

"Wait a minute, you say it was made out to *you?*"

"On the back, yes."

"You mean *you* didn't forge his signature on the endorsement?"

"Of course not. It was all signed when I first saw it, so I took it. I knew that was why he'd wanted me to go out there."

"You don't expect anyone to believe that?"

"Why not? It's the truth."

"Well, we'll not let anyone hear it until we can check certain things."

"Mr. Mason, I want you to call me to the stand. I want to tell them exactly what happened."

Mason shook his head. "Let us do the talking for a while."

"You think I'm lying, don't you?"

"Not necessarily."

"Yes you do."

"Well, you told us one story which didn't prepare us for being slapped in the face with this cashier's check."

"I just left that out. I didn't lie to you. There were some things I didn't tell you, that's all."

Mason said, "If I put you on that witness stand now they'll crucify you."

He turned to Etna. "Our time's getting short, Jim. We've got to do something."

"Let's make another try to get a continuance until tomorrow morning."

"The judge won't give it to us. He wants to get the case cleaned up today. He feels that it's only a preliminary hearing, that there's already enough evidence before the Court to bind the defendant over."

"Well, what are we going to do? We can't put her on the witness stand."

Mason said, "A lawyer runs into situations like this every once in a while, Jim. We've got to find some way of keeping things going until the judge has to take the evening adjournment."

"There isn't any way," Etna said. "They've tossed us the ball and we have no place to run. This business about the cashier's check and that clumsy forgery—we can't explain it, Mason, and if we don't explain it we're licked. I wish I'd never seen her—despite the fact that I needed the fee on that settlement. I . . ."

Mason shook his head. "You have to take them as they come, Jim. You can't skim the cream all the time. Every once in a while Fate hands you something."

"Josephine Kempton has had our loyal support. She has no right to make monkeys of us," Etna said.

Mason grinned. "Are you trying to be funny?"

Etna's smile was halfhearted. "I didn't mean it in exactly that way, but this story about the gorilla and—then we get the absolutely crazy story about this check—and she gets caught trying to conceal it!"

"Well," Mason said, "we'll try to stall until we can get things clarified a little."

"How are you going to stall?"

"I left myself an opening," Mason said, "in the cross-examination of the technical witnesses. There's one point that I don't think they know about. Ever hear of Dr. Gradwohl of St Louis?"

Etna shook his head.

"You should have," Mason said. "He was largely instrumental in founding the American Academy of Forensic Sciences, and he's been doing some research work lately that's going to give these boys a headache. I didn't intend to spring the point until I'd had an opportunity to brush up on the technical facts, but—here we go!"

Mason indicated the door to the judge's chambers which opened to let Judge Mundy re-enter the courtroom.

CHAPTER SEVENTEEN

JUDGE MUNDY GLANCED AT HIS WATCH. "WILL YOU PLEASE PROCEED as rapidly as possible with your case, gentlemen. I see no reason why we can't conclude the matter today."

Mason said, "If the Court please, we had arranged for a cross-examination of Philip Groton."

"Wasn't that simply as to a matter of his qualifications?" Judge Mundy asked.

"It has to do with his qualifications."

"Well, can't we stipulate as to Mr. Groton's qualifications? The Court has a full calendar tomorrow."

"I think, if the Court please, that the interests of my client require . . ."

"Very well, but the Court warns you, Mr. Mason, that it is not going to be patient with any tactics utilized purely for the purpose of delay. This is a preliminary hearing. It is not a trial in front of a jury. The Court is fully familiar with Mr. Groton's actual qualifications. The Court has heard him testify on dozens of occasions. Moreover, I think that Counsel are quite familiar with Mr. Groton's qualifications. Take the stand, Mr. Groton."

Groton returned to the witness stand.

Mason said, "In regard to this precipitin test for human blood, you are familiar with the mechanics of the test?"

"Naturally."

"Can you describe to the Court just what . . . ?"

"The Court doesn't need any description," Judge Mundy interrupted impatiently. "The Court is fully familiar with the process. By repeated injections of human blood an animal develops a defensive mechanism which immunizes him against that type of blood. If, therefore, a serum from the blood of that animal is maintained in a test tube and human blood is added to it, there is a reaction which results in a precipitation. That's all there is to it."

182

"Very well, Your Honor," Mason said, still keeping his smiling good humor. "I would like to have the witness testify to that rather than the Court."

Judge Mundy frowned angrily, then said, "Very well, ask the witness if you want to, but the Court knows it and you know it, and every person who has had any experience with scientific crime detection knows it."

"That is generally the case, is it?" Mason asked Groton.

"That is a general description, yes."

"Now then," Mason said, "when was this test first developed? Just answer the question briefly."

"If you don't mind," Groton said, "and so it will clear the matter in your own mind, Mr. Mason, I would like to tell you something about the precipitin test."

"Go right ahead."

"About the turn of the century," Groton said, "a gentleman named Uhlenhuth, a leading German worker in serology, first showed that if you inject a rabbit with the blood serum of another animal species, say man, you will iso-immunize him, that is, you will produce in his (rabbit) blood a substance that will react (or show up) only with the same animal species with which he has been injected, man's blood.

"Wassermann was one of the many who confirmed Uhlenhuth's dictum, and the test began to be used as a method for identifying human blood.

"Professor Nuttall, an American serologist, who was a professor at Cambridge University, England, took up the immense task of making a complete determination of the scope and field of the various tests, and in 1904 published his work in book form.

"Professor Nuttall produced anti-sera from rabbits injected in turn with blood from every known animal the world over, and in no case did he find any exceptions to the dictum that the test was specific, i.e., sera from rabbits injected with human blood reacted only with human blood, rabbits injected with elephant blood reacted only with elephant blood, etc."

Groton glanced at the judge and smiled, and the judge returned his smile as much as to say, "I guess that will put this lawyer in his place."

Mason said, "That's very interesting, Mr. Groton. Did you know that several of the German investigators had stated that the blood of the primates sometimes gave reactions weakly simulating the human blood reactions?"

"I believe that there is something to that effect in some of these books."

"And methods have been very much improved since the period of Uhlenhuth and Professor Nuttall?"

"Oh yes."

"Now then, are you acquainted with Dr. R. B. H. Gradwohl?"

"I have heard of him. I am not acquainted with him."

"He is the director of the St. Louis Police Laboratory in St. Louis, Missouri?"

"I believe that is right."

"Are you familiar with his experiments conducted during 1951 and 1952 with the improved technique now available?"

"No, sir. I am not."

"Are you familiar with a paper which was published first in the Laboratory Digest, Volume 15, February 1952, pages 4, 5 and 6, in which Dr. Gradwohl followed up this early suggestion and made precipitin tests with the blood of apes?"

"Why—now that you mention it, I believe that I did have the matter called to my attention at one time."

"I submit that if you are going to testify in this matter you had better keep up with the latest scientific advances in it," Mason said. "You will find that Dr. Gradwohl, with the new improved equipment, made a series of tests with the blood of chimpanzees, and found that he obtained exactly the same reaction in the precipitin test with chimpanzee blood that he got with human blood.

"To complete the chain of evidence he then injected rabbits with chimpanzee blood, producing an anti-chimpanzee testing serum, and found that this gave identical results with both chimpanzee and human blood samples."

"Well, I didn't know that!" Groton exclaimed.

"But you do have access to the scientific data by consulting a reference library?"

"I do. Yes, sir."

"And will you consult that library in case the Court takes an adjournment until tomorrow morning?"

"Oh, now come," Hamilton Burger exclaimed. "This is going far afield if the Court please."

"I don't think it is proper for Counsel to suggest to a witness that Court should adjourn in order to enable him to answer a specific question," Judge Mundy said. "Either the witness can answer a question or he can't, and that's all there is to it."

"Very well," Mason said, "I will now put my question directly to the witness. Are you prepared to swear on your oath, Mr. Groton, that the bloodstains which you found on the clothing of the defendant, and which you tested in the so-called precipitin test, were not stains made by the blood of a gorilla?"

The witness hesitated and fidgeted.

"Yes or no?" Mason said. "You're a professional expert witness. You're one who has qualified as an expert in dozens of cases. You're supposed to keep up with what's going on in the field. You're supposed to know what's true and what isn't true, so go ahead and state now on your oath—absolutely fairly, can you state that the bloodstains were not the bloodstains of a gorilla?"

Groton ran his hand through his hair, glanced uncomfortably at the district attorney.

"Oh," Hamilton Burger said, "I object, if the Court please. I think this has already been asked and answered. It's entirely extraneous. Not proper cross-examination."

"Objection overruled!" Judge Mundy snapped, his eyes on the witness.

Groton glanced again at the district attorney, then at the judge.

"No, I can't swear to it," he said.

"And for all you know the bloodstains may have been those made by a gorilla?"

"For all I know."

"You do know that one of those gorillas that had been liberated had cut his foot on a piece of glass?"

"Yes."

"And had done some bleeding?"

"I understand so. Yes."

"Then, as I understand your testimony, you are not now prepared to swear that the bloodstains made on the garments which you inspected were human blood?"

"Well, of course, if they could have been gorilla blood, they wouldn't have been human blood, that is, they might not have been human blood. And, of course, Mr. Mason, I'm assuming you're correctly reporting Dr. Gradwohl's experimental researches. Personally, well, I doubt if—I don't know."

"You're an expert?"

"Yes."

"You know you must testify on the strength of your own knowledge and research, not on what I tell you or what someone else tells you?"

"Well, yes."

"All right then, answer the question. Are you prepared to swear absolutely that the bloodstains which you analyzed were the stains of human blood?"

"I'd like to have a little more time in order to answer that question."

"Time for what purpose?"

"Time so that I can familiarize myself with the experiments of Dr. Gradwohl. You understand, Mr. Mason, that I am not a research scientist. I am a laboratory technician and a toxicologist. I follow the tests other persons have made, tests which have been published in authoritative books on the subject, and when I get certain results I evaluate those results in accordance with experiments and research work that has been made by others.

"If there is something new in this field of serology, and, now that you mention it, it does seem to me that I have heard the matter discussed recently—well, I feel that I owe it to myself and to the Court to make an investigation."

"If the Court please," Hamilton Burger said, "I don't think it makes a dime's worth of difference whether that was human blood or whether it wasn't."

"It depends on what value you put on a dime," Judge Mundy snapped. "The Court is very much interested in this phase of the examination, and the Court wishes to beg Mr. Mason's pardon for a somewhat natural assumption under the circumstances that this cross-examination was to be used as a means of securing a delay. Quite apparently Counsel has information of the greatest interest to this Court, information which certainly should be clarified. The Court is going to take a recess until ten o'clock tomorrow morning, and the Court is going to ask Mr. Groton to make every effort to ascertain the true facts in regard to these Gradwohl tests. Will you do so, Mr. Groton?"

"I certainly will. I'll telephone Dr. Gradwohl personally, get the evaluation of his tests, and go to reference libraries and read his paper on the subject."

"Under those circumstances," Judge Mundy said, "court is adjourned until ten o'clock tomorrow morning."

Chapter Eighteen

In the automobile, driving back from the courthouse, Della Street said to Perry Mason, "Chief, you certainly gave that expert something to think about."

"Of course," Mason said, "we are still up against the problem of accounting for the endorsement on the cashier's check. You'll note, Della, that that is a particularly damning piece of evidence because it is apparent, first, that the signature of Benjamin Addicks is a forgery; second, that Josephine Kempton is apparently the only person on earth who could profit by that forgery."

"Why do you say apparently?" Della Street asked. "She *is* the only person who could profit by the forgery."

Mason shook his head. "There is one other person who could profit by it."

"I'm afraid I don't understand—and how about her fingerprint outlined in blood on the paper?"

Mason said, "If she's lying she could very well have blood on her hands from killing Addicks. If she's telling the truth someone could have pressed her finger against the check while she was unconscious."

"But the blood?"

"A drop could have been put on her finger or the blood could have come from the gorilla with the cut foot, the one that was friendly to her."

"Is there any way of proving what did happen?"

Mason said, "We're going to do something about investigating that phase of the case, Della. I'm going to stop at this service station. You call up Stonehenge and see if the brother is there. I understand he arrived by airplane from Australia and is taking charge of the business matters which Benjamin left unfinished."

"And if he answers?" she asked.

"Tell him I'd like to see him on a matter of some importance," Mason said.

"But, Chief, shouldn't you take any matter up with him through his attorney? Isn't he . . . ?"

"The attorneys aren't representing him," Mason said. "The attorneys are representing the bank which is the executor of the will. I don't have any matter which is adverse to the estate to discuss with him. I want to discuss something that has to do with an entirely different matter. I want his help in finding certain clues."

"Aren't the police going to take a dim view of that?"

"Probably."

Mason swung the car into a service station and said to the attendant, "You might fill up the tank while we're putting a call through."

Della Street entered the phone booth in the service station, put through the call, and a moment later came running out to the car. "He says he'll see you any time, Chief; that he'd like very much to talk with you. It seems his name is Herman Barnwell. When shall I say it will be convenient?"

"Right now," Mason said. "Tell him we're on our way out there."

Della Street returned to the phone booth, and emerged after a moment or two, saying, "He certainly seems anxious to meet you, Chief. He said he'd read a lot about you in Australia."

"That's fine," Mason told her. "We'll have a talk with him and then we may learn a little more."

The attendant had finished filling the tank and was putting a final polishing touch on the windshield.

Mason paid for the gas, swung the car out from the service station and started threading his way in and out of the congested late afternoon traffic.

Della Street, long accustomed to Mason's driving, settled back in the seat, turned the rear view mirror on the right side of the automobile so she could keep an eye out for patrol cars.

Mason took advantage of every opening he could find in the traffic. Then, as he got out onto the less congested boulevard, gave the car more speed.

"This is the time that they wait to pick up speeders," Della Street warned.

"I know," Mason said tersely, "but I'm on a hot trail. I don't want it to cool off."

"What's the trail," she asked, "or are you keeping secrets from me?"

Mason said, "When I went out to call on Benjamin Addicks the day after he had his encounter with the gorilla, he was pretty badly upset and nervous. One side of his face was concealed with a bandage."

"That was the right side?"

"The right side. That's where the injuries were inflicted—most of them."

"Well?" she asked.

Mason said, "Aside from that bandage which covered the right side of his face and a small portion of the left side, he looked quite presentable."

"Well, why not?"

Della Street saw that Mason didn't want to answer any more questions, that he was giving his full attention to driving the car, and at the speed he was driving he needed all of his faculties.

"If I am successful in getting permission to start looking around the house," Mason told her abruptly, "I want you to keep away from me."

"To do what?"

"To keep away from me."

"How far away?"

"Some distance away. Under no circumstances are you to try to cope with any unexpected situation which may arise."

"What in the world are you talking about?"

"If we should find another gorilla," Mason said, "I don't want you to try to help me. No matter what the circumstances are, I want you to get out of there. Jump in the car, get to the nearest available telephone, and call the police."

"But, Chief, I don't understand. Do you think there's a gorilla hidden in the house? There can't be."

Mason said, "Hypnotism is something we know comparatively little about. Suppose you were able to hypnotize a gorilla. Then comes the problem of how to reach his mind. He'd do unpredictable things."

"Chief, you're spoofing me, trying to keep from frightening me. You don't, you can't believe all that stuff Mrs. Kempton said about a hypnotized gorilla killing Benjamin Addicks."

Mason grinned.

"You don't, do you?"

Mason said, "Della, I think there's a key clue which has been overlooked. I think that if you are with me, *and are in a position to escape*, we may learn what that clue is. On the other hand, if you are too close to me, we may find that we're both trapped. So please remain near a door and at the first sign of trouble start for the police."

"Trouble with whom?"

"A hypnotized gorilla."

"But what will happen to you?"

Mason grinned. "Courage is the best antidote for danger, Della, remember? I *think* I'm going to be all right."

She frowned. "I don't like this at all."

Mason turned into Olive Street. "Well, here we are, Della. Some change."

"I'll say there's some change," Della Street said. "The new tenant certainly seems to be far more sociable than his dead brother."

The iron gates were now standing wide open. The graveled driveway curved invitingly through the green of the grounds. There was no watchman.

Mason gave Della a last warning. "If Herman Barnwell should offer to show me through the house in order to help me look for clues, Della—and I'm almost certain he's going to prove very cooperative—I want to be sure you aren't with us. Stay near an exit and pretend that you are interested in paintings, interior decoration, anything except murders."

"I've been cudgeling my brains trying to find out why you want me to do that, but I still don't . . ."

"Here we are," Mason said.

He parked the car in front of the house. The door opened and a chunky, powerfully built man came out to greet them. His teeth flashed in a quick smile. He spoke with a very noticeable Australian accent.

"Ah, Mr. Mason, I believe. I am so pleased to meet you. When you telephoned I could hardly believe my good fortune. I have read accounts of many of your cases. And this is Miss Della Street, your secretary?

"It is indeed an honor to have you come here. Of course, you will understand I only arrived a short time ago. I haven't had an opportunity to go over the place well. It needs a thorough cleaning. I haven't been able to engage any servants as yet. In fact, my preliminary conversations with employment agencies indicate that it's going to be very difficult to do so."

"What are you doing with the gorillas?" Mason asked.

Herman Barnwell made an inclusive sweep with his arm. "They're gone. I sold the whole outfit, lock, stock and barrel, to a zoo. When that sale is reported in the press, I may have some success with servants—but do come in, and tell me what, if anything, I can do for you. It is indeed a pleasure to have you here."

He held the door open and said, "Right across that entrance hallway and into the main living room, if you will. I'll have to fix the drinks myself, I'm afraid—a little Scotch and soda? Or would you prefer a cocktail?"

"Scotch and soda will be fine," Mason said, "but we're in rather a hurry. I assume you're quite busy and . . ."

"No, no, not at all, Mr. Mason. I have had a preliminary conference with Mr. Hardwick, the attorney for the executor, and I have been over some of the accounts with Mr. Hershey, trying to get some idea of my brother's rather complicated businesss affairs. Of course, those are for the most part in the hands of the bank, but the bank wants to follow my wishes in the matter.

"It may interest you to know, Mr. Mason, that I have instructed the bank that under no circumstances are they to contest in any way the provisions in the will giving Mrs. Josephine Kempton a share of the estate."

"Of course," Mason pointed out, "she's being tried for murder and if she . . ."

"She didn't murder him," Herman Barnwell said calmly. "I know she didn't."

"You do?"

"Yes."

"May I ask how you know that?"

Herman Barnwell said, "I am satisfied, Mr. Mason, that Mrs. Kempton did not kill my brother. My brother was trying to hide from his past. There is no use for me to beat about the bush, Mr. Mason. You are far too wise to be trapped by superficial subterfuge. There was no measure of affection between my brother and me. I am not even going to try to pretend—perhaps to the public, yes; but to you, no."

"Benjamin was intensely self-centered. We spent some time in Australia. We had a mining partnership. There were legal difficulties. One of the persons who had conflicting interests in our claim was killed. He was murdered. I won't say Benjamin murdered this man. There were circumstances which pointed to it.

"But the police bungled the case. They thought *I* had committed the murder. I was tried and convicted. However, after conviction new evidence was disclosed which resulted in my obtaining a pardon.

"Benjamin, however, had completely disappeared. Fortunately for him he had never been fingerprinted and so he was able to elude everyone."

"And you didn't know where he was?" Mason asked.

"I thought he was dead. Benjamin had been very cunning. He had a small yacht. He put out to sea in that yacht when a bad storm was coming up. Two days later the capsized yacht was found floating. There was no trace of Benjamin. Naturally it was assumed that he was dead."

Mason frowned. "So he ran away and left you to face the murder charge?"

"Not exactly. The police misconstrued the evidence. My brother ran away."

Mason said, "I have reason to believe your brother may have had a gorilla which wasn't kept in the cages."

"What?"

"That's right—a gorilla only two or three people ever knew about."

"But—good heavens, Mr. Mason, where on earth could such a gorilla have been kept?"

"That's what I'd like to have you help me find out."

Herman Barnwell's eyes were pinpoints of concentration. "I'm afraid I don't follow you, Mr. Mason. The very idea seems preposterous."

"I'm not certain that I follow myself," Mason said, "but I wanted to look around a bit if I could. Naturally I'd want you to be with me. I doubt if the police ever did search the entire premises."

"By all means," Herman Barnwell said. "Just sit down, please, while I set the drinks—you know, Mr. Mason, I too have had an uneasy feeling that the police may have let their attention be diverted by the obvious. I have had the feeling that—however, I don't want to say things I am not prepared to prove, and I don't want to alarm your secretary. You want Scotch and soda? And you, Miss Street, I believe the same."

"The same," she said, "and if you don't mind, I'll look around here in the entrance hall. I'm very much interested in the Grecian urn where the articles were recovered."

"Make yourself at home," Herman Barnwell invited cordially. "Just help yourself."

He left the room, and a few moments later Mortimer Hershey entered. "Good afternoon, Mr. Mason. I just returned from court. I hardly expected to find you here."

He came forward and shook hands, then turned to Della. "How do you do, Miss Street?"

Mason motioned with his hand. "Della wanted to take a look in the stone urn in the reception room."

"Well, that's perfectly natural," Hershey said, laughing. "I can well understand that. You certainly did a remarkable job of deductive reasoning, Mr. Mason. And, incidentally, started a rather interesting chain of events."

Mason said, "I'm hoping I can do something along those same lines this afternoon. I was telling Mr. Barnwell I wanted to ascertain if a gorilla is here which wasn't kept confined in the cages."

Hershey laughed. "I think that's entirely out of the question, Mr. Mason. All of the animals here, with the sole exception of that one monkey . . ."

Della Street's high-pitched scream of fear knifed through the room.

"Chief! Behind you!"

Mason whirled.

Della Street came running into the room.

"What was it?" Mason asked.

"Behind you," she said, "I just had a glimpse of him through the door—a terrible, grinning gorilla . . ."

The roar of a shot sounded through the house. It was followed by a second and a third shot, and then silence.

Somewhere a chair overturned.

Della Street ran toward Mason.

"Get back!" Mason shouted. "Get back! Do as I told you! Follow instructions."

For a moment Della Street looked at him in dazed incomprehension.

Suddenly a huge gorilla appeared in the doorway leading to the kitchen, a gorilla with staring eyes, a fixed sardonic grin on his features.

"Good Lord!" Hershey exclaimed, then turned to run, paused to look back.

The grinning gorilla came shambling toward Mason. The knuckles of one huge, hairy hand rested on the floor. The other one held a glittering carving knife.

"Help! Help!" Hershey shouted, and started for the door, stumbling over a chair as he did so, falling flat. He grabbed Mason's coattails in order to pull himself up, shouting, "Run! Help! Get me out of this!"

The huge body of the gorilla came directly for Perry Mason.

Hershey produced a revolver. Trying to scramble to his feet, he fired three shots from a kneeling position.

The gorilla, its eyes fastened on Perry Mason, moved deliberately forward.

Babbling incoherently in fear, Hershey got to his feet. As he did so, he stumbled against Mason, throwing the lawyer off balance.

The gorilla lashed out savagely with the knife.

Mason side-stepped, suddenly grabbed the hairy arm which held the knife, and twisted it sharply.

For a moment it seemed that sheer surprise froze the muscles of the gorilla in awkward immobility.

Mason made the most of that moment. His right fist crashed

into the hairy midriff. His right knee came up in a savage knee lift.

The revolver roared again and a bullet whipped past Mason's head, crashed into the wall.

The big gorilla collapsed slowly, doubling forward, then toppling to the floor with a crashing impact which made the room tremble.

Mason turned toward Hershey.

The business manager raised the revolver, pointed it directly at Mason, pulled the trigger.

The hammer clicked.

Mason lunged, stumbled over the paw of the gorilla.

Hershey backed toward the hallway, hurriedly thrusting fresh cartridges into the open cylinder of the revolver.

Della Street appeared in the doorway, a stone image in her hands.

Hershey took another backward step.

Della brought the stone image down, hard.

Hershey's knees buckled. He dropped the gun, fell forward.

"Della!" Mason said sharply. "I told you to start for help at the first . . ."

"Did you think I'd leave you? Hurry, Chief. Get going. We've knocked him out and . . ."

Mason scooped up Hershey's revolver, then, stepping up to the big gorilla, rolled him over, fumbled with the back for a moment, and suddenly jerked a long zipper.

"Chief!" Della Street screamed.

Mason lifted the grinning head to one side, pulled back the skin of the gorilla and disclosed the limp body of Herman Barnwell.

"Well," Mason said, "perhaps now you'll consent to leave me in charge here, and go get the police."

CHAPTER NINETEEN

MASON, DELLA STREET AND PAUL DRAKE SAT IN MASON'S PRIVATE OFFICE.
Paul Drake, his eyes red from lack of sleep, but nevertheless
alert with interest, said, "Good Lord, Perry, it's a wonder you
weren't killed."

Mason said, "If I'd been absolutely certain, if I'd known what I
know now, I'd have gone to Lieutenant Tragg and told him the
whole story. I think he'd have searched the place and found the
gorilla skin."

"Of course, they must have been planning it for a long time,"
Drake said.

"Sure they had. As it turns out now, Benjamin Addicks had
caught both Hershey and Nathan Fallon in embezzlements—when
you come right down to it, he had given these men an enormous
amount of leeway. They had every opportunity in the world. Addicks was trying to cheat on his income tax by manipulating a lot
of his transactions on a cash basis, and Hershey and Fallon had
been taking a pretty generous cut.

"Of course, the disadvantage of trying to carry on a business the
way Benjamin Addicks was doing it, is that you don't have any
really accurate books. You yourself can't tell where your business
stands. You scramble it all up so there are no written records,
and you fool yourself as well as the government."

"How much do you suppose they got away with?"

"Hershey's confession says something over three hundred thousand dollars. That, of course, was small stuff to what they were preparing to do. Apparently they had been in touch with Herman for
some time. Herman offered them a fortune if they could manipulate it so that Benjamin was put out of the way under such circumstances that Herman would inherit the fortune.

"When you look at it carefully they did a pretty smooth job.
They overpowered Benjamin Addicks. They twisted the ligaments

in his leg. They inflicted cuts and bruises on his face, and then they bound him and gagged him.

"That was when Herman Barnwell took over, masquerading as Benjamin Addicks. That was rather easy to do because they were very similar in build, complexion and general appearance. There was quite a remarkable brotherly resemblance.

"The idea was that they would call in some disinterested witness who didn't know Benjamin Addicks personally. Because of the bandaged face and the fact that Hershey and Nathan Fallon would both identify Herman Barnwell as being Benjamin Addicks, they would then be in a position to go ahead with their scheme.

"Apparently they intended to bring James Etna into the picture as their disinterested witness, but it happened that I bought those diaries of Helen Cadmus, secured some newspaper notoriety from it, and therefore walked right into the middle of things. They decided it would be better to use me than James Etna.

"So they built up a background that Benjamin Addicks distrusted Nathan Fallon but had complete confidence in Mortimer Hershey. They had, of course, been practicing forging Benjamin Addicks' writing for a long time.

"Then it was all fixed that while Hershey and Fallon would prepare ironclad alibis for themselves so that they couldn't possibly be implicated in murder, Herman Barnwell, masquerading as Benjamin, would get Josephine Kempton out to the house. On some pretext or other, he'd leave her a minute and go unlock the cages of a couple of harmless gorillas. In the meantime, liquor had been forced down Benjamin Addicks until he was sufficiently drunk so that he had passed out. Herman got into this carefully prepared gorilla-skin suit—the only bad thing about it was that the head necessarily had a natural fixity of expression which was what made Josephine Kempton think she was looking at a hypnotized gorilla.

"They lured Mrs. Kempton up into the room. She saw this huge gorilla, saw him stab the unconscious body of Benjamin Addicks. They counted on Mrs. Kempton not being able to resist the temptation of appropriating the check, which had already been carefully forged, with an endorsement that showed it was a forgery.

"Of course, the endorsement being forged, the check couldn't be cashed. The money would return to the estate, and whoever inherited that estate would inherit the money on that check.

"The fact that I was able to show that Benjamin Addicks had been mistaken about the theft of the ring and the watch was a break for them. They decided to capitalize on that by incorporating that matter in the will which would give the whole thing an air of authenticity.

"They didn't get *all* the breaks. A few things went against them. One was that while I was there Sidney Hardwick came out to see his client, and the masquerader, who was supposed to be Benjamin Addicks, said that he felt too upset to see him—to see his own attorney, mind you, although he had previously given *me* an audience, and I was not only a stranger, but a man whose interests were completely hostile."

Drake said, "Then Josephine Kempton was telling the truth."

"The truth about everything except that cashier's check. She tried to hide that. Of course, Hershey, Fallon and Herman Barnwell knew that they had her the minute she took that check. It could either be found in her possession or she would try to cash it. As far as they were concerned they were perfectly willing for her to cash it. She could have taken the money and then Herman Barnwell, in checking into the business affairs, could have detected a forgery. The bank records would show the twenty-five thousand dollars had been paid to Josephine Kempton and there they had her.

"In other words, if the story of the gorilla murdering Benjamin Addicks went across all right, that was fine, that was the way they wanted it; but in the event anything went wrong, Josephine Kempton could be cast in the role of murderess. And in the event she wasn't accused herself, once she had cashed that cashier's check they had her absolutely in their power."

"Well," Drake said, "it was a bizarre scheme, but nevertheless when you realize the weird circumstances under which Benjamin Addicks lived, his attempts at experimentation with animal psychology, and—how do you explain that, Perry?"

"He'd killed a man in Australia," Mason said. "We have a lot to check, but apparently Herman's story to me was, in the main, true. Benjamin Addicks, or Barnwell, was rationalizing with his conscience. He probably felt he had been hypnotized. He may have been off the beam on that one subject."

"How did you get the lead on all this?" Drake asked.

Mason said, "Actually, Paul, I should have smelled a rat a lot sooner than I did."

"How come?"

Mason said, "I went out to see Benjamin Addicks. I saw a man who was introduced as Benjamin Addicks. I did not get a good look at his face. He was wearing dark glasses so I couldn't see his eyes. He had a bandage which concealed nearly all of his face. Actually, of course, I was talking with Herman instead of Benjamin. Herman had been here for some time, leaving an accomplice in Australia to answer cablegrams from Hardwick. That was all part of the carefully laid trap. Herman was a good enough actor to change his voice, and since I had never met Benjamin, they stood very little chance of detection—not one chance in a million. But they fell down on one thing."

"What?"

Mason said, "It was then Tuesday evening. The gorilla was supposed to have attacked Benjamin the day before. I had a glimpse of the cheek of the man with whom I was talking. That cheek was smoothly shaven. In court they introduced a photograph of Benjamin's face. I examined the photograph rather closely and saw that the lacerations were deep and painful.

"I felt vaguely uneasy about that photograph. I knew there was something wrong, but I couldn't tell what. It was, of course, the incongruity of the shaved cheek I had seen at the edge of the bandage.

"That the lacerations were too painful for the victim to have shaved, was shown by indisputable evidence—the fact that he *hadn't* shaved. Yet the man whom I saw had a cleanly shaven cheek more than thirty-four hours after the injuries were supposed to have been sustained.

"You can't be mistaken on that. A bandage, of course, will cover up skin, but as a person talks the bandage moves slightly, and if the skin under the bandage is unshaven, whiskers will be working out."

"Now what happens?" Della Street asked.

"Fortunately," Mason said, "we can prove that holographic will is a forgery. Hershey is simply dying to turn state's evidence. The other will then becomes effective, the one that Hardwick prepared. Of course, there's a clause in that will that Hardwick didn't want to tell us about, a clause leaving the bulk of the fortune to Helen Cadmus. Hardwick kept insisting that Benjamin Addicks make a new will because he thought Helen Cadmus was dead. Benjamin, however, had no real intention of changing his will because he knew that Helen Cadmus was very much alive, and he knew that he wanted to have her provided for in the event anything happened to him.

"So there you have a peculiar situation. A lawyer insisting that a client's will needed to be changed because the principal beneficiary was dead, and the client, knowing that she wasn't dead, stalling the lawyer along. After all, when Hardwick mentioned that he had been insisting that Benjamin make a new will because of certain complications which had arisen, I should have begun to guess what the situation was right then."

"But the marriage to Helen Cadmus is actually bigamous?" Drake asked.

"It is if his first wife is still alive, but somehow I have an idea she isn't. Hershey says that it's been eighteen months since anyone has heard from her. Before that she used to put the bee on Addicks about once every four or five months."

"Why did they pull this attack on you?" Drake asked.

"For the very good reason that they knew I was suspicious. They knew that Josephine Kempton had told me her story of the murder. They had an idea that I had begun to smell a rat.

"By the time court adjourned this afternoon I had begun to realize the significance of the shaven cheek that I had seen on the person whom I had interviewed. Then I began to get a glimpse of the truth. On the way out to Stonehenge I thought the thing through to a conclusion.

"I knew they would like to dispose of me. I knew that if they could kill me under such circumstances that Della Street could actually see a strange grinning gorilla, and run for the police, her story of the murderous gorilla would be believed because it would conform to Josephine Kempton's story.

"I knew, therefore, that they would let Della Street get a glimpse of the gorilla. If she should then start to run for the police, they'd let her go. That would leave me to cope with whoever was in the house. If there had been three men I might not have taken the chance, but there were only two—Herman and Hershey. Herman, of course, looked terribly formidable in the big gorilla skin. He was actually a pushover. He couldn't move fast carrying the weight of the gorilla skin, the awkward head, and all the padding. He could just about walk, manipulate the knife and that was all.

"So I gave them a chance. Herman set the stage, then went out to the private bar to prepare drinks. He slipped into the gorilla suit and appeared at the door long enough to let Della Street get a glimpse of him. Then he disappeared and fired several shots. Then, dressed in the gorilla skin, he appeared in the doorway with a knife.

"Under ordinary circumstances a man would have been completely paralyzed at such a formidable apparition. I should have turned to run, and there was good old Hershey to pretend that he was assisting me, falling all over things so that the gorilla would have a chance to close the distance.

"By the time Della Street arrived with the police, she would find two badly shaken men, both of whom would have sworn that they had seen a gorilla who had escaped through the grounds, and that the gorilla had killed me. They had both shot at him and they thought perhaps had wounded him—or, if they had needed to do it, Hershey could have shot me, claiming he had killed me accidentally while aiming at the gorilla."

"You were taking chances," Drake said.

"Some chances," Mason admitted. "I made up my mind that if it came to a showdown I would tell them that the jig was up, that Della was in on the secret and had gone to get the police."

Drake said, "Just the same, it took nerve."

"Perhaps," Mason said, "but it was the only way I could think of to get them to show their hand so I could have absolute proof.

"I think I'd better go get in touch with Helen Cadmus and let her know what the situation is—by the way, Della, you remember that I left a bill at the Chinese restaurant where we ate, and told the cashier I'd be back for the change?"

She nodded.

"I dropped in there to pick up the change and the man gave me your coin purse. It seems that you dropped it when you pulled your notebook from your purse."

Della Street's face suddenly colored.

"What is it?" Mason asked.

"The fortune paper that was in it."

Mason shook his head. "Apparently you must have put that paper some place else, Della. There wasn't any paper in it."

"Oh," Della Street said, relief in her voice.

"Well," Mason said, "you entertain Paul Drake, Della. Get out that bottle of whisky, and we'll have a drink on it. I'll go out to the switchboard and put through a call to Helen Cadmus. We can at least take a load off her mind."

Mason went out to the outer office, plugged in the telephone line, and, as he did so, took from his pocket the folded piece of rice paper from the fortune cake which had been delivered to him by the Chinese together with Della Street's coin purse.

On the paper appeared in fine print:

"If you marry him you will be very happy and present him with a man child who will be very like his father."

Mason hesitated for a moment, then, opening his wallet, pushed the folded piece of rice paper far down into a corner. Pocketing the wallet, he put through the call to Helen Cadmus.

THE END

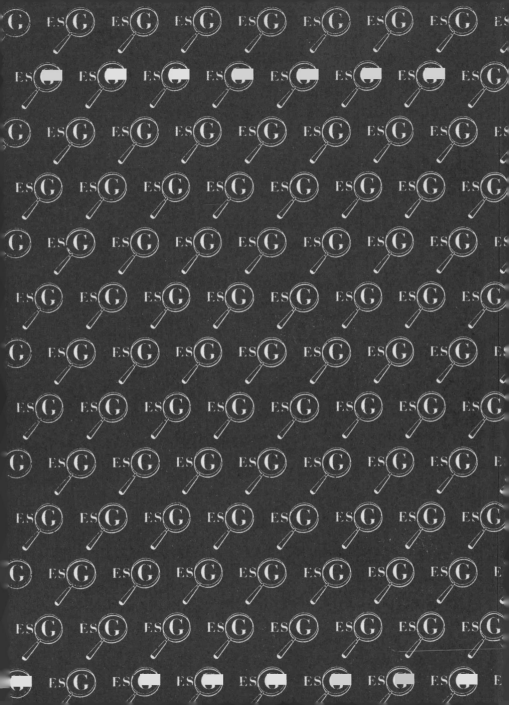